"Don't you see, Dos Cameron," Klaus taunted, "why none of us Stark boys are allowed on the ranch my pa helped to build? Are you blind? Your high 'n mighty ma laid down with my pa. You ain't no Cameron! You ain't no better 'n I am! You're my goddam brother."

Fireworks exploded in Dos's brain, and he lashed out blindly, sending Klaus sprawling against the gaming table. Cards and poker chips rained down around them, and an uncorked whiskey bottle shattered to the floor. Dos grabbed its neck and brought it up. Klaus never saw it. In his haste to jump Dos, he lunged; and the jagged bottle buried itself in his throat, slicing the jugular vein as neatly as if it had been a razor.

Dos scuttled backward away from the stream of blood. He had killed a man—his own brother! He was a bastard—not a Cameron, after all! Dos staggered to his feet and screamed, his wail of despair lonelier and more frightened than the cry of a trapped animal . . .

*Books by*
*Ronald S. Joseph*

THE KINGDOM
THE POWER
THE GLORY

Published by
WARNER BOOKS

# The Power

## RONALD S. JOSEPH

WARNER BOOKS

A Warner Communications Company

*To Gay Mongan*

# PART I

# 1893

# 1

It was a custom along the border, when a girl turned fifteen, to mark her coming of age; and in September, 1893, Maggie Cameron celebrated her *quincianera*.

A *quincianera* could be a simple family gathering enlivened by sugar-sprinkled cakes, hot chocolate, and music from a wheezy accordion.

Or it could be as elaborate as Maggie's. Preparations for the week-long fiesta had begun a full year before the event, for this was to be the biggest party ever given on the Lantana.

From replacing the velvet curtains in the smallest third-floor bed chamber to hand-polishing the thousands of diamond-bright prisms in the chandeliers that glittered in the honey-colored ballroom off the downstairs foyer, the mansion was completely refurbished—all forty-six rooms.

Throughout the blazing summer, perspiring maids wielding heavy flatirons pressed acres of bedsheets, tablecloths, and napkins, each bearing on one corner of its border an embroidered representation of the famous Lantana brand: the Crown of Thorns; and persnickety cooks culled the choicest beef on the hoof from the rest of the Lantana herd and moved them to a special holding area to fatten; likewise, their experienced eyes selected young goats, picking those kids just the right age to turn into delicious barbecued *cabrito*.

As is always the case, each new improvement seemed to call for another, and after the house was done, outbuildings that had appeared perfectly acceptable before, now cried out for attention. Carpenters and painters were hired to spruce up the barns and stables while cowboys kept busy completely reworking the stockpens and fences.

A week before the guests were to arrive, all was nearly ready, and an army of peons, swinging scythes, mowed twenty-five acres of surrounding pasture to manicured perfection.

When they were finished, their *caporal* called at the big house, and his mistress, Anne Cameron, rode out with him to approve the work, for no detail on the Lantana was beneath her scrutiny.

She was a striking woman, still a great beauty at forty-five, tall with a commanding posture that bespoke the iron strength of her will. Her hair was long and as yellow as sunlight, and her eyes—sharp and ever-watchful—were as green as meadow grass in the spring. Except for formal occasions when she couldn't avoid it, she dressed as she always had, in leather breeches, oxblood boots, and the common white shirts of the poorest *campesino*.

12

For her, only five things mattered in life: her husband Alex, her two children, her half-brother Carlos, and—in no less measure—the Lantana.

According to legend, Alex Cameron proposed to her by asking: "Will you give me your love?"

And Anne was supposed to have replied: "I'll do better than that. I'll give you Texas!"

The story was fanciful, to be sure, but it was too good a tale to die—and like most legends, it contained more than a grain of truth, for when in 1874, Anne Trevor took the handsome Scotsman as her husband, she *did* give him Texas—or at least a sizeable portion of it. Her dowry was the Lantana, the largest and wealthiest ranch the world had ever known, a cattle empire encompassing a million and a half acres.

Once fencing had begun, it had been her idea to pull up the cedar posts and restring the barbed wire anywhere from a dozen yards to a quarter of a mile beyond the original perimeter—a small deviation, barely noticeable to any but a sharp-eyed surveyor in the almost limitless *brasada;* but the Lantana's perimeter was so lengthy that when Anne traveled to Austin to refile her title, bringing it into line with her new borders, she found, to her immense surprise and satisfaction, that she had increased the Lantana's size by another half-million acres.

Throughout the 'eighties, she added to her holdings by purchasing land from ranchers who had fallen on hard times, or from widows who hadn't the inclination or the ability to carry on their late husbands' work, or from men who simply found her price too attractive to turn down—until, nineteen years later, the Lantana's two and a half million acres touched the Gulf to the east and sprawled halfway to Mexico to the south and west.

13

All this was hers—and her husband's—a fief, a feudal kingdom with barbed-wire borders—and Anne and Alex Cameron were its absolute rulers.

In addition to the legend of their engagement, there were other tales—born of rumor and speculation and nurtured by the common folk's love of gossip about the high and mighty. It was said, for example, that Anne's fence-riders, who vigilantly patrolled the Lantana's perimeter on horseback, had orders to shoot trespassers on sight. In fact, there *were* some killings, and perhaps a few innocent, wayward travelers did find themselves at the wrong end of a vaquero's gun. But most of those who lost their lives on Lantana soil were thieving rustlers caught with outlawed wire cutters in their saddle bags.

And it was told, with authority by people who claimed to know, that the Camerons had spent a million dollars on their mansion—as if its actual cost, somewhat less than six hundred thousand, was too paltry a sum for a ranch as big and powerful as the Lantana.

Old-timers related that Anne had been wild in her youth, a headstrong, untamed beauty who left a trail of broken hearts across the brush country. In truth, she had loved only once before meeting Alex Cameron —and it was *she* who had been jilted.

And there was a darker rumor, a story only whispered about, that said that Anne had carried on with her foreman, a man called Rudy Stark, and that the affair had continued even after her marriage to Alex. It was this rumor that led to speculation about the paternity of the Cameron heir—a boy called Dos. . . .

# 2

Dos Cameron took his mother's spanking new surrey and set off across the prairie, heading for the Lantana's private railroad siding some six miles west of the big house. As soon as he had cleared the last of the freshly whitewashed corrals, he heaved a sigh of relief, happy to be away from the frenzy of last-minute preparations for Maggie's fiesta.

The team of maids, who usually went about their work like silent, stalking cats, had lost all discipline in the mounting excitement. They ran to and fro, filling the corridors with whoops and giggles. Alex bellowed orders from the gallery, and Anne's raised voice could be heard throughout the downstairs. Cowboys tramped in and out followed by two frustrated twelve-year-old maids on hands and knees, fighting a losing battle to erase their dusty bootprints from the foyer's tiled floor.

The special train was due to arrive at mid-afternoon; so today there would be no siesta for anyone. Earlier, as the caravan of three-seater platform wagons rolled away from the big house to fetch the guests from the train, Alex sought out Anne and said, "Do you think it's proper to make the Governor ride in a wagon with everyone else?"

Anne shrugged. "He shouldn't mind. After all, he makes it a point to declare that he's just one of the people."

Like most big ranchers, Anne had no love for Jim Hogg, and she'd looked forward to making him ride with the hoi polloi.

But Alex said, "A snub would serve no purpose. Let's send Dos in your buggy to collect him."

Anne nodded. Alex was right, of course. Offending the Governor was pointless—and despite what they thought of his politics, the Camerons could afford to be generous.

The day was hot with a dry wind blowing from the south, the sky cloudless and almost white in the glare of the sun. There had been rain that summer, so the prairie grass had grown chest high, but by September, the season's heat had scorched all green from it, burnishing the waving blades to gold and sienna, and it stretched out on either side of the caliche road like vast carpet, split down the middle, its edges vanishing in the shimmering horizon.

Dos took his time, driving the horses at a leisurely pace even though the plume of black smoke in the distance promised that the train would beat him to the siding. It was the first time he'd driven the handsome surrey with its dark leather quarter top and English wool upholstery, and he wanted to prolong the pleasure even if it meant keeping the Governor waiting.

16

Dos was eighteen, yet already a bull of a man with broad, strong shoulders on a husky frame; and the work-hardened muscles of his arms and chest strained the bright plaid fabric of his shirt.

On first meeting him, one immediately felt a sense of impending danger, an impression of immense power barely controlled. His eyes—wide-set, green as Anne's, fringed with lashes so blond that they were almost white—held flashes of lightning like those that crackled from turbulent clouds on hot summer nights. He spoke quietly, but there was thunder in his voice, barely perceptible but subliminally present like that from a storm in a distant county.

Despite his build, he moved with the stealthy grace of a lynx on the prowl—and there were those who said that Dos Cameron was always on the prowl.

From the time he was twelve, he'd had almost any girl he desired, from the dark-eyed housemaids to the virginal daughters from Joelsboro. He was a lusty, exciting lover, and if any of his admirers complained, it was because he abandoned her so quickly for the next flirty girl who caught his eye.

In fact, as his surrey rolled up to the railroad siding, he was already wondering who among the many women climbing from the soot-smeared coaches would be his bedmate that night.

He never had a chance to decide, for among the passengers setting foot on the Lantana was a New York actress by the name of Nelda Flynn, a member of a touring company that had just given its last performance in San Antonio the night before. She had caught sight of Dos from the train window and had pushed and shoved her way past members of her troupe, jostling them roughly and knocking their hatboxes from their hands in her effort to be first to lay claim to Dos.

17

Nelda Flynn was forty-two, a closely guarded secret that wouldn't have been believed, anyway, for her forte was ingénue roles, and she suited the parts perfectly with a petite figure, an unlined, milky complexion, and girlish features framed by soft golden curls.

One of the repertory actresses, still bristling from having been shoved aside, tapped a friend on the shoulder and commented acidly, "Well, that's a new record—even for our *dear* Nelda. We haven't been here ten seconds, and she's already found herself a new boy!"

Her friend arched her eyebrows and nodded sagely, for it was common gossip in theatrical circles that Nelda Flynn had an insatiable appetite for men of a younger generation.

Nelda made a beeline for Dos, introduced herself, and added, "And whom do I have the pleasure of knowing?"

"I'm Dos Cameron."

Nelda couldn't believe her luck. "The owner of the Lantana!" she squealed. "I'm so pleased to meet you."

"The son of the owners, ma'am," Dos replied, amused yet flattered.

"Then, the heir apparent," Nelda said, not the least perturbed. "What a fine-looking surrey! May I invite myself to ride with you?"

"You're the person I've come for," Dos lied.

"Then you knew I was coming?" Nelda said, believing every word Dos said.

"My mother has a list of everyone who comes to the Lantana. No one crosses her fence without her permission."

"Well, I'm terribly flattered," Nelda said, climbing unassisted into the surrey and taking her place beside Dos. "Now, let's be on our way. Don't worry about my luggage. Someone will take care of it."

18

Dos grinned, laugh lines cutting white creases into his deeply tanned face. "Then, we're off," he said, slapping the reins and wheeling the surrey about, leaving the Governor behind to climb onto one of the creaking platform wagons.

Dos took the long way home, breaking off from the road to drive Nelda along the bank of a muddy arroyo. He halted the surrey and helped her down. Nelda popped open her parasol and strolled with him. High up in a salt cedar, a mockingbird whistled a sharp warning, sending startled sparrows flying like buckshot from the tree's ferny branches. In the distance, a fawn darted after its unseen mother, and farther off a single black buzzard hung motionless against the hard, blue sky.

Nelda pretended fascination, but in truth, she could hardly keep her eyes off the handsome youth at her side.

"How big is the Lantana?" she asked.

"Damn big," Dos replied.

Nelda laughed. "No, I mean it. How big?"

"All you can see—and then more. The whole place is called the Lantana, but each part has a name of its own. There's the Lovelace, the Piedras Blancas, and the Ebonal. And there's the Casa Rosa, the Cenizo, and the Hallelujah . . ."

"The Hallelujah?"

Dos smiled. "Nice name, isn't it? It seems the original settler was so tired and saddle-sore when he finally reached his spread that he fell down on his knees and hollered 'Hallelujah!' "

"I like that," Nelda said.

"And then, of course, there's the Trevor, a little piece of land—less than a hundred sections—that started the whole thing for our family. My grandfather

19

paid a nickle an acre for it the year before the War."

"Everybody on the train said the Lantana's like a state within a state. You've got your own towns and schools and churches . . . and even your own railroad station. They said people are born and die without ever setting foot on land the Camerons don't own. And they said your family rules like royalty."

"Royalty never worked so hard," Dos said, amused. He studied her, wondering as to her age, realizing that the color on her cheeks came from a box rather than from a young girl's natural blush.

She twirled her parasol, enjoying his stare. The sun glinted off his blond head, making it shine like silver. Unable to resist, she ran her gloved fingers through his closely cropped hair, then boldly let the back of her hand graze the outline of his jaw.

He reached out and took her by the waist, pulling her to him. She complied willingly, tilting back her head and parting her lips in anticipation of his kiss. She found to her satisfaction that it was surprisingly gentle —almost sweet. That was *one* reason she enjoyed young boys, but as his tongue touched hers, she realized he was more experienced than most. She locked her hands behind his neck and held him tight.

"I want you to make love to me," she said, breathless as they broke apart.

Her boldness caught Dos by surprise, but Nelda was a woman who'd never felt guilt and who cared nothing for her bad reputation. In fact, she had learned over the years that a bad reputation could be a definite asset.

"Not here, not now," she added. "But tonight. Can you arrange it?"

"I can," Dos answered.

Then, as he reached out for her again, Nelda turned quickly, bewildering him as she suddenly changed roles, dropping the mask of passion for that of coquette, making him follow her back to the surrey. She climbed up unassisted and handed him the reins as he joined her.

"We'd better go," she said. "They'll be missing us."

Their excursion had allowed the slower-moving platform wagons to reach the mansion well ahead of them, and when Dos and Nelda finally arrived, Anne and Alex Cameron were waiting at the top of the steps. For Nelda's benefit, Anne arranged her face in an expression of warm welcome, but her tapping foot alerted Dos to her hidden anger and warned him she would have a private word with him later.

Alex forced himself to be civil, but his fury lay closer to the surface—evidenced by the cloudy darkness of his eyes.

As Nelda pranced up the steps, Dos rushed through the introductions.

"We're honored to have such a celebrated person on the Lantana," Anne said, firing a pointed glance at Dos over Nelda's shoulder.

"It's my own pleasure, Mrs. Cameron, I assure you," Nelda simpered in her best ingénue style, not knowing how repulsive Anne found her act. "And how thoughtful of you to send your son in your covered surrey to carry me from the train."

"You've Dos to thank for that," Anne said with mock sweetness. "It wouldn't do for Miss Flynn to ride in an open-air wagon—would it, Dos?"

Dos squirmed beneath his mother's gaze. "I'll show Nelda to her room," he said quickly, eager to get away from Anne and Alex.

He reached for the door and ushered Nelda inside.

Throughout the confrontation, Anne had taken care to avoid Alex's eyes, but his muttered curse caused her to turn and face him.

"I'll take care of it, Alex."

"Aye! Don't you always?" His eyes went even darker.

"Please, Alex, not that again." She tried to make her voice sound casual, but strain echoed in every word.

"What am I supposed to do, Anne? Stand by in silence while you mollycoddle the lad every time he causes trouble?"

"I can handle him."

"Not very well, I'd say."

"That's not fair, Alex!" Anne's eyes flashed, and she transferred a good part of her anger from her son to her husband.

"Of course it's fair," he countered, determined that she should understand him. "And you're not so blind that you can't see. He's bad. He was born bad."

"No!" Her voice was a cry wrenched from the heart.

"Shutting your eyes to the truth won't make it go away."

"Perhaps part of it's *your* fault, Alex!" Anne said, fighting on behalf of her son.

"If you remember, Anne, *I* had nothing to do with it!" His words were barely whispered, but they sent Anne reeling.

No sooner had he spoken than he was filled with remorse. That wasn't fair! He saw how deeply he had wounded her, and he reached out to comfort her, but she yanked her hands away.

"I'm sorry, Anne! I'm sorry!"

She shuddered as though a chill wind had blown across the sun-bright landscape.

"Forgive me," Alex said quietly.

Anne shrugged, but her face was pinched, her eyes downcast.

"Anne, listen to me," he said. "Don't turn me away. . . ."

"Like you turn away Dos?"

"I tried, Anne. For years and years, I tried. You know that."

"I know that you favor Maggie. You always have. Ever since she was born, she's been your pet. You gave her all your love and seemed to have nothing left over for Dos. And don't think he doesn't know it."

"I could have had room for both."

"Could you, Alex? I don't think so."

Nor, in all honesty, did Alex. He let her remark pass without challenge.

They stood in silence for a moment. In the distance a wagon carrying new arrivals raised a trail of dust against the sky.

"If you'll welcome these good folk, I'll go inside," Anne said tersely, turning toward the door.

"Anne," Alex said as she reached the threshold. "I'm truly sorry for what I said."

She looked at her husband and nodded. "I know you are."

She slipped into the house that she and Alex had built nearly twenty years before. It was a massive Victorian structure with limestone walls and cypress trim rising three stories above the prairie. Its dark slate roof pitched and fell in high, pointed peaks and deep, narrow valleys, and at one end, a four-sided turret soared another full story above the highest gable. It was there, in a small room surrounded by windows beneath a mansard roof, that Anne had her office.

"Mama's grumble room," her daughter Maggie called it, because Anne retired to it whenever she was upset or angry. Yet it was more than that. It was Anne's sanctuary—a place of peace and quiet where she would think and plan, where she could reminisce or forget, as suited her mood, and where she could peer out—

through a brass army telescope—over the kingdom that she ruled.

She intended to go directly there, but voices at the top of the grand staircase warned her that guests were descending, and she ducked into a side parlor, wanting to avoid them until she had time to collect herself. Her half-brother Carlos, sitting by an empty fireplace, rose as she entered.

"Oh, Carlos!" she breathed in surprise. "I thought I was alone."

"What's wrong?" he asked quickly, noticing the pallor on her cheeks and the quiver in her voice.

"Nothing," she said, unwilling to discuss her argument with Alex. "I guess it's just all the excitement. The party's only now beginning, and I already feel as if I've been put through a wringer. I had no idea I'd invited so many people. They're elbow to elbow upstairs, and there're at least as many still to come. Thank God we don't have to put the Joelsboro folk up at night."

"Don't get all frazzled, Anne," Carlos said. "Everyone's going to have a grand old time."

"Everyone but me, I'm afraid."

"You most of all. Just wait till the music starts, and Alex opens the champagne."

She smiled hopefully and let him kiss her cheek. Carlos had a way of soothing her as no one else had, and her angry words with Alex and her consternation with Dos already seemed part of the distant past.

Carlos embodied the history of the settlement of the territory. He was a half-breed, a mixture of the old and new, an uneasy heritage that made him an enigma to most who knew him. His Gachupin mother, the beautiful Sofia, had been a patrician of Spanish blood whose title to the Lantana was already ancient by the time

24

Joel Trevor, the gringo homesteader, the father Carlos shared with Anne, had come to the state in search of land.

Carlos seemed more Spanish than not. Slim, no taller than Anne, but gracefully, powerfully built, he took his dark good looks from his mother. His nose was proudly aquiline, his lips were full and delicately formed just as Sofia's had been, and his thick black hair shone with blue highlights in the bright glint of the sun. Such beauty is seldom seen in a man—and even rarer, as in Carlos's case, when it is utterly masculine.

So on first glance, he seemed an extraordinarily handsome grandee, but his eyes betrayed the confusion of blood in his veins: they were Joel's eyes, silvery-gray like flint glass darkened by the sun.

Anne had reared him from babyhood and thought of him more as a son than as a brother. And Carlos loved her more than anything else on earth—even more than the Lantana, although in his mind the two were inextricably bound. He considered her both mother and sister and stood in awe of her beauty, her intellect, and her spirit—attributes against which he subconsciously measured all other women in his life.

At twenty-five, he was deemed the most eligible catch in Texas, and not a few young girls were drifting into spinsterhood in hopes of snaring him. But Carlos had met them all already—and found them wanting.

He had his flings, of course, but they were discreet and safe, women who would lay no claims on him, who had no designs on the Lantana, who merely wanted to sleep with him for his beauty. Because he loved parties and music and dancing, he was a regular at balls in San Antonio—the only real city he'd ever visited—and his appearance inevitably caused a heart-fluttering stir among the debutantes; but he always arrived and left alone, leaving belles and wallflowers alike sighing after him.

Although by rights he owned half the Lantana, he considered himself—as did Anne and Alex—one of the heirs apparent along with Dos and Maggie. He had no desire to assert his greater claim nor to enhance his position. His time would come soon enough.

He and Dos had grown up together, friends despite the seven-year gap between them, but they were as unlike as their differing appearances would lead one to expect. Never once had Carlos been involved in a brawl. Dos, at eighteen, could number his scrapes by the score. If Carlos had taken advantage of any local girl, no one was the wiser; yet often were the times Anne and Alex had to deal with an irate father complaining that Dos had dishonored his daughter. Hotheaded and impetuous, Dos sullenly endured Anne's reprimands and actively resented Alex's. But he would listen to Carlos. Perhaps it was the closeness of their ages, or Carlos's quiet, sympathetic voice—or maybe it was simply that Dos admired his young uncle and wished—without knowing how to achieve it—he could be more like him.

"Dos stood up the Governor," Anne said, not bothering to mask the irritation in her voice. "Not that I give a hoot about that big bag of hot air, but after all, Jim Hogg *is* the goddamn Governor. Instead, Dos picked up that floozy actress who practically invited herself down on the train. You ought to see her—forty if she's a day, yet dressed like Maggie did when she was twelve —all ruffles and bows! Utterly tacky! She *would* be the kind Dos would go after!"

"I'll talk to him," Carlos offered.

Anne hesitated, then sighed. "I was going to, but maybe you'd better. I'd probably tear him to pieces."

"Here, let's have a drink," Carlos suggested, pouring two stiff shots from a crystal decanter at the sideboard. "Just the two of us, in peace and quiet before we have to face the thundering herds."

Anne reached gratefully for the glass. "I need this," she said, tossing the drink down expertly. She didn't resist when Carlos offered to refill it.

The whiskey began to take effect immediately, calming her jangled nerves, and this time she sipped her drink instead of swallowing it at one gulp. She sank into one of a pair of wingback chairs in front of the empty fireplace and motioned for Carlos to join her in the other.

Gazing down at them from above the mantel was a life-size portrait of Sofia, Carlos's mother. Both of them looked up at it at the same time.

"God, she was beautiful," Anne murmured, gazing at the painting. Sofia was dressed in black silk with tortoise shell combs in her raven hair and a gossamer mantilla that hung in lacy folds almost to her ankles. Her enormous dark eyes dominated her delicate, pale face, and her lips showed only the faintest hint of pink. In one hand a rosary of shiny jet beads twined through her delicate fingers; the other clasped a bouquet of lantana, the only touch of real color on the canvas.

"I wish you had known her as I did," Anne said quietly. "She was the greatest lady who ever lived. If there's anything soft and gentle and good still left in me, it's due to her."

Anne lowered her eyelids, unable to look any longer at the woman she'd loved so deeply. Her glass was empty again, and Carlos moved to fill it.

"No," she said this time. "I don't want to be drunker than my guests."

"When does the orchestra start?" Carlos asked.

"Nine. Of course we'll have dinner first." Then suddenly she clapped her hand over her mouth. "Maggie! Oh, my God! I forgot all about her. I promised to help her dress!"

She sprang from the chair and headed for the door. "Oh, the poor thing! You know how nervous she gets. She's been dreading her *quincianera* as much as she's been looking forward to it!"

Anne hurried through the foyer, nodding to her gathered guests, but not stopping to chat. She darted up the stairs and went directly to Maggie's bedroom, slipping inside without bothering to knock.

"Maggie, dear, I'm sorry. I got sidetracked somehow," she apologized, shutting the door behind her. "But you'll have to hurry—we've got guests jammed to the rafters."

Maggie swung away from her vanity table with an exasperated sigh. "Oh, Mama, I'm not like you! It takes me hours!"

Anne smiled gently. "Here, let me help you," she said, taking the heated curling iron from the lamp chimney and rolling up a lock of Maggie's hair.

"I don't know why I was cursed with straight hair when both you and Papa are naturally curly," Maggie said, the faintest sign of a childish pout playing over her lips. "And you two—so famous for breeding!"

Anne laughed. "*Cattle* breeding, my dear!" she admonished. "That's what we're known for, not . . . well, not for what you made it sound like."

"You can tell even before a bull gets with a cow whether the calf'll be red or black, longhorn or shorthorn."

"That's cows. They're a whole lot more predictable than people. And furthermore, don't run around the ball tonight talking about breeding and bulls getting

28

with cows. That's all right just among us—that's our business. But there'll be a whole lot of city folk present who've never set foot on a ranch before, and talk like that will set their ears right back."

"Silly bunch."

"You're going to be around some of the finest people in the state."

"I thought *we* were the finest people in the state," Maggie teased, but there was a hint of self-assurance in what she said.

"We are," Anne replied. "But everybody knows that; so we don't have to remind them."

Maggie studied her mother's reflection in the mirror. Anne wore a gown of green silk that exactly matched the color of her eyes. The bodice was low-cut and sleeveless supported by shoulder straps of ribbon and lace, a style that was already out-moded, even in this remote region, but Anne cared little for fashion and wore her clothes with such casual aplomb that no one ever thought of her as looking out-of-date. Her yellow hair was pulled back from her face and fastened in a loose bun, and around her neck she wore a garnet lavaliere that had belonged to her mother and to her grandmother before that.

"You look beautiful, Mama," Maggie said. "No one would ever guess you were forty-five."

"You do have a direct way of speaking, Maggie," Anne said, putting aside the curling iron and examining her handiwork.

"No! I mean it," Maggie insisted. "We could almost pass for sisters. For half-sisters, anyway, like you and Carlos are half kin."

"Well, I take that as a compliment," Anne said, "and for that I thank you. But you'd oblige me by not ringing

29

a bell through the house and announcing my age to any and all who have ears to hear."

"Don't worry. No one would believe me, anyway."

Anne smiled and kissed Maggie's forehead. "You're lovely yourself."

Maggie sighed. "I wish I could believe that."

Anne looked surprised. "Why, just look in the mirror if you need convincing."

Maggie stared at her reflection. "Oh, I can see myself all right," she said. "But it's not what I really believe. I just can't help thinking of myself as sort of plain, like . . . you know that photograph of me? The one that German man took when I was nine."

"He wasn't German—he was Swiss. And his name was Herr Elmendorf."

"Well, anyway," Maggie went on. "That's how I see myself. When I close my eyes and think of me, that's what floats up in my mind. I look so donkey-faced—big eyes, long nose, funny chin! I wish you'd burn that picture."

"Well, you did look a bit mulish in that photograph," Anne said, only half-joking. "But let me tell you something you've probably forgotten. That night at dinner, Mr. Elmendorf called you to his side. He pulled your hair back away from your face and said 'Look at this child! Look at her bone structure—the wide forehead, the high cheekbones, the good strong chin, and these eyes the color of an Alpine sky. One day she'll be most striking!' "

"I do remember," Maggie murmured softly.

"Well," Anne said proudly. "Mr. Elmendorf was right."

Maggie tried to smile and squeezed her mother's hand.

"Now stand up," Anne said briskly. "You've got to get into your gown."

Fifteen minutes later Maggie stepped into her gilt leather slippers and was ready.

"Let's go, dear," Anne said. "Everyone will be wondering where we are."

But Maggie hung back, turning from side to side, examining herself in the mirror. Unlike Anne, she was dressed in the height of fashion, wearing a tea dress of eau de Nil satin with enormous gigot sleeves that made her eighteen-inch waist look even smaller. The plunging decolletage revealed the tops of her youthful breasts, and around her neck she wore a wide choker studded with milky moonstones. But still she was not convinced.

"What do you think?" she asked Anne.

"I think you're the prettiest thing I've ever seen."

"No, tell me really!"

"I'm telling you really. For the life of me I don't understand why you can't believe that!"

She stared in exasperation, hands on hips, wondering what she could say to convince her daughter that she *was* pretty, extremely so, and improving every day. There was nothing wrong with her that another year wouldn't remedy.

A little more height, a little less baby fat. Then, limbs that now seemed gawky would be deemed lithe and graceful. "Oh, how impatient children are! Especially girls! If you only knew what growing up will bring you, you'd cling to girlhood!"

Maggie took Anne's statement as a reprimand and lowered her eyes, no longer able to look at the beautiful woman in whose shadow she'd lived. No matter how hard she tried, she never hoped to match her mother's beauty—or to come even close! Why couldn't Anne be plain like other mothers? Even in that old dress, she

31

would look finer than any other woman at the party! She could wear her old leather pants and cotton shirt and still outshine them all.

Maggie's sigh perplexed Anne, and she felt the tug of impatience. "Come along, Maggie. Run downstairs and play hostess until I get there. I'm going to look in on your father."

They parted in the hall, Maggie taking a deep breath and heading for the grand staircase, Anne gliding toward the suite she and Alex shared.

She hesitated for a brief moment, then pushed through the door. Alex had changed into evening clothes, looking tall and strikingly handsome in his finery, a midnight blue vicuña tailcoat with rolled silk lapels and a brocade waistcoat the color of ivory.

He greeted Anne with a wary look, but she smiled and crossed the floor to join him. She had a long memory, but she knew the futility of grudges borne against one you love.

"You're mighty splendid," she said. "I see you've managed to knot your cravat without my help."

Alex's face softened with relief. So she *had* forgiven him, after all. His damned Scottish temper! When would he learn not to turn it against her? "I can manage a lot when I have to. I only ask you to tie it because it brings you close to me."

Truce! Anne thought gratefully. "You've always been overly randy—to use your Scottish expression."

"You've never complained."

"No. And I never shall. I wouldn't have you any other way!"

She slipped easily into his arms, and he kissed her lightly on the lips.

"My Scottish cowboy!" she murmured. "You're handsomer now than you were when I first met you. Just look at yourself—hardly a wrinkle, barely a touch of gray, and what little there is only adds distinction to your face."

Alex chuckled happily, relishing the sensation of Anne's compliant body against his.

The second son of a Scottish landowner, he had left the misty green Highlands to make his way in the New World, bringing with him little more than his own keen intelligence and a vision of empire in his wintry blue eyes. In the beginning, he lusted for the Lantana more than he desired Anne. They both knew the truth of this, although they found no reason to speak of it, for as the years slipped by Alex discovered Anne to be the true treasure of the Lantana; and their mutual love had matured and deepened, until now they felt themselves to be more than partners, more than a couple.

A glance between them across a crowded room could speak an entire conversation; a touch conveyed more than the thousands of I-love-you's they'd murmured to each other over the years.

So now, in their comfortable embrace, they found little need to talk. Alex kissed her again, his lips moving to brush her finely molded ear as lightly as a butterfly. She nuzzled into his neck and breathed deeply of the rich scent of bay rum and Havana tobacco.

"God, when I hold you like this I feel like a lad again," he whispered, his words tantalizing her ear, causing her heart to flip-flop so violently that she was afraid it would stop beating. "Damn! I wish we weren't already dressed."

Without a word, Anne reached up and loosened his cravat. Smiling, she unbuttoned his waistcoat, then, one by one, picked free the pearl studs down the front of his starched bib.

They spent an hour together in bed, making love

with a vigor that would have put Dos to shame, then lying spent and happy, dozing lightly until the darkening sky beyond their windows told them that the afternoon had passed and evening's violet shadows were beginning to pool across the land.

Anne preceded Alex downstairs, and as she greeted her guests, each one remarked that she had never looked more radiant. Anne smiled privately to herself, accepting their compliments and thinking: If you only knew why . . . if you only knew. . . .

# 3

The bronze, mellow-throated yard bell announced dinner, and no one except perhaps the New York visitors thought it the slightest bit odd that such an elegantly attired gathering would sit outside at long wooden tables to feast on barbecue and frijoles.

The Governor sat at Anne's table, and she made it a point to be more than hospitable toward him. Alex presided over another table, one seating at least fifty people, with Maggie at his side. They were surrounded by old friends, people Maggie felt most comfortable with; and it had taken only a "My, how bonny my lassie looks tonight!" from Alex to give Maggie the confidence that no lavish compliment from Anne could ever achieve.

Carlos captured the glances of every young girl—and most of the older women, too. His raven hair was combed back from his wide forehead, and beneath straight, dark brows his flint gray eyes, fringed with coal black lashes, glittered in the torchlight like multi-faceted jewels.

He was very Spanish tonight, very much the handsome grandee, in a formal black *charro* suit shot through with flashing silver embroidery, an intricate filigreed tracery on the tightly fitting garment that emphasized the graceful form of his body. His shirt was snowy white silk, knotted at the neck with a brilliant crimson scarf, the bright flash of color calling attention to the startling beauty of his face.

His twice-polished boots gleamed like patent leather, and on his heels he wore the jangling silver spurs, inlaid with gold, that had been Sofia's wedding present to his father.

There had been a scramble for his table, and he found himself flanked by the most determined girls in the territory. He gave each one an equal share of attention—paying compliments, finding it unnecessary to lie, for each in her own way was truly beautiful. He laughed appreciatively at their pleasantries, listened intently to their stories, and promised each one a dance. But that was all. Neither in manner, nor in words, did he imply more.

Dos was, of course, with Nelda. No formal suit for him, he wore instead a pair of skin-tight leather trousers, laced at the fly with rawhide thongs, and his shirt was a soft, loose-fitting cotton *camisa* opened nearly to the waist to show the iron-hard muscles of his chest.

His casual provocative attire had raised eyebrows, as he knew it would, and he realized, even as he dressed, that his appearance was one more thing Anne would add to her mental list to speak to him about. But he didn't care. The evening was young, and his tongue-lashing was hours off—*if* it even came at all, for Anne had been known to cool off as suddenly as she'd grown riled.

For the moment, he was determined to enjoy himself. His plate was laden with crispy *cabrito,* spareribs, frijoles, and flour tortillas dripping with butter. The beer was cold, the *picante* sauce fiery hot, and Nelda Flynn was at his side. What more could he want?

But Nelda had found something she wanted more than Dos. She had her ear cocked toward him—not in order to hear him better, but to give herself a clearer view across two crowded tables, for her eyes had suddenly fastened on Carlos.

*Oooh!* I've made a big mistake, she thought. That black-haired princeling is the prettiest thing I've ever seen in my life. Suddenly the golden bull at her side interested her no more than a bawling calf that had just been cut.

Dos, utterly unaware he'd slipped from favor, finished his dinner and snapped his fingers to have his beer stein refilled. Lounging indolently at the table, he bit off the end of a fragrant cheroot and bent forward to light it from a flickering hurricane lamp. While he busied himself, Nelda caught Carlos's eye. Her arched brow posed the question, and Carlos answered with a quick, almost imperceptible smile.

Why not? he thought. She wasn't half as tacky as Anne had described her. And he couldn't, for the life of him, see why Anne thought she was over forty. By torchlight, her complexion was as smooth and fresh as that of the young girls beside him; her lips were red, her cheeks rosy, and her daring neckline revealed the tops of her two taut, creamy breasts. Why not? Dos won't put up a fuss. He's never worried about losing a girl in his life. They fall all over him as it is, and he can have anyone he wants. No, I'll take the actress tonight. Dos'll manage. Then if he's still interested, he can have her later. After all, the party has a week to run.

Dos sat back, a wreath of blue smoke crowning his silver-blond head. He smiled contentedly, his belly full, the alcohol from his fourth beer streaming merrily through his veins, Nelda's nearness causing a pleasurable pressure against his thong-laced fly.

He reached out and let his fingers brush the bare flesh at the nape of her neck. She was undeniably beautiful, and more worldly than any woman he'd ever known. She spoke of New York and Philadelphia and Boston as if they were Brownsville or Laredo. She had been to San Francisco twice and her deliberately graphic descriptions of the notorious Barbary Coast sent the plain country folk around her into such wide-eyed shock that their last mouthfuls of beans stuck in their throats. All of which amused her immensely, and she imagined they couldn't be more scandalized if she stripped off her clothes and danced naked on the table.

Having secured Carlos with a mere fleeting glance, she saw no reason not to turn her attention back to Dos. He was pretty, too, and if she had time—and if Carlos disappointed her—she'd take him on in turn.

You little bull, she kept thinking as she watched him squirm on the bench trying to make the touch of his knee against her leg appear accidental; and she was fully aware—as he intended her to be—of the bulge in his leather breeches. You little seed-bull! If that half-breed uncle of yours weren't so perfectly beautiful, I'd be sleeping with you tonight. Ah well, keep yourself up, sweet Romeo, there's still half a chance I'll call to you from my balcony!

Dinner was over. The ballroom began to fill, but it

was mostly young folk. Their elders strolled about the grounds enjoying the welcome coolness of the night, needing the leisurely walk to help settle their dinner. Everyone had eaten too much—and some had drunk too much—and all of them needed a respite before the long night of dancing began. Neighbors—though they lived a hundred miles and more apart, they were neighbors still in this land of almost unimaginable distances —seized this interval to trade gossip, good news and bad, and to wonder stoically when the next drought would settle in. They talked, in their slow drawls, as quickly as they could, trying to cover it all, for it might be a year or two before they saw each other again.

Dos sensed the change in Nelda's attitude. Her eyes had ceased to flirt with him, and she appeared preoccupied. He attempted to interest her in a walk, thinking of a storeroom behind a barn where there was an old cot with a horsehair mattress and, if he recollected right, a Mexican *serape* for a blanket.

However, Nelda would hear none of it. "But the dancing's about to begin. Look, there's the orchestra."

"You that keen on dancing?"

"I started my career as a dancer."

Dos fell into sulky silence, but remained close by her side.

Nelda didn't mind his proximity—not as long as she could keep Carlos in view across the ballroom. It was still very early; she had plenty of time to make her move.

Outside, the long tables were mostly deserted, little groups remaining here and there chatting over coffee or brandy while silent servants drifted among them clearing away the debris of dinner.

Alex was still at his place, as was Maggie, along with friends from San Antonio, Dora and Marcus Buchanan, the Heimbeckers, the Froehlers, and the Quinns, all old-timers, rich ranchers, but whose holdings totaled together wouldn't make up a fifth of the Lantana.

Maggie's pre-fiesta jitters had largely dissipated in the company of her parents' long-time acquaintances, and she was enjoying herself just listening to them talk.

Anne moved to join them, waving her hand to keep the men from rising at her approach.

"Best *cabrito* I ever ate," Marcus Buchanan said, reaching across to pat Anne's hand as she settled herself between Alex and Maggie.

"Thank you, Marcus. The cook took care to select only the finest kids."

"You could tell it, dear," Dora Buchanan chimed in. She had grown enormously fat in later years and quite gray, but her face was still as pink and unlined as a baby's.

"We were talking about your train that brought us down here," Herman Froehler said.

"You folks certainly know how to do things right," his wife Christine added. "Imagine! Not just a car to hook onto the end of the Southern Pacific, but a whole train!"

"Well, when we finally got tracks down this way, we bought the parlor car from Mr. Pullman," Anne explained, referring to the beautifully appointed coach that had been built to her specifications. It was furnished with velvet couches and mahogany club chairs, gold-fringed curtains, concealed beds, a dining table, a galley, a lavatory, and electric lights. The outside was glossy midnight blue with gilt letters spelling out the name LANTANA superimposed over the Crown of Thorns brand.

"Then we thought, shoot, the thing can't run by itself, and what if we wanted to take off in it and no train was coming through that day? So Alex bought the locomotive—and if you have a locomotive, you have to have a coal car, and of course a caboose for the crew. So you see, the thing just grew like Topsie!"

Dora Buchanan laughed with amusement at Anne's impeccable logic.

"It's a damned comfortable way to travel," Samuel Heimbecker said, loosening the bottom two buttons of his waistcoat and stifling a belch with his damask napkin. "If I had one of my own, I'd never travel any other way."

"Nor I," Christine Froehler added enviously.

Anne smiled with satisfaction. She took an unconcealed delight with her train. When she first came to this region as a girl of twelve, it had taken the better part of a week in a bone-jarring wagon just to cover the distance from San Antonio. Now she could leave the Lantana in the morning and be ensconced in her suite at the Menger Hotel later that afternoon, fresh, rested, and ready to go out for the evening.

"Think of the old days," she said to Alex, referring not to her childhood, but to a time as recent as the year before when San Antonio was accessible only by stagecoach. "Things are certainly getting better. I *like* the modern world."

"Tell me about the old days," Maggie asked suddenly, almost the first thing she'd said all evening. "Tell me what it was like back then."

"No," Anne replied.

"Oh, please, Mama!"

Anne shook her head adamantly. "The old days were exciting, but they weren't much fun. You're lucky to be living when you are."

Maggie wrinkled her nose. "I'd like a little adventure."

"You wouldn't if you had to live through it. Am I right, Alex?"

"Aye, right you are," he agreed.

Maggie was not to be put off. "Oh, I've heard stories about you, Mama. Ramiro Rivas tells me everything."

"Well, he shouldn't. I pay him to be a foreman, not a storyteller. Besides, Ramiro is getting old. I wouldn't trust his memory."

"He told me you rode the Chisolm Trail. Is that true?"

Anne glanced at Alex. *He* knew, but she wondered, did the others? "What utter nonsense!"

"Oh!" Maggie exclaimed in disappointment. "I was hoping it was true. It made you seem so glamorous."

Anne's lips turned up in a half-smile. "I'm not at all glamorous . . . never was!"

Marcus Buchanan snorted a contradiction, remembering Anne in her twenties. Alex smiled and reached out to clasp Anne's hand.

"And Ramiro told me that every man in South Texas was crazy in love with you," Maggie pressed.

"Not true," Anne said, embarrassed in front of the others. "As a matter of fact, your father found me on the remnant table."

"Some remnant!" Alex laughed.

"They met at my house, Maggie," Dora interjected.

"Was it love at first sight?" asked Maggie.

Anne and the Buchanans joined Alex's laughter.

"Of course not," Anne said. "There's no such thing. And you'll do yourself a favor to remember that." She rolled her eyes to the star-jeweled violet sky. "Love at first sight! Think of all the trouble that silly notion has caused! Still, I imagine every schoolgirl believes in it."

"Do you, Maggie?" Alex asked gently.

Maggie sat back, subdued, feeling put down by Anne's response. "I don't know, Papa. It hasn't happened to me yet."

"And let's hope it doesn't," Anne said, rising, indicating it was time to relinquish the table to the waiting servants. They were the last still in the yard, and the orchestra had struck up the first tune of the evening.

Dora Buchanan hauled herself off her bench. "Good advice, my dear," she said to Maggie. "Look before you leap!"

"Why, Dora," Marcus said, offering his arm to his wife, "we married a week after we met."

They were ambling off toward the house, but Maggie heard Dora's trailing voice. "Things were different then, Marcus. Girls grew up quicker. Why, by the time *I* was fifteen . . ."

Maggie wished she had heard the rest. Were they really that different when they were her age? And if so, how were they different? What did they know that she didn't?

"Why so quiet?" Alex asked as they reached the steps.

"Just thinking," Maggie replied.

"Well, perk up, my bonny lass. This is your special party, and I expect you to shine."

Maggie forced a smile and entered the house.

The magnificent ballroom needed no adornment other than the masses of yellow, cream, and bronze chrysanthemums that bloomed from every silver vase Anne possessed. Overhead, the glittering chandeliers filled the spacious room with light, burnishing the honeyed walls an ever richer gold and reflecting brightly in the pellucid onyx floor that had come from the quarries near Oued-Abdallah. Potted palms framed the dais where the orchestra played, and linen-covered tables bore mountains of petits fours on Limoges trays and silver buckets of iced champagne.

It could have been the ballroom of any splendid mansion in New York or London or even San Francisco, but there were touches here and there to remind

43

you that this was cowboy territory, cattle country, the seat of empire—Lantana headquarters.

Mounted on the graceful proscenium arch above the dais was a set of longhorns with a spread of more than eight feet. Even now, the skittish, wild longhorn was growing scarce, killed off, interbred, supplanted by fatter, more tractable stock from England, Scotland, and India. Alex himself was partially responsible. He had imported Angus for their beef, Brahma for their strength, and bred them to the sturdy, drought-resistant longhorn and was well on his way to creating a new breed he called the Lantana cow.

The camelback sofas were upholstered with beautifully patterned horsehides, roan, chestnut, pinto, and brindle. In the parlors, Chippendale chairs rested on rare Mexican rugs whose colors rivaled the finest Persians, and a rack from a spectacular stag deer was as likely to hang above a mantel as a painting or an ornate gilt mirror. And even the paintings reflected the place, for they were Russells, Remingtons, and two gigantic Bierstadts.

These hard-working people knew little formality, and dancing had already begun before Maggie entered. Alex extended his hand to his daughter and led her onto the floor, but it wasn't a moment before a young lieutenant from Fort Sam Houston, splendid and ramrod-straight in full-dress uniform, intervened and swept Maggie from her father's arms and into his.

Marcus and Dora Buchanan joined Anne at the edge of the dance floor. Marcus offered her a glass of champagne, but she appeared not to notice. Dora, puzzled by the bemused expression on Anne's face, asked, "Darling? Is something wrong?"

Anne smiled wistfully and was unable to prevent her eyes from going suddenly damp. "What? Oh! No . . .

44

no. There's nothing wrong. It's just that I'm watching my little girl take her very first spin around the dance floor in the arms of a young man."

She bit her bottom lip and took a deep breath, fighting back tears.

On the other side of the ballroom, Maggie was breathless with excitement, perfectly happy to be in the arms of her handsome partner and to be waltzing on slippers that scarcely seemed to touch the floor. Then suddenly the dance was over, and she realized she didn't know what to do. For an instant she clung to the young lieutenant, then broke away in confusion. He saw her quick blush of distress and came to her aid.

"Let's go for a cup of punch," he said, offering her his arm and heading for one of the serving tables.

Anne witnessed the scene and murmured to Dora, "I do hope Maggie realizes that she shouldn't stay with the same boy all evening. I thought I'd taught her everything, but all of a sudden I realize there're so many more things she doesn't know."

Dora smiled wisely, having raised a daughter herself. "Don't worry. They seem to learn these things all by themselves. After all, *we* did, didn't we?"

Anne looked surprised. "Did we? I suppose so. I . . . I really don't remember."

The band was playing a polka, and Alex, knowing it was Anne's favorite dance, led her onto the floor. Her feet tapped lightly, in perfect rhythm, and for a moment as they dipped and swirled, she was supremely happy. Then suddenly Alex felt her stiffen in his arms and heard her breathe in disbelief: "I'll be damned! How did one of *them* get in here?"

Her concentration was lost; she missed the beat and stumbled against Alex.

"What's wrong?" he asked, catching her and seeing

that her face had paled except for two spots of red blazing on her cheeks—an infallible sign of anger in Anne.

"One of Emma Stark's boys is here," she hissed, abandoning any attempt to begin dancing again. "How the hell did he get past the gate guards? They know my orders!"

Alex followed Anne's eyes and easily picked out the boy she meant. All the Starks looked alike—burly and blond like their German father.

Alex's face was grim, ashen beneath the ever-present tan. "I'll get rid of him!"

"No! Let me," Anne said, catching his sleeve.

"Don't involve yourself, Anne," Alex warned. "Why provide grist for the mill?"

He's right, Anne thought, although nothing would give her more pleasure at the moment than to order whichever one of the Starks he was off the place. She had known them all as children, for they were born in the foreman's house not a mile from the old hacienda. But now that they were grown, she couldn't place names with faces. Except for Davey, her godson whom she had helped deliver and whom she'd named. He alone still acknowledged her when they chanced to meet on the dusty streets of Joelsboro. And Peter. She knew him by the badge—the sheriff's silver star. But the others—how many were there? Six? Seven? She couldn't remember. They had learned from Emma Stark's knee to cross the street if they saw Anne coming. For her part, Anne had standing instructions at the gatehouse to turn away any of Rudy Stark's kin who sought to enter.

Now, one had slipped through, and she watched as Alex crossed the onyx floor to confront him.

The boy had meant no harm. It was a lark—he'd heard about the party and rumbled through the gate past the guard with a group of young people in a hay-lined wagon from Joelsboro. He was laughing, enjoying his first taste of champagne and marvelling at the opulence of the mansion he'd never before entered.

Alex's hand gripped his shoulder like a vise and spun him around.

"I don't believe you were invited here, laddie," Alex said softly, keeping his voice down so others wouldn't hear.

"I thought everybody was," Klaus Stark said.

"Not you . . . not any of you."

Klaus's German pride blazed up in him like fire in a furnace. "We're as good as you!"

"It's my house, and you're not wanted here. Now go under your own steam, or I'll have my men throw you out."

The boy shook off Alex's iron grip. "I know why I'm not welcome."

"The reason doesn't matter. Get out!"

Klaus's glittering eyes taunted Alex. "Do you know the reason? If you don't, I'll be happy to tell you."

"Shut your bloody gob and leave my house!"

Klaus stood his ground and stared at Alex as long as he dared. Then spinning on his heel, he stalked from the ballroom.

Some of the young people had drifted outside to the gallery that surrounded the house. A few couples had found dark corners where they stood with arms locked about each other; one or two country boys with champagne-stunned brains lay sprawled on their bellies with arms outstretched in a vain effort to stop the porch from bucking like a wild bronco. Others—non-dancers mostly—leaned on the stone balustrade and stared out into the looming darkness. The night was so clear and calm they could see the diamond points of stars glittering almost to the horizon.

Then the twin main doors flew open, and they saw a figure hurtle down the steps, pausing to scream in a fury-filled voice: "Fuckin' rich sonsofbitches! I ain't forgettin' this!"

They watched, too stunned to move, as he grabbed a horse—whose it was, he didn't care—yanked it free of the hitching post at the edge of the lawn, and spurred it off into the night, heading for town.

Inside the house, Dos was searching for Nelda. On the pretext of wanting to powder her nose, she had given him the slip and joined Carlos. In a vain attempt at discretion, they had stolen through the kitchen and out the back, but in the inky darkness had nearly trampled over Virgil Jones grappling on the steps with one of the bright-eyed little kitchenmaids.

"Sorry, Virg," Carlos murmured quickly, clamping his arm around Nelda's tiny waist and hurrying her off.

" 'At's awright, Carlos," Virgil called boozily after them. "I weren't gettin' nowhere nohow . . . now c'mon, *señorita*, you purty little thang, move that hand an' lemme taste them sweet lips. . . ."

Carlos whisked Nelda out to the carriage shed and, hitching up Anne's new buggy, set off down the road toward the salt cedar arroyo Dos had visited with her earlier in the day.

The sparrows were gone or asleep, but what sounded like the same mockingbird called out drowsily, then fell silent. The only other song was the mournful cooing of a flight of whitewing enchanting the darkness. *"Hoo-hoo, hoo-hoooo!"* they called in plaintive sweetness to each other from the highest branches, and there was a soft, rapid flutter of wings as others settled in.

"When I was a child," Carlos said as he and Nelda stretched out on a blanket beneath the salt cedars, "I thought the trees themselves made that sound. I thought

48

it was marvelous that something besides animals had a voice."

Nelda was not a bit interested. She was only sorry that it was so dark because she wanted to look at this slim young man's body. She put her hand between his legs and shocked him into silence.

It took him a moment to recover, but when he did, he moved quickly. Her lacy, frilly dress seemed to have a thousand buttons but he flicked them open in an instant, pulling down her bodice and freeing her ribbon-trimmed camisole.

He stretched out alongside her and pulled her close against him. Since she couldn't see his body, she let her hands inform her. She traced the curve of his back between his shoulder blades down to his buttocks, noting with pleasure that he was almost hairless. She liked her men smooth, another reason for preferring the young ones.

Carlos buried his face in her neck, his finely shaped lips moistening her flesh, experiencing the taste of powder, finding it alluring and exciting.

He caught her earlobe between his teeth and chewed lightly. Nelda felt herself stirred at last and grabbed him tightly about the shoulders. Then his lips were on her eyelids, leaving one to caress the other, his warm tongue feeling her eyeballs flickering back and forth in rapid excitement beneath the tissue-thin lids.

Nelda groaned as he shifted on top of her, and she locked her silky legs around his hips. She slipped her hands between their bodies, palms up against his flesh, and ran them down his hard, smooth belly till she found what she was seeking.

*Ahhh!* It *never* fails! It's always the slight ones, the slim ones, the ones with bodies like this, that have the most! She wished she could see it. It was so hot between her palms she was astonished it didn't glow with its own fire.

Carlos seemed in no hurry, his lips only now having moved from her eyelids to her other ear. She felt her body churning, quickening, thrusting itself against him; her heartbeat was cannon fire in her ears, so loud she was sure she would be deafened. Then suddenly, surprisingly, she shuddered. But the plateau was momentary, and as his burning lips dropped to the cleft between her breasts she felt herself buoyed up once again as if on a column of flame. She blazed, felt her body ignite—and still he had not taken her!

Dos grabbed a bottle of iced champagne and left the ballroom acting on a tip that someone had seen Nelda heading for the kitchen door. He stumbled outside, his brain spinning with alcohol, and startled Virgil and the Mexican maid.

"Aw, hell," Virgil said in disgust. "I ain't gettin' nowhere, 'specially with all this goddamn traffic. Go ahead on, Dos, take her. She's a reg'lar spitfire, anyhow."

"I'm looking for someone else."

"That New York actress you been courtin'?"

"You've seen her?"

"Seen her? She dang near stomped on my face! I don't know where they went. They hitched up a buggy and struck off down the road. Forget her, Dos, an' try to get next to this one. She done whupped *me!* She's got those goddamn legs clamped so tight together, it'd take a crowbar to pry 'em apart. Maybe you're man enough. I sure as hell ain't!"

"Them?" Dos asked. "Who was with her?"

It took a moment for Virgil to switch horses. "With who? Oh . . . with that New York lady? Why that sneaky ol' Carlos, that's who."

Carlos! You sonofabitch! You stole my girl!

Dos stepped over Virgil and the reluctant maid and strode off across the yard. The moon, three days past full, had cleared the horizon looking as if one of the lopsided orange pumpkins had left the garden and floated into the sky. It threw the shapes of distant trees into sharp silhouette and spread inky shadows across the land, but Dos was immune to the fairylike beauty it created out of the desolate landscape. Nor did he need the moon to light his way. Even inebriated, he knew every inch of this land for thousands of acres around, and he could make his way blindfolded down any caliche trail that meandered past clumps of nopal cactus and mottes of gnarled mesquite.

A coyote howled lonesomely out of the darkness, and a barn owl replied with a querulous hiss from the rafters of the carriage shed. Dos paused at the head of the road, now gleaming white as salt, and opened the bottle of champagne. The cork flew off with the sound of a pistol shot and frightened the owl into flight.

Dos took a long pull at the bottle, belched up the effervescent bubbles, and shambled off down the road. It took him half an hour to reach the arroyo, and he saw the moonlight reflecting off the leather top of the buggy parked beside the row of salt cedars.

He dropped into the muddy arroyo and moved so silently not even the skittish whitewings nesting overhead were disturbed.

A low purring moan of passion brought him up short, and peering over the creek bank, he saw Carlos and Nelda. The actress's arms were locked around his uncle's bare back, and her hips were thrusting rhythmically against his flanks. Carlos's naked buttocks were pale in the faint light, and his lips were gently sucking one of Nelda's breasts.

Dos watched, fascinated, feeling his own excitement

rising within him, as Carlos shifted, half-rising on his knees. Nelda's moans turned into sharp little cries, each one longer and deeper than the one before until what sounded like a continuous growl filled Dos's ears.

He turned and made his silent way back down the arroyo, waiting until he was far removed before climbing onto its bank and retracing his steps back toward the house.

The image of what he had seen tormented him.

Dos swore and threw the nearly drained champagne bottle against a clump of spiny nopal. Had it been anyone other than Carlos, he would have torn into the couple, wrenching the man away from Nelda, dragging him into the dirt and ramming his big fists into his rival's face. But he didn't have the heart to fight Carlos. Not Carlos! The only man on the Lantana who took up for him whenever he stumbled into trouble, the only person, besides Anne, who stood between him and Alex's disgust and anger! No, not Carlos! Anyone other than Carlos!

Frustration welled up in Dos. He stood in the middle of the glowing road and bellowed like an animal at the tired old moon. Music and merry laughter from the big house reached his ears, taunting him, torturing him. He spun around and raced back to the cactus where he'd thrown the champagne, finding it as quickly as a bird-dog could spot its quarry. Sharp spines drew blood as he grabbed the bottle and pulled it out. There was little more than a swallow left, but he gulped it down, then turned and ran for the corral.

He chose a fleet, black stallion, saddled it swiftly, then spurring it with his booted heels, galloped off across the prairie.

# 4

Klaus Stark had gone directly to the Liberty Saloon in Joelsboro. A single-room, wooden building, one in a row of similarly false-fronted, frame structures that lined both sides of the town's rutted Main Street, it was something more than a bar where cowboys could wash down with liquor the choking dust they'd eaten all day. Near the entrance, by heavily draped windows, were baize-covered gaming tables for faro, blackjack, and poker. Along the side were cramped high-backed booths where cronies could meet, drink, and talk with a modicum of privacy, and at the rear was a raised platform, a rude stage where a fiddler or an accordionist might hold forth on weekends, providing music for the half-dozen foofaraw-gowned slatterns who passed themselves off as dancers.

Tonight there was no music, and the saloon was relatively empty, most of the townsfolk taking advantage of the rare opportunity to sample Lantana hospitality.

Klaus bypassed the only poker table in use and leaned against the gleaming mahogany bar. The saloon-keeper was slow in coming. He didn't like Klaus—or any of the Stark boys, for that matter. They held their liquor badly, and their hot-headed German tempers had been the cause of more than one ruckus in the place. And he could see by the look in Klaus's eyes that he was already properly oiled.

Too proud to call out for service, Klaus waited with uncustomary patience and passed the time until the saloon-keeper placed a bottle in front of him by giving the once-over to the girls who sat gossiping at a table in front of the stage. It was the usual bunch, Fat Fanny with her flaming red hair and gold teeth that glittered more brightly than Montezuma's treasure house; the sallow-skinned Hester with her crossed eyes and hunched shoulders; Ethel, who steadfastly denied she was pregnant even as her swollen belly kept her more than a foot away from the table; Guadalupe, who could guarantee a cowboy a case of crabs; and the nasty-tempered Cora, who kept a stiletto in her boot and a pearl-handled Colt .41 in her lace-trimmed bag.

There was another girl at the table, new to the Liberty Saloon, but familiar to Klaus, for he had met her once or twice in his brother's apothecary.

Her name was Lorna Rivers, and she lived with her parents in a rented adobe hovel on the dusty edge of town. Her father had once been a gentleman, a stock-broker in Philadelphia before gold fever seized him and led him west to Denver, where he made a quick fortune out of the Lost Smoke mine only to fritter it away on women, cards, and stables of fine horses. Liquor allevi-ated the pain of sudden poverty, and when he wasn't drunk, he rendered himself senseless with opium. He married a woman who was part-squaw and who relished the bottle as much as he did.

Whenever he had a few dollars in his pocket, he'd head for a local saloon with his family in tow. While his wife drank herself numb, he'd play poker—and Lorna, with nothing else to do, would hang around the table and watch.

She taught herself numbers from the spots on the cards, and almost without knowing it, she learned the perils of betting on an inside straight and the chances a person had of getting a winning hand against another fellow's pair. And without ever holding a hand of cards, she grew to understand why her father always lost.

Her parents had no love for Lorna, but she was a convenience, for without her they would have starved. Early on, she'd learned to pick through rubbish bins behind butcher shops and grocery stores for cast off bones with fat and gristle that hadn't yet spoiled and wormy vegetables that could be trimmed and used for stew. And later, she'd learned to steal, developing a sixth sense that told her when the shopkeeper's eyes were averted. Then she'd deftly take what she needed and drop it into the lining of her ragged coat. Only once had she been caught and beaten, when the lining tore and three fresh apples gave her away by thumping like billiard balls onto the floor. That very day, she swiped a needle and thread and taught herself to sew.

She regarded her parents with silent loathing and vowed a thousand times to run away. They roamed the land, moving a dozen times a year, and with each new town Lorna prayed that her father would sober up and find work, that they would install themselves in a house that didn't leak, whose dirt floors didn't turn to mud whenever it rained and that wasn't so numbingly cold whenever the winter winds blew.

She didn't believe in miracles, but she hated to abandon her dream—she longed to be like everyone else, with a home she could call her own; she yearned for the company of friends and the chance to go to school. But the time for school had passed, and she turned sixteen without ever learning to read or write. Nevertheless, there remained a lingering hope for friends and a home—and she was at an age when she could think about marrying. If only they stayed in one place long enough to meet someone! *Anyone!* For in the month since coming to Joelsboro, she had grown desperate.

Her father had begun to look at her in curious ways, had touched her breasts when her mother was too drunk to see. Lorna had fended him off, and on each occasion he had buried his head in his arms and wept with contrition. But she feared him now more than she hated him and swore to herself that she was leaving for good.

Finally, a week ago, as her mother lay in a stupor on a squalid mattress on the floor, her father came at Lorna with an even more frightening look in his eyes. His big hands grabbed her shoulders, then tightened around her neck. She struggled to break free, but his grip was too strong. Her legs gave way beneath her and she sank to the floor, her mind reeling before blackness overcame her.

When she came to, she cried out at the pain that burned between her legs, and she found her father snoring in alcoholic sleep, lying beside her, his filthy trousers bunched around his ankles.

She touched herself where the pain was worst and brought her bloody hand before her horrified eyes. She didn't weep, although the agony was great enough to blur her vision. Nor did she pity herself, for she supposed she'd known this day was coming. Instead, she hauled her aching body from the floor and cursed her father.

"You goddamn bastard!" she breathed, her lips trembling with fury. "Who needs you? Who wants you? I hope the two of you die and burn in hell! And *still* that would be too good for you!"

Reaching for her tattered shawl, she wrapped it tightly around her shoulders and left her father's house forever.

It was midnight, and she staggered in pain down the dark alley to the rear of the Liberty Saloon. She knew the place and what sort of establishment it was—but where else was a girl like her to go? The local church? She had never laid eyes on the preacher—and as far as she knew, she'd never been baptized. Anyway, she'd starve before she asked for charity.

So, she knocked at the back of the Liberty Saloon, and Ethel opened the door to her.

"What brings you here, miss?" Ethel asked.

Lorna raised her chin resolutely. "I'm looking for work."

Ethel nearly slammed the door, for on first glance in the shadowy alleyway, Lorna appeared no older than twelve. Her straight black Indian hair framed her thin, heart-shaped face and fanned out over her narrow shoulders. Her lips formed a pale cupid's-bow that would have been as sweet as a baby's had the sharpness of her pointed chin not given her a look of hungry determination.

It was that look, the raised chin jutting out boldly, and the enormous brown eyes that dominated her pinched face that caused Ethel to pause and examine the girl more closely. She moved to the side and light spilled over her shoulder.

"You ain't as young as you look, are you?"

"I'm sixteen." The chin rose another inch.

"Skinny for sixteen."

"Nothing a square meal or two wouldn't remedy."

"You hungry?"

"I always am," she said, stating the simple fact.

The utter lack of self-pity in Lorna's voice stirred sympathy in Ethel's soul. "Come in. I'll get you a plate of something."

Lorna didn't budge. "I came for a job . . . not a handout."

"Grateful little piece, ain't you?"

"I just want to earn my own way."

"Well, we'll have to put some flesh on them bones before any man would take a second look at you. Now quit being so all-fired proud and git yourself inside."

Lorna stepped into the Liberty Saloon, and Ethel closed the door behind her. Fanny and Hester scraped back their chairs and sauntered over, eyeing Lorna with curiosity.

"Look what the cat drug up," Ethel said, crossing her arms over her enormous belly.

Fanny took one glance at Lorna's shabby clothes and held her nose delicately. "For heaven's sakes, Ethel, don't let her in here! She'll scare the customers."

"Let her outside and she'll scare the horses!" Hester said.

"I won't stay where I'm not wanted," Lorna spat, turning and reaching for the door.

"Hold up a minute, girl," Fanny said, waddling between Hester and Ethel. "We was just funnin'. Don't pay us no mind. What's your name?"

"Lorna Rivers."

"She's hungry," Ethel advised.

"I bet she is," Fanny said. "Nothing but a bag of bones. Well, take her upstairs, and I'll scare up some food. I think Jack's got some of that ham left over."

58

Lorna's enormous eyes widened. Ham! She couldn't remember the last time she'd tasted it!

"How does that sound to you, miss?" Fanny asked. "A little ham, some cold black-eyed peas, maybe a tortilla with butter?"

"Anything," Lorna murmured. Did they eat like this all the time? From the size of Fanny, it appeared they did.

"Take her upstairs, Ethel," Fanny said, obviously the one who gave orders around the Liberty Saloon. "And get her out of them clothes!"

"What'll I give her to wear?"

"Anything! A horse blanket'd be better. Just get those nasty rags off her . . . and burn them. That's all we need in this establishment . . . lice!"

"I don't have lice!" Lorna countered, raising her chin so high the dark bruises on her neck came into view.

"Oh, honey!" Hester said, staring at her with her crossed eyes. "Who done it?"

"My pa," Lorna answered without shame.

"I hope you killed him for it," Ethel said.

"I wish I had."

"Take her upstairs," Fanny said, her voice suddenly soft and kindly. "I'll get her dinner."

That night, Lorna slept with a full belly for the first time in years.

The Liberty Saloon slatterns, even the foul-tempered Cora, were horrified at the livid marks that ringed Lorna's neck, and the sight of the bloody drawers that Ethel took outside on the end of a stick to be burned told them the rest of the story.

They took her in and coddled her. The somber, serious Hester saw to it that she was properly fed. Guadalupe gave her a silver crucifix to wear around her neck, and Ethel, now in her eighth month, presented her with all the dresses she could no longer squeeze into. And at last, the vibrant, sharp-tongued Fanny brought a smile to Lorna's lips with her biting wit.

Lorna put on weight like a stray cat suddenly nourished with cream. Her cheeks filled out so her face no longer seemed all eyes and chin; her small breasts rounded and firmed, and her bony hips took on a curving, pleasing shape beneath her hand-me-down dresses.

For her first appearance at the Liberty Saloon, Lorna chose a yellow satin gown with lacy sleeves and a ruffled bodice.

"That was my favorite outfit," Ethel said approvingly. "I wore it all the time before the summer's awful heat swole me up so bad."

Cora's derisive snort brought a sharp look from Ethel. "Keep your cracks to yourself, bitch!"

"I ain't said nothin'," Cora claimed, her face deceptively innocent. " 'Cept it must've been one powerful summer!"

"You oughtta know. You were here."

"But I sure as hell didn't get *that* hot!"

"Hush up that bad-mouthin'!" Fanny ordered, fussing with Lorna's straight hair until she managed to crimp it into some semblance of curl. Then Guadalupe took over, dusting Lorna's face with sweet-smelling chalky powder and outlining her large, dark eyes with kohl. Her lips, they decided, were too naturally pink to require the touch of crimson-colored almond oil the others always used, but they did permit Guadalupe to dab Lorna's cheeks with a bit of rose-scented rouge.

When she took her place at their table in the Liberty Saloon, she looked more like a child playing grown-up than a member of their worldly profession—but she had no illusions. She knew that after a while, when the poker game palled, or when one of the players had had enough to drink, the men's attention would come her way; and, as she sat at the table in front of the empty stage, she wondered which one of the long, lean cowboys would take her out the back door and upstairs to a cot-furnished room next door.

Then Klaus Stark entered the bar, and Lorna hoped it would be him. At least she knew him, and she thought that would make it easier.

"Go grab ahold of him if you fancy 'im," Fanny urged, having followed the direction of Lorna's eyes. "He ain't too good at it, but then you prob'ly ain't either. 'Sides, he don't play rough, which is more'n I can vouch for about those sidewinders around the poker table. And, you gotta admit, he's a damn sight purtier. Prob'ly don't smell as bad, either."

Lorna laughed despite her nervousness. "What do I say to him?"

"Ask him to buy you a drink."

"I've never touched liquor!"

"Don't worry! You won't foul your pretty lips now. Old Jack'll pour you a glass of sweet tea. Now git!"

Fanny touched Lorna's hand affectionately and sent her from the table.

Klaus pretended he didn't see her coming, and only when she was standing shyly by his side did he turn and look at her.

"Hidey, there, Klaus," she said forcing a smile, wondering if he knew who she was beneath all that powder.

"Well, if it ain't Lorna Rivers," he said, his voice deep and lazy. A slow grin played across his lips, and his startling blue eyes disconcerted her.

"Why won't you buy me a drink?" she blurted out.

"Never said I wouldn't. Jack! How 'bout a glass?"

Jack Lynch, owner of the Liberty Saloon, filled a tumbler from a special bottle he kept next to his cash box and set it in front of Lorna.

"I didn't ask for no drink," Klaus protested. "I said bring me a glass . . . empty."

"Oh, this'll do," Lorna interjected.

"A glass, Jack," Klaus repeated, and the saloon-keeper reluctantly complied, not wishing to rouse the boy's hot temper.

Klaus filled the glass from his bottle and pushed it toward Lorna. "Down the hatch."

He tilted back his head and drained his shot glass. Lorna touched hers to her lips and recoiled as the fiery liquor burned her tongue.

"That'll grow hair on your chest," Klaus said, reaching for the bottle again.

She started to reply, but was interrupted by the thunder of hooves outside the saloon. Both she and Klaus looked to the door as Dos burst in. His blond hair was disheveled and his cheeks were flushed. His loose-fitting cotton *camisa,* opened to the waist, had pulled out of his trousers, and his boot heels clattered on the wooden floor as he strode up to the bar.

"Gimme a drink, Jack," he shouted to the other end.

Jack brought him a bottle and a glass. "How come you ain't out at the Lantana for the fancy doin's?"

"I had a bellyful of those fancy doin's," Dos said, filling his glass and sloshing red-eye onto the polished bar. His hand was unsteady as he brought his drink to his lips.

Lorna had seen Dos only once before, on the day a month ago when she first rode into Joelsboro with her parents. She had stared in awe as he pranced by on a nervous red thoroughbred, looking like a fairytale prince with sunlight glinting off his silvery lashes and flashing in his bright green eyes—in appearance very like the boy at her side, but infinitely more handsome . . . bigger, stronger, and with a strapping chest and narrow hips encased, then as now, in skin-tight leather breeches.

"Who *is* that?" Lorna asked Klaus, for although she had heard of the Lantana, she knew nothing of its owners.

"One of the fuckin' Camerons," Klaus said, the grim set of his jaw signaling the anger that still blazed in him.

Dos heard, as Klaus meant him to, and stared down the bar, his already flushed cheeks growing even redder.

"What's your beef, Klaus?" he demanded.

Klaus's hand gripped his glass. The glitter of his eyes matched Dos's.

Jack Lynch saw what was coming. "Git outta here, both of ya!"

Neither man moved. They stared at each other like two bulls ready to charge.

Like Lorna, the poker players sensed trouble and laid down their cards to watch. In the rear, the women rose from their table and waited.

"I asked you a question," Dos insisted.

"If I ain't good enough to visit your place, you ain't good enough to drink around me!"

Dos had no idea what he meant, but it didn't matter, for he smelled a brawl, and in his frustration, he looked forward to it. His hands were already clenched, and his feet were spread in a ready stance.

"I got booted off your goddamn place," Klaus explained, his voice a menacing growl. "You people have a welcome for everybody else in Joelsboro—but not for the Starks."

He took a step toward Dos, who held his ground. Jack Lynch grabbed Klaus's arm, but his grip was thrown off. Lorna backed up, her dark eyes wide, realizing now that nothing could prevent the fight.

"Know why? Know why, Dos Cameron? Ain't you

never figured out why Rudy Stark's boys ain't allowed on the ranch he helped to build?"

Dos *had* wondered—had even asked, only to be told that the Starks were no good, old-time enemies to be kept at bay. Now here was one of them challenging him, goading him into a fight he had no intention of avoiding. His fingers dug into his clenched fists, aching for the first blow. But Klaus prolonged the moment, keeping his distance until the right instant as if he hadn't primed Dos sufficiently, as if his own blood weren't hot enough to begin the fray.

"You dumb shit!" Klaus shouted. "Everybody else knows! Everybody knows but you!"

"Shut up, Klaus!" Jack Lynch warned, for he, too, knew. But his voice was feeble, and neither Dos nor Klaus heard him.

Klaus's face was dark with hate. "The whole world knows your ma was my pa's whore!"

Dos bellowed with rage. He swung his big fist, snapping Klaus's head to the right, but Klaus was on him in an instant, catching Dos's jaw with his knuckles, causing Dos's teeth to slice into his tongue. Blood filled his mouth, nearly choking him until he spewed it out, splattering Klaus's shirt with red.

Klaus's knee jammed into Dos's belly, sending the boy reeling backwards in pain. The women screamed and backed up against the stage. The poker players, enjoying the brawl, shouted encouragement but gave the fighters room, while Lorna stared white-faced in horror as Klaus flew against Dos, knocking him to the floor. Klaus knelt on Dos's chest and crashed his fist into his jaw, and with every blow he shouted out his fury. "Don't you see? . . . Are you fuckin' blind? . . . Your high-'n'-mighty ma laid down with my pa! . . .

You ain't no Cameron! . . . You ain't no better'n I am! . . . You're my goddamn brother!"

Dos screamed in horror as fireworks exploded in his brain. Him! A Stark! Not a Cameron after all! Not part of Alex! So that's why—that's the reason for the hate! It was a shock, but he didn't doubt it for a moment. All these years, and he never knew! He wasn't Alex's, after all! He was Anne's and Rudy's ever-damned bastard!

He lashed out blindly, blood flowing from his mouth, his left eye already swollen shut, the tender flesh around it rapidly blackening.

He bucked with his knees, sending Klaus sprawling against the gaming table. Cards and poker chips rained down around them, and an uncorked whiskey bottle shattered on the floor. Dos grabbed its neck and brought it up. Klaus never saw it. In his haste to jump Dos, he lunged, and the jagged bottle buried itself in his throat, slicing the jugular vein as neatly as if it had been a razor. Blood, so dark it was almost black, shot out in a stream, propelled by Klaus's thumping heart. It squirted across Dos's chest, warm, sticky, mingling with his own blood. It spattered across the hardwood floor and obliterated the marks on the fallen cards.

Klaus gasped in shock, rocking back and forth on his knees, his throat so full of blood he could not cry out for help. Through eyes already dimming, he watched the pulsating dark thread spew the arc of his life away.

The others in the saloon stared, transfixed, unable to stir themselves to action. Lorna gripped the bar so tightly her knuckles went white, and she had to force herself to breathe.

Dos scuttled backward away from the stream of blood, horrified at the realization that Klaus was going to die and that it was he who had killed him. His expression mirrored Klaus's agony, and Lorna thought she had never seen so tragic a look on a man's face. The bright, golden prince had turned to clay; his features twisted and sagged as if time had magically accelerated and he was growing old in an instant. The awful, bright blood bubbled from between his lips and fell in thick drops from his chin. But it was his eyes that mesmerized Lorna. Those strikingly green eyes that had flashed like wet emeralds the first time she saw him. They'd been bright, blazing with confidence and aplomb. Now clouded over, they seemed to be sinking deep into his skull, their beauty enshrouded by dark veils of grief, horror, pity, and hopelessness.

Dos staggered to his feet and screamed. His voice, a demonic wail of despair more lonely and frightened than the cry of any trapped animal, echoed with desolation and self-loathing. Its ferocity stunned Lorna, even more than the sight of Klaus's moribund body.

Dos still gripped the shattered bottle. With another cry he swung it above his head and hurled it blindly. It sailed across the saloon, striking a shelf high up above the bar, sending glasses flying against a kerosene lamp that blazed in one corner. The lamp teetered, then plummeted, shattering as it hit the floor. The volatile oil spread quickly and ignited with a whoosh, setting fire to the heavily swagged red velvet draperies that covered the saloon's front windows.

Fanny screamed, and the other women followed her panicky rush for the back door. The poker players, shocked into action at last, began beating the flames with their coats while Jack Lynch grabbed a dishpan of soapy water and threw it on the fire; but this only spread the burning oil, and crackling flames began to blacken the pinewood walls.

"Let's clear out!" someone cried, and the men abandoned their smouldering coats to follow the women out the back. Seeing that the building was hopelessly doomed, Jack Lynch raced after them, and no one—in their excitement and fear—noticed that they'd left both Dos and Lorna behind.

Dos stood dazed, rooted to the spot, oblivious to the fiery tongues that licked the walls and blistered the paint on the tin-tiled ceiling. And Lorna, still spellbound by Dos's tragic eyes, clung to the bar, her fingernails gouging deep scratches in its polished surface.

The temperature soared. Flames engulfed the tables and chairs behind Dos, the scattered playing cards blackened and curled, turning to ash without ever catching fire, and the pools of blood—Dos's mingled with Klaus's—darkened and began to dry on the floor.

Suddenly the tin ceiling flared, raining drops of blazing paint from the swirling clouds of smoke that were quickly filling the room. A spark set Dos's sleeve afire, rousing Lorna at last from her catalepsy, snapping her mind into sharp focus. She sprang from the bar and slapped out the flames on Dos's shirt with her bare hands, ignoring the pain, knowing only that she had to get Dos and herself out of the inferno.

The entire west wall was a sheet of fire, and burning ceiling tiles began to sag and drop, setting new blazes behind the bar. The wagon wheel chandelier spun in the maelstrom of blasting hot air, and its stubby tallow candles dripped puddles of wax on the floor below. The thickening smoke choked Lorna and seared her lungs even as her nostrils told her that the stench she smelled was her hair—and Dos's—singeing in the heat.

She tugged at him, locking her blistered hands in his, but he was as immovable as a block of stone. She looked up at him, her eyes pleading with fear. "Come on! Let's get out of here!"

He remained stock still, paralyzed, gazing unblinkingly at the ring of fire that was enclosing Klaus's dead form. Lorna pulled her hand free, made a tight, tiny fist, and brought the back of her knuckles against Dos's bloody jaw. His head jerked to the side, and when he flung it back, she saw that she had broken his trance. He looked at her—his eyes still veiled with sorrow and despair—but he *looked* at her and realized at last what was happening.

"We've got to get out of here!" she cried, grabbing his hand again.

This time he moved. He stumbled along with her through the strangling smoke and the shower of sparks falling like brimstone from the buckling ceiling. Lorna gasped and coughed, clutching at her aching chest. The back door seemed so far away.

We've got to make it! Come on! Come on! Hurry! I can't breathe in here any more! Come on! We're nearly there—only a few more feet! Please, God, don't let me die like this!

Then her hand was on the doorknob and the door flew open. Tumbling into the alley, their ears still full of the roar of the fire, they sucked breaths of sweet cool air into their tortured lungs.

In front of the building, the other survivors huddled together, too shocked by the suddenness of the calamity to react; but shortly the excited clamor of the town's church bell, ringing out from the high steeple, brought others to the scene, the scanty few from town who had not trekked out to the Lantana for the fiesta. They initiated a bucket brigade—cowboys, merchants, drifters, and the taffeta-gowned girls from the saloon, forming a line, swinging pails of water from hand to hand in an effort to douse the flames. In their excitement they failed to realize the hopelessness of the endeavor. They continued to splash water against the saloon's flaming

68

walls long after clearer heads would have seen that the building was lost; and their preoccupation prevented them from noticing the flickering burning embers that swarmed like a cloud of agitated fireflies and settled on the cedar-shingled roof of the dry goods store next door. Most of the sparks consumed themselves in their flight through the cool night air and ended up as gray ash dying with a final curl of pale smoke; but a few bright sparks found new energy in the dry shingle roof, and it wasn't until too late that Fanny glanced up and cried, "My God! *Look!*"

The buildings on Main Street stood shoulder to shoulder, sharing common walls, and it dawned on everyone simultaneously that the fire would have its way, that it would blaze from one end of town to the other, leaving them helpless to stop its course.

Far away, on the porch of the Lantana's big house, two lovers kissed in the shadows. As their lips parted the girl raised her eyelids and spotted a strange glow in the sky.

"What's that?" she asked.

Her beau turned and saw a baleful orange smear just over the horizon as if another waning moon were about to rise. "It looks like Joelsboro," he murmured. "It looks like the whole damned town is goin' up in flames."

Then he left his girl and dashed inside to tell Anne. Running back out with him to the porch, she took a quick glance.

No doubt about it! It was Joelsboro, and a fire—a big one!

She hurried inside to alert Alex and ran with him to the stable. They saddled their mounts and were already speeding off across the prairie when the big yard bell began clanging its alarm.

Long before they arrived, Anne realized with a leaden heart that there would be little she or her men could do to stem the course of the flames. The blaze in the sky rivaled a summer sunset, and even as she and Alex jumped their horses over the dry bed of Sandia Creek, some four miles from town, she smelled the powerful stench of burning wood and saw the pall of hazy smoke rolling toward them like a morning fog. They galloped into town and reined up in the middle of Main Street. Anne clapped her hand over her mouth and cried, "Oh, God, Alex! The whole place is on fire!"

At that moment, the walls of the dry goods store collapsed with a mighty roar, sending flames, sparks, and smoke billowing high above them.

"The buildings are going like dominoes," Anne said, speaking more to herself than to Alex. The saloon had nearly burned itself out, while a vortex of fire swirled above the ruins of the dry goods store, and it was clear that the barbershop roof was soon to go. The adjoining apothecary shop was well ablaze, as were the feed store, the café, the two-storied Commercial Hotel, and most of the other shops and establishments that lined the northern side of the street.

A cry of agony escaped Anne's lips as she saw the first puffs of gray smoke begin to pour from the schoolhouse—the last structure in the line of doomed buildings. She had built the school, and it had taken her years to lure a teacher there; now her heart ached as she anticipated its certain destruction.

"Oh, Alex!" she cried, turning to her husband.

Alex reached across to clasp her hand, knowing that nothing he could do or say would ease her pain.

She desperately loved this little town. She had permitted it to spring up on her ranch. She had encouraged its growth, building and donating to the town at least half the structures that were now going up in flames; and on her own initiative, she had redrawn the boundaries of her ranch, pulling back her fences so that the town stood on free ground with adjacent land available to any settler who filed for title. And, as final immutable evidence of her love for the community, she had named it Joelsboro—in memory of her father.

Alex understood her tears, as did the ranch hands who rode up behind her into town. They found her sitting astride her mount looking like a grieving queen, her proud face, illuminated by the fire, showing grit and determination mingled with sorrow at the senseless destruction of a beloved corner of her kingdom. They reined up beside her, consciously forming a solid ring around her—a gesture that bespoke both protection and honor. And, in sympathy with her misery, they kept silent.

At last, Anne brushed her tears away with the back of her hand and spoke to them. "There's not much we can do about the fire. But we can help save the other side of the street. Go spell those folks with buckets. They're bound to be dog-tired."

Her men sprang forward in loyal obedience, joining forces with the townspeople, who cheered their appearance.

For a moment, Anne and Alex were again alone together. Then the clatter of hooves on hard ground announced the arrival of Carlos and Maggie.

Maggie reined up at her mother's side, her face pale with fright and excitement. "Oh, Mama! It's awful!"

Anne bit her bottom lip to keep from bursting into tears again. "It's not the end of the world, Maggie. They'll recover. And I'll help them."

But as she spoke, her mind flew back two decades to when the gracious old hacienda had burned to the

71

ground, and she repeated the same sentiment she had spoken then: "We'll rebuild, and we'll make it better than it ever was before!"

Carlos had remained only a moment at Anne's side before quickly tying up his horse and hurrying down the street to join the firefighters.

"Come," Alex said, addressing Anne and Maggie. "There's nothing we can do here now." He spoke softly to his horse, and the three of them rode out of town bound for home.

News of the fire had ended the ball, and the guests who hadn't ridden into Joelsboro with Anne's vaqueros were already asleep in their beds; yet lights still blazed in the downstairs windows to welcome the Lantana's owners home.

Upon reaching the house, Anne walked wearily up the steps, her shoulders bent, her ballgown soiled with soot and dust, her long blond hair—set free by the wind —falling in loose tangles down her back.

Alex looked at her tired, sad face and said, "Let's go to bed, Anne."

"I don't feel like sleeping just yet. You go on ahead. I'll come up later. Right now, I think I'd like to be alone." Then, turning to Maggie, she kissed her daughter's forehead. "You, too, Maggie dear. Get some rest. And don't worry. The party will go on tomorrow exactly as planned."

Touched by her mother's concern, Maggie said, "If you want to call it off, Mama, I promise I won't mind."

Anne smiled sweetly. "There's no reason to call it off. All the guests are here, and we'll carry on as usual. Besides . . ."—she brushed Maggie's windblown hair back from her forehead—"you only turn fifteen once."

Anne left them and passed through the kitchen for a cup of hot chocolate to take upstairs to the turret, her private realm, her "grumble room," where no one, not even Alex, ever came without being asked.

It was late—or rather early, for the clock on her roll-top desk showed it was getting toward four. She opened a mahogany humidor and selected a slim, black Havana cigar, bit off the end, and lit it with a match she struck into flame on the arm of her wooden rocker, an arm well-scratched from countless matches being drawn across it. She puffed and to her immense satisfaction blew out a perfect smoke ring. Cigars were her private vice, known only to Alex, although she suspected the children knew it, too. It was a habit she'd picked up early in her marriage when she would light stogies for Alex and find herself more and more reluctant to give them up. She smoked only in her office—and only when alone.

But at that moment, as she watched the pale gray smoke ring expanding as it floated toward the ceiling, she couldn't help thinking, "Oh, I wish Alex could see that!"

She relaxed in her rocker with her eyes closed. Once, like a flicker of a shadow, Dos crossed her mind. She'd scarcely seen him all evening. Had he taken off with some girl to spend the night down by the creek? He'd done it before. Or was he playing cards with the cowboys in the bunkhouse? No, they were in town, fighting the fire. The fire!

The flames played across her memory, and she thought no more about Dos.

After sprawling into the alley, Dos and Lorna had lain there, gasping for breath, their brains still stunned from smoke and terror, until the clamor of the church bell roused them and brought them slowly to their feet.

The building blazed behind them, and Lorna could

73

see that the shingles next door were already catching fire.

"We've got to move on," she said, her mind the cooler of the two. "Come with me."

She reached out automatically for his hand, then winced, feeling for the first time the painful burn on her palm. Dos followed her down the alley, leaving behind the swirling smoke that rolled between the buildings like an earthbound cloud. He didn't know where she was leading him, nor did he care. His brain was still muddled with champagne, and shock mercifully blocked the agony of his split tongue and the angry blisters on his arm beneath the blackened tatters of his cotton shirt.

Lorna urged him on, impatient with his slowness. "Hurry! Hurry! We've got to get out of here."

Like weary ghosts they moved through the darkness to the public stable at the edge of town. It was deserted, as she'd figured it would be, for it was clear that everyone in town was fighting the fire. She unlatched the door and drew Dos inside. Four horses snorted and swung their massive heads, peering with curiosity from stalls side by side. Lorna prised the lid from a tin box and grabbed a fistful of sugar cubes to calm the animals, making her way down the stalls, letting the horses nibble from her blistered palm.

"The tack is over there," she told Dos. "Saddle up the two black ones—they'll be the hardest to see in the night."

But when Dos didn't move, she realized she'd have to take charge. She bridled the two black geldings and grunted as she heaved the heavy saddles onto their backs.

Dos watched her dumbly, only vaguely aware of what was taking place, and she knew it was useless to ask him to help. When she finished with the second cinch, she

74

crept into the stableman's office and took two Winchesters from the glass-fronted gun case. In the drawer below, she found a box of rounds and a nearly full bottle of tequila. Reappearing, she slid the rifles into their saddle holsters and secured the ammunition and the liquor in a leather wallet that she strapped to the back of her saddle.

"Mount up," she ordered, and Dos did as he was told. Then she slid her slippered foot into her stirrup and swung atop her horse. Her yellow satin gown rustled and flounced around her, and the stirrups felt strange without boots. "Now, aren't I a sight!" she muttered and shook her head in disgust. "I'll have to find me some proper clothes somewhere."

She reached across and grabbed Dos's reins, leading his gelding out of the stable and around the side of the building. "I know you can ride," she said to Dos. "I saw you once struttin' down Main Street. But can you manage now, or do I have to lead you?"

"I can manage," Dos replied, his voice dull and husky, but Lorna heaved a sigh of relief. Getting him to speak seemed a major triumph.

"All right," she commanded. "Let's raise dust!"

She let her horse set the pace, an easy lope that brought them half an hour later to a winding creek where they paused to let their mounts drink.

The ride and the rushing air had cleared Dos's brain, and as they sat side by side at the creek, he looked across at Lorna and said, "You better go on back now."

"I'm not going back."

"You can't come with me."

"Tell me why not."

"I killed a man. They'll come hunting for me."

"I know."

75

"I'm on the run."

"I know."

Dos stared at her bewildered. Her powdered face was streaked with soot; her fire-singed hair lay in disarray about her head; greasy smoke stains grimed her yellow dress, but her enormous dark eyes flashed in moonlight like a girl at her first ball, and her pointed chin was raised defiantly in his direction.

"Who are you?" he asked.

"My name is Lorna Rivers."

Dos shook his head. He'd never heard of her. "You'd better go home."

"I have no home."

Her horse had drunk its fill, and she pulled back on the reins. "We ought to move on," she said.

"You sure you want to come with me?" Dos asked. He spoke quietly, his voice barely audible across the short distance between them.

"I'm sure," Lorna answered. She looked across at him. *He may be a killer . . . he may be bad . . . but bloody and beat up as he is, I still think he's the finest man I ever saw!*

"They'll try to hunt us down. We'll be on the run."

"I know," Lorna said simply, feeling her spine tingle with love and excitement.

Dos continued to stare at her, not really understanding this girl whom he didn't know or why she was so eager to cast her fate with his.

Accepting her decision, he took a deep breath and said, "Then let's head out!"

They sloshed through the creek and upon reaching the other bank, spurred their horses into a gallop, leaving the flames of Joelsboro behind them and making tracks across the moonlit countryside.

# 5

Anne must have dozed, for when she reopened her eyes, the cigar had gone out, its fine ash barely an inch long in the little brass tray on the table at her side.

Outside, morning clouds were breaking up and scuttling swiftly southward. Anne sat up in eager anticipation of the first glint of sunlight. The cloak of night lifted around her, exposing the surrounding terrain. She owned all that she could see, and then more, for the sun was already shining on her coastal land to the east, and her vaqueros in the hilly west were still sleeping beneath a canopy of night.

But Anne missed the moment of sunrise that morning, for she glimpsed a shadowy movement in the yard below and recognized Carlos returning from Joelsboro.

She took her cup of chocolate, barely touched and

long since turned cold, and hurried down the spiral stairs to hear his report of the fire.

She met him in the kitchen, sitting at the big oak table sipping coffee. The old cook, Azucena, stood off to the side busying herself with stacks of Alex's fine Spode china decorated in the red, green, and yellow colors of the Cameron Clan's tartan.

Carlos's face was soot-smudged, his shining black hair wild and tousled, and his eyes red-rimmed and swollen from smoke. Fine ash still clung to his clothing, and his cheeks and chin were stubbled with a day's growth of whiskers.

Anne stood in the doorway for a moment, then entered and handed her cup to the cook.

*"Café, señora?"* Azucena asked.

Anne shook her head, dragging a chair up to the table. "Just reheat that chocolate, Azucena. That'll do me fine."

Carlos cleared his throat and met his sister's gaze. "The whole north side is gone," he said.

Anne nodded. "I figured there was no saving it."

"The other side was spared."

"Thank God for that," Anne murmured. "Was anybody hurt?"

Something in Carlos's eyes sent a chill of fear up her spine. She reached across the table and grabbed his hands. *"Dos!"*

"No! Not Dos!" Carlos said quickly, hating what he had to do, for even as he saw the instant relief in Anne's eyes, he feared that what he was about to tell her would crush her very soul.

He got it over as quickly as he could, blurting it out before she had a chance to think about what he was saying.

She sat for a moment immobilized, her face drained

of color, her pupils constricting until there was no black in them at all. Then suddenly she screamed, her voice echoing off the kitchen walls as if someone had plunged a dagger into her breast.

Carlos was around the table at once, only to have her lash out at him, pummeling his face and his chest with her clenched fists, and all the while her hideous, tortured voice cried, "My son! My son! No! It's a lie! A goddamned lie!"

Azucena crossed herself and scurried out of the way as Anne sprang past Carlos and made for the drainboard. With a wild sweep of her arms she sent the stacks of Alex's lovely china crashing, shattering on the polished terracotta floor; then, before Carlos could stop her, dozens of thin-stemmed Waterford crystal glasses joined the rubble at her feet. The terrible noise of destruction brought Azucena's corps of kitchen helpers gaping wide-eyed at the door in time to see Carlos finally catch Anne and shake her, pinning her arms behind her back, until she was jostled out of her hysteria. She fell against her half-brother, her body heaving with dry sobs.

He held her close, his heart aching for the woman he loved more than anyone else. Anne, the indomitable, whose sturdy shoulders had borne the burden of so much tragedy, grief, and pain—and still remained unbowed.

Until now . . . until now? She seemed bent and small against him, vulnerable and drained of strength.

His lips brushed her hair in a gesture of comfort. He was ashamed to find that he was almost glad the calamity had occurred. In the past, she had been the one to console, to soothe, to set matters right. She always thought she was invincible, that there was nothing she couldn't overcome. But she had to meet her match someday, he thought; and he was grateful he was there to take care of her. He wanted to be her solace.

However, Anne surprised him. As he held her against him, he felt a shudder seize her body, not a trembling weakness, but the throbbing of resurging power within her, welling up from that mysterious spring in her soul from which she always drank in times of crisis. Its vital waters had never failed her in the past, and now to his astonishment—how could he have ever doubted it?—the well had not gone dry!

She straightened her shoulders—an automatic gesture that Carlos had seen her perform a thousand times before—and left his arms, heading for the door.

"I must go tell Alex," she said simply, but at the door she turned and gazed into Carlos's eyes. "If it had to be someone . . . why did it have to be one of the Stark boys? That will cause nothing but unending trouble."

Maggie's *quincianera* was over almost before it had begun—called off in the face of tragedy and scandal. Even as Alex stood on the porch watching the guests stream from the house in wagons and buggies, a fence-rider rode up with a poster he'd found nailed to the Lantana's gatepost.

WANTED FOR THE MURDER
OF KLAUS STARK
JOEL "DOS" CAMERON
Age: 18 Fair Hair Powerfully Built
Anyone having knowledge of this
DANGEROUS KILLER
Should Communicate With
PETER STARK
Sheriff of Zamora County

A curious attitude had seized many of the revelers who only the night before had gratefully—even greedily —feasted on the Lantana's hospitality. Dos's crime released long-pent-up resentment and envy of the Cameron wealth and power, and they found themselves satisfied, even delighted, that the fates had finally struck the family a crippling blow.

Not caring if they were overheard, perhaps even hoping they would be, they voiced their opinions even before they were clear of the house.

"Wonder what good all their money will do 'em now?"

"Shoot! They'll buy their way out of it!"

"Course they will! The law weren't made for rich folks."

"The Camerons make their own law," a woman volunteered, and like the others, her voice carried through the window of the upstairs bedroom where Anne sat consoling Maggie.

"They'll spirit Dos back onto the ranch and dare a Ranger to come get him."

Maggie moaned, and Anne reached out to her. "Don't listen to them, darling."

But it was impossible to ignore the voices.

"Ought to be shot like a coyote."

"Shootin's too good for the likes of him."

Each remark tore through Anne, and she recalled Alex's own comment when she broke the news to him. His face had grown hard with disgust, and he said, "The boy has bad blood . . . he was born with it. We're better off rid of him."

Rid of him! Dos! Her first-born whom she loved with a desperation even she could not comprehend, for whose transgressions she experienced a dagger of guilt —even as he felt none—and for whom she always found

81

forgiveness, thinking perhaps it was *her* fault Dos was the way he was.

Rid of him? *Never!* Not while she had breath in her body!

What good was Lantana money and power if not to protect its own? The voices were right! She *would* find Dos and spirit him back to the ranch. And she *would* dare the Rangers to try to take him. Not only the Rangers . . . but Peter Stark, too, for she knew he would be the more formidable adversary.

The challenge almost cheered her, and had Maggie not looked so mournful, Anne would have smiled.

Dos and Lorna had ridden all night, and by dawn, when the moon hung ghostly white in the lavender western sky, they had covered nearly fifty miles—still on Lantana soil, on the section called the Ebonal, but approaching the ranch's farthest border.

The anesthetic of alcohol and shock had worn off, and Dos grimaced with pain at every jog of his black gelding. Lorna's reins cut into her burned palms, and her leather straps were slick with blood.

"There's a house out here somewhere," Dos said, peering through the morning light with his one good eye—the other was black and swollen shut, dried blood matting the silvery lashes. It had been three years since he visited this part of the ranch, but he remembered a shack where he and his vaqueros had taken shelter when a violent norther had screamed across the prairie, raising dust high enough to meet the roiling bellies of the overspreading clouds. "It's not much, but it's got a well, and we can catch some sleep with a roof over our heads."

They rode on, and just as the sun was beginning to

burn hot on their backs, Lorna spotted the roof on the horizon. As they approached, Dos saw with relief that the house was deserted. It was a dilapidated structure slanting so precariously that he was certain it would never withstand the force of another storm. The next big wind would blow it over, scattering its weathered siding and sending its rusted tin roof cartwheeling across the countryside along with the rolling tumble-weed.

After they dismounted and tied up, they went to the well into which Dos dropped a stone and heard the gratifying sound of it splashing into water. They found a bucket, so dried out that it leaked more water than it carried, and filled a trough for the horses to drink. Dos's hands were terribly swollen, knuckles raw and nearly bleeding, and Lorna had to disregard her own pain and help him haul bucket after bucket from the well. They too slaked their thirst, then, carrying a bucket into the house, Lorna tore a strip from her petti-coat and dabbed the worst of the dried blood from Dos's face.

His jaw ached, his split tongue nearly filled his mouth, and even after the caked blood was cleaned from his lashes, he was unable to open his battered eye.

Lorna ripped more cloth from her petticoat and bandaged her burned hands, wondering why she had not thought of doing that before.

Then they stretched out on a horse blanket and slept, waking only when the sun was molten red on the western horizon.

Dos ached even more intensely, as if sleep had served only to revitalize his pain. Lorna held his head in her lap and stroked his short blond hair.

"Why did you come with me, Lorna?" he asked, looking up into her dark eyes.

She thought about it for a moment before answering. What could she say about her past? That her father was a brutal drunk, her mother an ignorant, unloving sloven who never seemed to mind—as Lorna did—that they were paupers eternally drifting from one hellhole of a town to another? Would he understand if she said that until she presented herself to the girls at the Liberty Saloon she'd never owned more than one dress at a time in her life? Would he believe her if she told him that the slippers she had on were the first she'd ever worn, and that the thin-soled boots that preceded them had been stolen because there was no money to pay for them?

She looked at Dos, her ravaged prince, and replied simply, "I wanted a different life."

Her answer seemed to satisfy him—and she was grateful, for he seemed content to have her with him and didn't say that she should go home again.

By nine that night, they left the Lantana behind and as they rested their horses on a sage-covered rise, Dos said, "We've got to make plans. We've got to figure out what we're going to do and where we're going to go."

Lorna looked to the south. "We could go to Mexico."

"Have you ever been there?"

"No."

"It's a dangerous place—full of bandits and desperados."

"Well, *we're* desperados, aren't we?"

Dos looked at her, momentarily surprised as if she'd given him a revelation. "I guess we are."

"Then let's go to Mexico where we'll feel at home," Lorna said. "Nobody will look for us there."

So it was decided. They spurred their horses and struck out across the countryside, heading south.

# 6

In the weeks that followed, Anne never ceased to hope for word from Dos. Too worried and distracted to tend to business, she left the management of the ranch entirely in Alex's hands, and she and Carlos rode to the far-flung corners of her empire to call on her vaqueros—to question them as to whether they had news of Dos. They stayed a night on the Ebonal, then rode south to the Hallelujah and the Cenizo. They camped outdoors on the Lovelace section and holed up in an abandoned *jacal* on the Piedras Blancas. Everywhere they went—including the Casa Rosa and the Trevor—the story was the same. No one had seen Dos. No one had a word about him.

Dispirited and weary after more than two weeks criss-crossing the *brasada,* Anne and Carlos headed for home, arriving at the mansion on the second day of October.

Alex greeted them in the foyer, and in response to his questioning look, Anne shook her head and said, "Nothing to report."

She turned, heading for the stairs, intending to go up to her turret room where she could be alone with her thoughts. Then she looked back over her shoulder and asked, "How's Maggie?"

"She's well," Alex replied. "She's upstairs in her room."

Anne's brow furrowed. "Why isn't she at school?"

"Perhaps you ought to look in on her and ask her yourself," Alex said.

"I will," Anne murmured, and she climbed the stairs to Maggie's room.

She found her daughter sitting by a window reading a battered copy of *Les Misérables*. When Anne entered, Maggie dropped the book and ran to her. "Oh, Mama! I'm so glad you're home!" She hugged her mother and buried her face in her breast.

"What's the matter, darling?" Anne asked, stroking Maggie's hair, aware that the girl had burst into tears. "What's wrong, dear? Why aren't you in school?"

"I'll never go back there," Maggie sobbed.

"Because of Dos?" Anne asked, already knowing the answer.

"Yes," Maggie said. "That's all they talk about. They won't let it drop. They call him a murderer, and they call me a murderer's sister."

"Poor Maggie," Anne said softly.

"Please, Mama," Maggie pleaded, lifting her eyes to Anne. "Don't make me go back! I can't stand it, and I hate everyone there!"

"It'll get better, Maggie," Anne ventured.

"No! No, it won't! I *know* it won't!"

Anne held her daughter in silence for a long time. At

last, she said, "All right, dear. You don't have to go where you don't want to. But you have to have some schooling."

"Maybe we could get a teacher to come here."

"Maybe," Anne replied gently. "We'll look into it. Now, I'm going upstairs to my office. . . ."

Maggie smiled through her tears. "To your grumble room."

Anne smiled back at her and hugged her lovingly. "To my grumble room. I need some time to think."

Relieved that Anne had been so understanding, Maggie dried her eyes and returned to her book—a story she had read many times before, but now, because of Dos, the flight of Jean Valjean from Javert held special significance for her.

Anne climbed the spiral staircase and let herself into her private domain. She sat in her rocker and smoked a cigar. For the first time in weeks, she felt a measure of peace. The early autumn day was warm, and a soft breeze from the distant Gulf drifted through the room.

She remained there, rocking and thinking, until the dinner bell called her downstairs.

The old cook, Azucena, made a rare appearance in the dining room, serving the meal herself in honor of Anne's return.

"Welcome home, *señora*," she said, setting the food in front of Anne. "You were gone too long. We missed you."

"*Gracias,* Azucena," Anne replied warmly, and she pressed the woman's hand in gratitude.

Alex poured wine for everyone, including Maggie, but the dinner was not festive, and they ate in silence. When dessert was served, Anne cleared her throat and addressed Alex, "I've been thinking. Maggie doesn't want to go back to school in Joelsboro—and I don't blame her. But she'll have to study somewhere. It might not be a bad idea for her to go away."

"Oh, Mama, no!" Maggie exclaimed, putting down her spoon and staring wide-eyed at Anne.

"Darling, all you've ever known is the Lantana. . . ."

"And I love it!" Maggie interrupted.

"So do I. So do we all," Anne said. "But it's really only a small part of the world."

"It's big enough for me," Maggie declared.

Anne nodded. "It *will* be . . . later, when you're grown and settled down with a husband. But a young woman should know more about the world than what you can learn here on the ranch."

"You did very well without," Maggie argued, dreading the thought of leaving the Lantana for a strange city far away.

"I had no choice," Anne countered. "Ask your father how much better off he is for having seen other places—Scotland, England, Italy, and all the big cities of this country."

" 'Tis true, Maggie, dear," Alex said. "Your mother knows what she's talking about."

"What about you, Carlos?" Maggie asked, looking across the table for support from her uncle. "You never went away to school."

"No . . . but I wish I had."

Anne looked up with surprise. "I didn't know that, Carlos. You never told me."

"I felt I was needed here . . . to help you and Alex."

"Aye, and a big help you've been," Alex said with affection. "But I daresay we could have managed for a while without you."

"If we'd only known," Anne said, reaching across the table to touch Carlos's hand.

Maggie sat back quietly, hoping the conversation would not return to her.

"It's not worth discussing now," Carlos said. "The time's long past when I could have gone. But still . . . I wish I could have known other places besides the Lantana and San Antonio."

"You see, Maggie," Anne said. "Listen to Carlos." Maggie glowered at her uncle. "I don't want to go."

"It wouldn't be for long," Anne promised. "A year . . . maybe two. You really ought to study art and music—the finer things that will give you the polish other young girls your age are getting. Manners, books, how to entertain. You'll need to know these things. The frontier days are over—gone as sure as the longhorn is going. We'll soon be entering the twentieth century, and you'll have to keep up with the changing times."

"But nothing ever changes on the Lantana."

"How can you say such a thing? We're as modern as can be. We've got the train and gaslight and central heat, and there's word we'll even be having telephones before long. Talk about change! You should have seen it when I came here!"

"Or even the way I remember it," Carlos said, for his memory still held the image of the old hacienda with its vast cooking hearths and big tiled cisterns for catching rainwater off the roof. He recalled the open range, before barbed wire, when grass grew higher than his head and mesquites were as rare as waterholes. And he remembered the cattle drives, when old Ben Talley and his cowboys herded the Lantana's longhorns north, raising a cloud of dust that darkened the sky for hours. "Yes, there's been change."

"And all for the better," Anne said decisively. "I've said it before, and I'll say it again. I like this modern world! And you, Maggie dear, are going to spend more time in it than I. So, all the more reason why you should be prepared."

"And it wouldn't be that you'd never come home," Alex said. "You'll have holidays—and all summer. We'll send the train for you. Won't we, Anne?"

"Of course we will. And we'll visit as often as we can."

Maggie could see that further argument was futile. Her dessert sat practically untouched before her, but she had lost all appetite. "Where?" she murmured miserably. "Where would I have to go?"

"Well, San Antonio is too close," Anne said. "You'd find the same trouble there that you found in Joelsboro. There's Galveston to consider. They have a fine school there. And even New Orleans wouldn't be too far away."

"It's far enough," Maggie muttered.

"Well, we don't have to decide now," Anne said, closing the discussion and folding her napkin beside her dessert plate. "For the moment, forget about school. You don't have to go back to Joelsboro."

The servants began clearing the table. Anne rose and moved to Maggie's side, stroking her daughter's hair and hugging her shoulder. "Don't be miserable, dear. You'll get used to the idea, and before long you'll be looking forward to your new adventure. Believe me—you will."

Maggie doubted it. She cried herself to sleep that night—and every night for weeks afterward. Alex worried about her. Seeing his daughter so unhappy softened his resolve, and late one night, lying in bed beside Anne, he said, "Maybe we shouldn't send Maggie away, after all. She hates the idea . . . and she's still very young."

"She's nearly grown," Anne replied softly. "When I

90

was her age, and Papa was away fighting Yankees, I ran our ranch by myself."

"Aye," Alex agreed, his soft Scottish burr a pleasant whisper in Anne's ear. "But things were different then. You said yourself that you had no choice."

Anne turned on her side and faced her husband. "That's exactly the point, Alex. Things *are* different. We've got the money to give Maggie the better things in life, and it's our duty to do it. Believe me, I know how she feels. I was twelve when my mother died, and Papa planned to send me to convent school in San Antonio. I was heartbroken—I couldn't stand the idea. But I understood his decision and realized why I *had* to go."

"But he changed his mind," Alex said. "He kept you with him after all."

Anne nodded. "Only because Rudy and Emma Stark went to work for Papa, and Emma was willing to take care of me."

"Maybe we could hire a tutor to teach her here on the ranch. That would make her happy."

"I'm sure we could find someone," Anne replied. "But I think it would be better for her to go away. She knows nothing of the outside world, and there's so much to learn."

Alex saw that Anne's mind was made up. "Then let's not send her far," he said.

"I was thinking about New Orleans," Anne murmured. "There's Ursuline Academy and Sacred Heart. And, of course, there's the LaForet family. They'd take her in and introduce her to the finest people."

"Aye . . . they'd treat her well," Alex agreed.

"Then it's decided?" Anne asked.

Alex nodded and whispered, "I suppose it's for the best, but . . . but I hate the idea of losing her so soon."

"We won't lose her," Anne reassured him. "She'll be back. The Lantana's her home."

The autumn flew by—much too quickly for Maggie, bringing ever closer the day when her trunks would be loaded aboard the family's palace car and Alex would accompany her on the train to New Orleans. Both Ursuline and Sacred Heart Academy had accepted her, and letters of consultation with the LaForet family had persuaded Anne to entrust Maggie to the nuns at Sacred Heart.

"They'll try to make me a Catholic," Maggie said.

"No, they won't," Anne said. "Besides, being a Catholic isn't all that bad. Your uncle Carlos is a Catholic."

"Only because his mother was."

"That's the only reason anybody's anything," Anne declared.

Maggie shrugged. She had long since realized that there was no chance of changing Anne's mind. Convent school in New Orleans was in her future whether she liked it or not, and as her departure date approached, she even found herself looking forward to it. Lately, in secret, she had browsed in the family library, pulling out books and encyclopedias that described New Orleans. She was intrigued by exotic sounding words like "Vieux Carré," "Place d'Armes," and "Faubourg Marigny." She studied maps of the Crescent City, tracing the curving streets that followed the bend of the Mississippi, outlining for herself the boundaries of the Garden District and the French Quarter, imagining the former to be a civilized Eden and the latter a miniature reflection of Paris. The story of the Evangeline Oak sparked romantic daydreams, and she speculated on the mysterious Mardi Gras krewes—Comus,

Momus, and Proteus. . . . Almost despite herself, she found her interest piqued. Not that she dared confess this to Anne—she was too stubborn to admit that her mother might have been right. So, daily, she raised petty objections that she knew Anne would brush aside. It was a bit of a game—recognized as much by both— and the exchanges between them grew light and good-humored.

"I'll have to learn to make the sign of the cross and when to stand up and kneel at mass."

"Well, that's a bit of knowledge that won't hurt you," Anne countered.

"And they'll probably make me go to confession," Maggie went on. "I've heard terrible stories about what goes on in that little closet between priests and young girls."

"Oh?" Anne said, raising her eyebrows, looking interested. "Tell me about them."

"I *couldn't!*" Maggie exclaimed. "They're too awful!"

Anne nodded sagely. "Hmm, I'm sure they are."

"And I'll probably get converted and become a nun. How would you like that? A nun for a daughter?"

"I think you'd look lovely in black and white."

Maggie rolled her eyes toward the ceiling and gave an exasperated sigh.

And on another occasion: "New Orleans is a wicked town," Maggie said. "I'll probably be ravished before I even get out of the train station."

"Really?" Anne said, smiling broadly. "Well, if the town's *that* exciting, send for me!"

Maggie looked shocked. Anne laughed happily and drew her near, hugging her tightly. "Oh, my dear, you're going to like it there. I know you will!"

"Maybe I'll like it so much I'll never come back."

"Do you think that's possible?" Anne asked, her

voice suddenly strained. She'd already lost one child; she couldn't bear to lose the other.

Maggie relaxed in her mother's arms. "No," she whispered. "I could never stay away from the Lantana."

Anne kissed Maggie's cheek. "I didn't think you could."

Autumn drew to a close, the cool dry days of November giving way to December. Although Anne continued to cast her net far and wide for news of Dos, she was forever drawing it back empty. There were rumors, of course—that he'd been seen in Laredo, Del Rio, San Antonio, and even on the Lantana itself—but they all proved false. Anne no longer believed the tales that reached her ears.

"We'll hear from him eventually," Carlos reassured her.

"I hope so," Anne said. "I don't care where he is, and I don't really care what he's doing. All I want is to know that he's safe and well. Nothing else matters."

But as autumn ended and the bleak, joyless Christmas holiday passed into memory, this assurance had not been granted her, and on the last day of the year, she found herself saying goodbye to Maggie with a heavy heart.

She watched long after the train carrying Alex and Maggie away disappeared and until the smoke from its stack vanished into the haze that blurred the horizon. Then turning, she climbed into her buggy and drove back to the house. Carlos watched her enter, but saw by her expression that she wanted to be alone. And later, as he crossed the yard, walking from one corral to another, he glanced up and caught a glimpse of her in her turret office high above the roof. She was standing at the window, staring out at the empty landscape that surrounded her.

# 1894

# 7

After fleeing Joelsboro, Dos and Lorna entered Mexico at Mier, where they remained until year's end, putting up in a single rented room behind a noisy cantina. To Lorna, the nearly one hundred dollars Dos had in his pocket was an astonishing fortune which she fully expected to last them for a year. But they needed clothing—boots and breeches for Lorna, and hats and jackets for both of them; and almost before she knew it, the fortune had dwindled to less than half.

"Where has it gone?" she asked, truly surprised, counting the coins in little stacks on top of the *serape* bedspread.

"On cheap sombreros like this," Dos said, fingering the inside band that was already coming loose. "I must have a dozen hats back home—all Stetsons, too."

"Here, give it to me," Lorna said, taking a needle

and thread she'd purchased at the market. "I'll mend it so you won't know the difference."

Dos watched her as she worked, her dark brows furrowed in concentration, her pink tongue caught between her lips, her fingers moving deftly as she reattached the band to the hat.

He knew she loved him, although she'd never expressed it in words. She hadn't needed to, for he saw it in her eyes whenever he looked up quickly and caught her staring at him. Such times always embarrassed her, he realized, for she would glance away and her cheeks would flush until they were as pink as her lips.

What he didn't know was that she had vowed not to speak her love aloud—not until she heard him say it first. Her decision wasn't born of pride, but rather of superstition. She felt somehow that telling him how much she loved him—before he told her how he felt—would doom their love, perhaps even drive him away. And more than anything else, she wanted to remain beside him.

So she kept her silence—and hoped.

They had grown intimate. He took her to bed the first night they spent in Mier. Her inexperience was obvious, and when Dos asked her if she were a virgin, she replied that she was, knowing that technically it was not true, but in her heart she had never slept with a man.

Lovemaking for her was pleasant and joyful, filling her with a sense of giving and sharing, and she was happy in the warmth of Dos's arms, but she'd never felt the passion that so obviously seized him when they lay locked in each other's embrace.

She wondered why, but it didn't really trouble her, for she imagined that women felt things differently from men. And most of all, she was content to see him satisfied.

By the first of January, their money was running out, and they had grown bored with Mier. Without any plans, they packed up and set out on horseback, heading south, seeking warmer weather more than anything else.

They wandered aimlessly, spending nights huddled together outdoors under the stars, the rugged peaks of the Sierra Madre dark hulks against the sky, the howl of coyotes breaking the almost palpable silence that surrounded them, the loneliness of its wail echoing the growing unhappiness in Dos.

"Maybe we should go back," he said one night as they lay beside a flickering campfire.

"They'll find you and arrest you," Lorna murmured, and her heart went cold at the thought of losing him.

Dos's thoughts shot ahead. Was he going to be on the run for the rest of his life? Never go home? Never see the Lantana again?

Lorna sensed his sadness and reached out to touch him, tracing the outline of his mouth with her fingertips. "We'll get by," she promised.

"I'm down to less than ten pesos," Dos said. "We shouldn't have spent so much in Mier."

"It was bound to go sooner or later, I suppose. We'll have to find work."

"Where?" Dos asked. "I can't do anything but cowboy, and no Mexican *hacendado* is going to hire on a gringo."

"We'll find something," Lorna assured him. "Don't think about it now. Let's wait till morning."

When the sun rose over the mountaintops, they ate the last of their cold tortillas and saddled their horses.

"I wonder where we are?" Lorna asked.

"About a hundred miles south of the Rio Grande. I figure Monterrey's not too far off."

"Are we going there?"

"It's no good hitting a strange town stone broke."

Lorna pretended to think, but she already knew what she was going to say. Long after Dos fell asleep she'd lain awake turning their situation over and over in her mind, trying to find a solution. Finally, she said, "Dos, if we need money, we'll have to steal it."

"You're crazy!"

"No, I'm not. I'm making sense. It's either that or starve. Or . . . go back to Texas."

Dos closed his eyes and leaned against his mount. "God, Lorna! You shouldn't have come with me. Look at the mess I've got you into!"

She kept silent, but her heart told her she would rather be with him, lost in the badlands of Mexico, than anyplace else on earth.

He opened his eyes and looked at her. "I'm sorry."

"Don't be. There's no reason for it. I made my decision. I could leave any time I wanted. Now, let's mount up and head out. We can make plans as we ride."

The rugged terrain made the going slow, and they were silent for the first few miles. From time to time, Dos would look across at Lorna, his heart filling with admiration and respect.

Where did she get her strength? Her calm? Her reserve? How could she be so sure things would be all right? And why did she love him so?

Gratitude welled up in him, and he wished he knew the way to repay her. She had saved his life and nursed his wounds, and now on the bleakest morning of his life, she was sticking by him. Suddenly he knew he would do anything to take care of her, anything . . . even if it meant . . .

"Okay," he said. "We'll hit a bank."

He caught Lorna's quick glance and thought he saw in it a flash of hope . . . even excitement.

"One of these little Mexican banks shouldn't be too hard to handle."

Lorna kept silent and redirected her gaze straight ahead, but the corners of her lips curled in a slight smile, and her sharp little chin lifted.

They rode all day, climbing higher and higher through a pass in the mountains, and as darkness fell they had spoken scarcely a dozen words to each other. As they were searching for a place to camp, they spotted the lights of a town flickering in the valley below.

"Is that Monterrey?" Lorna asked.

"It can't be," Dos replied. "It's too small."

He lapsed again into silence, staring at the distant lights, while Lorna made a campfire and spread their blankets on the stony ground.

Dos was up before dawn, and Lorna woke to find him crouched before the fire in an effort to ward off the chill of the mountain air. Even this far south, the region was regularly swept by northers cold enough to turn their fingers blue and set their teeth to chattering.

"What I'd give for a good cup of coffee," Lorna said, drawing the blanket tightly around her shoulders. "I won't even let myself think of bacon and eggs."

"We'll have coffee," Dos said. "And eggs—a big plate of *huevos rancheros*. We're going into that town below and we'll order anything we want, 'cause if things go right, it won't matter how much we spend."

He smiled at her, and caught the glitter of adventure in her eyes.

They rode off into the valley. For a moment, Dos was afraid the town was too small to boast of a bank, but as they circled the plaza he saw, opposite the church, a yellow stone building with iron-barred windows and a sign reading: BANCO de COAHUILA.

"We're in business," he said, reining up at a *loncheria* cater-corner from the bank. The little café was already open, and Dos and Lorna took one of the three tables situated on the sidewalk. While they waited to be served, Dos allowed a street urchin to polish his boots, tossing the boy one of the last remaining pesos.

Lorna cleaned her plate and ordered more, but Dos, too nervous over what he was about to do, found himself suddenly without hunger and left his breakfast virtually untouched.

He watched the street carefully, planning his move. The plaza was beginning to fill—as vendors set up shop on the corners, old men with nothing better to do took their places on their favorite benches, and mantilla-veiled women, leaving the church after morning mass, took advantage of the opportunity to exchange gossip as they ambled toward the open market.

An imposing buggy rolled up the street, depositing a well-dressed man in a dark suit and black sombrero on the curb outside the bank. The man fumbled with his keys, then swung back the heavy iron gate and unlocked the doors. Two customers who had been waiting outside followed him in.

"It's now or never," Dos said, throwing the rest of his money on the table beside his plate.

They rose and led their horses across the street. "I'll take care of it," he said. "Just cover me."

He took a deep breath, trying to settle the butterflies in his stomach. Then he yanked his Winchester from the saddle holster and flew into the bank with Lorna close behind.

The banker looked up, his face pleasant, a smile of greeting on his lips, as yet unaware of the rifle in Dos's hands.

102

"Hands up!" Dos ordered. "You there!" he said to the customers. "Get against the wall."

Eyes wide with sudden fear, the banker gave a little gasp and went pale.

"Money!" Dos barked. "Hand it over!"

Terror paralyzed the banker, and Dos rammed the rifle through the teller's cage, rattling the bars. *"Dinero!"* he commanded. *"Pronto!"*

The banker snapped into action. With trembling fingers he grabbed a canvas bag and emptied a drawerful of cash.

*"Más!"* Dos said.

The banker shrugged helplessly. *"No hay más!"*

"Sure there's more!" Dos shouted, waving the Winchester toward the safe behind the banker. His palms had begun to sweat, and the rifle felt slippery in his hands.

Out of fright, the banker moved suddenly to cross himself, alarming Dos, and his finger squeezed the trigger. The shot went wild, ricocheting off the steel safe and shattering the overhanging lamp. The customers cowering against the wall screamed and covered their heads.

There was a cry from the street outside, and Dos reached through the teller's cage, grabbing the money bag. Lorna wheeled about and ran ahead of him, stopping on the threshold to brandish her Winchester menacingly at the crowd in the street. At the sight of her rifle, they dropped to the cobblestones. Dos dashed out, and he and Lorna swung into their saddles.

Before the crowd in the plaza could react, they dug their heels into their mounts and thundered out of town, not slowing until they were sure they had lost themselves in the rocky foothills to the south.

Their horses were staggering with fatigue as they reined up behind a wall of rugged boulders. Dos slumped in his saddle, but Lorna dropped to the ground and ran over to him.

"Dos! Dos!" she cried. "We did it!"

Her delighted laughter echoed off the surrounding crags, sounding like a child on Christmas morning. "Let's see it, Dos! Show it to me!"

He reached inside his shirt and slowly withdrew the canvas bag. Lorna took it from his fingers and yanked back the drawstrings.

"Oh, Dos! Look!" she exclaimed breathlessly. "There's gold in here! Gold pesos and silver!"

Dos swung down from his stirrups and stood by her side. Lorna was reaching into the bag, letting the coins slip through her fingers and jingle into a pile.

"Let's count it," Lorna said. "I'm dying to know how rich we are!"

When Dos didn't reply, Lorna looked up at him, seeing in his eyes a wild, almost ferocious glitter.

"Is something wrong, Dos? You look so strange!"

He shook his head, but a slow smile crossed his lips. He hunkered down next to her and dipped his hand into the bag. Gold and silver coins filled his palms. Opening his fingers, he let them trickle through. They flashed brightly in the sun and rang against the stone like a hundred tiny chimes.

"I enjoyed it, Lorna," Dos said in a husky, almost inaudible voice. "I *liked* it! It was fun!"

Lorna watched him transfixed—wondering at the look of ecstasy on his face.

"Did *you* like it, Lorna?"

"I loved it. I felt strong and good."

"It was one of the greatest things I've ever done," he went on. "It's like I've been waiting all my life to feel what I felt inside that bank. I was scared—really scared. My hands were wet, and my heart was jumping in my chest—but, Lorna, believe me, it was grand!"

Lorna gazed at him with tears of wonder in her eyes. She could see he was aroused, and she felt the fires of passion rising within her, too. The danger and daring had electrified them both, and without a word Dos put his arms around her and lowered her onto the flat surface of the boulder, unbuttoning her blouse and pulling off her trousers. The sun-baked rock warmed her back and buttocks. He pinned her arms against her side and began kissing her wildly as if desperate to devour her. Gasping for breath, she writhed beneath him, flushing with pleasure as his newly grown silken beard caressed her cheeks. Dos released her hands, and her arms wound around his back, feeling the hard muscles flex within her embrace.

He made love to her with an urgent, almost violent, intensity, riding her as if she were a barebacked pony. She bucked, but he held her close, nearly crushing her with his heaving chest. At last, Lorna cried out, shouting to the mountain peaks.

Her mind reeled as a tremendous shudder swept through her body, shaking every fiber, every nerve, causing her heart to flip-flop and her soul to quiver with joy and satisfaction.

There! That was it! That was what *he* felt every time they made love! Now, at last, she felt it too—the passion, the pleasure.

Now they shared it together—she and Dos! Her heart ached with love, and tears of happiness trickled between her closed eyelids.

For a long time they lay motionless side by side, letting the mountain air dry the sweat that slicked their naked bodies. Lorna dozed, her head on Dos's shoulder. Later, when she awoke, she saw that he had dressed and that the sun was sinking rapidly in the west.

"Are we going to stay here for the night?" she asked.

Dos rose to his knees and looked out, not replying.

Lorna pulled on her trousers and buttoned her blouse. "Dos?" she asked again. "Are we going to stay here or . . . ?"

*"Sh!"* Dos whispered, grabbing her shoulder and pushing her back down.

"What is it?"

"They followed us," he breathed. "I heard them—down at the bottom of the hills."

A tingle of fear raced up Lorna's spine. She turned and raised her eyes toward the rocky mountain that loomed almost straight up behind them. "Oh, God!" she thought. "They'll trap us here. We'll never get away!"

Dos scrambled in a crouch over to the horses and pulled the rifles from their holsters. Rejoining Lorna, he dumped a pile of rounds between them and handed her a weapon.

"Don't shoot until I tell you to," he said.

They waited in silence—hearing only the high, dry whistle of the wind in the mountain peaks above.

"Dos!" Lorna whispered. "Are you sure? I don't see anyone."

"They're there," he said, his expression calm but an edge of excitement in his voice. "They're waiting till just before the sun goes down—when we've got the light in our eyes."

He watched. Nothing moved on the dry and barren countryside, while in the sky an eagle soared high overhead, and the sun slipped nearer the horizon.

Suddenly there was a shout, an unseen man's voice calling out, "Surrender, *amigos!* We have you surrounded!"

Then, as if to illustrate, two dozen rifles went off one by one, spaced as regularly as the ticking of a clock, their sharp reports first ringing out in the boulders, then traveling in a circle, up the side of the mountain, behind Dos and Lorna, and then back down to the boulder where they had begun.

When the echoes, died away, the voice called again: "You see, *amigos*? We are all around you. We have you in our sights. Throw down your rifles!"

Lorna looked to Dos. His face was tense and flushed. "They've got us, Lorna," he said quietly. Then with a curse of resignation, he hurled his rifle onto the rocks below. When Lorna followed suit, he took her hand and raised her up beside him.

They stood exposed and vulnerable. The countryside looked as bare and lifeless as before, but after another moment, their captors revealed themselves, appearing from behind outcroppings of rocks and dense clumps of concealing brush.

"It was wise of you not to fight," a man called.

Dos and Lorna turned their eyes in his direction and saw a tall, dark man, dressed in black with a carbine in his arms and a pair of Peacemaker .45s dangling from his hips. Obviously the leader, he made no move to approach, but the other men left their posts and converged on the pair. Like their leader, the men wore only black and kept their rifles leveled at Dos and Lorna while two among them moved forward and bound the couple's wrists with rawhide strips.

When he was satisfied they were securely tied, the leader lowered his carbine and said, "*Vámanos!*"

"Do you think they'll hang us?" Lorna whispered as she stumbled after Dos down the rock strewn side of the foothill.

"I don't know," Dos breathed. "I don't understand it. They had us trapped. If they wanted to kill us, why didn't they just go ahead and shoot?"

"There must be a bounty on our heads. We'll end up in a Mexican jail."

Dos didn't answer. They had reached the bottom of the mountain where the desolate terrain flattened and stretched westward. The sun was close to setting, and long purple shadows crept across the land.

The leader paused and whistled. Out of the glare of sunset came another man leading a string of horses. "Put them in their saddles," the leader said, and Dos and Lorna were hoisted onto their black geldings.

When all had mounted, the leader gave a signal, and the whole band trotted forward, away from the mountain.

Dos noticed, before Lorna did, that instead of taking them back toward town, the men were leading them off across the flat land, heading west, following the sun.

"Are you scared?" Dos asked.

"I don't think so," Lorna answered. "No . . . I know what scared feels like. And this is different." Nevertheless, her cheeks blazed red and her pulse raced wildly. "Funny thing, Dos," she added. "I *ought* to be scared . . . but I'm not. You're gonna think I'm crazy, but what I feel, what I *really* feel is . . . excitement!"

She looked at him quickly. It took him a moment to react, then he threw his head back and whooped with laughter.

Their captors glanced at them sharply.

Neither Dos nor Lorna noticed. They were gazing into each other's eyes, laughter bubbling from Dos's throat. Then Lorna joined him, her bright, mirthful giggles playing counterpoint, rising to the fading sky, discharging their tension. They laughed until their sides ached and tears flowed down their cheeks.

Utterly bewildered, one of the Mexicans looked at

a *compadre* and tapped the side of his head. *"Locos . . . muy locos!"*

They rode for an hour. The sky turned violet, then sparkled with stars. At last, Dos and Lorna saw lights in the distance.

"An hacienda," Dos said.

They were led to the house and helped roughly from their saddles. The leader had already dismounted and stood waiting for them on the porch—a narrow gallery with a red tile roof supported by ax-hewn beams jutting out from the whitewashed adobe wall. The front door was open despite the chilly night, and Dos could see into a small central room lighted by a blazing fireplace.

With an almost courtly gesture, the leader extended his hand and said, "Please . . . enter."

He had a lean, hard body, but the silver in his hair betrayed his true age. His face was leathery, as dark as a polished saddle, and Lorna noticed as she crossed in front of him that his eyes were flat and cloudy—almost sorrowful—as if he'd seen too much pain and grief in his nearly sixty years.

He closed the door behind them, and Lorna turned to face him. Her shoulders ached and the rawhide chaffed her wrists tied behind her back. *"Señor,"* she said boldly. "Is this an example of Mexican hospitality."

He looked at her blankly.

"The least you could do is cut our hands free!"

Dos stared at her with admiration, proud of her spunk.

"Certainly," the man said. He pulled a knife from a scabbard inside his boot and, with a quick flick of the blade, severed the rawhide that bound them. They rubbed the red welts on their wrists and shrugged away the tightness in their muscles.

The room was sparsely furnished—a handmade oak table with four straight-back chairs, a rusting iron chandelier fitted with a dozen stubby candles, two chests against one wall, and a long hard bench against the other. Two well-worn rugs covered the tiled floor, and in one dark corner a multi-hued parrot swung from a perch in a cage fashioned from woven twigs.

The man motioned for Dos and Lorna to sit, indicating the chairs at the table, but he continued to stand, resting his elbow on the mantel above the fireplace.

"Now, tell me," he said. "Who are you, and why are you here in Coahuila?"

Dos saw no reason to lie. "I'm Dos Cameron. We ran into trouble in Texas and thought it best to lie low in Mexico for a while."

If the name Cameron meant anything to the man, Dos couldn't tell from his expression.

"I'm Miguel Escobar," the man said. "Have you heard of me?"

"No," Dos answered.

Escobar smiled wryly. "Such is fame. In these parts even little children know my name . . . and fear it."

Lorna looked to Dos, a flicker of caution in her eyes. Dos took her hand and held it.

Escobar went on: "But perhaps you haven't heard of me because I take care not to venture north of the Rio Bravo."

"What is your business?" Dos asked.

"The same as yours. *Señor* Cameron," Escobar replied, taking a handful of sunflower seeds from a bowl on the mantel and offering them one by one to the parrot. "I rob banks . . . *and* unwary travelers who venture through these parts. It's a precarious living. The area is poor, and like a hunter where game is scarce, one must

110

be careful not to take more than the land can provide."

"I think I see your point," Dos said. "We've butted in on your territory . . . like poachers."

Escobar smiled. "You're a man of understanding, *Señor* Cameron. The little bank you robbed is poor and must be cared for. We take from it only once or twice a year. Any more than that would disturb confidence among the people, and they would begin to keep their money in hiding places they consider safer. No money . . . no bank, and we would find life more difficult than it already is."

"So when you heard we robbed it, you came after us?" Dos said.

Escobar nodded.

"How did you know where we were hiding?"

"Where else but the mountains, and where else in the mountains but at the foot of Chipinque? It's as far as a good horse can gallop without exhaustion, and it affords an excellent place to hide." The parrot took the last of the seeds from Escobar's fingers, and the man returned to his position beside the mantel. "Oh, you're not the first. There have been others who've robbed the Banco de Coahuila—grand name for such a tiny bank! —and they have always sought refuge at the foot of Chipinque. But you were luckier than they."

"How's that?" Dos inquired.

"We caught you sleeping and were able to surround you without a fight. The others were, unfortunately for them, more alert."

"So you shot them?" Lorna asked.

Escobar lowered his head. "They always fired first."

There was a moment of silence. Escobar sighed and Dos thought he recognized an expression of true contrition on the man's face.

"Why didn't you shoot us?" Lorna asked.

Escobar looked surprised. "It wasn't necessary. I'm a *bandido,* not a murderer."

"And what are you going to do with us?" Dos asked.

"Let you go," Escobar replied.

"Now?"

"If you wish. But I suggest you stay the night here and leave in the morning when both you and your horses are refreshed."

Dos eyed Escobar suspiciously. "It can't be as simple as that, *señor.* You must have conditions."

Escobar sighed again with a world-weary smile. "Alas, life is never simple. There are always conditions."

"What are they?" Dos asked.

"Two only," Escobar replied. "First, you leave the money behind. I'll see that it's returned to the bank. It would be unwise to pump the well dry."

"And the other?"

"You must leave Coahuila. It's *my* territory and not rich enough to support both of us."

"That's all?"

*"Es todo,"* Escobar replied, simply.

Dos smiled. "You're a good man, Escobar."

Escobar smiled at the compliment. "Now, if you'll come with me, we'll go to the kitchen and see what my woman has prepared for supper."

The next morning, Escobar saw Dos and Lorna off. "Here is a little money," he said, slipping a gold coin into Dos's hand. "It's not much, but it will sustain you for a few days."

*"Gracias, señor,"* Dos said.

"Do you know where you're going?" Escobar asked.

Dos shook his head. "I expect we'll just wander. But we'll clear out of Coahuila. We owe you that much."

112

"Return to your own people," Escobar said. "It is not good to be a stranger in a foreign land."

Dos and Lorna thanked him and bade him farewell. They spurred their horses and set forth. After a few moments, Dos turned his head and looked over his shoulder. Escobar was standing alone on his porch gazing after them. Dos touched his hat brim in salute.

Escobar raised his hand in reply.

That evening by campfire, Dos held Lorna and watched the spangled universe in its slow march across the velvet sky.

He smiled to himself, pulled her closer, and murmured, "Honor among thieves."

"What did you say?"

"Nothing . . . I was just thinking out loud." But later, he said, "He could have shot us, but he didn't. He's a true gentleman." Dos shook his head in wonder and was silent for a while. Then, unable to put Escobar out of his mind: "Poor sonofabitch! It must be hell to be a bandit in a poor country."

# 8

Jeanette LaForet Drouet poured coffee from a silver pot and handed a delicate Limoges cup to Alex. "Are you sure you want to leave tomorrow?"

"I must," he replied. "I've already wired Anne to expect me. Besides, I only intended to stay in New Orleans long enough to make sure that Maggie was settled."

"Well, I believe she's fitting in perfectly, don't you?"

"Aye, that she is. She and Elise took to each other right away."

"Oh . . . Elise! She's never known a stranger."

"She's a bonny lass, Jeanette. You must be proud."

Jeanette laughed. "Always the Scotsman, Alex! I do believe that's the first time anyone's ever called my Creole daughter a bonny lass! But you're right, I am proud of her . . . just as you're proud of Maggie. I can see it in your eyes."

Alex smiled. "The Lantana's going to seem empty without her."

Jeanette rose and stood by the mantel. A cheerful fire dispelled the January gloom that chilled New Orleans beneath a blanket of low, dark clouds. Alex watched her and found it hard to believe that she was nearing forty. Her hair was as black and glossy as it had been almost a quarter of a century before when they first met at his father's estate in Scotland. Not a line marred the creamy smoothness of her complexion, and her dark eyes were still as luminous as they'd been that night so long ago when she threw herself into his arms and declared her love for him.

Jeanette read his thoughts. She smiled wistfully. "Do you ever think of it, Alex?"

"What?" he asked, knowing full well what she meant.

". . . how it would have been, if we'd married?"

"You wouldn't have Elise . . . nor I Maggie."

"It was for the best, wasn't it, Alex?"

He nodded.

She crossed the floor and took his hand in friendship.

"Did you love André?" he asked. She still wore black in mourning for her husband.

"Very much," she replied.

"And I love Anne . . . now more than ever."

"I can tell. And I'm happy for you."

They fell silent; then Jeanette withdrew her hand and refilled Alex's cup.

The next afternoon, Alex boarded the Lantana train. As his attendants, Felipe and Jose, loaded his baggage, he embraced Maggie and kissed her forehead.

Suddenly his heart ached at the thought of leaving her behind. He looked into her smooth, innocent face and saw a child; and it seemed to him that she was still far too young to be cast forth into the world.

115

"Are you sure you want to stay?" he asked impulsively.

Maggie's face registered surprise.

"I mean," he went on quickly, "that if you want to come home with me, you may."

"But what would Mama say?" asked Maggie.

"I'm sure we could smooth things over with her," Alex replied. "I know she already misses you as much as I'm going to."

Maggie smiled, touched by his words. But she was already fascinated by New Orleans and by the people she had met recently. Had he asked her the same question the first day or two after they'd arrived in town, she would gladly have climbed the steps into the palace car and ridden back with him, but now she knew she wanted to stay. "I need to be here. Mama's right."

Alex sighed unhappily, but forced a smile. We'll come see you . . . Easter . . . if not sooner."

"I'll count the days."

They embraced again, and Alex climbed aboard the train. The locomotive whistled shrilly and pulled out of the depot. Maggie watched after it, waving farewell to Alex until the train rounded a curve in the track and disappeared.

Then she turned and headed for the cabriolet where Jeanette and Elise sat waiting.

Elise looked very much like Jeanette; but in many ways, she reminded Maggie of Carlos. Her sleek raven hair gleamed with blue highlights, just as his did. Her olive skin was clear and smooth, and her nose curved in the same patrician arch.

Latin blood! Maggie thought. How dashing it makes them look! Almost exotic! And she wished with a twinge of envy that she had a drop of it in her veins, too.

Oh, well! she thought, taking her seat in the carriage with a sigh. I guess I'm doomed to be a plain Jane.

Misreading Maggie's mood, Jeanette smiled kindly and took her hand, expecting to have to comfort the girl. "Are you going to cry?"

"I don't think so."

"There's no reason to," Jeanette assured her. "We're your family now, and we'll love you and take care of you as if you were one of our very own."

"We'll be like sisters!" Elise said. "I always wanted a younger sister—and now I have one."

There was a scant year's difference in their ages, but Maggie had already despaired of ever achieving Elise's sophistication. There had been parties almost every night since Maggie's arrival, and she had noted with helpless admiration how easily Elise flirted with the boys. She had a knack for drawing them into a circle around her, for leading them on, making each one feel she preferred him to the rest of the crowd, while Maggie found herself on the verge of panic in their presence —these forward, handsome young men whose lazy drawls belied their fiery natures. Elise could chatter mindlessly and keep them enthralled, while Maggie stumbled even over her own name and hoped they mistook the blush on her cheeks as a sign of vivacity instead of embarrassment.

Maggie sighed again, more deeply, and wondered if she would ever be able to manage. Jeanette and Elise respected her silence, believing her thoughts to be with Alex speeding homeward to the Lantana.

Their carriage rolled along St. Charles Avenue into the Garden District—not the civilized Eden Maggie had once imagined, but a neighborhood of mansions set among magnolia, oak, ivy and azalea. Shortly, the

117

driver pulled up outside Jeanette's two-story home, a sprawling stone residence with a spacious gallery that girdled the first floor and a circular turret that reminded Maggie of Anne's grumble room.

Maggie's room was on the second floor, across the hall from Elise's. Its walls were covered in gleaming lemon silk, made even more cheerful by a crackling fire beneath a mantel of polished rosewood; and, situated between two tall windows overlooking the back garden was an enormous, downy-soft, canopied bed draped with oceans of yellow organdy that billowed out onto the Aubusson rug. Lavella, the upstairs maid, had turned back the quilted comforter, and Maggie was about to slip into bed when Elise knocked softly on the door and stole into the room.

Like Maggie, she wore only a lacy camisole and bloomers and a pair of brocade slippers on her feet. "Are you too tired to talk?"

"No," Maggie said, but in truth she had been looking forward to her nap. The almost constant round of parties over the past two weeks had taken their toll, and she imagined she detected dark circles forming around her eyes.

"I was just thinking," Elise said, curling up in a chair before the fire. "If we're going to be sisters, really sisters, we ought to get to know each other better."

"There's not much more to know about me."

"Oh, I don't believe that. I know! If I tell you a secret—a deep, dark secret—then you can tell me one. That way, we'll have to trust each other . . . like sisters should."

Maggie wasn't sure she wanted this intimacy, but Elise had already begun.

"It was last summer at Bay St. Louis—we always go to Bay St. Louis during the summer—and I was bathing in the Gulf. It was overcast, and we'd had some rain, so everyone else was indoors. But I love the water more than anything; so I went out alone. Then, in a little while, my cousin Gerard came down to the beach. He's four years older than I am, and one of the handsomest boys you'll ever see. Anyway, we played in the waves for a while; then he got this strange look on his face and put his arms around me. . . ."

Maggie listened, fascinated.

"Then the next thing I knew, he kissed me right on the lips and touched me."

"Where?" Maggie breathed.

"I told you. At Bay St. Louis."

"No, I mean where did he touch you?"

"Can't you guess?"

*"Elise!"*

Elise giggled. "Isn't that awful?"

"Did you slap him?"

"It never crossed my mind."

Maggie sat back, scandalized.

"There!" Elise said, utterly pleased with herself. "That's something I've never told anyone else before. Now you're the only one who knows."

"Gerard knows."

"Oh, he doesn't count. Besides, I haven't seen him since. He went off to Harvard and won't be back till next summer."

"And will you let him do it again?"

Elise shrugged. "I don't know. I may have a special beau by then. But that's neither here nor there. It's your turn."

"For what?"

"To tell me *your* secret."

"I don't think I have one . . . not like that, anyway."

Elise looked disappointed, even irritated. "That's

hardly fair, Maggie. If I'd known that, I wouldn't have told you about Gerard and me."

Maggie felt guilty, as if she had taken something for nothing. And she desperately wanted to be friends with Elise. She sorted through her memory, but everything she came up with paled in comparison with Elise's confession. "Not much has happened to me," she said tentatively. "But I could tell you about my brother."

"Does anyone else know?"

"In Texas, everybody does. But no one here."

"That's good enough," Elise said, leaning forward, eager to hear.

Maggie bit her bottom lip, apologizing to Dos in absentia for betraying him. "He . . . he's a wanted man!"

"Wanted . . . by the police?"

"Well, by the sheriff, at least."

"What for?"

"He . . . he killed a man."

"No!"

"And, there's more. He burned down half a town."

Elise scooted from the chair and sat at Maggie's feet enthralled. "He must be terribly bad."

Maggie frowned. "I suppose he is, but he was always good to me. And I still love him."

"Oh, Maggie! That's so exciting!" Elise's face glowed with admiration.

Her reaction astonished Maggie, but it pleased her even more. And she was almost thankful to Dos for raising her esteem in Elise's eyes.

"You're so lucky to have a wicked family," Elise said.

"Only Dos. My parents and Carlos have never done anything bad."

"I know your parents . . . but what about Carlos?"

"He's handsome, and gentle, and quiet. . . ."

"Then I prefer Dos. Oh, I wish I could meet him!"

"No chance of that, I'm afraid. No one's heard a word from him. I suppose you'd call him a desperado."

Elise sighed dreamily and hugged her knees. "A desperado! I'd give up every one of the LaForets to have a desperado in the family. The closest we've ever come was a great-uncle of my mother's who strangled a woman."

"Well, that's *something*," Maggie said, trying to pay a compliment.

"Oh, it hardly counts! She was only a quadroon, and they say he didn't know what he was doing. He was mad as a hatter, and they locked him up in an asylum until he died."

"I'm sorry."

"Me too."

"Elise . . ." Maggie said.

"What?"

"You won't tell, will you?"

"About Dos?"

Maggie nodded. "That's why I had to leave Texas."

"Don't worry, Maggie. I'll keep it in my heart." She rose and kissed Maggie's cheek. "Our secrets will bind us together . . . like true sisters."

"Thank you, Eise."

Elise paused at the door. "I promise I won't tell about Dos . . . but I'm going to dream about him."

After Elise left, Maggie drew the heavy draperies tightly across the windows and curled up in bed. The fireplace cast a warm glow throughout the room, and ghostly shadows danced across the ceiling.

Drowsily, through flickering eyelids, Maggie watched them, and they began to take on shapes. There was Elise, her hair piled high, her arms outstretched. And then there was Dos! They drifted together and began to spin slowly in time to phantom music. The ceiling fell away, and Dos and Elise were alone in a vast hall dimly lit by candles that burned with soft, golden flames. They danced in silence in each other's arms, dipping, pausing, gliding as if floating in air.

Is this real? Or is it a dream? Elise's dream? How can that be? And where am I? Where. . . ?

Two hours later, Lavella woke her, calling her name softly and saying that her bath was already drawn. Maggie came to consciousness slowly, puzzled and confused, and hardly rested.

"Got to hurry, Miss Maggie," Lavella was saying. "Time to get dressed. Don't forget about Mr. Emil's party tonight."

Maggie groaned. She *had* forgotten. Another party! She would be glad when school started and she could get some rest. She dragged herself from bed and went to her bath. When she returned to her room, wrapped in a thick turkish towel, she found her underclothing laid out neatly on her remade bed.

No sooner had she slipped these on and sat before her vanity to fuss with her hair than there was a soft knock at the door, and Elise entered, already dressed and coiffed.

"I don't know why I can never be on time," Maggie apologized, glancing at the mantel clock. "It takes me hours to get ready. It always has."

"I'll help you," Elise offered. "What are you going to wear?"

"I thought the violet," Maggie said.

Elise pulled it from the armoire and scrutinized it critically.

"Don't you like it?" Maggie asked.

"It'll look lovely on you . . . when you're forty. It

looks like something my spinster aunt Suzanne would wear. Oh! I hope I haven't hurt your feelings."

"No! That's all right. I want to know about these things."

"Well, if the neckline were any higher, it would cover your chin. And the color! It's all wrong for you. You'll look like you're in *demi-deuil.*"

"*Demi*-what?"

"Half-mourning, like *maman.*" She turned and rummaged through the armoire. "Let's see what else you've got. Hmm . . . not bad. Oh! Here's one that will do perfectly, and the blue exactly matches your eyes." She held it against her and turned from side to side in front of the mirror. "Look, Maggie! See how prettily it hangs. Oh, please wear it! It'll be beautiful on you."

"It's awfully low in the bodice," Maggie murmured, concentrating on a wayward curl that persisted in falling wrongways across her forehead.

"But that's the best part," Elise breathed with a touch of mischief and daring.

Maggie twisted the curl into place and said, "If I had a figure like you, Elise, I'd wear it, but I'm afraid I don't have enough on top to hold it up."

"Well, we can fix that!"

"How?"

"Stockings, of course," Elise replied. "Don't think they're only for wearing on your legs."

She crossed over to the chest of drawers and chose a pair of silk stockings. "Here," she said, rolling them into little balls. "Stuff these into the top of your corset."

Maggie did as she was told, then studied herself in the mirror.

"See?" Elise said. "Now you're as big as I am."

"Elise!" Maggie breathed, the truth dawning on her. "Do you. . . ? I mean, is this what you. . . ?"

Elise giggled happily. "Of course, *chérie*! All the girls do it!"

Maggie continued to examine her reflection. "But don't you think mine look a little lumpy?"

"They won't . . . once you put the dress on." She snatched the blue gown from the bed and helped Maggie into it. "There . . . there, you see? Very becoming, and . . . daring!"

Too daring, Maggie thought, and she tried to hitch the bodice higher.

"Oh, now, don't spoil it!" Elise scolded. "What's the use of wearing a dress like this if you're not going to show off what you have?"

"What I don't have, you mean," Maggie said.

"Well, that's another secret we'll share," Elise replied. She stood in front of Maggie and yanked the bodice back down so that the tops of Maggie's breasts rose tantalizingly above the gown's deeply cut neckline. "Now, here," Elise went on, reaching into her beaded evening bag and producing a silver-capped vial of wildflower perfume. "Put a dab of this behind each ear and on both wrists."

"I've never used scent," Maggie said.

"Well, it's high time you started. *Everybody* wears it in New Orleans."

Maggie applied the perfume as Elise directed.

"And now," Elise said, "just a drop between your breasts."

Maggie tried to mask her shock at Elise's suggestion. "But who's going to smell it down there?"

Elise laughed. "You never know, *chérie!*"

Feeling wicked and very grown-up, Maggie moistened her finger with perfume and rubbed it into her cleavage.

"Now you look absolutely beautiful and smell divine," Elise declared. "And you'll be glad you do because Victor is going to be there tonight."

"Victor?" Maggie said, puzzled. "I don't remember him. I've met so many people in the past two weeks."

"You haven't met Victor yet," Elise said. "If you had, you'd remember, I assure you. He happens to be the most exciting man in New Orleans."

Maggie reached for her slippers, waiting for Elise to elaborate.

"His name is Victor Durand," Elise went on, not attempting to mask the tone of adoration in her voice. "He's an artist—a very good one—and he lives in Paris. But every year, he comes to New Orleans to do portraits."

"Did he paint the one of you in the drawing room?" asked Maggie.

"Yes," Elise answered. "And the one of *maman* that hangs above the fireplace. Oh, Maggie, I can't tell you how exciting it was to be able to sit and look at him while he painted me. My heart beat so loudly, I'm sure he could hear it."

"Are you in love with him?"

"Everyone is!" Elise declared with a sigh. She lowered her voice to a whisper. "I dream about him, Maggie. I dream that one day he'll crush me in his arms and kiss me!"

"Elise!" Maggie's eyes grew wide.

"It's true, Maggie! You'll know what I mean when you see him. You'll understand."

Jeanette called to the girls from downstairs, urging them to hurry, saying that their carriage was waiting to take them to dinner.

They gave each other a final glance in the mirror and raced down to join Jeanette.

Emil LaForet lived in the Vieux Carré in a three-

125

story house on Royal Street just behind the cathedral. He was a short, balding man with piercing eyes and an ample paunch that bespoke a fondness for comfort and good food. By contrast, his wife Catherine was a tall, pale blonde, a "Saxon" instead of a Creole. They greeted Jeanette and the two girls warmly and ushered them into the downstairs salon where a dozen other guests were already gathered.

Their faces were familiar to Maggie, for the same people seemed to attend every soirée. She spoke to each in turn, following Elise around the room, and was momentarily cornered by a feisty dowager aunt who demanded to know exactly what Maggie thought of New Orleans and, in particular, the LaForet family.

Maggie had barely begun to extol the beauties of the city—delighting the old woman—when Elise interrupted with, *"Pardonnez-nous, tante Virginie,* but I simply must have a word with Maggie."

The woman gave her great-niece a sharp look, but Jeanette appeared at her side with a bowl of smoked almonds and a bit of gossip she considered too spicy for the girls' ears; so the elderly Virginie let Maggie go and popped an almond into her mouth turning eagerly to Jeanette to hear of the latest *scandale.*

"What is it?" Maggie asked.

"It's him!" Elise whispered. "Victor! He's here!"

Maggie looked toward the door. Victor Durand stood with his back toward them, shrugging off his cape and handing his cane and top hat to the LaForets' maid.

"Don't be surprised if I faint dead away!" Elise breathed tremulously, and Maggie couldn't suppress an amused smile, for she was sure that Elise, bold as she was, had never fainted over a man in her life.

Then Victor turned, and Maggie felt a twinge of

126

disappointment. He was handsome enough in a pale, tousled way, but since coming to New Orleans, Maggie had met far better-looking men. What in the world entranced Elise so? His eyes? They were deep-set and luminous beneath fine, straight brows. His forehead was wide and smooth, but so white that Maggie was sure the man had never been out in the sun. His mouth was ruddy with a sensuously full bottom lip that made him seem in a continual pout. Perhaps that's it, Maggie thought. He looks a bit like Lord Byron, a bit bohemian—that must be his attraction!

Elise was not alone in making a beeline toward Victor. No sooner had he appeared than the guests began a general rush toward him. Maggie watched from the periphery and discerned another reason for his popularity. He appeared to look not at, but *into* a person, and he spoke to each in turn in a way that seemed almost private, as if the two of them were alone despite the crowd.

At last, he was presented to her. He took her hand and brushed it with his lips, a daring thing to do to an unmarried girl, and Maggie blushed fiercely; but he performed the act with such grace that no one could object. Maggie felt his fingers clasp hers, and when he released her hand she sensed, uneasily, that he had taken something from her.

He moved away, surrounded by a circle of women, but from then until dinner was announced, Maggie imagined she could feel the touch of his lips on the back of her hand.

At the table, he was seated across from Maggie with Elise on his right. No sooner had they taken their places than he reached out and moved a towering bouquet of hothouse roses that interfered with his view of Maggie.

"The flowers are beautiful," he said, "but I find you far more interesting to look at."

Maggie blushed again, and Elise interceded for her. "Really, Victor! You're embarrassing Maggie. Country girls aren't used to fast-talking swells."

Maggie understood that Elise was only trying to help, but she resented being called a country girl—even if she *did* feel like one—and she wished she had the gumption to reach across and replace the vase of roses.

Instead, she said, "Oh, where I come from, cowboys are pretty fast-talking themselves. I'm used to that sort of thing." Then realizing how her last statement must have sounded, she tried to make amends. "I mean, not *really* used to it . . . they don't say things like to me all the time, but, I . . . they. . . "

She floundered about trying to extricate herself, and only the first course saved her. She attacked the soup with fury, concentrating on the bowl and trying to keep her spoon from trembling. She knew Victor had his eyes on her—laughing, no doubt, thinking what an idiot she was!

Oh, I *am* a country mouse!

But when she at last summoned the courage to look up, she saw that Victor was not laughing at all, but was staring at her with a kind of wonder and interest.

She smiled, tentatively, grateful to him for not mocking her, and he smiled back warmly, genuinely.

Elise saw it all and nearly burst into tears. So Victor would never be hers after all! Maggie had won him with her artlessness, and suddenly she remembered a conversation Victor had had with Jeanette. "I love painting children," Victor had said. "Although they're surrounded by our corrupt and decadent world, they have such freshness, such innocence. That's true beauty.

128

And the sad thing is—what touches me most—is that it cannot last. Once we, too, were as trusting and naive. Oh, Jeanette! I can't even remember that time of my life!"

Well, it's too late for me! Elise thought, shrugging and returning to her soup. And after a year in New Orleans, Maggie won't be so innocent, either!

The meal progressed. Victor was drawn into a long conversation with Virginie and Jeanette, and Maggie relaxed a bit, but was constantly aware of Victor's eyes returning to her again and again. Each time she caught him studying her, her heart gave a little flutter, and she chastised herself for allowing him to draw her under his spell. At last the lemon ice was replaced by cheese and coffee. Then liqueurs were served, flashing in their tiny glasses like Ali Baba's jewels, topaz brandy, diamond anise, emerald crème de menthe, and ruby-like maraschino. It was well past midnight, and one by one, the dinner guests began drifting away, heading for home and bed.

Jeanette collected Elise and Maggie. *"Allons, mes enfants, il faut rentrer chez nous."*

Victor was on his feet, following them to the door. He held Jeanette back and murmured something in her ear. Elise, standing by her mother, heard her reply: "Well, I really don't know, Victor. It's up to her, after all."

"Will you speak to her about it?"

"I see no harm in that."

"Please, do!"

"Good night, Victor."

*"Bonne nuit,* Jeanette."

As their carriage rolled through the lamplit streets, Elise could contain her curiosity no longer.

129

*"Maman?"* she asked. "What did Victor say to you as we were leaving?"

"He inquired about Maggie."

"About me?" Maggie exclaimed.

"He found you lovely, dear, as indeed you are. And he asked if he might paint you."

"What did you say?"

"I told him it was a matter between the two of you," Jeanette replied. "What do you think? Would you like to have your portrait done?"

"Well, I . . . I don't know," Maggie stammered. "I mean, I would have to ask Mama and Papa. I imagine it's awfully expensive."

"Not so much that it would worry them," Jeanette advised. "In fact, it might be a nice thing to do."

"I'll have to think about it."

Jeanette patted her hand. "Take your time. There's no hurry."

They rode the rest of the way in silence, Maggie feeling oddly troubled, Elise bursting to get alone with Maggie, and Jeanette thinking only of bed.

The girls went upstairs, and Elise followed Maggie into her room and shut the door behind them.

"He's mad for you!" she whispered.

"Don't be crazy, Elise. He's twice my age."

Elise hugged herself and sank into the chair by the fireplace. "Oh! I should be jealous, but I'm not. It's too much fun to watch!"

"I thought you were in love with him."

"I am—but then, everybody is. It's not something you can take seriously. But you, Maggie! Now that's a different story. He couldn't take his eyes off you. I watched him carefully."

Maggie threw herself onto her bed. "He made me so nervous. His eyes seemed to drill right through me."

"Are you going to let him paint you?"

"I don't know."

"You really should—after all, he asked. And Victor *never* asks! He's got more commissions than he knows what to do with."

"I imagine posing is terribly boring."

"No, no, it's not! At least, not when you're posing for Victor. You just sit there and stare into his dreamy eyes. It's heaven!"

"Oh, Elise, I just don't think he's that attractive."

Elise rolled her eyes in exasperation and got up to go to the door. She paused and turned. "I suppose you realize . . . he's going to try to seduce you."

Maggie looked horrified. "What makes you say such a thing?"

"I can tell it," Elise said. "Are you going to let him?"

"Of course not!"

"Well, if you do, will you tell me about it?"

"Elise!"

Elise smiled mischievously. "Oh, you're *so* lucky!"

Maggie reached for her pillow, and Elise ducked out of the room just as it sailed toward the door.

Victor left Emil's and strolled down the *banquette* to a bar where he knew he would find his friend Fernand. The place was crowded, blue with smoke and smelling of Herbe Sainte, wine, and beer. An accordionist was playing on a raised platform in a corner, and two or three couples danced in the narrow space between the tables.

*"La vie bohème, n'est-ce pas?"* Fernand said by way of greeting as Victor joined him and signaled for a glass of Burgundy. "Doesn't it make you nostalgic for Paris?"

"Any other time, it would," Victor said. "But not tonight. I've just met the most beautiful girl."

"At Emil LaForet's? Which one of his nieces is it this time?"

"No, not a LaForet. A girl by the name of Maggie Cameron—a Texan."

"Oh, a little cowgirl! Was she wearing chaps and boots?"

"She was in blue that matched her eyes. And her face is one of the most beautiful I've ever seen. Innocent, naive, and . . . pure."

"All of which you hope to change, no doubt."

Victor said nothing, but the corners of his mouth curled in a smile.

"Oh, Victor!" Fernand said, amused and a bit envious. "The spider spins his web, eh? You really should be ashamed of yourself—preying on little girls. You're nothing but a *vieux marcheur!*"

# 9

Alex had telegraphed from New Orleans that he would be back on the Lantana mid-week; so when Anne heard a horse riding up to the house late Wednesday afternoon, she left her desk and raised a turret window to shout a welcome. But instead of Alex, she recognized Peter Stark and saw the low-lying January sun glint off his silvery sheriff's badge. Anne withdrew hastily, confident she hadn't been seen, and paced the office floor.

Ever since Klaus's death, she had expected Peter Stark—it was inevitable that he would eventually call on her, and she had personally instructed her gate guards to let him pass without question. But why did he have to turn up when Alex was absent? She didn't want to see him alone—and her blood turned to ice when she thought what he might have to say.

After a moment, she heard a knock at her turret door. "Who's there?"

"It's Dolores, *señora*," one of her housemaids replied. "There is a man to see you."

"Tell him I'm not in."

"He says it's important. He has news of *Señor* Dos."

Anne caught her breath and thought: *I must know!* She opened the door and brushed past her maid. "I'll go to him."

When she entered the parlor, she found Peter Stark gazing out of the window, his back to her.

"Good afternoon, Peter."

He turned and her heart skipped a beat, then raced on wildly. If the light had been dimmer, she might have sworn he was Dos! How alike they were! How much like Rudy!

"Good afternoon, Mrs. Cameron." He touched his hat in greeting.

Oh, God! Even the voice!

"The place is looking good," he went on. If he noticed her pallor, he gave no indication. "Course I don't remember it too well from the old days. I was pretty young when Papa died and Mama moved us away."

"Of course," Anne said curtly, desperate to avoid further mention of Rudy and Emma.

"I wasn't sure your men would let me past the gate," Peter said. "But they gave me no trouble."

"They had orders to let you through. I've been expecting you, but I must admit I thought you'd come sooner."

"I figured it'd be better to give both of us time to . . . to get used to what happened."

Anne reached out to him from across the room, a

gesture he recognized as sincere, and felt the tension within him lessening.

"Oh, Peter, believe me," she said. "If it was in my power to undo. . ."

"I know, ma'am. I feel the same way."

A long silence stretched between them. Then Anne said: "Dolores tells me you have news of Dos."

"Just a rumor. I came out to see if you'd heard it, too. Or . . . if you knew more."

"I don't know anything about him. I haven't heard a word since . . ." She paused. She couldn't say it.

Peter understood. "I've been tipped off he might be headed back this way."

"Back this way? Back from where?"

"Mexico, ma'am. Story I heard said that a man looking a lot like Dos robbed a bank down Coahuila way."

"Dos wouldn't rob a bank!"

"There were folks who never thought he'd kill a man, either."

His whispered words lashed Anne like a whip, and she had to grip the back of a chair to keep from reeling.

He watched her without pity. He didn't hate the Camerons as his mother did—he'd been too young to know first-hand the reasons behind the enmity between the two families. But Emma had carefully coached her children to distrust this powerful family and to resent the Lantana's might and wealth. It galled him to know that his authority as sheriff ended abruptly at their barbed-wire boundaries and that, without Anne's permission, there weren't enough guns in Joelsboro to get him past her gate.

Anne recovered quickly. Straightening her shoulders and lifting her chin, she said, "I'm sorry, Peter. I think

135

of Dos as any mother would; and of course, you think of Klaus and the job you have to do."

"That's the reason I'm here, ma'am. It's my job . . . and I was hoping for your help."

"Help? In what way?"

"If you should hear from Dos, you might give him a word of advice."

"What's that?"

"Tell him he'd do best to give himself up."

"Do you honestly think I'd tell my own son to turn himself in?"

"Yes, I do, ma'am, because you're a smart woman. And you know that if Dos *is* on the Lantana, he's pretty much safe from arrest. Now, the Lantana's big, but not big enough to hold Dos forever. Sooner or later he's gonna hanker for the pleasures of town, and he'll go roaming. And then it's only a matter of time before I catch up with him."

He saw fear flare up in Anne's eyes, and he wondered if it was the first time in her life she'd ever been afraid.

"Don't worry, Mrs. Cameron," he said. "I won't shoot him. I'll see he has a trial."

"You have great faith in the law."

Peter nodded. "Yes, ma'am, I do."

He buttoned up his coat and started for the door.

"Peter!" Anne called, halting him on the threshold. "Do I have your word?"

"On what?"

"That you won't shoot him."

"On my honor."

Anne stared into his eyes and saw he was telling the truth. "Then you have *my* word. If Dos shows up here, I'll turn him in to you."

Peter headed out into the cold. The sun had set,

and the horizon was gray and bleak. He mounted his horse and set off for Joelsboro.

She's a fine woman, he thought. It's a crying shame we can't be friends.

And nothing his mother had told him about Anne was able to smother the spark of admiration that kindled within him.

Anne was still awake when Alex arrived home at midnight. He was full of stories about Maggie in New Orleans, and Anne let him talk, knowing his heart ached for his daughter as much as hers longed for her son.

He told her in detail about the parties they had attended, what everyone wore, what food was served, and what they had talked about. And he told her not to worry about Maggie—that Jeanette and Elise had fallen in love with her immediately and had taken her under their wings.

But as they crawled into bed and he took her into his arms, he whispered in her ear, "Oh, Anne! I'm going to miss her so."

Long after his regular breathing told her he was asleep, Anne remained awake, her eyes staring into darkness.

Never once had he asked about Dos!

Burned into the headboard behind her pillow was the Lantana brand—the Crown of Thorns. She traced its outline with her fingertips, then using her wedding ring, she gouged the wood, adding another thorn to the crown.

Dos and Lorna *were* on the ranch, hiding out on the spread known as the Casa Rosa, named for the little adobe house where they sought shelter. Its walls had once been pink, but years of sun and sand had scorched the paint until the bare earthen bricks were the color of bleached bones.

They shivered with cold, but avoided building a fire for fear the smoke would attract attention from a wandering vaquero.

"Would they turn you in?" Lorna asked.

"No. But they would tell my mother, and she would try to find me. I don't want to put her through that."

The sentiment surprised Lorna. It was the first time he'd revealed anything that sounded like guilt or remorse.

"You must love your mother very much."

Dos looked away, silent.

Say it, Dos! Say it out loud! Love! What keeps you from using that word!

Lorna bit her lip and gathered her coat more tightly around her shoulders. She loved him now more than ever, and pitied him because he was afraid to love her back.

The sun was low on the horizon; outside the windows the sky was coppery, streaked with flaming clouds. A norther had blown through the night before leaving the air clear and bitter.

"We can't stay here forever," Dos said. "Someone's bound to come along and spot the horses."

"Where will we go?"

He shrugged.

"We could go west," Lorna said.

"California?"

"Why not? It's far away."

He thought for a second. She watched him closely, wanting to reach out for him, to cradle his face in

138

her palms, to run her fingers through his hair, to hold him tightly.

But just as she raised her hands, he stood up and pulled on his glove. "Well, if we're ever going to go, we might as well leave now. It'll be cold, but at least we'll have the darkness for cover."

"Can we make it off the ranch before sunrise?"

"Probably not. But we'll be damn' close."

They rode all night, leaving the Casa Rosa behind and crossing three-quarters of the Ebonal before the rising sun behind them cast long shadows toward the west.

By mid-morning they crossed the farthest boundary. Dos reined up and looked back over his shoulder. This part of the Ebonal was high rolling plains studded with sage and bristly clumps of dead grass. The leading edge of the latest norther had met up with warm air from the Gulf and was being pushed back, dividing the sky with a line of ragged clouds that dragged their gauzy gray tatters along the horizon. They might bring rain. Dos hoped not, for it was miserably cold, and he knew they would never find shelter in this desolate land.

Nevertheless, he hung back as the clouds crawled farther across the sky, grazing the sun and spreading a deepening shadow across the *brasada.*

Lorna watched him, reading his mind. Their flight to Mexico had not seemed final to him—it had been a spur-of-the-moment escape, a quick retreat with Lorna leading the way. But now, leaving the Lantana for the second time, it dawned on him that it would probably be for good. Never again would he sleep in his bed in the big house, or drive Anne's surrey, or sit down at a meal prepared by Azucena. He had swum for the last time in the pond at Bitter Creek and had ridden his last bronco in a Lantana rodeo.

That was all over now . . . or would be if he didn't turn back.

He thought of Anne. He would never see her again. Or Carlos.

Or . . . Alex!

That decided him. He faced west and spurred his horse forward.

Lorna started to speak up, started to say, "Dos, wait! Let's go back. Everything will be all right!"

But she knew it wouldn't; and knew, too, that if they *did* return she would lose all chance of keeping him forever. She remained silent and followed him out across the open prairie beneath the gathering clouds.

It rained on them that afternoon and throughout the night. At first, they huddled together, shivering under a *serape* until they were so soaked that it didn't matter any more. Blue with cold, they mounted and rode on with fingers so numb they couldn't feel the reins beneath their gloves. The next day dawned cloudy, but dry, and there was a noticeable warmth in the southern wind. They gnawed on jerky and caught a few hours of sleep before pushing ahead.

The going was slow. The rugged land rose with every step the horses took, and it was five more days before the snow-dusted peaks of the Davis Mountains appeared on the horizon.

"Where are we, Dos?" Lorna asked.

"I don't know."

"It's beautiful. I didn't know Texas had mountains like this."

They were resting their horses on the rocky edge of a crag. The first sun they'd seen in a week broke

140

through the clouds and filled the valley below. A cold wind, smelling of snow, howled around them and cut through their clothing. They were saddle-sore and exhausted, and the leather of their boots had dried hard as iron.

They stood there for a moment, drinking in the grandeur of the view before climbing back onto their horses and heading into the valley.

It was early evening when they rode into Alpine.

"Not much of a town," Lorna observed.

"No . . . but they've got a hotel. It's going to feel good sleeping out of the cold for a change."

"Oh! A bed! And a bath!"

The hotelkeeper didn't bat an eye when they checked in. He'd seen worse-looking travelers before, but he judiciously made Dos pay in advance. Lorna lounged blissfully in the hotel's only tub while Dos led their horses across the street to the municipal stable. When he returned to their room, he found her sitting at the dresser peering at her reflection in the mirror.

"Traveling's hard on a girl," she said stroking her hollow cheeks with her fingertips. "I could sure stand a dab or two of Guadalupe's sweet-smelling rouge."

Dos looked at her silently. With nothing to sustain her on their journey but jerky and rainwater, she'd lost so much weight that her face was pinched and her body was as gaunt as it had been the evening she first went to the Liberty Saloon.

He reached in his pocket and counted his change. "We've got nearly four dollars left. We ought to be able to live high off the hog for a couple of days."

Lorna smiled into the mirror at him. "Let's don't throw that money away on food. Now that we're in a town, I can get us anything we want to eat . . . and it won't cost us a cent."

Dos caught her meaning and shook his head. "Lorna, you're a born thief."

Her eyes went distant. "No. I wasn't born that way ... but I learned."

Dos felt a tug of tenderness for her. He crossed the floor and, standing behind her, slipped his arms around her shoulders. A thrill raced through Lorna as his lips grazed her still damp hair.

The lingering fragrance of lilac soap filled his nostrils, and he murmured, "Mmm, you smell sweet."

"Well, you certainly don't," Lorna said, only half-teasing.

"Reckon the water's still hot?"

"Warm, anyway," Lorna replied.

Dos grabbed her towel and hurried from the room.

An hour later, as spruced up as they could be in their travel-soiled clothes, they crossed the street and strolled into the Bighorn Saloon. A group of cowmen looked up as they entered, and finding Lorna too pretty to ignore, began vying for the privilege of buying her and Dos a drink.

"Personally, I never touch anything stronger than root beer," Lorna said coyly, "but my friend would probably appreciate something more potent."

"Set 'em up, Tom," one of the men said, slapping a five-dollar gold piece on the copper-covered bar. Then turning to Dos and Lorna, "The name's John Stoney. That ugly galoot's called Jake. An' them there's Willy, Gene, Buster, an' Nick."

"Pleased to meet you," Lorna said graciously. "And I'm Belle Starr."

The men laughed, and Stoney inquired, "An' the gentleman with you? I suppose it's none other than ole Jim July!"

142

"Him in the flesh," answered Lorna, pleased with the game.

"Hell, you ain't Belle Starr," Buster said. "Everybody knows that injun July done her in some four or five years ago."

"Well, then, ain't I the prettiest corpse you ever saw?"

Their laughter made Lorna jolly and expansive. "We're on the dodge," she volunteered in a conspiratorial whisper that alarmed Dos. But before he could halt her, she went on, "My friend here killed a man to save my honor, and then we were involved in a little fracas down Mexico way."

The men grinned, not believing a word of her prattle.

"You're some card, ma'am," Jake declared, reaching for the bottle and refilling Dos's glass.

"Did someone mention cards?" Lorna asked innocently, batting her eyes and giving each of the half-dozen cowmen a soulful look. "I'd just love a hand of cards. Who knows how to play Mexican Spit?"

A well-worn deck of cards, edges carefully trimmed, was produced, and Lorna riffled the deck with artful clumsiness.

"Wait a minute, boys!" she said, pushing the deck away. "We haven't even started, and already I'm in over my head. My friend and I are so dead broke we're about to sell our saddles."

"I'll be more'n happy to stake you, ma'am," Buster offered, madly infatuated with Lorna.

"Well, I couldn't allow such a thing. We pay our own way—always have, always will," Lorna stated, straightening her back and raising her chin in a display of moral correctness. "But we do have two horses

143

we'd be willing to sell if someone has a hankering for a couple of fine black stallions."

"Lemme take a look," Buster said. "I could use me two more horses."

"Lorna! Have you gone loco?" Dos intervened.

"Go on," Lorna told Buster, ignoring Dos. "They're right next door at the stable."

Dos dragged her aside, hissing into her ear, "What the hell are you up to?"

Her eyes flashed a warning to him. *Stay out of it, Dos! Trust me!*

He let go of her and fell back.

Turning to the men, Lorna reached for the cards. "I just love Mexican Spit, but if you boys want to teach me a new game, I'd be willing to learn."

Dos watched in amazement. He'd never seen her simper so. She was playing the coquette and the innocent at the same time, and the cowmen were buying it. And Dos noticed that her accent had developed a distinct moonlight-and-magnolia drawl.

"We mostly play seven card stud," Jake said.

"What's wild?"

"Nothing."

"Well, that doesn't sound like too much fun, but I'd be willing to give it a turn."

Buster reentered the saloon. "Them horses ain't stallions . . . they're geldings!"

Lorna batted her enormous eyes. "Well, I'm sure I wouldn't know about such delicate matters."

"Aw, it don't matter nohow. They're fine-looking critters. What would you folks say to twenty apiece?"

"Sold!" Lorna declared, reaching across the table to seal the contract with a handshake.

"Lorna!" Dos warned.

"Give twenty to my friend, Jim July," Lorna said,

"and count me out another twenty in chips. Now will someone kindly explain the rules to me?"

Dos dropped into a chair and sighed with resignation, convinced Lorna had lost her mind. She'd just sold their only horses and was recklessly aiming to give the money back to the men.

"Wish me luck, Dos!" Lorna called out gaily, and picked up her hand.

By midnight, she had turned her twenty dollars into nearly a hundred. She bluffed the other players at every turn and was such a gracious, flattering, seemingly surprised winner that they actually enjoyed losing to her. Dos watched with amazement, and grudging admiration, as she parlayed a pair of sixes to triumph, forcing Buster, the new owner of two geldings and who held a pair of jacks king high, to fold.

"Full house," Lorna lied, slipping her unseen cards back into the deck and shuffling just as clumsily as before. "Lucky at cards, unlucky at love."

The cowmen looked to Dos, who tried to appear appropriately guilty.

"I'm out," Buster said abruptly.

"I'll take the horses as collateral," Lorna said.

"Well, I'll put up one," Buster replied.

Lorna smiled sweetly and pushed twenty dollars in chips across the table. "Are you bucks sure you don't want to play Mexican Spit?"

The next morning, Dos and Lorna rode out of Alpine atop their horses, and in Lorna's wallet were gold and bills worth more than two hundred dollars.

"You had me scared there for a minute," Dos said. "That was a helluva chance to take. How'd you know you could pull it off?"

" 'Cause they were drinking, and I wasn't. I figured

they'd get good and oiled and start making mistakes. And I also figured that playing with a girl would rattle 'em nicely."

"But poker's not easy . . . and you knew what you were doing. How'd you learn?"

A bitter memory clouded Lorna's eyes. She spoke softly: "Watching my daddy lose taught me how to win."

# 10

Letters on cream vellum embossed with the Lantana brand arrived regularly for Maggie at Jeanette Drouet's home. There were always two in every envelope, one from Alex and one from Anne. Anne's handwriting was broad and black, as decisive and devoid of frills as her mind. Alex's elegant Carstairs script was beautiful and light, looking as if the nib of his pen had only just grazed the paper's surface.

Anne's letters were newsy and informative: " . . . Carlos is in San Antonio all this week, supposedly on a shopping trip but actually to be on hand for Sara Dixon's debut party . . . We had snow last night! Snow! Can you believe it? It didn't stick, but everyone was so excited to see the flakes falling from the sky that we stood outdoors for an hour just watching and didn't even think about the cold . . . Azucena passed away

147

on Sunday and the funeral was yesterday. The poor old soul just worked herself to death. I've decided that Gloria will be the new head cook. . . . And speaking of death, I don't think Ramiro Rivas is long for this world. He hasn't left his bed in more than a month. Anselmo has been serving as foreman, and I expect will take over officially if and when his father goes to meet his Maker. . . . Your calico had four kittens behind the woodbox in the kitchen and is quite a devoted mother . . ." And always: "No news of Dos."

On the other hand, Alex, filled his letters with personal thoughts—memories, hopes, and expressions of love: " . . . Sometimes I wonder at the ways of fortune, how a man from the Scottish Highlands could end up in this strangely beautiful part of the world (Do others see its beauty as I do? Do *you*?) blessed with a magnificent wife and a lovely daughter who is always in my heart. . . . Except for one brief visit shortly after I married your mother, I have never been back to my ancestral home. My American family and the Lantana have been home enough for me. Yet, I hope there's *no* place on earth you grow to love so much that it would take you permanently away from us. . . . It's hard to believe you've been gone four months already—four months to the day. As one grows older, time flies. Don't you think that's unfair? With one's term on earth growing short, it would be better if time slowed down. . . . I can't tell you how disappointed I am that pressing business forced us to cancel our trip to New Orleans to see you, but think! Soon you'll be back on the Lantana! And be ours again for the entire summer! . . ."

And never any mention of Dos.

Maggie accumulated the letters, bound like *billets-doux* with blue ribbon, in an enameled box on top of her dresser, and in the stillness of night when she was

148

most likely to be lonely or homesick, she would take them out and read them through, Anne's first because they took her back—almost physically—to the Lantana, then Alex's which she devoured as food essential for her soul.

It wasn't that she was unhappy in New Orleans. She was far too busy for that. The nuns at Sacred Heart were demanding taskmasters, and although Maggie found French and Latin easy and enjoyable, she had to devote long hours studying arithmetic and memorizing the sometimes bewildering catechism responses that, even though she was a Protestant, she was expected to repeat by rote when called upon in chapel by Father LaPlante.

And then there was the constant round of parties. The LaForets appeared to know or to be related to nearly everyone in town, and they seemed to have an insatiable need to congregate, the mandatory but pleasant Sunday mornings at LaRivière, afternoon tea at one or another of the grand houses lining St. Charles Avenue, dinner at *Tante* This's or *Cousine* That's, theater, opera, and of course, the exciting, but eventually exhausting Carnival balls. The parades, especially that of the Krewe of Comus with its prancing flambeau carriers lighting up the narrow French Quarter streets, the gowns, the dainty favors which the ladies received from the masked revelers, and the extravagant tableaux that were the highlight of every ball—all this had dazzled Maggie, but she woke up on Ash Wednesday morning grateful that the Catholic Church had had the good sense to invent the season of Lent.

Except that in New Orleans, Lent turned out to be more talked about than observed. No sooner had Maggie recovered her breath from Carnival than the succession of matinées, soirées, teas, and dinners re-

149

sumed—smaller, less elaborate affairs in grudging deference to the season, but nevertheless demanding one's presence. And there was the portrait. She sat for it every Thursday afternoon after piano lessons and before tea —with Elise lounging nearby watching as Victor's eyes studied Maggie's face between brush strokes on the canvas.

Victor seldom spoke while he painted, and he insisted that Maggie sit perfectly still, so the hour passed in almost total silence, driving Maggie to utter distraction. She still could not see what Elise found so totally absorbing about the man. Oh, he could be charming, and he had a pleasant smile, and she couldn't deny that his dark eyes were very appealing. But he never once caused her heart to thump out of control, as always happened when she saw some of the handsome LaForet cousins.

"How much longer, Victor?" she asked impatiently.

*"Encore un instant* . . . don't move!" He touched the tip of his sable brush into a smear of rose madder and applied it to the canvas. "Now . . . we're through for the day."

"Oooh!" Maggie stretched and yawned. "I'm stiff as a board. I didn't know having my picture painted would be so painful."

"Just wait till you see it. It will all be worthwhile."

"Let me see it now. It's almost done."

"No . . . you know my rule. Not until it's finished," he said, covering the canvas with a cloth. "That's a lesson I learned the hard way. If you show a picture before you're through, your sitter will say, 'I don't have eyes like that!' or 'My lips are not that thin!' or 'You've made my hair look like mouse fur! Do it over!' "

Maggie giggled.

"It's true. That actually happened. And do you know what? Her hair *did* look like mouse fur!"

"What did you do?"

"I painted it over and gave her an even more luxurious head of mouse fur. She was perfectly delighted."

Maggie and Elise laughed gaily.

Victor slipped the canvas in his case and closed the latch.

"Won't you stay for tea?" Elise asked hopefully. In her heart, she'd already given Victor over to Maggie but that didn't prevent her from relishing his company.

"I must be off, unfortunately," he said. "I promised Madame Landry her portrait a month ago, and I'm still not finished."

He bade the girls goodbye and departed. It was true that he was late with Juliette Landry's picture, but he had no intention of working on it that afternoon. Instead he went back to his flat in the Quarter, changed clothes, and dropped in at the Brasserie Charbonneau for a glass of wine.

He was not alone for long, for Fernand spotted him at the bar and took the seat beside him.

"How goes it, Victor?" he inquired, slapping his friend on the back and calling for a glass of red.

Victor's dark, moody eyes stared straight ahead. *"Je suis chipé pour cette fille."*

"Crazy about what girl?"

"That little Texas beauty I'm painting now."

"Ahh . . . the same old story. Last year it was the Keppner girl, and the year before that you were in love with Charmaine Robillard. . . ."

"Not in love . . . infatuated."

"Call it what you will, but they're always mere babes in arms. What is it about these children that attracts you so?"

151

"Their purity . . . their innocence. They seem to be of another race, even of another world."

"Like angels?" Fernand was kidding him, but Victor's face was serious.

"Yes . . . like angels."

"Oh, Victor! Victor! You're really too much. Lusting after angels!"

"I can't resist it."

"I suppose she's mad for you."

"On the contrary."

"Oh! So you haven't turned her head?"

"Not a hair's-breadth."

"It must be quite a blow," Fernand said, smiling to himself.

"I haven't given up hope."

"You'd better work fast. When do you depart for Paris?"

"At the end of the month."

"Not much time."

"Too little . . ."

"And when you return, *mon vieux,* you're likely to find that someone else had already plucked the ripened fig from the branch!"

"You, Fernand?"

"Never! I detest children!" He drained his glass and signaled for another. "But tell me, Victor. How do you handle the contradiction? Their innocence and purity attract you. But after the . . . I suppose we could call it the 'inevitable conclusion' . . . after that, where is their innocence?"

"That's the problem, Fernand. That's the maddening dilemma."

Maggie sat for Victor twice more; then one afternoon when she and Elise arrived home from school, Jeanette

152

met them in the foyer and said, "Come into the sitting room. I have a surprise for you."

The girls followed her into the room, and there, resting against the back of a chair, was Maggie's portrait. It was ornately framed, and dabs of paint, still wet, glistened on the canvas.

Elise clapped her hands together and cried, "Oh, it's wonderful!"

But Maggie hung back, feeling sure there had been a terrible mistake.

The face of a young woman gazed back at her from the canvas with blue eyes flecked with silver light, high cheekbones carefully modeled and curving to a strong, determined chin; the lips were full, the palest pink, curled in the barest trace of a smile, giving the face an enigmatic expression as if the sitter had just been presented to a stranger and wasn't yet sure whether they would become friends. There was an air of grave dignity to the portrait, and somehow a hint of private sadness—despite the smile. But most of all—the sitter was beautiful. Truly beautiful!

"That doesn't look like me at all," Maggie murmured.

"What do you mean, dear?" Jeanette asked.

"It's you exactly," Elise said.

No! she thought. No! Not me at all! It couldn't be. I'm that donkey-faced girl in the picture that Swiss photographer took of me. Big nose . . . big eyes . . . awful chin. Not this . . .

She stared at the portrait.

. . . not this beautiful person!

Then she thought with wonder: Is this how Victor sees me? Does he think I'm really that . . . ?

She couldn't bring herself to believe it.

"You're not happy with it?" Jeanette asked, disappointed, for she thought the portrait was magnificent.

"It's wonderfully done," Maggie said. "But I don't think it looks like me at all."

She turned away, thinking: Mama and Papa will probably like it, though. It will make a nice present for them.

"The painting came with a note from Victor," Jeanette said, producing an envelope.

Maggie tore it open and read:

Forgive me for not delivering your portrait in person, but I'm off today for Paris. I hope we meet again when I return this fall.

I shan't be surprised if you hate the picture. I tried my best, but found it impossible to capture your true beauty. Perhaps I shall have another opportunity. . . .

"What does he say?" Elise asked.

Maggie folded the letter and slipped it back inside the envelope. "That he's left for Paris. That's all."

She went upstairs alone, and after she shut the door behind her, she reread Victor's words.

" . . . impossible to capture your true beauty."

Did he really mean that? Or was it just flattery?

She sat at her dresser and stared into the mirror.

"Maybe it's true what they say about the eye of the beholder."

She sighed, troubled, confused; then rising, she slipped the envelope into the box where she kept the letters from the Lantana.

Later, an urge drew her impulsively downstairs to the solarium where she had posed for Victor. It was quiet and deserted now. Winter sunshine streamed through the polished windowpanes, making a checkerboard of the floor.

Elise's voice from the doorway surprised her. "Thinking of Victor?"

Maggie turned quickly. "Of course not!"

"I thought maybe that's why you came in here—to revive fond memories."

"That's not true at all," Maggie said, but as soon as she'd uttered the denial she wondered if she were lying—not to Elise, but to herself.


When school ended for the year and Maggie returned to the Lantana, she was shocked to learn that Alex had suffered a perilous bout of pneumonia during the spring, and his recovery had been extremely slow.

"You should have told me!" she said to Anne.

"You would only have worried, and there was nothing you could do."

"I could have come right home."

"Your father didn't want that. Now, go see him. He's waiting for you."

Maggie moved to the door, but Anne reached out suddenly and held her back. "Don't say anything about how he looks!"

Maggie's spine tingled with apprehension. She opened the door and slipped inside. It was late evening, and the gas lamps in the dim room had not been lit. Alex lay in bed propped against pillows, his head turned toward the violet sky outside the open windows.

"Papa," Maggie whispered, almost afraid to come closer.

He shifted on the pillows and looked in her direction. "Maggie? Is that you?"

The thin reediness of his voice alarmed Maggie and set her heart to thumping in her chest.

"Papa! I'm home!"

She ran to his bedside and embraced him, burying her face in his shoulder.

"Oh, my bonny Maggie! It's so good to have you back!"

Maggie couldn't hold back her tears. She went limp against him and sobbed.

"Hey, what's all this?" Alex chided softly. "Tears instead of smiles? I thought you'd be happy to be home again."

"I am, Papa. I just hate to see you sick."

"I'm much better now, my darling. And with you here again, I'll be up and about in no time."

"I hope so, Papa."

"The room is so dark," he said. "Light the lamps so I can look at you."

Maggie struck a match and touched it to the gas jets on either side of the bed. A warm yellow glow suffused the room.

She steeled her nerves and turned back to Alex, but nothing could have prepared her for the sight of him. She gasped involuntarily and had to bite her lip to keep from crying out.

He looked twenty years older. His face was gaunt with hollow cheeks and sunken eyes, and beneath the bedspread his body was shockingly thin and wasted. His hair reached nearly to his shoulders and was streaked throughout with white.

But he seemed unaware of his appearance. Instead, he looked at Maggie and smiled—a grotesque expression on his cadaverous face.

"Maggie!" he breathed in wonder. "You grow more beautiful every day! Come. Hold my hand."

156

She knelt beside the bed and laced her fingers through his. How weak his grip is! Like clasping hands with a sleeping child! And his eyes! Oh, Papa!

"My darling Maggie," he whispered. "How happy I am to have you home at last."

"I'll never leave again," she said. "I'm going to stay here with you forever."

Alex chuckled lightly. "Oh, you'll soon be longing for city life again . . . just wait and see."

Maggie started to protest, but the door behind them opened and Anne entered.

"You mustn't tire your father," she said.

Maggie resented the intrusion, but when she looked to Alex, he nodded and said, "Aye, I must have my rest. But I'll soon have my strength, and the two of us will ride about the place like we used to in the old days."

"I'd like that, Papa," Maggie said rising.

"Will you share breakfast with me in the morning?"

"Of course, I will, Papa. Tomorrow morning . . . and every morning."

Having Maggie home worked wonders for Alex, and he seemed to rebound miraculously. By midsummer, it took all of Anne's coaxing and cajolery to keep him from plunging headlong into his old, strenuous routine. Nevertheless, he had grown strong enough to relieve Carlos of some of the burden that had fallen to him during Alex's illness.

Doing the work of two men had tired Carlos, and it showed in his face. He slept poorly, and his shoulders were stooped as if the load had grown too heavy.

Maggie saw it and tried to help, but the vaqueros resented taking orders from a girl, and after a few days, she abandoned her efforts and settled in at the house.

With each day that passed, she found herself more

and more alone. Anne busied herself in her office for hours at a time. Alex shed the pallor of illness and grew robust again, and as his health improved, he began spending long days away from the house. And Carlos was so weary when he came in at night that he dawdled through supper, oblivious to what he ate, and trudged to his room to throw himself in bed.

So preoccupied were the others, that no one noticed Maggie's boredom, and she found herself looking forward impatiently to Elise's weekly letters chronicling the events of her summer. Gerard had come home from Harvard, and Elise had written: "I hope you have a secret for me because I've got a confession to tell you that will curl your hair!"

That's *bound* to be good! Maggie thought, and she regretted that her letters to Elise were so dull and repetitive. A sudden rainstorm that washed away a bridge over Bitter Creek was the most exciting bit of news she could offer.

And as Alex grew stronger, Maggie's resolve to remain on the Lantana faded and she looked forward to autumn when she could return to New Orleans.

I guess I'm not such a country mouse, after all, she conceded as she sat on the porch of the big house and gazed across the yard to a corral where Carlos and a band of vaqueros were breaking a dappled filly. The men's shouts echoed through the dusty summer air, and the stubborn pony's hoofbeats sounded like a wild, erratic tom-tom.

She smiled wryly, admitting to herself that she actually missed the LaForets' relentless round of parties, and . . . yes! She had to concede that she even missed Sacred Heart. Next year—she promised herself—I won't grumble about catechism, and I won't imitate the way Mother Matilda waddles down the hall!

Carlos left the corral, and Maggie called out to him. Stripping off his gloves and tucking them into his belt, he crossed the yard and leaned against the porch railing. Fine white dust clung like flour to his dark lashes, and he looked tired beneath his tan.

"Not your favorite kind of work, is it, Carlos?" Maggie said.

Carlos sighed wearily. "I'd rather do almost anything else than break horses."

"Dos was crazy about it."

"I wish he were here right now. That little filly'd be broke in no time."

"Do you think he'll ever come back?"

"I hope so," Carlos said. "We need him."

"Because of Papa?"

Carlos nodded.

One of the vaqueros called to him from the corral. Carlos sighed and pulled his gloves from his belt. "I've got to get back to work."

"Carlos."

He looked to her.

"Why don't you come with me?"

"To New Orleans?"

"Yes. A week . . . or two. You'd have a wonderful time. And you'll need a vacation by then."

"I need one now."

"Then it's settled?"

"Let me think about it."

"No, don't think!" Maggie said. "Just say you'll do it. We'll take the train, you'll meet my friends, and we'll have so much fun. And for a week or two, you won't have to think about the ranch, or cows, or . . . or breaking fillies."

Carlos grinned broadly. "That's mighty tempting."

"Promise you'll come with me."

Carlos winked at her. "It's a deal!"

Maggie flew down the steps and hugged him. "Oh, Carlos! I can't wait to show you New Orleans!"

By the end of August Alex had resumed most of his old duties, and Carlos and Maggie were able to leave the Lantana with a clear conscience.

They wired ahead and Jeanette Drouet was at the depot to meet them.

"I'm so glad to meet you at last, Carlos," she said, escorting them to her waiting carriage. "I've heard so much about you from Anne and Alex."

"Where's Elise?" Maggie asked.

"Still in Bay St. Louis!" Jeanette sighed with exasperation. "I can't get the girl home. You know how crazy she is about the beach."

Hmm! Maggie thought, remembering Gerard. I certainly do!

Jeanette went on: "But I wrote her that you were returning today, and I imagine she'll come flying back."

Their carriage rolled homeward and Carlos stared at the city with wonder. He had never seen so many people or such traffic. St. Charles Avenue was choked with buggies, and noisy, clanging streetcars clattered up and down the neutral ground. Huge trees covered the street with a canopy of green, and the mansions were grander than any he'd known in San Antonio.

Maggie chattered happily throughout the drive, pointing out the sights, the homes of friends, and the academy where she went to school. And she was pleased to see that Carlos was immensely impressed.

The whirlwind of parties began that evening with dinner at Emil and Catherine's in the Vieux Carré. From the moment he arrived, Carlos set every woman's heart aflutter, and Maggie noted with pride that *he* was

160

no country mouse. He chatted and flirted as confidently as if he'd been born on Audubon Place, and *Tante* Virginie was so charmed that she surreptitiously switched place cards to insure that Carlos sat beside her.

Dinner was gay and lively, and Maggie listened avidly to gossip about what friends had done all summer. Then she heard Catherine LaForet, at the far end of the table, mention the name of Victor Durand. She pretended to listen to Emil's story about a spinster cousin who had caused a scandal by running off to Baltimore with a defrocked priest, but her ears strained to hear what Catherine had to say.

" . . . arrived last week. I invited him tonight, but he had another engagement. He's so much in demand, you know. And I understand his visit to New Orleans is going to be brief this time . . . two months at the most. He's had to turn down commissions right and left."

Maggie arched an eyebrow. So, Victor's back! I wonder if he would have broken his engagement and accepted Catherine's invitation if he'd known I was going to be here, too. Not that I really care! But it might have been interesting.

Then she heard Jeanette say, "Well, I'm luckier than you, Catherine. I've snared him for Saturday."

Emil finished his story and looked expectantly at Maggie.

What had he said? Am I supposed to laugh or look shocked? She opened her eyes wide and muttered, "My word!" and saw by Emil's pleased expression that she had reacted properly.

Saturday! She and Victor would be thrown together again, and she wasn't sure if she was pleased or not. She would have to say something about the portrait. She couldn't tell him that she'd cared so little for the

161

picture that she'd left it behind at Jeanette's instead of taking it back to the Lantana. No, that wouldn't do at all. But he'd said in his note, which she still kept locked in her letter box, that he was unsatisfied with the portrait himself and that he hoped she would sit for another.

She had no time for further reflection, for Emil had launched into another story and she'd already missed the beginning. She *had* to listen this time; she might not be so lucky again to guess the appropriate reaction.

Elise arrived that Saturday, only an hour before Jeanette's reception. She burst into Maggie's room, and they squealed with delight, hugging each other, and talking all at once until Maggie shushed her and demanded, "Tell me about Gerard."

"First a secret from you!"

"Oh, Elise! *Nothing* happened to me. Nothing at all!"

"How dull!" Elise said sympathetically. "I hope I *never* have to go to Texas."

"I know," Maggie replied. "You'd hate it there. But tell me, Elise! I've been dying to know about you and Gerard ever since I got your mysterious letter."

Elise threw herself on the bed and hugged the pillow. Her face went solemn and she seemed to gaze far out into space, striking a pose that would have done Bernhardt proud. "I'm no longer a girl. I'm now a woman . . . and in fact, I'll probably soon become a mother."

*"Elise!"*

"Yes," Elise said, holding out her hand for silence. "I let Gerard have his way with me."

"You didn't!"

"I'm afraid so. I'll be the next family scandal."

"Your family seems to have so many."

"It must be in our blood."

"Well, tell me about it," Maggie urged, her curiosity overcoming her shock.

"It was late one night. I heard a noise on the veranda and when I went out to investigate, I found Gerard, who'd gone outside to smoke. There was a big moon, and, oh, Maggie, he never looked so handsome. Well, one thing led to another, and before I knew it, I was in his arms. And then . . . then he started kissing me. I don't know what made me do it, but I opened my mouth and let our tongues meet."

"And then . . . ?" Maggie breathed.

"And then *what?*" Elise asked sharply.

"And then what did you do?"

"I cried all night, of course."

"Just for that?"

"Don't you understand?" Elise said impatiently. "Aunt Jane was visiting."

Maggie was terribly confused. "Who's Aunt Jane? Gerard's mother?"

"Don't you know anything, Maggie? Aunt Jane! The curse! My period! I was having my period. And everyone knows that if you touch tongues with a boy—if you let him kiss you like that while Aunt Jane's visiting —you're bound to get pregnant!"

Maggie's confusion gave way to gales of laughter. She hugged herself about the waist and dropped into a chair, tears of hilarity glistening down her cheeks. "Oh, Elise! I'm sorry, but that's too much! And I always thought you were so sophisticated . . . so much more than I!"

"What's so funny, Maggie?" Elise demanded, sitting up straight on the bed and flinging the pillow to one side. "Here I am in a terrible predicament, and you're laughing!"

"You're *not* in any predicament," Maggie managed to say. "You can't get pregnant that way."

"Of course you can!"

"No . . . no, you can't! Believe me. I was raised around animals, and I know how it works."

"Animals aren't people."

"That's true . . . but it's all done the same way."

Elise sat on the edge of the bed, looking doubtful and dejected.

"Why, Elise," Maggie said, rising and going over to her. "You look disappointed. Did you want to be pregnant?"

"No, of course not. I was worried to death. But . . . but are you *sure* that people make babies the same way animals do?"

"I know it for a fact."

Elise thought about this for a moment, then wrinkled up her nose. "How utterly disgusting!"

Maggie laughed again and hugged her friend. "So even though you let Gerard kiss you while Aunt Jane was visiting, you're not a woman yet, Elise."

Elise looked at Maggie mischievously. "If I'd known *that,* I'd have let him kiss me more!"

Maggie rose and plopped down on the stool in front of her dressing table. "You've let me down, Elise," she said, scrutinizing her reflection.

"How?"

"Ever since I got your letter, I've been counting on curly hair!"

Jeanette's reception had begun a good half-hour before Maggie was dressed and ready to go downstairs. Elise, despite her late start, was gowned and waiting. "I feel so frazzled," Maggie said, winding a rope of pearls around her neck and giving her reflection one

164

last hasty glimpse. "One of these days I'm going to learn how to put myself together as fast as you can."

"You're getting better," Elise said, linking her arm in Maggie's and heading for the staircase. "If you live long enough, you may actually get to see how a party begins."

They had reached the landing, when Maggie heard Elise gasp and felt her yank back sharply on her arm.

"Who in the world is *that?*" Elise whispered, her voice almost a hiss between clenched teeth.

Maggie followed her gaze, her eyes settling on Carlos, who was engaged in conversation with Virginie and Catherine.

"You mean my uncle?" Maggie asked.

"He's your uncle?" Elise asked in disbelief. "That's Carlos?"

"Yes. Why?" But when she looked at Elise, she immediately knew the answer.

Elise had gone pale as ivory. Her hand fluttered to her breast as if she had to fight for breath, and her pupils had grown so large that her eyes looked like shining black agates.

"Elise! Are you all right?" Maggie asked in alarm.

"I don't think so. Let's go back upstairs!"

She staggered against Maggie as they turned and climbed back up.

"Elise! You look awful!"

"I *know!*" Elise exclaimed in a trembling voice. "I *can't* go down like this. Quick, Maggie! Help me change. I've got a new gown, a pale pink satin I haven't worn yet. It'll look much better on me. And . . . oh, my hair! Why did I stay out in the sun all summer? I should have listened to *maman!*"

She fretted all the way back to her room and would probably have stayed there all evening if Jeanette had not grown suspicious and come upstairs to investigate.

"What in the world is keeping you?" she asked.

"Do you want your daughter appearing at your party looking like the corpse of Marie Laveau?" Elise demanded.

"I keep trying to tell her she looks beautiful," Maggie said.

"You both do," Jeanette said impatiently. "And if you don't get downstairs quickly, you'll miss the party entirely."

"Oooh!" Elise moaned, splashing herself liberally with rose cologne.

"And if you use any more of that scent," Jeanette warned, "you'll draw flies!"

Maggie's laughter drew a stern stare from Elise.

Oh, this is too much fun! Maggie thought. The sophisticated Elise, reduced to jelly! And on account of Carlos!

But there was a greater surprise in store for Maggie, for when they appeared downstairs, she saw an expression on Carlos's face she'd never known before.

He was across the room, surrounded by women, and he looked up, glanced away, then looked again. His mouth opened as if someone had struck him a blow, and Maggie could almost hear the intake of breath that caused his chest to heave. He excused himself from his circle and crossed the room toward Elise.

"This is my uncle, Carlos Trevor," Maggie said in a voice that sounded strange even to herself. But she realized something momentous was happening, an event utterly beyond her control, like two stars colliding. "My friend, Elise Drouet."

Carlos bowed gracefully, and when he straightened, Maggie saw lightning in his eyes.

*"Encantado, señorita."* There was thunder in his voice.

*"Enchantée, monsieur."* And an answering echo in Elise's.

Jeanette's eyes locked with Maggie's.

Carlos extended his hand and led Elise away, leaving Maggie and Jeanette staring dumbfounded at each other.

Maggie spoke first. "My mother said there's no such thing as love at first sight."

Jeanette shook her head. "I think we've just seen it."

# 11

Victor had been watching Maggie for five minutes. He saw Carlos and Elise slip off together and wondered at the curious look that passed between Maggie and Jeanette. Then, when a guest snared Jeanette, leaving Maggie alone in the crowd, he excused himself from his circle and made his way across the room.

"Why, Victor, hello! I was told you were back in New Orleans."

"It's wonderful to see you, Maggie." He spoke quietly, intimately, as if they were the only two present. It was obvious he'd found the sun that summer, for his face was healthily tanned. His lips seemed ruddier, and his touseled curls fell in pleasing, casual disarray across his forehead.

Had he grown more handsome? she wondered. Or was her memory playing tricks on her?

168

Victor caught a passing waiter and handed Maggie a glass of champagne.

"I understand you're not staying long," Maggie said.

"Two months."

"It hardly seems worth the trip."

He didn't reply. Instead, he cupped his hand beneath her elbow and steered her away from the party onto the balcony. The night was warm despite the breeze that ruffled the leaves above them, and far down the avenue a streetcar bell clanged nervously.

He faced her, standing so close she could smell the bay rum on his cheeks. "Maggie, I only came back for one reason. I'm preparing for an exhibition in Paris, but I simply couldn't stay away."

"Why, Victor?" But she already knew the answer.

"I want you to pose for me again."

Maggie sighed and tried to turn away, but he brought her back around and gazed into her eyes.

"You hated the portrait, didn't you?"

"No. I didn't hate it." She paused, then decided to tell the truth. "Victor, I just didn't think it looked like me."

"Nor did I."

"You made me so beautiful."

He stared at her in honest astonishment. "But that's exactly where I failed! I couldn't make you beautiful enough."

"Victor, you're teasing me. I know how I look."

"Do you? I doubt it."

Maggie glanced around uneasily. "I think I'd like to go back in."

"Certainly," Victor said, opening the door for her, but as she brushed by him, he caught her hand. "Say you'll do it, Maggie. Promise you'll pose for me again. I want to show it at the Paris exhibition. It will cost you nothing."

"I really don't think so, Victor."

A look of desolation filled his eyes, and his shoulders sagged. "Then I've made the trip for nothing."

Maggie was furious with herself for feeling guilty. She knew it was unreasonable—she owed Victor nothing—yet she couldn't shake it. After all, he was asking for so little . . . a few hours of her time. Nothing more.

"I'll think about it," she conceded, more as a way to placate him than as a promise. But as soon as she'd spoken, his eyes brightened with hope.

She started to turn away, but over his shoulder she spotted Carlos and Elise strolling alone in the front garden. Elise paused beneath an oak and let Carlos take her in his arms. Their two figures melted into a single shadow as Carlos bent his head and kissed her.

Maggie felt a pang of envy.

Victor seemed to be waiting for her to speak. She turned on her heel and without meeting his gaze, said, "All right, Victor. I'll do it."

Late that night, Maggie lay abed, her light still burning, for she expected a visit. Surely Elise would be crossing the corridor bursting to share her latest secret.

Soon there were footsteps in the hall; then a soft knock.

"Come in, Elise," Maggie said, sitting up eagerly and shoving a pillow behind her back.

But it was Carlos who entered. He was still dressed in his evening clothes with his collar opened and his tie hanging loose.

"Were you asleep?" he asked quietly.

Maggie shook her head, surprised to see him.

"Did you have a good time?" he asked.

"Yes. Did you?"

He didn't answer straight off. Instead he dragged a chair beside her bed and sank into it. Taking a pencil-thin cigar from a silver case, he lit it, and as the smoke curled around his head, he closed his eyes.

For a moment, Maggie thought he was drifting off to sleep, but she saw a smile slowly forming on his lips.

She leaned forward, smiling herself. "You're in love, aren't you, Carlos?"

He opened his eyes—those startling gray jewels that glittered more brightly than ever.

"You're in love with Elise!"

"You know me well . . . how well do you know *her?*"

"She's a sister to me."

"Then you'd like her to be part of our family?"

Maggie threw back her covers and hugged him. "Oh, Carlos! Is it true? Does she love you, too?"

He laughed happily. "She says she does."

Maggie perched on the edge of the bed, her heart beating so fast she could hardly breathe. "Oh, I always *knew* there was such a thing as love at first sight. Mama was wrong!"

"Anne!" he breathed. "Do you think she'll approve?"

"Of course she will! And Papa, too! Oh, Carlos, tell me! How did you know it was love?"

His eyes sparkled with wonder. "I just knew. When I looked across the room and saw Elise, I felt that I'd been looking for her all my life. I would have recognized her anywhere. You know what it's like when you've had a dream and forgotten . . . then later in the day, something you see, or hear, brings it back to you all at once?"

"Yes! I know what you mean."

"It's as if I'd loved Elise in another life and suddenly found her again in this one!"

They sat in silence for a moment; then Maggie asked, "Have you proposed?"

Carlos grinned. "I didn't need to."

"You mean you both just *knew?*"

"We started talking about our children . . . just as naturally as if we were already married."

"Oh, Carlos! I'm so happy for both of you. And you know what?"

"What?"

"You'll have beautiful children!"


Too smitten with Elise to tear himself away from New Orleans, Carlos sent the train back to the Lantana without him. When it arrived, one of the attendants rode to the big house with a letter. Anne read it and reported to Alex.

"Carlos doesn't say so, but I think he's falling in love."

"Are you sure you're not being too romantic? There're lots of other reasons for a young man to want to stay on in New Orleans."

"That may well be, but I doubt it. Listen to this." She unfolded the letter and read. " 'There was a marvelous party at La Rivière last Sunday. Elise Drouet and I took a pleasant stroll along the banks of the bayou. . . .' "

"It's only natural for a girl to show off her family's plantation."

"Wait," Anne said. "There's more . . . 'Elise toured me through the French Quarter and we had lunch in the courtyard of a restaurant beneath trees hung with moss.' "

"They have to eat."

Anne rolled her eyes. "Oh, Alex! Can't you read between the lines? Here! Look at this letter. Elise said this. . . . Elise did that. . . . Elise and I went here and there. . . . Every other mention is of Elise."

Alex glanced over the pages. "Anything about Maggie?"

"Not one blessed word. Now if that doesn't tell you something, I don't know what will."

Alex smiled. "So, Carlos has found somebody at last."

Anne sat down close to him. "I hope so. It's time he had a wife."

"And Elise is a wonderful girl."

"Hmm," Anne murmured, thinking. "I just wonder how she would take to life on the Lantana. It'll seem mighty rustic to her after New Orleans."

"Aye," Alex agreed. "She'd like San Antonio much better."

Anne looked to her husband. "You're still considering opening an office there, aren't you?"

"We really should. So much of our business takes place there. It would be more convenient . . . and efficient. And Carlos could run it."

"That would be perfect. And I'm sure Elise would take to San Antonio right away."

"You've as much as gotten them married off."

Anne laughed. "I must be a romantic! Ah, well, let's just sit back and see what happens. Perhaps it's only a fling."

But in New Orleans, both Jeanette and Maggie knew better. As the days passed and Carlos postponed his departure again and again, it became clear to everyone that his relationship with Elise had grown serious.

Jeanette was wise enough to accept the inevitable. She was already planning Elise's wedding.

And in the busy days that followed, as she came to know Carlos better, she not only accepted the idea of the marriage, but welcomed it.

She had but two real regrets. She dreaded the thought of Elise leaving home and living so far away. And she wished, vainly, that the couple would put off the wedding until Christmas at the earliest. But Carlos was

173

pressed for time; he was needed back in Texas, and Elise wouldn't hear of his leaving New Orleans without her.

So banns were announced the very next week; and after an exchange of telegrams, Anne and Alex packed and left for New Orleans.

When the day arrived, it seemed that everyone in New Orleans rode up the River Road to the reception at the LaForet family plantation. La Rivière never looked lovelier. The mansion glowed in the afternoon sun, and the rose garden was a riot of bloom. A full orchestra alternated with a string quartet to provide music throughout the day, and the continuous pop of champagne corks resounded like firecrackers on a string.

In her white satin gown, Elise moved radiantly among the guests, pausing here and there to accept a toast, and though they were not always together, she never let Carlos out of her sight.

"We're going to live in San Antonio," she said in reply to a question.

"And you once told me you never wanted to go to Texas," Maggie reminded her.

"I'd go to the moon with Carlos! Or any place else he chose."

"Why San Antonio?" someone asked.

"The Lantana is opening an office there. It's been decided, and Carlos will head it."

"You'll like San Antonio," Anne said. "In some ways it's very like New Orleans."

Elise was blissfully happy. "As I said, I'd go to the moon with Carlos."

"You may think you're there when you first see the Lantana," Maggie said.

"Oh, Maggie!" Alex said. "Have you come to think of our ranch as that remote?"

"Not to me," Maggie assured him, linking her arm in his. "But the *brasada*'s awfully different from New Orleans."

"I'll say," Anne declared. She liked the city, found it lovely and exhilarating, but she'd never been able to shake the claustrophobic feeling it instilled in her— narrow streets canopied with trees, the noise, the traffic. . . . She couldn't stay there long without yearning for the Lantana's big sky.

A voice at their side turned their heads.

"Hello, Victor," Maggie said. "I'd like you to meet my parents, Mr. and Mrs. Cameron."

Victor bowed, brushing Anne's hand with his lips.

"Victor painted the portrait I just gave you."

"It's marvelous," Anne said. "We'll treasure it."

"A perfect likeness," Alex added.

"You're too kind," Victor demured. "I've persuaded Maggie to sit for me again. We should already have started, but for the wedding. However . . ." And he turned to gaze at Maggie. "As of tomorrow, you'll have no excuses."

"You've finally trapped me, Victor," Maggie said, her lack of enthusiasm obvious.

Victor merely smiled.

Just before sunset, Carlos and Elise prepared to depart from La Rivière. Anne embraced Elise, then turned to Carlos.

"I'm so happy for you, my darling."

Carlos slipped his arm around his bride's waist. "Our happiness is just beginning."

They climbed into the carriage amid shouts from well-wishers and headed away down the long horseshoe drive.

Tears streaming down her cheeks, Maggie watched

after them, blowing kisses and waving farewell until they rounded the bend and disappeared from view.

Alex turned to Jeanette, whose own tears were a sign of both joy and sadness. "I wish your father had lived to see this day. He would have been pleased by this union of—as he'd have said—'two dynasties'."

Jeanette nodded in agreement. "Dynasty . . . yes. It was a word he liked. It was a concept he believed in. He would have been extremely happy."

"That leaves *you* now, Maggie," Alex said, taking his daughter's hand. "But don't go getting any wild ideas. We want to keep you for a while longer."

Maggie sniffed and brushed away her tears. "Don't worry, Papa."

Despite Maggie's efforts to persuade Anne and Alex to prolong their visit, Anne had had enough of New Orleans, and Alex was impatient to get back to the Lantana. At noon the next day, they boarded their train and left for home.

The frantic days before the wedding had left Maggie little time to think about herself. But after returning from the depot and climbing the stairs to her room, she suddenly realized how alone she was going to be with no Elise across the hall to turn to when she needed a friend, to help her choose a gown or a hat and advise her how to wear her hair. And no more late nights spent gossiping, and trading secrets.

Secrets!

Maggie sighed with loneliness. Secrets! Oh, Elise! Now you have Carlos to tell your secrets to. And I . . . I have no one!

She stretched out on the bed, burying her face in the pillow, and wept.

# 12

The next afternoon, chaperoned by Clarisse, one of Jeanette's housemaids, Maggie went by streetcar to Victor's French Quarter studio.

They entered the courtyard, and Victor met them at the top of the graceful, circular stairs.

"I didn't know we would have an audience," he said, referring to Clarisse.

"You couldn't expect me to come here alone."

Victor made no reply. He ushered them in and closed the door behind them.

"So, this is where you work," she said.

"And live," Victor replied. "I gave up my apartment when I went to Paris last."

"Where do you cook?"

"I seldom do. My friends here are more than hospitable. But, if I must, I use that old contraption at the end of the room," Victor said, indicating a dented, rusting wood stove with a flue that ran up to the ceiling.

Maggie's eyes made a circuit of the studio. It was a spacious rectangle, illuminated by six tall french doors opening onto a balcony that overlooked Chartres Street. The oddly pleasing odor of oil paints, turpentine, and lacquer permeated the atmosphere. Scores of canvases rested against one another, and drawings in pen, pencil, charcoal, and pastel were pinned to the walls like so many notices affixed to a billboard. In the center of the room, a large, cluttered table bore bulging sketchbooks, crumpled paint tubes, and several vases filled with brushes.

Victor watched her eyes pause briefly on a shabby velours curtain that hung from the ceiling toward the far end of the room.

"And what's beyond that?"

"My bed."

She glanced away quickly.

Victor selected a prepared canvas and propped it against his easel. "I've already made sketches . . . from memory. Time is short; so we'll start right in. Your maid may sit in that chair by the wall."

"And where do you want me?"

"On that divan," he replied, indicating a lumpy Récamier sofa with worn upholstery. "Don't worry about how it looks. In the finished picture, it will be covered with splendid gold brocade. Now, just stretch out there, and I will arrange your pose."

He bent over Maggie, wondering if his expression betrayed his pleasure at being able to touch her. As he raised her arm and placed it along the curved back of the divan, his hand lingered on her wrist, reluctant to abandon contact with her warm, satiny flesh. Cupping her calves in his palms, feeling their supple curves be-

178

neath the fabric of her skirt, he crossed her legs at the ankles, then gently lowered her other hand to her lap. "Now your head," he directed. "Look directly at me. I want it full-faced, bold and unashamed."

"Unashamed of what?"

He ignored her question. "Are you comfortable?"

"Yes."

"Good. We'll begin." He reached for a brush and touched it to his palette.

The session lasted three hours. Clarisse sat in her straight-back chair yawning with boredom, pitying Maggie for having to sit so still, and wondering how the confused swirl of rusty brown paint that Victor applied to the canvas would ever turn out to be a picture of the girl.

There seemed to be some sort of a head—but it was more of a blob attached to a vague shape that she supposed would become Maggie's body.

Clarisse smiled to herself. "Lordy, if a person looked like that, they'd scare the devil!"

Maggie was no less bored. As before, Victor wouldn't allow her to move or speak except during the infrequent breaks he gave her to stretch her bones.

At last, he threw down his brush and said, "Enough for today. I'll see you tomorrow at the same time."

"I suppose you won't let me see what you've done."

"Not until it's finished."

She put on her hat and walked to the door. "Let's go, Clarisse. I hope supper's early tonight. I'm famished."

They left. Victor waited a moment, then went outside to stand at the balcony. Despite having stared at her steadily for the past three hours, he felt his heart give a jolt as he saw her appear on the banquette below.

I must be mad not to leave the child alone! But her

179

beauty . . . her innocence! She makes all the others who came before her pale by comparison!

He watched hungrily after her as she threaded her way down the street, keeping her in sight almost until she reached Canal.

Then he ducked back inside the studio and stared at the canvas. Here, at least, he could preserve Maggie at the perfect moment in her life—the child on the brink of womanhood . . . the innocent at the threshold of knowledge! As he gazed, the picture seemed to complete itself before his eyes, and the image sent a thrill up his spine.

Oh, Maggie! Forgive me! But it has to be done!

When Maggie reached home, she learned that Jeanette had gone to help out at the home of a niece who was ailing. She dined alone and later curled up in a chair in the drawing room waiting for Jeanette's return.

Although the servants were in their quarters, she felt she'd been left by herself in the big house. She tried to read, but the pervading silence distracted her and the words made no sense. Snapping the book closed, she climbed the stairs and went to her room. It was early yet, but she dropped onto the bed.

It was hard to imagine that Elise was gone for good, that she would never again steal across the hallway after Jeanette had retired for the night, to sit cross-legged on the floor and chatter gaily.

What did we even talk about? Maggie wondered. Little things . . . silly things! But now they seem so important!

Oh, Elise! I already miss you terribly!

She fell asleep without knowing it, and woke in the middle of the night, still dressed. She peeled off her clothes, drew a nightgown over her head, and slipped beneath the covers. Only now, she couldn't sleep.

She thought of Elise and Carlos—and of the life they now shared.

They'll never be lonesome again. No matter how late at night, they'll always have each other to turn to.

Maggie's throat tightened, and she made no attempt to hold back her tears. She cried into her pillow and felt sorry for herself because she had no one.

She woke the next morning, still downcast and ashamed of her self-pity. At least there was school to occupy her, and she had a number of friends there. Perhaps one of them would take Elise's place in her life. And—for the next couple of weeks—there were the afternoon posing sessions with Victor.

The latter thought surprised her. Was she actually looking forward to sitting rock still for three or four hours every day while Victor, in his stern manner, forbade her even to speak?

Oh, well, at least it's something. Then she smiled to herself and shrugged. I *must* be bored and lonely!

Whatever the reason, she began to anticipate the streetcar ride with Clarisse down to the luminous studio on Chartres Street, and as one week passed and another began, she found she was no longer impatient with posing. It required nothing of her, and she could let her mind wander as it pleased. Autumn had arrived, and the weather grew lovelier by the day. She thought about the new dresses Jeanette's seamstress was creating for her and the round of parties that would begin when the nights grew longer and cooler. She mused idly about Anne and Alex and mentally reviewed the letters from them that had already begun to arrive. And she wondered about Victor, especially about his other life— the greater part of each year he spent in Paris.

Where did he live? Who were his friends? And did he have a woman there who pined for him while he was away?

She wanted to ask him, but he always set to work as soon as she appeared at the studio, and by the time the session ended, she had to hurry back to Jeanette's for supper.

Her pose required her to look directly at him, and she began to examine his face as intently as he studied hers. It amused her to watch the play of concentration across his features. His eyes would narrow, then appear to lose all focus, only to snap back again bright and alert as if some sudden sound had jolted him from a reverie. His lips would part; he would catch the tip of his tongue between his teeth as if what he were doing were extremely difficult, reminding Maggie of a child struggling to tie his laces. And at times, she wanted to break her pose and reach out to him to brush back the unruly curls that tumbled across his broad forehead.

And she wondered how his hair would feel beneath her fingertips. Was it as soft and silky as it looked? And was his forehead as smooth to the touch as it appeared?

Toward the end of the second week, as Maggie and Clarisse left the streetcar to make their way into the Quarter, Clarisse cleared her throat and said, "I shouldn't be speaking up, Miss Maggie, but I ain't too sure about that picture Mr. Victor's painting of you."

While Victor was adamant in refusing to allow Maggie to view the progress, he seemed not to mind at all that Clarisse sat behind him and watched every brush-stroke.

"What do you mean, Clarisse?"

"Well, at first I couldn't tell nothing about it. It was just a mess. But now I can see what he's doing, and . . ."

"And what?"

"Well, it 'pears that you ain't got no clothes on."

Maggie laughed. "I think that's the way they do it, Clarisse. They have to draw the body first, to get the form and shape. Then they paint the clothes. It's sort of like dressing a doll."

"Hmm," Clarisse said, unconvinced. "Well, he sure is goin' to town on the body."

Maggie laughed again. "Let's hurry, Clarisse. You know how perturbed he gets if we're even a minute late."

She looked ahead and spotted Victor on the balcony. For a moment, their eyes locked, and Maggie felt an odd sensation in her breast, a quickening, a sudden breathlessness.

*"Oouf!"* she exclaimed, slowing her pace. "I think I've laced my corset too tight."

Victor went to work as soon as they arrived, speaking barely a word to Maggie as she entered. But after about twenty minutes, he laid down his brush and gave Maggie a rest.

"I have some shopping that needs to be done," he said. "Do you think Clarisse could manage? I don't want to cut our session short."

"I'm sure she could," Maggie answered.

Victor turned to Clarisse. "Can you read?"

"Yessir, I can."

He tore a sheet from a sketchpad and scribbled a long list, handing it to Clarisse along with some money. "No need to hurry," he said as she made for the door. "We'll be here all afternoon."

With Clarisse gone, he went back to the easel and painted for a few minutes more. Then laying aside his brush again, he said, "Would you like to see the picture?"

183

"You mean it's finished?"

"No, I still have much to do."

"But . . . I thought you never showed . . ."

"I don't usually. But I have to know what you think."

Maggie rose from the divan and walked around the easel. She was too startled to examine the likeness of her face, for all she could see was her naked body stretched out langorously across the canvas.

"Oh, Victor!" She laughed, thinking it was a joke. "Hurry and put clothes on me!"

"There won't be any."

"What?" She looked up shocked.

"It's a nude, Maggie," he said with quiet intensity.

"But . . . but . . ."

"And I can't go any further unless you . . . pose properly for me."

"You mean without my clothes?"

He nodded.

"You must be crazy!"

"No, Maggie! Listen to me! It's done all the time. Some of the world's greatest paintings are of nudes. There's nothing lovelier than the human form."

"But, Victor! Those are pictures of gods and goddesses! Not real people!"

"The models were real. Come, Maggie, do it for me."

She almost laughed in his face, but he reached out and took hold of her arms, and she felt the same odd sensation she'd experienced when she caught sight of him waiting on the balcony. Her breath quickened, and her heart seemed to skip every other beat.

She tried to break free, but her legs went weak and she slumped forward against his chest. Before she knew it, his arms were around her, supporting her, holding her tightly. And then, his lips touched hers.

Her brain spun in confusion. She wanted to tear herself away, knowing she couldn't allow this, but her body seemed paralyzed. Fright and surprise sent chills up her spine, but she clung to him trembling as wave after wave of unfamiliar pleasure swept over her.

Again his warm lips sought hers. She turned her face, but his tongue lapped at the fine molding of her ear, and she felt her blood turn to liquid fire in her veins.

She gasped—terrified, yet strangely secure in his arms. Her mind reeled, and, in the chaos of her thoughts, he seemed to be both a threat and a protector.

He lifted her off her feet and carried her the length of the studio to his bed behind the curtain. She sank into the pillow and he hovered over her, his face so near it was a blur. She felt his breath on her neck, then his lips on her throat. She wanted to struggle but was powerless to move. With one hand he traced the contours of her face while the other went past her throat and gently settled on her breasts.

She felt something give way within her, and her body flushed with passion. She curled her arms around his back and cried out. His lips covered hers, silencing her.

Maggie saw a burst of light, a blue-white flash against the ceiling; then thunder from a sudden storm rocked the studio.

Victor raised her from the pillow and quickly freed the buttons down her back, dropping her clothing into a pile on the floor.

Trembling with awe and excitement, he studied her nubile body; her skin was flawless, her youthful figure taut and lithe, her small, girlish breasts round as apples, pale as ivory.

He groaned—almost sorrowfully—and settled her back against the pillow.

Thunder roared again, and a stinging rain peppered the windowpanes.

An hour later, Clarisse returned, drenched to the skin, her shopping bag bulging with the items Victor had sent her for.

"I would've been back sooner," she grumbled, " 'cept I got caught in the rain. But I bought everything you wanted."

"Good," Victor replied.

Maggie stood at the french doors, her back to the room. The storm had passed, and the autumn sky above the rooftops was clear and blue.

"Come, Clarisse," she said quickly. "It's time we went home."

Victor halted her at the door, his dark eyes searching her face. "Tomorrow?"

Maggie shuddered and left without answering.

During the walk to the streetcar, Clarisse glanced sharply at Maggie. "Something wrong, Miss Maggie? You're pale as buttermilk."

"It was the storm," Maggie lied. "The thunder scared me."

"Yes'm," Clarisse agreed. "Scared me, too." But she didn't believe Maggie's story for a moment.

Victor sat drinking wine at the Brasserie Charbonneau. His friend Fernand arrived and tried to engage him in conversation, but Victor was unresponsive, his thoughts far away.

Fernand watched him for a moment; then a slow, wise smile crossed his lips. "Ah, I understand, *mon vieux!* You've finally managed to pluck the fig. Was it as delicious as you'd hoped?"

Victor's dark eyes settled on his friend. He paused a

moment before answering. "Even more, Fernand. Even more. . . ."

As the streetcar carried her closer to home, Maggie grew extremely nervous, unable to control her agitation. Would her eyes reveal what she had done? Would Jeanette be able to detect it? The nuns and the girls at school— would they know simply by looking at her?

Why couldn't I stop myself? she wondered miserably. Why couldn't I have just said no and left the studio forever? Why did I fall to pieces and let Victor have what he wanted?

It had never occurred to her that she wouldn't go to her marriage a virgin. Now, in one brief afternoon, she'd thrown all that away. She'd changed—would never be the same person she was before. She trembled with guilt and regret. Would any man ever want her now—any man other than Victor?

When she arrived home, she learned with relief that Jeanette would be out for the evening. Thank God, I don't have to see her now! I'd probably burst into tears, and then she'd know everything!

She went directly to her room, feigning illness; and when Jeanette returned and looked in on her, Maggie pulled the covers up high and pretended to be asleep.

But she lay awake throughout the long night, crying and hating herself for what she'd done. The next morning, her red eyes and pale, drawn face convinced Jeanette that she was truly unwell, and it was decided to keep her home from school.

She stayed in bed that day, and the next, and throughout the weekend, and as the lonely hours passed, the terror and distress of that afternoon and Victor slipped away from her, and her mind was left with the memory of a pleasure she'd never known before—never even suspected existed. And she found that the mere recollection was strong enough to drive away the demons of guilt and regret who visited her when the house was quiet and dark.

On Monday, she rose and dressed and met Jeanette at breakfast with the declaration that she was feeling better. She went to school, and that afternoon caught the streetcar with Clarisse and headed for the Quarter.

Victor seemed grateful to see her, but then she discerned a different expression on his face, one—if she'd had to guess—that hinted at some secret sorrow or regret.

As before, Victor scrawled out a shopping list and handed it to Clarisse. The maid looked mulish and suspicious, but obeyed, and as soon as she shut the door behind her, Victor took Maggie in his arms.

"My darling, my sweet, *ma petite!*" he breathed into her ear. "I was afraid you were never coming back!"

"Oh, Victor!" Maggie murmured. Her voice shook, and her legs were as weak as before.

Without another word, he took her to the bed, and they made love. Afterwards, drained and satisfied, Maggie yearned to linger in the comfort of his encircling arms, but Victor seemed recharged with energy. He coaxed her out of bed and posed her nude on the divan. Then, with more than his usual intensity, he set to work on the painting.

He worked in a frenzy and didn't stop until they heard Clarisse's footsteps on the circular stairs.

"Oh, my God!" Maggie exclaimed, springing from the divan.

"Here!" Victor said, tossing her his dressing gown. She wriggled into it just as Clarisse entered. The woman took one look and understood everything. Wordlessly, she deposited the shopping bag on the cluttered table and stood, arms crossed, waiting.

Maggie ducked behind the velours curtain and hastily dressed. She patted her hair into place and reappeared, struggling to appear as natural as possible.

"I'm ready, Clarisse," she announced, making for the door.

On the street outside, Clarisse followed a half-step behind Maggie. They were nearly at Canal, when Maggie pulled up and faced the woman.

"Are you going to tell?"

Clarisse's face was stony, but she stared Maggie straight in the eye. "No'm. I learned a long time ago to keep my mouth shut."

Maggie sighed with relief. She reached out to pat Clarisse's arm in gratitude, but the woman pulled away.

"I said I'd keep quiet, Miss Maggie. I didn't say I was approvin'."

And later, as they stepped from the streetcar and crossed the avenue in front of Jeanette's house, Clarisse said, "My sister lives on Rampart. From now on, if you want me to, I'll go there while you're at Mr. Victor's."

Maggie merely nodded.

The weeks stretched into a month, and the season's first real cold spell sent a chill through the city. As Maggie entered Victor's courtyard and began climbing the circular stairs, she caught the scent of paints and linseed oil, fragrances she had come to associate with Victor himself, for they clung to his skin and hair and were as sweet to her as perfume. And when he let her in, she reveled in the studio's glowing atmosphere that bathed walls and polished floor with northern light.

Victor took her into his arms, and she tasted wine

on his lips even before he poured a glass for her. Then they undressed and lay together in his bed.

Victor had taught her about lovemaking—gently at first, leading her slowly and expertly until she was a confident, joyous, ardent partner who pleased him as no one ever had before.

Afterwards, he rose and pulled on his clothes while she moved, shivering, to her place on the divan.

"I'll make a fire," he said.

"That would feel good." She already missed the recent warmth of his body next to hers.

Victor packed the old stove with kindling and crumpled paper and lit it with a match.

"Oh, Victor!" she cried in alarm.

Sparks had showered from the loosely fitting door and sparkled threateningly on the floor. Victor stamped them out with his boots and banged the door with a poker until it wedged into place.

"That old stove's dangerous, darling," she said. "It's liable to cause a fire."

"I wouldn't need it if you weren't so cold-natured."

"That's easy for you to say, standing there fully dressed . . . but I have to pose stark naked."

"Nude, *chérie* . . . not naked."

"Saying 'nude' doesn't make it any warmer!"

He smiled at her. "Well, it won't be long now. A few more sessions and the picture will be finished. Then I'll be leaving for Paris."

He had already booked passage back to France, and his stay in New Orleans would be over in less than a week.

At his words, Maggie's mood turned as cold as the day outside. She flew into his arms and pressed her cheek against his chest. "Oh, Victor! I don't want you to go!"

His lips kissed her bare shoulder. "I must *chérie*. I've already put off my departure twice. I have work to do in Paris. There's the exhibition. If I don't go now, I'll be too late."

"But what about us?"

"I'll be back."

"I'm going to be so lonely without you."

He gazed at her—that oddly sorrowful look she had seen from time to time and never understood.

"I love you, Victor."

He kissed her forehead and brushed a tear away, like a father bidding good night to an unhappy child. Then he led her to the divan and arranged her pose. She lay there in silent misery, propped against a mound of pillows, wearing nothing but a strand of pearls.

Moving quickly to his easel, Victor took up his brush and began to touch the canvas with quick, sure strokes, flicking here and there over the nearly finished face, working frantically to capture Maggie's expression before her mood changed. A highlight applied here to the eyes made them glow. A minute alteration to the line of her lips, and suddenly the mouth was both determined and petulant—and a darkening of the brows, no more than two or three brush strokes, transformed the visage and made it appear mysterious and compelling.

He stepped back suddenly, then dropped his brush onto the table at his side. "That's all for today."

Maggie sat up puzzled. No more than five minutes had passed, and she was used to posing for an entire afternoon. "But you just started!"

"Nevertheless, I'm through for the day!" He crossed to the couch and knelt down beside her, resting his head on the pillows.

"Did it go badly?" she asked.

191

"No." He slipped his arms around her and nuzzled her warm breasts. "No, it went magnificently!"

Maggie sighed with renewed joy—knowing he was pleased with her, happy to be a part of his life and his art.

With the rest of the afternoon before them, they made love again on the couch, then lay in each other's arms on a quilt before the glowing stove, sharing wine from the same glass while they watched the afternoon fade in the sky.

Maggie had never known such contentment. I want to live with him forever, she thought, to be his wife, share his work, have his children. We'll travel back and forth between Paris and New Orleans; and I'll take him to the Lantana where he'll paint Mama and Papa. And we'll hang the pictures above the big fireplace so there'll always be a bit of Victor there.

Then suddenly she giggled.

"What is it?" Victor asked.

"Nothing," she replied. But she had conjured in her mind the image of the big parlor at the Lantana with her nude portrait hanging above the mantle.

She could have remained in his arms forever—indeed, she wished it were possible—but the cathedral bells tolled five o'clock, and she rose reluctantly to dress.

"I hope," she said as she was leaving, "I hope Elise is as happy with Carlos as I am with you."

He bent to kiss her, and as his face neared hers, she saw again that strange, troubled look.

That night at dinner, Jeanette laid down her fork and said, "Maggie, I'm not too pleased with you spending so much time at Victor's. Now, I know that Clarisse is with you all the time, but I don't think it's good for a girl your age. There are so many other things you should be doing. You'll forget all the music you learned if you don't pick up your piano lessons again, and there's the dancing class you said you wanted to take."

Maggie lowered her lids. She hated being deceitful to Jeanette, but she knew she could never confide in her.

"I'm learning French beautifully," she said. "Victor and I converse in it all the time."

"Well, I'm sure you could learn just as much from the nuns . . . without Victor's help."

Maggie glanced up, trying to look casual. Did Jeanette suspect? Had Clarisse broken her promise and spoken to her after all?

But Jeanette's face was placid, and Maggie breathed a silent sigh of relief.

"Well, I feel you've been taken advantage of. He's totally dominated your time. I would have thought he'd have been through with the picture long before now."

Maggie nodded. Best not to say anything. In a few days, Victor would be gone, and Jeanette would be pacified. Jeanette tossed her napkin beside her place and rose. "We must hurry and dress. Emil has invited us to his place for champagne before the opera."

Maggie dreaded the evening ahead. She would rather curl up with a book than get fitted out in an evening gown and endure three hours of Rossini. But she was afraid begging off would stir up Jeanette more than ever. So she mumbled a docile, "Yes, ma'am," and followed Jeanette from the room.

They were watching the middle of the third act when the fire wagons raced by, the panicky clamor of their excited bells sending a shudder through the audience.

A nervous rustle filled the opera house. More than once, hungry flames had devoured the Vieux Carré, eating their way through the closely packed structures, taking their toll in human life and laying waste to some of the loveliest buildings in the city. Nothing—neither flood, hurricane, nor the dreaded fever—was as feared as fire in the French Quarter.

The singers held the stage, but here and there worried people rose from their seats and scurried up the darkened aisles. Emil touched Jeanette's hand and whispered, "Catherine and I are leaving. It might be our house on fire."

"We'll come with you," Jeanette replied, rising and signaling Maggie to follow.

They hurried down the street, surrounded by a growing throng, lured forward by an orange glow in the sky.

"It's not Royal," Emil judged. "It's beyond that. It looks like it's on Chartres."

Maggie's heart rose to her throat. Victor!

They raced down the narrow banquettes, chasing the fire, and as they turned in front of the cathedral, she clapped her hands over her mouth and cried, "Oh my God! It *is* Victor's!"

Flames were shooting from the roof and smoke boiled from the french doors that opened onto the balcony. In the street below, the firemen had leaped from their wagons and were frantically dragging hoses to hydrants.

Suddenly Victor appeared, a dark silhouette on the third-floor balcony. He carried something in his arms, leaned over, and released it. Sketchbooks and unframed canvases fell to the street, where people quickly snatched them up and dragged them aside to safety.

"Victor!" Maggie screamed, but he dashed back inside.

"Victor!"

Emil had to grab her to prevent her from running into the burning building.

"Let me go! Let me go!"

He shook her hard, snapping her head back and forth. "Don't be a fool!" he shouted.

She slumped against him, sobbing. Then Victor reappeared, dragging a large canvas which he heaved over the wrought-iron railing. It caught the wind, swooped, flip-flopped, and skidded onto the banquette just as the firehoses began to spew water. Jeanette burst through the crowd, took hold of one side of the canvas, and hauled it back with her.

Victor swung one leg over the balcony, wrapped his arms around a drainpipe and began to shinny down. The pipe groaned, and a cry rose from the crowd as it began to pull away from the wall. Victor slipped, falling nearly a full story to the pavement, but as the throng rushed toward him, he staggered to his feet, dazed but unhurt.

Maggie tore herself from Emil and raced to his side, throwing her arms around him and holding him tightly as she sobbed against his chest.

"The picture!" he murmured. "Where is the picture?"

With Maggie holding onto him, he moved through the crowd to where Jeanette, Emil, and Catherine were standing.

"The picture?" he demanded. "Did you save it?"

Jeanette's face was hard as stone. At her feet lay the finished portrait of Maggie lying nude on the divan.

"It's just as well he's leaving," Jeanette said. She was pacing the floor of Maggie's bedroom. Her eyes flashed and her jaws were set grimly. "I would have forbidden you to see him again. Ever again! Your parents would be outraged. I'd send you home if it were possible to do so without explaining why."

"But I love him, Jeanette," Maggie wailed.

"You're too young to understand what the word means." She looked at the broken-hearted girl and was overcome by a wave of sympathy. She knelt beside Maggie and slipped her arm around her waist. "Darling, darling, I know what you're going through. My heart cries for you, but it's for the best. You can't possibly believe me now. But years hence, maybe even sooner, you'll find it in your soul to thank me."

"Never!" Maggie bawled. "I hate you. I'll always hate you for what you've said and done."

Jeanette refused to let the words hurt her. She hugged Maggie tightly and rocked her back and forth. "Poor Maggie . . . poor Maggie," she cooed, knowing nothing she could say would comfort the girl. "Poor Maggie . . ."

# 13

No matter where their travels led them, Dos and Lorna had an unerring instinct for knowing exactly when they'd worn out their welcome. Just when the local tavernkeeper grew fed up with Dos's brawling and after Lorna had successfully emptied the pockets of the town's best poker players, the pair would pack up their few belongings, saddle their horses, and hit the trail.

Since leaving the Lantana, they'd zigzagged back and forth across the territories of New Mexico and Arizona, sizing up each new town as they rode down its wide main street, judging just how long it would take them to squeeze the melon dry. And they made it a point never to work in a town that boasted more than one church. They still had their sights set on California, but were in no particular hurry, figuring California would be waiting for them when they got there.

Heading north from Prescott, the couple camped for a week on the rim of the Grand Canyon, then struck out westward into Nevada, working their way up to Carson City, and crossing the Sierras before the big snows began to fall.

Their money was low, and Lorna decided it was time for another big game. They'd stopped at a place called Parrita, a one-time gold town nestled in the foothills with a dwindling population of diehard miners, their hard-faced wives, and a handful of taxi dancers huskier than Dos.

As they left their rooming house and crossed the street to the saloon, Lorna scrutinized the town and told Dos, "This ought to be good for a couple of hundred dollars. Enough to get us to San Francisco in style."

"You've gotten pretty cocky, haven't you?"

Lorna gave him a sharp look, "At least I've kept us out of the poorhouse."

Dos had to agree. He'd worked from time to time, wrangling for shorthanded ranchers, but Lorna's poker winnings were their bed and board. She'd had off nights, to be sure, when the cards simply weren't there, and a time or two they'd been down to their last double eagle; but her bad luck had never really stretched into a serious losing streak. Just when they thought they'd have to sell the horses—this time for good—Lorna would come up winners, and they'd ride out of town with a wallet full of money.

They entered the Parrita saloon, a dismal, one-room tavern with half a dozen tables and a long bar. There was no music that night, and the sour-looking taxi dancers sat together yawning with boredom.

Dos and Lorna launched into their much practiced

act. Lorna flirted with the miners and cajoled them into a game while Dos stood helplessly back acting like a man who'd lost control of his woman.

"I expect you're gonna wipe me out," Lorna simpered, fumbling with the cards. "All you men, so rich with gold."

The miners laughed good-naturedly, and a gloriously bearded man by the name of Stu cut for her deal. She won the first hand, then the second and the third. Then her four of a kind went down to Stu's straight flush. Lorna whistled with admiration and anted up.

Dos watched as the next six hands in a row ate up her winnings. Then she won again, modestly, and he saw her smile confidently to herself.

But Stu was her nemesis, and the rest of the evening was a disaster. For every pair she held, he laid down three of a kind. When she played a straight he had a flush; when she drew to a flush, he turned up a full house.

Dos tried to persuade her to quit, but she set her jaw and tapped the table for her cards. And lost again to Stu.

At last they were down to their saddles. Dos called her aside while the miners watched them, amused. "It's not your night. Let's clear out of here," he said softly between clenched teeth.

But Lorna refused to listen. "I've been down worse. It's that damned fellow named Stu, hiding behind that beard of his! If I could see his face, I'd know what he was thinking."

"Let's go, Lorna. A couple more minutes and you'll have us on foot!"

Lorna bridled. "I ain't run us up a tree yet!"

199

It was after midnight when they trudged back to their rooming house.

Dos was grim. "Well, you've finally done it. You didn't just run us up the tree. You got us stranded on a limb."

Lorna burst into tears. "I'll never play with a bearded man again!"

"You should've known when to quit, Lorna. I mean, when the money runs out, that's time to fold and walk away. For Chrissakes, you lost our saddles, our horses . . . if I hadn't dragged you out of there, you would have put up our clothes!"

She threw herself into his arms. "I'm sorry, Dos! I tried my best!"

His heart softened. He stroked her hair and let her cry against his chest.

"I'm so ashamed," she sobbed. "I guess I got carried away. I just couldn't believe my luck wouldn't change for the better. One more hand . . . if I could've hung in there for one more hand . . ."

"One more hand and we'd have been buck naked."

She looked up at him and saw he was smiling. "Do you hate me?"

"Course not."

"You got a right to."

"But I don't."

It was the closest he'd come to saying he loved her. She buried her face against his chest and wept.

"Don't cry any more, Lorna. It's not the end of the world. We've come back from worse. Think of Mexico when we got captured by Escobar and his gang. Think of the fire."

She sniffed, unconvinced. "But what are we going to do? We don't even have a horse for the both of us!"

He was silent for a moment, holding her tightly, running his fingers lightly through her hair. "We're going to go back to what we really like to do."

She raised her eyes, hopefully. "What?"

A slow smile crossed his lips. "Did you happen to notice, as we rode into town, that there was a little ol' bank on the corner?"

Her eyes widened.

"We still got our guns."

She started to laugh.

"What's so funny?" he asked, puzzled.

"I forgot all about them. If I'd remembered, I'd've bet those, too!"


The next morning, with the excitement of the heist overcoming their jitters, they robbed the Parrita Bank of nearly three thousand dollars. Grabbing the two nearest horses, they galloped out of town before the teller could wriggle free of his bonds and shout for help.

They rode all day, leaving the foothills behind, heading into the beautifully peaceful valley. Although winter was but a few weeks away, the weather was splendid, bracingly cool with a cloudless sky as blue as any Dos had ever seen.

At one point, while they rested their horses, he spread his arm wide, tilted his head toward the heavens, and shouted, "God, it's grand to be rich!"

Lorna giggled and reached across for his hand. He took her into his arms and kissed her. "We're going to buy you some new duds, Lorna. And some for me, too. We can't show up in Frisco looking like we just rode in on a bale of hay."

"We have to be careful, though, Dos," Lorna cautioned. "Lawmen all around these parts will be looking for us."

Dos thought for a moment, chewing on a blade of dried grass, and as he gazed toward the western horizon, he devised a plan.

Early the next morning, as Lorna watched with misgivings, Dos honed his knife to razor sharpness and shaved his beard.

"I hate to see it go," she said.

"I was kind of used to it myself."

"It always felt so good when we kissed, all soft and tickly."

Dos paused and smiled. "When the dust settles, I'll grow it back."

After he finished, he sheathed his knife and saddled up his horse. "Now you wait for me here, Lorna, and try not to get spooked. I'll be in and out of Sacramento as fast as I can. And when I get back, we'll have some fancy new clothes so we won't look a thing like those two no-good drifters who robbed the Parrita Bank."

"Bring me something pretty."

"I aim to."

"And, Dos . . . bring me a box of face powder and a pot of rouge."

Dos made a face. "Aw, hell, Lorna! I'll feel like a jackass buying something like that."

"And some scent!"

He sighed, knowing she'd have her way. "Any particular flavor?"

Lorna grinned. "You decide. It's you who'll be smelling it."

He nudged his gelding into motion and set off at a high lope for Sacramento.

Lorna spent the day in the secluded grove of trees where they'd slept the night before. As the afternoon wore on, the sky clouded over, and long before sunset, it grew dark as twilight. She had promised Dos not to get spooked, but as the light failed around her she began to worry.

Wonder if there're bears around here. Or wolves! She shivered and her arms tingled with gooseflesh. Oh, hurry, Dos! I don't like being out here all alone! And what if he didn't come back? What if he'd dropped into a saloon and taken up with a pretty Cyprian who promised to show him a good time? It could happen. Dos had an eye for women.

Her mind filled with regrets. She imagined Dos, glowing with half a bottle of redeye under his belt, snuggling up to a henna-haired taxi dancer who had her eye on his money.

Oh, God! The money! He's gone off with every penny we took from the bank! Her worry turned to indignant anger. Damn! How dare he! Right this moment, I bet he's kicking up his heels, having a high old time, while I'm shivering and shaking in a woods full of wolves! I should've gone with him. Sacramento's supposed to be a big place, I could've easily lost myself in the crowd. Why did I let him persuade me to stay behind? Damn!

A far-off sound caused her to tense. She strained her ears and peered into the darkness. Nothing! Then she spotted a pinpoint of light, a yellow glow bobbing slowly in the distance, and soon heard the thud of plodding hooves. And something else: a *creak-creak-creak* of turning wheels.

Lorna patted her horse and bribed him with a fistful of sugar cubes to keep quiet. Then, slowly, she pulled her rifle from its holster and flattened herself against a tree trunk. The lantern came closer, rocking and weaving in the darkness. Wondering if she had the courage to shoot, she cocked the rifle and waited.

The creaking ceased, and the lantern held steady.

Then she heard a chirpy whistle, two quick notes followed by a long, slurry tone. *Whip-poor-will! Whip-poor-will!*

She stayed stock still.

*Whip-poor-will! Whip-poor-will!*

She raised her rifle and pointed it at the light.

"Oh, for Chrissakes, Lorna, it's me, Dos! Where are you hiding?"

"You scared me half to death, Dos Cameron!" she yelled.

His merry laughter infuriated her. Raising her rifle, she fired into the treetops.

*"Hooo-hay! Whoa!"* Dos shouted.

Lorna came running toward him, the dried grass rustling beneath her boots.

He caught her in his arms. "So you got spooked after all?"

"You would be, too," she cried accusingly. "Out here all alone with all those wolves!"

"Wolves?"

"A whole pack of 'em. I never saw so many in all my life."

Dos didn't believe her for an instant, but he kept her in his arms and whispered soothingly into her ear until she calmed down.

"See what I bought?" he asked.

"A wagon?" she asked, trying to penetrate the darkness.

"A wagon?" he repeated with genuine umbrage. "Hell no! We're too rich for a wagon. I bought us a brand new, four-seater, leather top surrey, just like my mama has!"

They spent an extra night making love and dozing lightly under a blanket beneath the trees. At sunup,

Lorna rolled over and took Dos's face between her hands.

"You look all naked without your beard." She pursed her lips and kissed his stubbled cheeks. "But you're still a mighty handsome man."

Dos grunted happily and nuzzled close to her. Her hair held traces of the lilac perfume he'd brought back from Sacramento.

"Hmmm, you smell like a field in spring," he murmured.

"I hope you mean a field full of flowers . . . not some old cow pasture."

He laughed sleepily and hugged her close.

Later, when they'd dressed in their new clothes, he remembered something. Going to the surrey, he rummaged about and returned with a copy of the *Sacramento Bee*.

"We made the front page, Lorna," he said, shaking out the newspaper.

"Read it to me." She sat by his side and peered over his shoulder, although she couldn't read a word on the page.

" 'Bank Robbery in Parrita' . . ." he began. " 'A pair of unsavory characters, armed with rifles, relieved the Bank of Parrita of more than four thousand dollars in a daring morning raid yesterday! . . .' "

Dos stopped and looked at Lorna. " 'Four thousand dollars!' Now, I ask you, would you keep your money in a bank that couldn't count better than that?"

Lorna laughed. "What else does it say? Does it tell about us?"

"Aw, they got it all wrong," Dos said. "Listen to this: 'The man, a wild-eyed, blond-bearded desperado, bound the teller while his female companion, an Indian child of not more than twelve, wielded a Remington

205

rifle.' Now, in the first place, I don't have wild eyes."

"But you are a desperado."

"Well . . . they were just guessing there. As far as anybody in Parrita knew, we were just a pair of saddle tramps pushing through. Anyway . . . you're no Indian, at least not much of one, and you're a damn sight older than twelve."

"And I was wielding a Winchester," Lorna added.

"It's got so you can't believe anything you read in the papers. A bunch of fairy tales, if you ask me. I've got half a mind to write 'em back and set the story straight."

"Do it, Dos," Lorna urged. "Soon as we get to Sacramento, send that paper a letter!"

Two days later, the following appeared in the *Bee:*

To the Editor.
Dear Sir,

In the interest of truth, I submit the following. I robbed the bank at Parrita, accompanied by my kid brother, who resents the implication that he is an Indian girl of but twelve years. He is a young man of sixteen who chose female attire as a means of disguise. Furthermore, we only came away with five hundred dollars. If you're wondering where the rest went, I suggest you have a good, hard talk with the teller himself.

We're recent immigrants to these parts and expect to be written about in your paper often. In the future, we humbly hope you'll report the true facts.

Believe me to be
Yours truly,
The Wolf.

"The Wolf!" Lorna cried when he read it to her. "Where'd you come up with a name like that?"

"From all those wolves that nearly ate you up!"

She laughed with delight and clutched the paper to her breast. "Oh! I wish I had some schooling! I'd like to read the letter for myself!"

During the next two months, Dos and Lorna lived in splendor in the finest suite at the Hayden House. In public, Lorna comported herself with the worldy nonchalance of a woman of means. But in private, she revealed her excitement and awe to Dos. "Look at these curtains! Feel them! Do you think they're real silk? . . . And that chandelier! I'm sure it's crystal. When the sun comes through those windows, you can see little rainbows in every prism! Imagine! Lorna Rivers with a real crystal chandelier over her head!"

She chided Dos for eating steak every night, while she sampled—and enjoyed—abalone, smoked salmon, saltimbocca, and Peking duck. She doted on desserts, surprising waiters by ordering two or three after each meal just so she could learn about babas, soufflés, and cherries jubilee.

"You're going to get fat," Dos warned.

"Good," Lorna said, stuffing her face. "I'm glad for the opportunity."

And Dos was glad for her, too.

Every few weeks, a new letter would appear in the *Bee,* setting the record straight concerning the latest robbery at a nearby, small-town bank. And each one was signed: "The Wolf."

"We're getting famous," Lorna said, having overheard a couple dining at the next table talking about "the Wolf Pack," as Dos and Lorna had come to be called.

"Too famous," Dos said. "I think it's time we were moving on."

"Oh, Dos! I feel all settled in at the Hayden House. It's my first real home."

"A hotel's not a home."

"Well, I've stayed there about as long as I've stayed anywhere else."

"Nevertheless, we're going to be spotted if we hang around here much longer. And don't forget what that bandit Escobar told us. . . ."

"You mean about pumping the well dry?"

Dos nodded. "I think we've taken about as much out of this territory as we can."

Lorna was gloomy. Her neapolitan ice cream lay melting on her plate.

"Don't you think it's time we finally went to Frisco?"

She looked up, brightening. "Can we buy a house?"

"I don't know why not. We're so rich I'm surprised our heads don't hurt."

"A house . . . with a fence?"

"As tall as you want."

She smiled at him. "Then, let's go!"

# 1895

# 14

Jeanette was worried about Maggie. A few weeks after the new year, she wrote to Elise in San Antonio.

... Perhaps it was having you with us over the Christmas holidays, and then losing you again that has sent her into a funk. Or maybe she's concerned over Alex's latest illness. (By the way, I think you and Carlos did the right thing in telling her it was a simple cold. She would be even more despondent knowing he had pneumonia again.) In any case, she hasn't been herself at all since you and Carlos went back to San Antonio. She mopes, eats very little, spends most of her time in her bedroom (crying, I suspect from the looks of her eyes), and today I received a note from Mother Matilda that Maggie's school work is not up to standard.

Although I know I should inform Anne, I think I'll let the matter simmer for another week or so. She has her hands full taking care of Alex at the moment.

So, please, don't breathe a word of this to the Lantana. If matters don't improve shortly, I'll write Anne myself. Perhaps a visit back to Texas would perk Maggie up. I'll let you know what I decide.

Love,
Maman

She sighed, folded the letter, and slipped it into an envelope. She had another worry, too, one so enormous she found herself unable to write about it in her letter to Elise. For the past few weeks, she had been aware that Maggie was stealing money from her purse . . . never much at any one time, but as of the moment, something over fifty dollars had been taken.

Then this morning, Jeanette noticed that her topaz dinner ring was missing from the jewel box on her dresser. Anguished and perplexed, she knew she could not let the matter pass. She had no choice but to speak to Maggie. But, how she dreaded the confrontation!

When Maggie returned from school, Jeanette took a deep breath and headed upstairs to see her. The girl was pale, but no paler than she'd looked the past few weeks. Her eyes were wide, and she seemed startled to see Jeanette.

Jeanette clenched her hands in an effort to compose herself. "Maggie, dear, I thought we should have a little talk."

Maggie stared silently.

"You know I love you as much as if you were my own child. And you know that there is nothing you could do that would change that."

Maggie nodded almost imperceptibly.

"Maggie, darling, don't you have something to tell me?"

Maggie looked suddenly frightened, and her voice trembled as she answered, "No, Jeanette."

"Are you sure . . . absolutely sure?"

Maggie nodded again.

"It would be easier if you told me . . . easier for both of us."

"There's nothing, Jeanette. I promise."

Jeanette probed Maggie's eyes. It was clear she was lying, but suddenly Jeanette lost her courage and couldn't bring herself to confront Maggie with her discovery. Instead, she sighed deeply and moved to the door. "Darling, I think there *is* something you need to tell me. I already know what it is. But if you don't wish to talk about it right now, I'll wait. When you decide you care to discuss it, come to me."

Maggie let her leave the room without a word. But as soon as the door closed, her face contorted with misery and she threw herself on her bed, ragged sobs shaking her body. How does she know? How does she know, when I only just found out myself?

A voice echoed in her brain—the voice of the doctor she'd visited at his shabby Irish Channel office. "No doubt about it, young lady," he'd said, almost smiling as he talked. "You're pregnant. Three months along, at least. You'll be showing soon."

When she burst into tears, he'd risen and come close to her, speaking quietly, almost in a whisper. "If you don't want the baby, I can help."

213

Maggie had wailed, "How?"

"I can get rid of it for you."

"But what happens to me in the meantime?"

"No, you don't follow me. I can get rid of it now."

Maggie understood at last what he was saying.

"You're young . . . there'll be no danger. I assure you of that. However, it will cost."

"How much?"

"I couldn't do it for less than a hundred dollars," the doctor said, judging from Maggie's expensive clothing that she could meet the exorbitant fee. "If you can raise the money, come back. But I warn you, you can't wait much longer."

Maggie had stumbled from the office, too shaken to care about the spectacle she made of herself as she headed back to St. Charles Avenue weeping into her handkerchief. The next morning she had taken the first of the money from Jeanette's purse.

And now, believing that Jeanette had somehow discovered the fact of her pregnancy, Maggie felt certain that it was only a matter of days before she would inform Anne and Alex. The thought horrified her. They mustn't know! Ever! Anne would be outraged—might never forgive her. And Alex! It would break his heart to learn that she was pregnant.

After the fire at Victor's, when Jeanette had seen the portrait, Maggie expected her to write to Anne and Alex. But she and Jeanette had reached a silent truce, an unspoken agreement, and the matter remained a delicate secret. But now, Jeanette would surely have no choice! She was bound to reveal everything!

She sat bolt upright in bed as the solution struck her. I'll go to Victor! That's the only way. He'll take me in and care for me. He'll marry me, and I'll be able to keep my baby. Her resolve gave her strength.

She left the bed and dried her tears. Taking a small valise from the top of her armoire, she packed it as full as possible and hid it back in the armoire.

That evening, Lavella knocked on the door announcing supper. Maggie sent her away, saying she wasn't hungry. Then Jeanette appeared, her brows knit with worry. "Maggie, dear. We've got to get to the bottom of this."

Maggie regarded her with suspicion and kept silent.

Jeanette shook her head. "I think the best thing is a visit to the doctor. I'll make an appointment tomorrow."

Maggie kept her expression under control, but now she knew there was no turning back. Jeanette's doctor would surely confirm her pregnancy; and then, the worst would happen!

Maggie waited until Jeanette had retired for the night; then, leaving a hastily scrawled note on her pillow, she bundled herself up in her warmest coat and dragged her valise out of the armoire.

She crept silently downstairs and headed for the side door near the servants' quarters. A floorboard creaked beneath her feet, and she heard Lavella's sleepy voice demand, "Who's that traipsing around in the hall?"

Maggie slipped outside just as Lavella's door opened, and hurried across the garden toward the avenue. The night air was cold and damp, and a delicate mist made soft halos around the streetlamps. Less than a minute after she reached the neutral ground, she caught sight of the streetcar's lamp rocking down the track.

"Hurry!" she whispered. "I can't get caught now! Hurry!"

The streetcar stopped two blocks away, discharged a passenger, and rolled on toward Maggie.

An hour later, she was aboard the night train bound for New York.

Maggie was among the last of the voyagers to disembark after the ship docked at Le Havre. She had been in luck when she reached New York and had found a steamer sailing for France immediately, but she hadn't counted on her low funds buying her such a dreary cabin in steerage which she had to share with five other women. Nor had she counted on the storm which kept her ill and miserable in her cabin for the entire crossing.

Now, as she looked around her, she saw that the sun had vanished once again, hidden by low, threatening clouds scuttling inland off the Channel. Grateful for her French lessons at Sacred Heart, Maggie managed to purchase a third-class train ticket to Paris, an expense that used up most of her remaining money; and as she climbed aboard and claimed her seat, she closed her eyes wearily and hoped that the worst was over at last.

The train clicked across the French countryside, its monotonous rocking motion lulling her to sleep, and when she opened her eyes again, she saw that they were pulling into Paris's Gare du Nord.

Lugging her little valise, she threaded her way through the milling crowd to the carriage rank outside. She gave the driver Victor's address and climbed in. As they rolled through traffic, she took a small mirror from her purse and examined her face, horrified to see how savagely her seasickness had affected her. Her cheeks were hollow, and fatigue had left dark smudges under her eyes. She bit her lips to bring color to them and tucked a few straggly locks of hair beneath her hat. Then, with a sigh that surrendered her future to fate, she dropped the mirror back into her purse and snapped it shut.

The *fiacre* lumbered over a bridge crossing to the island floating mid-stream in the Seine—the Ile St. Louis where Victor lived. The driver pulled up before a townhouse of gray stone, and Maggie saw on the brass plaque affixed to the door the name: *VICTOR DURAND*.

The driver helped her to the pavement, and she climbed the steep steps, pausing a moment before reaching for the knocker. Soon, she heard the echo of footsteps crossing the foyer and the click as the latch was released. The door swung open, and Victor's maid, a stout middle-aged woman wearing a starched white apron, inquired, *"Oui, mademoiselle?"*

"I'd like to see Monsieur Durand."

"Who shall I say is calling?"

"Maggie Cameron."

The maid bobbed her head and disappeared. A moment later Victor burst into the foyer.

"Victor!" Maggie cried, rushing toward him.

But he stepped back, holding her at arm's length. His face was pale, his dark eyes wide as he stared incredulously. *"Mon dieu! Ce n'est pas possible!"*

Maggie felt a tremor of despair. "Victor, tell me you're glad to see me. Lie if you have to! I won't be able to stand it if you say you're sorry I've come."

"Oh, Maggie!" he breathed, ignoring her plea. "How could you have done this? This could be disaster!"

The *fiacre* had started to roll away, and Victor brushed past Maggie shouting, *"Attendez, monsieur!"* Taking Maggie's elbow, he steered her from the house back to the carriage, then with a quick muttered word to the driver he climbed in beside her.

"What's happening, Victor? Where are we going?"

She studied his face. He looked more frightened than angry. "I would have sent word that I was coming, but there wasn't time. I left before anyone could stop me."

"You told no one?"

"I wrote a note . . . but I didn't say where I was going."

"Then you must cable immediately and tell them you're sailing for home right away."

Maggie cried out. She had prepared herself for his anger, had understood his shock, but it never once occurred to her that he might send her back.

"I—I can't go, Victor," she murmured through her tears. Her sobs filled the interior of the carriage.

Victor seemed to soften. He slipped his arm around her and let her rest against his shoulder. As if in a dream, she smelled again the scent of paint and oil that clung to his hair—that special fragrance she had grown to love.

The *fiacre* slowed to a stop.

"Where are we?" Maggie asked, blinking back tears.

"This is the hotel where you'll be staying."

"Why can't we be together?"

"It's out of the question, Maggie. I can't explain at the moment." Handing her a handkerchief, he added, "Dry your eyes. I'll go in and arrange for a room."

After a few moments he returned with a liveried porter for her valise. "Go with him, Maggie," he said.

"You're leaving me here alone?" she asked with alarm.

"Not for long," Victor assured her. "But I must go home now. I have an appointment I can't possibly avoid. I told you—back in New Orleans—that I would be extremely busy here. Too busy . . ."

"How long will you be gone?"

He shook his head. "I have no idea."

"But tonight?"

"I'll try."

"Tomorrow?"

"Oh, yes. Certainly tomorrow."

He bent and kissed her lightly on the cheek, then sent her into the hotel with the porter.

Her second-floor room overlooking the street was drab and chilly, and the cold winter wind billowed the curtains away from the rattling windows. Lacking the energy and the will to unpack, Maggie sat fully clothed in a stiff-backed upholstered chair hoping vainly to hear Victor's knock at the door.

She dozed fitfully, waking from time to time to the sound of rain drumming against the windowpanes. Once, dreaming that Victor had returned, she opened her eyes, her heart racing, only to find herself still alone. At last, when her watch told her it was well past four a.m., she hauled her stiff body from the chair, put out the light, and threw herself onto the bed without bothering to undress.

It was not until noon the next day that Victor reappeared. Maggie's breakfast—a croissant and a bowl of *café au lait*—sat untouched on a table beside the chair.

"I wasn't hungry," she explained in response to his inquiring look.

"You have to eat something, Maggie," Victor said. "I know a small café down the street. . . ."

"We need to talk, Victor."

He stood silently beside the window, making it clear he would rather avoid this conversation.

"You're so mysterious, Victor . . . so cold. Not at all the man I knew in New Orleans."

As he turned she saw a cloud of impatience cross

his face. "It's the surprise at finding you here, Maggie. . . ."

"It should have worn off by now," she countered.

". . . and the fact that I'm so busy."

"Too busy to put up with me?"

He looked almost relieved that she'd put it into words. "I knew you'd understand," he said quickly. "You see now what a bad idea it was for you to follow me here. I've no time for anything but work."

"You had plenty of time in New Orleans."

"Ah, but New Orleans is different. It's a small town. The pace is slow. One works a little and one plays a lot. But Paris is like New York. One must be quick to survive here."

"And I'll be in your way." Maggie's cheeks flushed with anger.

He crossed the floor and took her hands. "You can't stay here, Maggie. I would hardly have a moment for you. You'd be left by yourself most of the time, and Paris is a terrible place for a young woman alone, especially a woman unfamiliar with the city. You might wander into the wrong quarter where any number of things could . . ."

"So you want me to go back to New Orleans."

Victor smiled with relief. "For your sake, *chérie!* I'll book passage this afternoon."

"What if I tell you that I can't?"

"What do you mean you can't?" Victor said brusquely. "Of course, you can! Naturally your parents are going to be angry. Jeanette also. But they'll be angrier still if you stay."

"That's not what I meant."

He stared at her silently, waiting.

"I'm pregnant, Victor."

She watched him carefully. His face sagged, and his

220

eyes filled with that strange sorrow she'd seen so often in the past. He went to her and took her gently in his arms, rocking her as one would comfort a child.

"I understand," he whispered in her ear. "No, I don't suppose you can go home now."

After Victor had hastily left her with vague promises of plans to be made, Maggie stayed in her room. The afternoon passed, and with the dismal twilight came a chilly drizzle which misted the window where she stood hoping for a glimpse of Victor in the street below. He had promised to return, but didn't say when.

The streetlights blinked on, reflecting in the spreading puddles that dotted the pavement, and the winter wind whistled shrilly between the buildings. At last, unable to endure the awful solitude, Maggie pulled on her coat and determined to go to Victor. She went downstairs and asked the concierge for directions to the Ile St. Louis.

"I'll have the porter summon a *fiacre*," he offered.

Maggie thought of her empty purse. "No, thank you. I'll walk."

"But surely mademoiselle would prefer to ride. It's cold out . . . and raining."

Maggie didn't reply. She turned and left the hotel. The bitter weather caused her to catch her breath and clutch her coat tightly about her throat. For the first block or two, the rain was a light, swirling mist, but soon it turned to sleet that stung her cheeks and slicked the pavement. She walked slowly to keep from slipping and huddled from time to time beneath an occasional awning.

She hoped she was following the concierge's directions, but soon the narrow winding streets became a

221

labyrinth, dead-ending where she thought they should go through, twisting and turning, changing names, until after an hour's wanderings, she realized she was hopelessly lost.

Then to her dismay, she turned a corner and saw up ahead the entrance to her hotel. She had wandered in a circle, achieving nothing but a chill that numbed her entire body.

Her clothes were soaked through; her leather shoes were cold and hard, and her sodden hair had tumbled down around her shoulders, the tangled strands freezing in the bitter wind. She staggered into the lobby, and the concierge who had been coolly correct and polite to her before now stared at her bedraggled figure with distaste and suspicion.

"Are there any messages?" she managed to ask.

Her shoulders sagged as he replied, *"Monsieur* Durand was here. He said he would call again tomorrow."

Maggie trudged upstairs and peeled off her wet clothing, and the effort of pulling a flannel nightgown over her head left her weak and breathless. For the first time she was aware of a gnawing hunger, but when she looked across the room, she saw that her untouched breakfast roll and her bowl of coffee had been removed.

She curled up beneath the blanket and buried her face in the stiff roll that passed for a pillow. Oh, God! she prayed. Please let me to go sleep! Maybe then I won't feel the hunger!

But she awoke in the middle of the night burning with fever, her chest aching, her throat parched and sore. She reached to her nightstand for a drink of water but found the carafe empty. When she tried to rise to refill it at the sink, she sank back into the bed too weak to stand. Huddled beneath the blanket, Maggie waited for dawn.

The maid appeared at last with her breakfast, but despite her hunger, Maggie was unable to choke down the single croissant that lay in a chipped plate on the tray. With trembling fingers, she managed to bring the bowl of *café au lait* to her lips, and for a while the sweet, milky coffee warmed her belly and stilled the pangs of hunger.

Later, when the maid reappeared to remove the breakfast tray, she looked at Maggie and inquired: *"Mademoiselle est malade?"*

Maggie nodded and said, "I took a chill in the rain yesterday."

"Shall I call a doctor?"

"No," Maggie replied, knowing she could not pay him. "I'll be all right."

The maid departed but returned a moment later with another blanket which she spread on the bed and tucked in around Maggie's chin. "Keep warm, *mademoiselle,*" she advised. "The fever will pass."

Maggie stayed in bed most of the day, waiting for Victor and hoping the fever would break, but her fever rose as the afternoon grew late, and she began to fear pneumonia. She struggled weakly from her bed and dressed herself, the effort taking the better part of an hour, and by the time she pulled on her coat, her clothing was soaked with perspiration.

This time when she sought directions from the concierge, she asked him to draw her a map, and she set off once more for Victor's house. The sky was overcast, and the wind was even colder than the day before, but at least there was a break in the rain.

She was unable to walk more than a block or two at a stretch before resting, and by the time she reached the Seine, night was setting in. Forcing herself forward, she crossed the bridge to the island where Victor lived.

Upon reaching his house, she brought the knocker against the door—once, twice, before her strength gave out and her arm fell limply to her side. It seemed an eternity before footsteps sounded in the foyer, and when the door opened, she found herself again standing before the maid.

"*Monsieur* Durand," Maggie muttered, barely able to speak.

The maid's eyes narrowed suspiciously. Maggie's hair, damp with sweat, clung to her cheeks. Her face was deathly pale in sharp contrast with the dark circles that ringed her haunted eyes. "Wait here."

"Who's there, Yvette?" called a voice from within the house.

"Someone inquiring for *monsieur*," the maid replied, moving aside so that Maggie caught sight of a woman entering the foyer. She was a beautiful brunette, with long sleek curls worn about a perfectly oval face. Her silk dress rustled softly as she approached the door, and her diamond brooch sparkled in the light of the overhead chandelier.

Maggie stared at the lovely young woman. She opened her mouth to speak, but her voice failed.

"Are you one of Victor's models?" the woman asked. "Have you posed for my husband?"

Maggie staggered backward, as if she had been struck a blow, and grasped the handrail for support.

*So he's married! And has been all this time!*

*Madame* Durand stared at Maggie, wondering if the girl were crazed with alcohol or opium. Most of the girls who posed for her husband were poor creatures from the slums, barely a cut above prostitutes, and she understood that many of them were addicted to absinthe or worse. She always felt sympathy for them, even as she was unable to comprehend their way of life. And it was obvious to her that the girl standing before her was in trouble, for she was trembling violently and her forehead was slick with sweat.

*Madame* Durand asked again, "Are you one of my husband's models?"

Maggie's thoughts flew back to New Orleans, to the afternoons she had spent at Victor's studio, posing nude on the divan while he stood behind his easel, brushing paint on the canvas.

"Yes," she murmured. "I've posed for him."

"Are you ill?" Madame Durand asked.

Maggie nodded almost imperceptibly.

"Please, tell me your name," the woman said kindly. "I'll send Yvette for my husband."

But Maggie didn't respond. Her haggard face still registering shock, she backed down the steps and hurried away as quickly as she could. At that moment, Victor joined his wife and the maid at the door. He followed their gaze down the street and caught a glimpse of Maggie as she turned the corner beneath the glow of a streetlight.

"She's one of your models," his wife said. "You must go after her. She's ill."

Without returning for his coat, Victor bounded down the steps. When he reached the corner, he peered into the darkness and shouted, "Maggie!"

There was no answer, but he saw a shuffling silhouette up ahead. However, Maggie proved elusive. By the time he reached the next intersection he'd lost her again in the gloom.

"Maggie!"

He chose a street leading toward the Seine and rushed forward.

As Maggie reached the bridge, a violent coughing fit racked her body, and she slumped against the balustrade clutching her burning chest. She swayed as she tried to catch her breath. Silence surrounded her, broken only by the river's current lapping against the banks.

Slowly, she made her way to mid-span. She had never known such cold or pain. Gazing down into the river from the bridge, she watched its sinuous gray flow beneath the gauzy veil of wintry fog. It seemed to beckon her, to promise her ease and respite from all her misery.

Victor rounded the corner in time to see Maggie haul herself onto the stone railing and struggle to swing her legs over the other side.

"No, Maggie! Wait!"

But she never heard him. The river was darkly beautiful and inviting, offering peace beneath its shrouded surface. She placed her hands against the railing and with the last of her strength pushed herself away.

For a moment she felt weightless, buoyed on a cushion of air. Then, plunging feet first, Maggie hit the water. She surfaced, rolled over onto her back, and let the current take her. In her heart she felt nothing but gratitude and release.

Victor flew down the stone steps to the bank, his eyes frantically sweeping the fog-swathed river.

Maggie's sodden clothing had begun to pull her under, and only her gaunt, white face floated above the swirling water. He sprinted ahead of her drifting form, then jumped into the river, thrashing wildly in an effort to reach her before she sank from sight. He lost her for a moment as a wavelet splashed over her face; but

226

when she reappeared, he swam furiously, catching up with her just as she began to go under again.

Locking his elbow beneath her chin, he paddled back toward the bank. Gasping with exhaustion, he managed to haul her onto the quai-side steps before collapsing alongside her. The cold was numbing, and it was long moments before he was able to sit up and examine her.

She lay still and quiet, her face pale, her long, dark hair plastered to her cheeks and shoulders. He gasped in horror and remorse, certain he'd reached her too late, but then her head flopped to one side, and he heard a hoarse, ragged gasp. He rose slowly, lifted the light burden in his arms, and carried her up the steps to the street.

The first *fiacre* that appeared rolled on without stopping, the driver taking one look at the bedraggled pair and snapping his whip alongside his nag. But Victor managed to halt the next one and, by paying in advance, persuaded the hackman to accept them. Together they placed Maggie's limp form on one of the seats, and Victor climbed in beside her.

"To the *Maison* Dollois," he instructed the driver. "The rear entrance."

The driver gave Victor a knowing look and climbed back onto his perch.

Babette, the cook at the *Maison* Dollois, answered the knock at the back door. *"Monsieur* Durand!" she cried in alarm. "You're soaked through! What has happened?"

"Summon *Madame* Dollois for me, please," Victor murmured.

*"Toute de suite, monsieur,"* Babette said, bustling off.

In another moment, Marie Dollois appeared in the

kitchen. She was a tall, svelte woman, middle-aged, with russet hair piled atop her head and sharp, lively blue eyes. Her lavender satin dress was deeply cut, and her bare bosom was covered with a dozen strands of smoky pearls.

*"Mon dieu, Victor!"* she gasped.

"I need your help, Marie."

"Certainly! What can I do?"

Half an hour later, Maggie was bedded down beneath a plush quilt in an enormous fourposter, and a doctor was just finishing his examination.

"Well, *Madame* Dollois," he said as he straightened up and removed his stethoscope from his ears. "The girl is gravely ill. Pneumonia."

Victor closed his eyes and held his head in his hands.

"What can I do, Dr. Lanoux?" Marie Dollois asked.

"Mustard plasters, warm foot baths, and keep her as comfortable as possible. Her youth may save her. If she regains consciousness, give her a little nourishment—hot soup or meat broth."

"Very well, doctor," Marie Dollois said.

Victor rose from the chair he'd occupied since Maggie was placed in bed. "I must go home now, Marie. My wife will be concerned about my absence."

"I'll take care of the girl," Marie Dollois assured him.

"I'll return in a day or two . . . to see how she is."

"In the event that she . . ." Marie Dollois left the rest unsaid.

Victor shook his head. "Whatever happens, you mustn't send a message to the house."

"Of course not, Victor. I understand."

*"Merci,* Marie," he said, then departed quickly.

Dr. Lanoux took another lingering look at Maggie's

inert form. He sighed quietly and began packing his instruments into his bag. "I'll call again tomorrow."

"Thank you, doctor," Marie said.

He reached the door, then paused. "I was just thinking . . . as long as I'm here . . . do you suppose it would be all right . . ."

Marie smiled warmly. "Of course, dear doctor. Make yourself at home in the salon below. Take anyone you want. There'll be no charge. . . ."

Dr. Lanoux returned her smile gratefully and let himself out of the room.

The salon was a large cheery room with red flocked wallpaper, a crackling fire in the hearth, and a brilliant crystal chandelier that flung sparks of color from its polished prisms.

As the doctor let himself in, a dozen exquisitely gowned young women turned their heads and looked at him.

"*Bon soir,* Nicole," he said to a ravishing brunette who lay languidly against the satin cushions of an overstuffed divan. "*Comment ça va,* Antoinette?" he greeted another, a sprite-like blonde in blue silk cut low to reveal the creamy smoothness of her small breasts. But his eyes sought out and found Thérèse, a slender redhead with emerald eyes and a complexion that reminded him of purest alabaster. She moved toward him, knowing that he had chosen her from among the others.

"*Bon soir, docteur,*" she said, linking her arm in his. "A glass of champagne?"

"Could we have it served in your room?" he asked.

Thérèse laughed brightly. "Ah-ha! My little doctor is impatient, *n'est-ce pas?*"

He smiled sheepishly and nodded, trying to ignore the other girls giggling behind his back.

"Pauline," Thérèse said, addressing a maid in attendance. "Bring champagne to my room." Then turning back to the doctor, she asked, *"Eh bien, monsieur,* shall we go upstairs?"

Throughout the next day, Maggie managed to hold her own, but the following evening she took a turn for the worse, and Dr. Lanoux, who had been hastily summoned, informed Marie Dollois that he feared the end was near.

"She is simply too weak," he said regretfully. "I would be surprised if she lasted the night."

"The poor darling!" Marie murmured softly, wringing out a cloth in cool water and placing it on Maggie's burning forehead. "To die alone . . . among strangers."

Having done everything he could, Dr. Lanoux excused himself, leaving Marie with Maggie. The older woman spent the rest of the night on a hard chair beside the bed watching her patient carefully, changing the damp compresses on Maggie's fevered brow, and listening with dread to the girl's ragged breathing. The doctor had given up hope; yet Marie Dollois was obstinate. She felt intuitively that if she could bring Maggie safely through the night, the girl would live. She watched and waited, wishing for the dawn that seemed so painfully long in coming.

With a weary sigh, she rose to add a log to the fire, poking at the embers until she was sure the wood had caught; then as she turned back toward the bed, she halted abruptly with a cry in her throat. Maggie's eyes were open, staring at her. And outside the window, the darkness of night had given way to the first gray glimmer of morning.

Marie hurried to the bedside and took Maggie's

hand, which lay dry and limp in her palm. "Oh, *ma petite . . . ma petite!*" Marie breathed. "You've made it! You're going to live!"

Maggie's lips parted, but she was too ill to speak. Her face was little more than a skull, and her sunken eyes were bright with fever.

Marie yanked on the bellpull and told the drowsy maid who appeared at the door to fetch a bowl of *café au lait.* "With plenty of sugar . . . plenty!"

When the coffee was brought up, the maid supported Maggie's back while Marie spooned the sweet warm liquid into Maggie's mouth. "Drink, *chérie,*" the older woman coaxed. "It will give you strength."

She watched with satisfaction as Maggie slowly sipped the coffee; and not knowing whether it was her imagination or not, she thought she saw a faint flush of color appear on the girl's sallow cheeks.

"I knew you would live," Marie murmured. "I was sure that if you made it through the night, you would recover."

Maggie's mind was too clouded to wonder where she was and who this woman might be. But she sensed a feeling of calm and well-being—and her heart filled with gratitude. When she could drink no more, the maid carefully settled her back on the pillow, and Marie resumed her vigil beside the bed.

Late that afternoon Victor called at the *Maison* Dollois and took tea with Marie in a private salon downstairs.

"She's lucid, but still extremely ill," Marie informed him. "I don't think you should visit her just yet."

Victor seemed almost relieved. He wasn't at all certain he possessed the courage to face Maggie, and he dreaded the time when they would have to meet again.

"Who is she, Victor?"

"An American girl named Maggie Cameron . . . one of my former models."

"And do you know why she leaped into the river?"

"She's pregnant."

"By you?"

His silence answered her question.

Marie gave him a hard, reproachful look. "But, Victor, she's only a child herself!"

He shook his head almost imperceptibly. "No, Marie. She's a child no longer." As he rose to leave, he asked, "Does she know where she is? Is she aware of the nature of your house?"

Marie Dollois's voice was cold. "No, Victor. She believes she is in the home of a wealthy woman . . . that's all."

He reached for his hat and made his way to the door.

"Victor," Marie said, halting him, "I'll relieve you of the burden. I'll take care of her myself. There's no reason for you to come here again."

"*Merci,* Marie," he murmured, and his voice was so laced with gratitude that Marie Dollois's lips curled with scorn.

When the door clicked shut behind him, Marie rose and tossed back her head. "*Salaud!*" she swore. "He's like all men . . . a coward!"

# 15

When Jeanette discovered the note the day after Maggie ran away, she thought of the nude portrait and immediately suspected that Maggie had left for Paris; and when the maid Clarisse broke down and tearfully confessed her knowledge of Maggie's affair with Victor, Jeanette was certain.

She dispatched a frantic telegram to Elise and Carlos begging them to come to New Orleans at once. When they arrived two days later, they found her wild with anguish. She showed them the note and told them everything she knew.

Carlos sat with his head in his hands, his thoughts with Anne and Alex, who had yet to be informed. Elise paced the floor, wringing her hands and berating herself. "It's all my fault! I threw them together. It seemed such fun at the time . . . so harmless! I never thought it would end like this. Never!"

"Anne and Alex will be horrified when they hear," Jeanette moaned.

Carlos stirred himself and looked up. "We have to keep it from them . . . at least until we find out the whole story. Anne's strong and will be able to take it, but Alex is very ill. The shock might kill him."

Elise dropped to her knees beside Carlos and clasped his hands. Her face was twisted with grief and remorse. "Oh, Carlos! What are we going to do?"

"You and I will go after her and bring her home," he said with grave calm. "It's the only way. I'll go down to the steamship office right now and make arrangements. While I'm gone, write a letter to Anne and Alex. Make up any excuse to explain our sudden trip. Tell them it was a caprice, a foolish lark on our part . . . anything except the truth."

They embarked the next day—two somber, solitary passengers on a festive ship bound for France.

The voyage lasted two weeks, and in the meantime at the *Maison* Dollois, Maggie was slowly, steadily regaining her health. When Marie considered her well enough to accept the truth, she told Maggie of her rescue by Victor, and she confirmed that he was indeed married and had been for years.

Maggie moaned and rolled over in her bed, burying her face in the pillow.

"When you're strong enough to travel, *ma petite,* I'll send you back home where you belong."

Home! Maggie's heart yearned for the Lantana. Yes! She wanted to go home, back to Anne and Alex. She knew she was going to break their hearts, but it was a grim consequence she'd have to face. There was nothing left for her in Paris—there had been nothing to begin with, really. At least on the ranch she might have a chance to make amends, might be able to pick up the pieces and reconstruct her life. And as she hugged her pillow tightly, she wished that by some magic she were back on the Lantana again.

Oh, Papa! I was your little girl. And now I've betrayed you! Can you ever forgive me? You must! You must! I have no one else to turn to!

Marie Dollois sat by her, stroking her hair until Maggie dropped off to sleep.


Carlos and Elise arrived in Paris that afternoon. Less than an hour after checking into their hotel, they learned Victor's address and set off by *fiacre* to the residence on the Ile St. Louis.

"I'll stay in the hack," Elise said, not trusting herself with what she might say to Victor.

Carlos mounted the steps alone, and when Victor came to the door, Elise sat farther back in the carriage, not wishing to look at him.

"Hello, Carlos," Victor said calmly, as if he'd been expecting him.

"I've come for Maggie. Send her down immediately."

"She's not here."

"You're lying to me."

"No! I swear it." Eyeing Carlos's hard-set face and clenched fists, Victor stepped back and half-closed the door. "Tell your driver to take you to the *Maison* Dollois. He'll know the address."

Without another word, Carlos spun on his heel and returned to the hack, calling to the driver, "To the *Maison* Dollois."

The driver looked at him strangely. "Is *monsieur* certain that's where he wishes to go?"

"Is there something wrong?" Carlos asked impatiently.

The driver arched his eyebrows and shrugged, giving

a look over his shoulder at Elise. "No, *monsieur,* not at all."

"Then let's be off." Carlos settled back beside Elise. "He put her at a hotel, or she had the good sense to go there herself. At any rate, we'll have her back with us in a few minutes."

The *fiacre* crossed onto the Right Bank and rumbled through the streets, pulling up at last in front of an imposing five-story residence.

"The *Maison* Dollois," the driver informed them.

"It doesn't look like a hotel, Carlos."

"It must be. Look . . . there's the name above the door. Are you coming with me?"

"Yes," Elise said, following him out of the carriage. "She'll need some comforting."

The maid answering the door regarded them inquiringly.

"We're looking for Maggie Cameron," Elise said.

"I'll send for *madame,*" the maid answered, starting to close the door.

"May we wait inside?"

The maid hesitated an instant, then allowed them to enter before hobbling upstairs in search of Marie Dollois. In the foyer's bright light, Carlos and Elise saw that the walls were covered with paintings of demure nudes with opalescent flesh, rosy cheeks, and moist pink lips. At the foot of the stairs was a lifesize bronze blackamoor bearing a torch, and off to the side were the double doors leading to the main salon from which emerged the sounds of deep-throated male voices mingled with the quick, light laughter of young women.

Carlos's blood ran cold, and he looked to Elise, wondering if she shared his suspicions. Without caring whom he might disturb, he strode to the doors and pushed them open. It took only a glance to confirm his fears. A dozen beautiful girls in daringly cut ball-gowns were entertaining a group of men lounging on plush sofas and sipping champagne. Thérèse, the red-head with emerald eyes, looked up, spotted Carlos and smiled invitingly.

Carlos pulled the doors shut quickly. When he turned to Elise his face was pale, his lips bloodless. "My God!" he murmured.

"What is it, Carlos? What's wrong?"

Before he could answer, Thérèse poked her head into the foyer, saying, *"Entrez, chéri!* Don't be shy." Then, spotting Elise, she raised her eyebrows and sucked in her breath. *"Oh-là-là!* I'm afraid there's some mistake."

Marie Dollois's voice from the landing interrupted them. "Thérèse! Leave us alone!"

Thérèse ducked back into the salon.

"Carlos!" Elise breathed, understanding at last. "This is a brothel!"

As Marie Dollois reached the bottom of the stairs, Carlos broke away from Elise and rushed to the woman, demanding, "Where is my niece? Where is Maggie?"

"Follow me. She's upstairs. She's been ill."

Carlos brushed past her and took the steps two at a time.

"Wait, *monsieur,* I'll take you," Marie Dollois called, but Carlos was already gone; and as she climbed the stairs after him, Elise could hear him shouting, "Maggie! Maggie! Maggie!"

Maggie was in bed asleep, but the commotion in the hallway outside roused her. Someone was charging through the corridor, banging loudly on every door, while one of the maids protested excitedly, *"Qu'est-ce que vous voulez, monsieur?* What is happening?"

Then Maggie heard her name. Sitting up, her heart thumping wildly, she cried out, "Carlos!"

Her door flew open and Carlos stormed in. The sight of her, pale, thin, and defenseless, swept all anger from his face, and he rushed to the bed and embraced her.

"Oh, Carlos! Thank God you've come. Take me away, please. Take me home!"

"How did you end up here, Maggie?"

She tried to explain, but she was crying too hard to reply.

Quickly, he lifted her from the bed and without bothering to look for her slippers or to cover her with a coat, he hurried her from the room.

Elise had reached the far end of the corridor. Seeing Maggie, she cried out and ran to her, taking her into her arms. "Oh, Maggie, darling! Come with us! Let's get out of this place."

Maggie was strong enough to walk on her own, but Carlos and Elise half-carried her downstairs, past Marie Dollois, and out onto the street to the waiting *fiacre*.

During the ride to the hotel, Maggie wept uncontrollably, unable to answer Carlos and Elise's questions, not really hearing what they had to say, knowing only that they had come for her, that she was back among family again, and that she would soon be going home.

Later that evening, when she was relatively calm, she told the story in bits and pieces, leaving out nothing, not noticing that each revelation caused Carlos's face to harden even further.

Elise was heartbroken. She took the blame on herself and begged Maggie's forgiveness, but Maggie shook her head and said, "It was my own fault. I was foolish . . . stupid. And I loved him so!"

"He'll answer for this," Carlos said grimly.

"No," Maggie replied. "He's not worth bothering with. Let's forget about him and leave here as soon as possible."

Elise held onto Maggie's hand. "I'll buy you some clothes tomorrow, dear. And we'll sail on the first ship leaving for America."

Maggie sank back into her pillow and closed her eyes. "Home! Do you think Mama and Papa will take me back?"

Elise looked to Carlos. "Of course, they will. Now sleep, *chérie*. No more talking tonight."

When Maggie's breathing grew regular, Elise and Carlos retired to their own bed in the adjoining room. But at midnight, Elise woke to find Carlos sitting alone by the window, staring into the darkness outside.

"What are you thinking, darling?" she asked drowsily.

Without turning to look at her, he said, "Don't worry yourself, Elise. Go back to sleep."

She woke again two hours later and saw him still by the window. She wanted to go to him, but her limbs were so heavy with sleep that she lay pinned to the bed and her eyelids closed again. Then, toward dawn, she found that the chair was empty and Carlos's side of the bed hadn't been slept in at all.

Thinking he must be with Maggie, she rose and peered into the other room, but he was not there, either. As she turned, perplexed, wondering where he had gone, her eyes glimpsed a folded note on the mantel.

She opened it and read:

My dearest Elise,

If all goes well, you will never see this letter at all. You will wake to find me lying by your side.

However, if the worst happens, please don't blame Maggie, and try to find it in your heart to forgive me for doing what I deem necessary to avenge her honor. It seems the only way to make Victor pay for what he has done.

Remember this: no man ever loved a woman more than I love you!

Carlos

Elise gasped with horror. Grabbing her robe she flew downstairs into the deserted lobby, waking the concierge with her frantic cries.

"Where do men duel?" she shrieked.

*"Madame!"* the concierge exclaimed, backing up, thinking surely she was mad.

"Tell me quickly!" she demanded. "My husband's life is in danger!"

"Traditionally in the Bois de Boulogne. But—"

She spun about without letting him finish and raced into the street, rousing a dozing hackman outside the hotel. "Take me to the Bois de Boulogne as fast as you can. Hurry! Hurry! There's not a moment to spare!"

The *fiacre* lurched forward and sped through the dark, empty streets. "Faster! Faster!" she cried, wishing she had the driver's whip in her hand.

They reached the edge of the park, and the driver called down to her, "The Bois is large. Where do you wish to go?"

"Just drive! I'm looking for my husband!"

However, no sooner had she spoken than she heard a pistol shot. She flinched, then flinched again at the sound of a second report.

The *fiacre* pulled up short, and Elise burst from it, running in the direction of the shots. A cold morning mist filled the park, and Elise stumbled forward over

240

the wet grass until she caught sight of several men huddled in two groups in a clearing among the trees.

"Carlos!" she shouted.

One of the men broke away from his group and rushed toward her.

"My darling!" she cried in relief, holding out her arms for her husband, but when the man neared, she found herself facing a stranger. She froze in her tracks. She wanted to ask for Carlos, but her throat was paralyzed.

The man reached out for her. *"Madame* Trevor?"

She was unable to manage a nod.

The man took her elbow, urging her forward. "Quickly, *madame.* Go to him before it's too late."

But she couldn't move, couldn't force herself to put one foot in front of the other, and the man had to pull her along. Carlos lay on the cold, damp ground, a bullet wound oozing blood from his chest.

She dropped to her knees and cradled his head in her lap. His eyes—those gray jewels she had cherished from the moment she met him—had turned glassy. His flesh was already waxen, his lips as pale as the morning mist.

"Elise," he whispered. Then his eyelids fluttered and closed.

Elise raised her head toward the sky and screamed.


The banging door woke Maggie. She looked up and saw Elise standing just inside the room. Elise's hair was in wild tangles about her head. Her robe was grass-stained and wet with streaks of blood already darkening on the fabric. Her eyes flashed demonically and her trembling hands formed claws that seemed to want to reach out and tear Maggie apart.

241

"You whore!" Elise screamed. "You jezebel!"

"Elise! What are you saying! Carlos! Carlos! Come quickly!"

"It's no use calling for Carlos! You've killed him!"

Maggie's hands flew to her mouth.

"He called out Victor . . . to avenge your honor, or what little there was left of it! Now he's dead. And Victor, too! You've killed them both."

"No! It's not true!" Maggie rushed from her bed, reaching for Elise, but Elise fended her off with a stinging slap against her cheek.

"Don't come near me . . . ever! Because of you the gentlest, most loving man in the world is dead! You killed him as surely as if you yourself fired the shot!"

Maggie cowered against the bedpost.

"I never want to see you again," Elise said, her voice low now, a vicious growl. "Nor shall Anne and Alex. They could have forgiven you for being a whore! But for killing Carlos . . . never!"

She slammed the door between the two rooms.

Maggie felt herself go faint. She grabbed for the bedpost, then pitched forward onto the floor, unconscious.


Anne and Elise stood in the little graveyard where Joel, Martha, and Sofia lay buried. Now the mahogany coffin bearing Carlos's body was being lowered into the ground. Behind them was a crowd of weeping mourners, peons, cowboys, and townspeople who came out in the cold February rain to pay their respects. Alex, too ill to attend, lay in bed back at the big house, biter tears filling the creases around his eyes and spilling onto the pillow.

They're all gone now! Anne thought. Carlos forever

. . . Maggie, too. Even if I could find it in my heart to forgive her, I know she won't return. And Dos? Maybe someday . . . but that won't last, either. They'll take him off to prison, and I will have lost him once again.

She heard Elise sobbing at her side and slipped her arm around her waist for support. Elise is also leaving me, going back to Jeanette. And there's not even a baby on the way. Nothing of Carlos left behind. Carlos, my brother and my son. The last of Sofia, the last of the Lantana's Spanish heritage. Oh, Carlos, how I'll miss you!

It's just me and Alex again . . . like it was at the beginning. Only this time, we're no longer young. We've got nothing to build for, to work toward, to look forward to. Nothing except us . . . and the Lantana!

She raised her eyes from the casket, not wishing to witness it disappearing forever into the earth, and gazed through the rain at the cold, wet prairie.

What's it all been for? she wondered.

The sound of sodden dirt being shoveled onto Carlos's coffin brought forth fresh sobs from Elise.

"Come, dear," Anne said, leading her away. "It's easier if we leave now. I know . . . I've been through this before."

As she and Elise moved toward their buggy, Peter Stark came out of the crowd. Rain dripped from his hat; his silver star hung from his lapel.

"You have my sympathy, Mrs. Cameron. It seems we only meet on sad occasions."

Anne thought of Dos. "And I fear the next time we meet, Peter, it won't be any happier."

"I haven't forgotten my promise. I won't harm Dos. You've already seen enough tragedy in your life."

Anne managed a feeble smile. "Thank you, Peter."

She squeezed his hand and moved away. Then, spotting the ranch's blacksmith, she beckoned him over and said, "Send for all the branding irons, and when you get them, add another thorn to the crown. Make it longer and sharper than the rest so when I see our mark, I'll know which one is for Carlos."

Elise left for New Orleans the next day, and a week later a letter from Maggie arrived on the Lantana. Anne kept it overnight unopened in her desk; and the next morning, still without having read it, she sealed it in another envelope and mailed it back.

# PART II

# 1903

# 16

San Francisco suited Dos and Lorna admirably. They purchased a comfortable two-story house on Green St. that afforded them a spectacular view of the bay and the golden hills of Marin beyond; and Dos saw to it that the tiny yard was encircled by a high iron fence that after a year or two was festooned with garlands of fuchsia.

The couple took to the city's roisterous nightlife with unabashed gusto, making the rounds from restaurant to music hall to saloon, seldom returning to their bed before dawn broke over Mt. Diablo.

They were a dashing, striking pair—Dos, burly and golden blond wearing a top hat and a silk-lined cape; Lorna, petite and dark, her brown eyes flashing, always looking for the next excitement, her little pointed chin jutting out like the prow of one of the trim, sleek cutters that sailed through the Golden Gate.

Dos presented them as Mr. and Mrs. Joel Rivers, and as soon as they moved to the city, they abandoned robbery. To Lorna's great amusement, however, Dos liked to say to any new aquaintance who was rude enough to inquire about his past that he was "formerly involved with banks." And if the acquaintance pressed further, asking, "Banks? Oh, really? Where?" Dos would roll his eyes and say, "Good Lord! Everywhere! Too many to number!"

All of which only served to enhance his reputation as an immensely wealthy young man from "parts east" who had no reason to trouble himself with work.

As a matter of fact, soon after arriving in San Francisco, Dos made friends with a down-and-out Irishman named Malloy whose dreams of a saloon on the city's North Beach were hampered only by a decided lack of cash. Dos, flush with stolen money and nowhere to invest it, staked the Irishman, and in less than six months, Pandora's Box was firmly established as the wildest, most exciting saloon in town.

Dos kept in the background, a silent partner, but Pandora's earned more than enough to keep him and Lorna is style.

He should have been utterly happy—as Lorna was —but on occasion he suffered pangs of nostalgia for Texas and the Lantana. He wondered about Anne and Maggie and Carlos. And even Alex . . . for his years of exile had smoothed the rough edges of his feelings. Once or twice he tried writing to Anne, but the words blocked up within him, and the letter paper ended up crumpled in the basket beside his desk.

And Malloy was troubling him. Originally grateful and content with their business arrangement, the Irishman pressed more and more often for a greater cut of the pie, the thirty percent Dos had granted him no longer satisfactory.

Dos wished he could be rid of the man, but Malloy held a trump that Dos himself had stupidly dealt him. Shortly after meeting the Irishman—in a moment of drunken expansiveness that Dos could never forgive himself for—he had bragged about the source of the money that had gone into Pandora's. He'd told Malloy everything, naming the banks he and Lorna had hit and describing the taunting letters signed "The Wolf," that he had sent to the newspaper. Malloy had been a good listener, taking it all in. And when Dos awoke the next morning with a throbbing headache and recalled the night before, he cursed himself for his indiscretion.

In all the time since, Malloy had never again brought up the subject, but Dos knew he hadn't forgotten. And he wondered when the echo of his blunder would resound.

"Why don't you sell out to Malloy and be rid of him?" Lorna asked. They were sitting down to breakfast, although it was well past noon. Lorna poured coffee and slid the morning newspaper across the table to Dos.

"He's not inclined to pay. He wants me to hand it to him, and I'll be damned if I'll give him the place for free."

"He's worked awfully hard. We haven't had to turn our hands."

"I'll grant him that, but without me . . . without us and our money, Malloy couldn't afford to get through the door at Pandora's, much less own a third."

Lorna sighed. She wished to be free of Malloy even more than Dos did. Lately his attentions to her had grown pointed and aggressive. Twice in the past month

251

he had come to her and suggested that they meet in private. She withheld this information from Dos, fearing his temper, but when she rebuffed Malloy the last time, he had smiled confidently and said, "You won't be able to put me off forever, Lorna. I've set my hat for you . . . and mean to have you."

Dos sipped his coffee absently and unfolded the paper. He skimmed the first page and turned to the second. Lorna saw the change in his expression and heard his cup clatter to the saucer.

"What is it, Dos?"

"My God!" he said softly, putting his palm to his forehead. The headline was brief, and although he had barely glanced at it, he knew instinctively what the two short paragraphs would say.

"Dos! Tell me!"

His eyes flickered over the article, to confirm his premonition. Then he looked up to Lorna and said, "It's my father. He's dead."

"Oh, Dos!"

Dos took a deep breath and read aloud: "Noted Rancher Dies. Mr. Alex Cameron, owner of the famed Lantana Ranch in Texas, expired in San Antonio last Tuesday of pneumonia. A Scotsman by birth, Mr. Cameron came to possess this nation's largest cattle ranch and is credited with the development of the Lantana cow, a sturdy breed combining Brahma, Angus, and the native longhorn. He was sixty-three.

"Surviving Mr. Cameron is his widow, Mrs. Anne Trevor Cameron, a Texas pioneer."

Dos closed his eyes, and Lorna kept silent, waiting for him to speak. At last, he rose and stood at the window. A thick fog had rolled through the Golden Gate and obscured the bay, and only the deep-throated foghorns interrupted the quiet.

Without turning, speaking more to himself than to Lorna, he said, "I didn't know I would feel like this. I thought I hated him. Now I suppose I really didn't, after all. It hurts. It really hurts. I wish . . . I wish. . . ."

He left the sentence unfinished.

Lorna left the table and joined him at the window, her hand slipping into his. "You should write to your mother, Dos."

He thought for a moment, then said, "No . . . she would think I was writing only because Papa is gone at last. It would look like I had been waiting for him to die."

Lorna understood.

"I think I'll take a walk," Dos said. "I'd like to be by myself for a while."

Lorna nodded.

At the door, Dos turned, a puzzled look on his face. "I can understand why the article didn't mention me as a survivor. But what about Maggie? And Carlos?"

It was a question Lorna couldn't answer.

Dos strolled the misty streets. A feeble sun tried unsuccessfully to break through the patchy fog overhead, and the mournful foghorns kept up their plaintive knell.

Alex dead! It just didn't seem possible. How would Anne live without him? Dos could imagine her taking to her turret office, locking herself in with only her grief for company. He could picture her—as he'd so often seen her—standing alone at one of the lofty windows, gazing out at her land.

He wondered what she looked like now. She was fifty-five, and he hadn't seen her in a decade. Was she still beautiful and strong, or had the years taken their toll?

His thoughts flew back to the day he left the ranch for good, and he recalled turning around and staring at the Ebonal for one last look.

From that moment until this, nothing about the Lantana had changed in his mind. It existed exactly as it did the day he and Lorna set out for the West. Now he knew that nothing about it would ever be the same, and the sorrow that pervaded his spirit was caused as much by the inevitability of change as it was by Alex's death.

"I wish . . ." he murmured miserably to himself as he turned around and retraced his steps back home. "I wish I had been able to make peace with him before it was too late."


A month later, Lorna turned twenty-six, and Dos presented her with a jaunty, two-seater Oldsmobile. That night, with Lorna driving erratically but courageously, they set off in the noisy, sputtering machine for Pandora's.

"How do I stop?" Lorna screamed as they neared the saloon.

Crowds on the sidewalk cheered their approach, and a frightened horse whinnied and dragged its buggy in front of them. Dos paled, but Lorna yanked on the steering stick and missed the buggy by inches.

"The brake!" he shouted.

"Where? How?"

They shot past Pandora's, delighting the crowd as Lorna steered the contraption in a dizzying circle and headed back the other way.

"Dos!" she hollered. "Help me!"

"Turn the damn thing off!" he yelled back.

"How? Show me!"

But it was too late. Scattering the crowd in front of Pandora's, they bounded over the curb, crossed the sidewalk, and barrelled through the doors, raising a hue and cry among the startled customers.

The automobile chugged through the saloon, sending people fleeing from its path, and collided head-on with the raised stage where Nola Winn and her all-girl orchestra were finishing a number. The car backfired loudly, expelling a cloud of blue smoke, then died.

The unflappable Nola Winn raised her right hand and led her girls in a fanfare. "Ladies and gentlemen! I present Mr. and Mrs. Joel Rivers!"

Dos and Lorna, dazed but unharmed, looked at each other and, with the cheers of the exuberant crowd ringing in their ears, threw back their heads and howled with laughter. Even Malloy was amused and ordered a round on the house; and Dos and Lorna spent the rest of the evening grandly holding court from the seat of their car.

But the next day, determined that Dos should bear the full cost of damages, Malloy called at the house on Green St. Lorna was there alone, but when she informed Malloy that Dos was out, he insisted on coming in anyway.

He was a thin, saturnine man with sallow skin and lank black hair and lips only too ready to curl into a sardonic smile.

"Well, you two were quite the show last night," he said, helping himself to a shot of whiskey and taking a seat in the parlor.

His expression told Lorna that his initial amusement had evaporated.

"I hope we didn't wreck the place too badly."

"More than I'd care to pay for," he said. Then

reaching into his coat pocket, he said, "Here's a list of items damaged. Will Joel be back soon, or should I leave it with you?"

"He's off having the automobile repaired. I don't know when to expect him."

Malloy's heavy lids veiled the look in his eyes, but Lorna realized her mistake. "I have to go out myself. So, if you'll just leave your list on the table, I'll see that—"

Malloy was out of his chair and beside her in an instant. "Lorna! Give in! Can't you see how much I want you?"

She was unafraid, but her face was stony. "My husband would kill you if he heard you say that."

"He's not your husband. I know the whole story."

"It doesn't take a few words from a preacher to make a marriage."

"No," he said slowly. "But it would only take a few words from me in the appropriate place to bring the whole charade to an end."

"What do I care if people know we're not properly married? I've never put much store by what others think or say."

"I'm not talking about your marriage . . . or the lack of it. I'm referring to your former career—to the banks you and your so-called husband robbed."

"You're talking blackmail, Malloy," Lorna said defiantly.

He shrugged. "I believe that is the correct term."

"It'll get you nowhere."

"It may get you and Joel in prison."

"Go to hell, Malloy!"

The smile dropped from his face, and his lips twisted with anger. "No woman ever said that to me before."

256

"Then I'm glad to be the first . . . and I'll say it again. Get out of here and go straight to hell!"

"You'll regret this, Lorna," he whispered menacingly. Then shoving past her, he stormed from the house.

Lorna watched through the lace curtains as he bounded into his buggy and whipped his nag into motion. As he clattered off down the street, heading for town, a sudden chill of fear raced through her.

She had handled him badly, and the last look on his face told her he would make good his words. He was bound to cause trouble . . . after all, with Dos out of the way, he stood to gain everything.

She let the curtain fall back into place and paced the floor, thinking: Dos! Hurry home! We've got to make plans!

But Dos was occupying his usual booth at Tadich Grill, enjoying a plate of fried clams and a schooner of beer. It was there, half an hour later, that Martin Hale, a reporter for the paper, caught up with him. They were old friends, having spent countless nights prowling the saloons of North Beach together, and Dos had standing orders at Pandora's that Martin was never to be handed a bill.

Now Martin, breathless from an uphill run from Portsmouth Plaza, slid onto the bench in Dos's booth and faced him. "Joel, you're in trouble! Lorna, too! I've just come from the courthouse. Malloy is over there talking his head off, claiming you're the Wolf who was robbing banks around here a while back. Says he knows it for sure. They're issuing a warrant right now."

Dos stayed calm. "Do I have time to finish my beer?"

"You don't even have time to pay the check. Go on, get out of here quick! I'll take care of it."

Dos rose and extended his hand to Martin. "Thanks, friend. We probably won't meet again. And that goddamned Malloy'll start making you pick up your chits at Pandora's."

Martin smiled ruefully.

Dos leaned close, speaking softly. "It's true, you know. I am the Wolf . . . and Lorna, too. Now, when you write the story for the paper, put in a line that says I wasn't such a bad guy after all."

Martin watched him hurry through the restaurant and head out into the street.

When the police arrived at the house on Green St., they found it unlocked but deserted. And on the door, in Dos's handwriting, was a note that said,

"Missed us!

the Wolf Pack."

# 17

Pascal Chareau let himself into the elegant town-house in the Place de Furstemberg, a short distance from the church of Saint-Germain-des-Prés. In his arms were a bouquet of yellow roses and a ribbon-tied box of dark chocolates.

"Is that you, Pascal?"

"Yes, Maggie. I'm sorry I'm late."

Maggie swept into the foyer. At twenty-five, she had triumphantly fulfilled the long-ago prediction of Elmendorf, the photographer. She was, to many, the most striking beauty in Paris. Her mahogany hair, rich and lustrous, glinted with deep red fire; her eyes were bluer than the sky above Mont Blanc; and her extraordinary height, like her mother's, commanded every eye.

She took one look at Pascal and smiled warmly. "Oh, Pascal! I still have the flowers you brought me last time, and if I ate all the chocolates you bring through that door, I'd be bigger than Notre Dame."

"Now don't scold me for doing what I like to do," he said happily, handing her the bouquet and carrying the candy into the parlor. "It gives me pleasure, and you must humor me. After all, I'm an old man."

"You're not so old, Pascal."

He arched his eyebrows. "I'll be sixty-seven next October."

"I know . . . I know. October thirty-first. Halloween."

"Allo-een," he repeated, trying to imitate her English.

"Oh, you're impossible. You'll never learn English."

"I don't need to. Your French is perfect." He opened the chocolates and popped one into his mouth. "Allo-*wheen!*"

"*H*allow . . . *e*eeen!"

"When all the goblins come out. . . . I suppose that's an appropriate day for my birthday."

Maggie smiled sweetly and bent to kiss his cheek. "There, goblin! That's for the flowers and the chocolates."

But she thought to herself: You're no goblin . . . you're more like an elf.

Pascal was one of the tiniest men she'd ever seen. Even in his raised heels he stood no higher than her bosom, and she was sure that he didn't weigh more than a hundred pounds. His hair was totally white and sat like a wispy haze about his head. But his eyes sparkled with wit and intelligence, and his laugh was as robust as that of any cowboy Maggie had ever known.

They had met eight years before, through the good offices of Marie Dollois, and Pascal had immediately installed Maggie in the lovely townhouse she had grown to think of as home.

At the beginning of their relationship he was shy

with her, perching on the edge of the sofa as if at any moment he might jump up and run away, chattering on about his wife and four sons who, like him, were in government service though nowhere near his rank of minister, betraying his nervousness by breaking into sudden sweats that slicked his forehead and by glancing quickly away whenever she looked at him.

Maggie had fully expected him to claim her as his lover. Marie Dollois had explained it all to her beforehand, and Maggie, penniless, alone, an exile from both her family and her country, had sorrowfully consented. There seemed no other way.

But Pascal surprised her. He paid her bills, brought her presents, and visited her at least once a week. But after his initial nervousness vanished, he sat beside her and patted her hand. "My dear, I don't want a mistress. I have a wife who is as much woman as I need. But I never . . . never had a daughter. It's the tragedy of my life. Would you, please, be my daughter?"

Maggie loved him from that moment on. He called on her whenever he wasn't required at home, never arriving empty-handed, always cheerful, bringing the latest government gossip, complimenting her beauty and utterly enjoying her company.

The evenings seldom varied. They would have a glass of champagne, dine together, then Maggie would bring out the chessboard and they would play in silence until Pascal pulled out his watch and declared that it was time for him to go home.

The rest of the time was Maggie's to do with as she pleased. She had discovered a love for art, and studied the museums from top to bottom. She met the new young painters and joined them at the cafés in Montmartre. When Pascal learned of her interest, he set aside an allowance for her so she could buy their pictures,

261

and the walls of the townhouse on Place de Furstemberg were soon covered with paintings by Dégas, Renoir, Cézanne, and their colleagues.

Pascal would view them with dismay, shaking his head and lamenting. "What a waste of money, my dear! These pictures are the ugliest things I've ever seen. Still . . . if they give you pleasure . . ."

"Oh, they do, Pascal!"

"For the life of me, I don't know why."

And this evening, as he bit into another chocolate, Maggie said, "Look! I have a present for you."

Pascal's eyes lighted up.

Maggie reached behind a chair and pulled out a portrait of herself. "It's by a man named Bonnard."

His dismay and puzzlement were obvious.

Maggie laughed. "Oh, Pascal, believe me . . . one of these days you'll grow to appreciate these artists."

"Never! They don't even know how to draw. And the colors . . . horrid! Oh, bring back David, Ingres, and Delacroix!"

"You don't like my little present?"

He smiled unconvincingly. "Of course, *ma petite,* because it's of you." He squinted at the canvas. "At least, I *think* it's of you. But why couldn't he have painted it more . . . realistically?"

Maggie lowered her lids. "Once an artist painted me realistically. It was a disaster. I much prefer this."

"Then I love it, too," Pascal said. "But, of course, you know you must keep it here. I couldn't possibly take it home. My wife would be most curious."

Maggie abandoned her memories and smiled at Pascal. "I'll be most happy to keep it here. After all, this is your house, too."

The dinner bell rang. Maggie helped Pascal rise to his feet. "Tonight, Pascal, we're having your favorite."

"Oh?"

"Chili. Good old Texas chili with Mexican rice. I made it myself."

Pascal suppressed a belch. "Wonderful, *ma petite!* Who would have thought that a man reared on *pigeon à la crème d'aïl* would be so enamored of . . . chili?"

Pascal played chess very well, but Maggie was better, and he never seemed discouraged that she almost always won. In fact, he took more pleasure in her victories than she did herself.

But tonight, she committed one of her rare errors, and he had her king in check in two more moves.

"What a stupid mistake," she chided herself.

Pascal smiled benevolently, feeling almost guilty that he'd won. By way of consolation, he offered, "I have a little surprise for you, if you'd like."

Maggie looked up, forgetting the lost game. "What kind of surprise?"

Pascal shook his head mysteriously. "I don't think I should tell you now. But be ready Saturday morning, very early, and I'll come by to pick you up."

"Oh, Pascal! Don't make me wait till Saturday. Tell me now!"

But he was adamant. "No. It will be more amusing this way."

Pascal adored his "little surprises." At first they were simple pleasures—a trip to Versailles, a ride down the Seine in a *bateau-mouche,* even a bizarre visit to the sewers. Then the surprises grew more elaborate, as if there were nothing too difficult to arrange for Maggie's pleasure—a telephone for the townhouse, an all-day excursion through the countryside in a chauffeur-driven Peugeot, dinner at the top of the Eiffel Tower in the company of Gustave Eiffel himself. Even a meeting with the Prince of Wales as he toured the nightspots of Montmartre.

Pascal plopped his top hat on his head and reached for his cane. "Don't forget, Maggie. Saturday morning."

"I can't wait."

The next day, wearing a somber dress, Maggie took the yellow roses Pascal had brought her and rode across town to the Père Lachaise Cemetery. It was a duty she performed every week, regardless of the weather, no matter what else she had to do. She left her carriage and made her way down one of the chestnut-lined avenues until she reached a small stone marker, a carved cherub holding a scroll on which was chiseled

### ALEXIA CAMERON
Died at Birth
August 12, 1895

She laid the roses at the cherub's feet and stood back, eyes lowered, hands clasped. She had long since shed all the tears she had, but she was never able to visit the grave without heartache and longing for the child whom she had never nursed, the baby girl who would never grow up, the granddaughter Alex and Anne would never know they had.

Maggie had realized at the moment the child was born that something was wrong. Dr. Lanoux and the midwife had whispered excitedly and worked frantically over the infant. But she never once drew a breath, never once cried out.

They let Maggie hold the baby briefly, and Maggie saw that she was sublimely beautiful, perfect in every way, except . . .

For that short moment, Maggie tried to pretend that all was well, that the infant was merely sleeping, but then the midwife bent over her and took the child from her arms, and Maggie realized she would never hold her daughter again.

Marie Dollois, in an attempt to comfort Maggie, tried to convince her that it was better this way, that a fatherless child would have a hard time in the world. But Maggie refused to believe that. "No! No matter what, living is better than dying. And my poor little girl never even had the chance!"

Maggie remained at the grave for a few minutes more, then turned and headed back to her carriage.

Saturday morning, her telephone jangled, waking her. It was Pascal.

"You're not up . . . not dressed yet! Hurry, Maggie! I'll be by for you in half an hour."

"When you said early, you meant it, didn't you?" Maggie yawned, seeing that the sky outside her windows was still black.

Precisely thirty minutes later, Pascal's carriage rolled into the Place de Furstemberg, and Maggie flew out to meet him, gloves, hat, and coat in her arms.

"You know I need more than half an hour to dress," she fussed, climbing in beside him. She swiveled around. "Could you finish buttoning me up?"

Pascal chuckled and poked the tiny buttons through their loops while Maggie pinned her hat onto her head and pulled her red kid gloves over her hands. "Now, help me into my coat. There! Oouf! What a lot of trouble it is being a woman! One of these days they're going to make things easy for us, a dress all of one piece that you can step into and be done with it. No corsets! Maybe then I'll be able to get ready on time!"

"I doubt that you'll be able to manage it even then,

265

Maggie. It doesn't matter, anyway. Your tardiness is one of your charms."

"I'm glad you're patient, Pascal. Now tell me! What is the little surprise this time?"

"You're going on a trip . . . a trip like you've never taken before. It's utterly unique. You'll see."

Beyond that, he would tell her no more. The carriage rolled through the early morning traffic and headed for the countryside north of Paris. From time to time, Pascal would pop his head out of the window and check the sky.

"Hmm," he said with satisfaction. "Beautiful weather, lovely day for such a trip."

Maggie was bursting with curiosity, but the more she begged Pascal to end the mystery, the more smug and adamantly silent he became.

At last they left the city behind and reached an area of gently rolling, grassy fields. Maggie felt the carriage slow and heard the driver call to Pascal that they had arrived.

Pascal climbed out first, then helped Maggie down. She looked around and saw a group of men standing around what appeared to be a huge red and yellow tarpaulin tangled with ropes lying on the ground.

"What in the world . . . ?" she muttered. But Pascal had raised his hand and shouted, "Bryan! We've arrived!"

One of the men broke from the group and strode toward them across the field. "Hallo, Pascal!" he shouted back. "It's a perfect day for it, isn't it?"

Maggie studied the man as he approached. He had chucked his coat, and she could see that he was built like the statues of Greek athletes she had seen in the Louvre. His dark, curly hair was closely cropped, and as he came closer she saw that his features were just as classically chiseled, like the marble busts of young Roman noblemen she had always admired.

But he was English, for though he had called to Pascal in French, she had detected the accent.

At last he reached them, and Pascal made the introductions. "Maggie Cameron, may I present Bryan Carrington?"

Bryan bowed, brushing her hand with his lips, and said, "I'm very pleased to meet you."

His voice was rich and melodious, and when he straightened, Maggie saw that he was smiling warmly.

"We shall be ready to go soon," he added.

"Pascal has been so mysterious," Maggie said. "Where on earth are we going?"

Bryan laughed. "Nowhere on earth, Maggie. We're going up there!" He tilted back his head and raised his hands to the sky.

"It's a balloon, Maggie," Pascal explained, bursting with pleasure and pointing excitedly to the object in the field. "I've arranged with Bryan to take you on a trip through the air in that magnificent balloon."

Maggie gasped. She wasn't at all sure she wanted to fly. It seemed terribly dangerous and utterly unnatural, but she swallowed her trepidation. Pascal was far too delighted with his "little surprise" for her to dare disappoint him. "How marvelous," she managed to say, hoping she sounded appropriately enthusiastic.

They walked into the field where the balloon was beginning to fill, its colorful silk coming to life, billowing, rising like a wakened giant, freeing itself from the earth, stretching for the sky. It was an awesome sight, and Maggie stared open-mouthed as the bright fabric inflated and pressed against the webbing that held it captive.

Bryan left their side to supervise the final preparations. At last, when the balloon was full and floating majestically, straining impatiently at the tether ropes, Bryan returned. "We're ready." He held out his hand to help Maggie into the basket.

"Are you sure this is sturdy?" she asked weakly, feeling of the thin wicker.

"Absolutely," Bryan assured her. He reached out and took two heavy coats from one of his assistants. "It will be cold up there."

Maggie was already shivering.

"All right, then," Bryan called. "Set us loose."

"Pascal!" Maggie cried. "Aren't you going, too?"

"There's no room for me," he shouted back. "I'll follow you in my carriage. *Bon voyage!*"

The balloon gave a little bounce, then rose like a soap bubble. As the ground dropped away, Maggie felt a sinking sensation in her stomach and closed her eyes quickly. "Oh, my!" she exclaimed. "I don't want to do this! Let me out, please!"

Bryan laughed softly. "Don't be afraid, Maggie. I'll take care of you. I've done this a hundred times before. Now open your eyes and take a look around. It's a sight most people have never seen."

Maggie gripped the rim of the gently swaying basket and forced herself to peep through one eye. "I don't see anything but sky!"

"Look down, Maggie! Look down."

She gasped and opened her eyes wide. They were passing over a farm—a miniature farm with a tiny stone house, playtoy cows, little white specks that looked like chickens, and a magically small farmer who waved his pitchfork in greeting. Then a minuscule spotted dog raced out into the yard and barked.

Maggie laughed out loud. "I can hear it! I thought it would be totally quiet up here!"

Suddenly she loved flying. She turned to Bryan and said, "It's wonderful! It's marvelous! How free we are!"

The balloon rose higher, and as the panorama of Paris appeared before them, Maggie couldn't contain her enchantment. She picked out the landmarks, the Eiffel Tower, the Arc de Triomphe, the not-yet-completed Basilica of the Sacred Heart on Montmartre hill, and of course, the crescent-shaped Seine that divided the city.

The air grew chilly as they climbed still farther above the earth, and Bryan draped a heavy coat over her shoulders; then, pointing to a road below, he showed her Pascal's carriage keeping pace with the balloon.

They sailed lazily over the Bois de Boulogne, over the Longchamp racecourse and Auteuil. The Eiffel tower passed off to the left and far below. They floated above the Invalides and hung for a moment over the Tuileries Gardens before a gentle cross-wind nudged them back across the Seine.

"Oh, look, Bryan!" Maggie cried excitedly. "I see the Place de Furstemberg where I live. Oh, it's so little!"

Her elation pleased Bryan immensely, and her beauty excited him. Had he not told Pascal to meet them in the Bois de Vincennes, he would have kept the balloon up for hours just for the opportunity of watching Maggie, of sharing her joy and being near her. He couldn't remember when he'd seen a more beautiful woman, and he was captivated by her freshness and spontaneity.

"We're free as birds!" Maggie shouted to the wind. "Soaring like eagles!"

But eagles have to come back to earth. As Notre Dame slipped by on their left, Bryan began releasing hydrogen.

"Oh, this is the most thrilling thing I've ever done," Maggie said breathlessly. "I hate for it to be over!"

"We can do it again . . . anytime. Just let me know."

He smiled warmly and covered her hand with his. Maggie looked up at him, her eyes sparkling, and she realized that the butterflies in her stomach had nothing to do with their swaying descent.

He was so utterly handsome, so open and friendly, and seemed as uncomplicated as his wide, smooth brow would suggest. She smiled back, then broke into laughter, wondering: Was it the altitude that made her feel so giddy? Then Bryan laughed, too, boyishly, exuberantly.

Notre Dame slipped by on their left; then they crossed the Seine again, settling slowly toward the Bois de Vincenne as Pascal's carriage rolled through the Porte de Reuilly.

The basket seemed to graze the treetops, then landed with a bump in a clearing near the bank of Lac Daumesnil.

As the great balloon bobbled and collapsed behind them, Pascal came hurrying across the meadow.

Maggie shouted from the basket, "Pascal! You must do it sometime! You must! It's the most amazing sight you'll ever see. I'll never be able to think of the earth in the same old way!"

Pascal was wreathed in smiles. "You enjoyed it?"

"I loved it!" she cried, giving him a kiss on the forehead. "Oh, Pascal! Thanks for my little surprise!"

He sighed with feigned anxiety. "I'm afraid I've outdone myself this time. What shall I give you next? A voyage to the bottom of the sea?"

Maggie laughed. "No . . . just let me go back up in that balloon again one day."

"It shall be done."

Maggie turned to Bryan. "Thank you for the most exhilarating voyage of my life. I'll never forget it!"

During their carriage ride home, Maggie was too excited to talk of anything other than the balloon trip, but later, as she and Pascal lunched, she asked, "Who is Bryan Carrington, anyway? I was so busy looking at the sights I hardly said a word to him."

"His father is Lord Carrington, the London banker. We've been friends for years. I hunt on his estate when I'm in England and show him the nightlife when he's in Paris. Bryan is something of a blade, I should say . . . not that there's anything wrong with that when you're young and rich. I was one in my time, believe it or not. But Bryan has the reputation of being a bit of a daredevil as well. You've seen his prowess with airships, and this year he drove an automobile at more than a hundred kilometers per hour. . . ."

"My word!"

". . . and when he was eighteen, he swam the English Channel. Lord Carrington and I were on the sands of Calais with a bottle of Dom Pérignon to greet him. However, I imagine that when the time comes to assume his father's title, the boy will settle down. After all, he'll be in charge of one of the wealthiest banks in the world."

"He sounds a bit like my brother, Dos," Maggie said, ". . . without the badness."

"Oh, no. There's nothing bad at all about Bryan. All in all, a charming man."

Yes, charming! Maggie thought. Oh, Pascal, do you realize what you've done? I like Bryan Carrington very much. I hope he liked me . . . and I hope I see him again soon.

She felt a twinge of guilt in Pascal's presence and wondered what he would say if she opened her heart to

271

him. She watched him as he filled their glasses once again and could see how contented he was in her company.

No, she couldn't say anything that might disturb his happiness. He had been far too good to her and asked for so little in return. The least she could do was to pledge him her loyalty.

But despite Maggie's pledge, she couldn't erase Bryan Carrington from her mind. That same month they met again by chance at the Jockey Club, and when he asked if he might call on her, she couldn't help saying yes. Thereafter, he visited frequently at the Place de Furstemberg. And soon, on nights when Pascal stayed at home with his family, Maggie and Bryan were meeting regularly for dinner.

Maggie wanted him to have no illusions; so very early on, she told him all about her past, but it made no difference to him at all, and he confessed that he owned a painting by Victor Durand and liked it very much.

Then one day he surprised her by showing up at the house with the portrait Victor had painted of her.

"Oh, my God!" she whispered, a shudder shaking her body. "I don't know how you found that, but get rid of it! Burn it! I never want to see it again!"

"But it's beautiful, Maggie. Don't hold it against me, but I want to keep it for myself."

In time she grew used to the idea and no longer flinched when she went to Bryan's flat in the Faubourg St.-Honoré and saw it hanging on the wall.

Through Bryan, she met the English colony in Paris and charmed them with her open Texas ways beneath her thin French veneer.

Bryan loved her before she fell in love with him. For too long she had lived with a wariness of growing too close to a man to admit her feelings for him. Without putting it into words, she had vowed that no man would hurt her as Victor had.

But one evening, as Bryan took her home from the racecourse, he took her hand and said simply, "I understand your fears. I won't pressure you. But I'll wait."

With that statement, her barriers began to fall. She melted into his arms and let him kiss her.

He went upstairs with her. They drank champagne, then walked arm in arm to her bedroom. Maggie undressed, as nervous as a new bride, and lay down on the bed. Bryan sat beside her, tracing the curves of her body with his fingertips until she felt her skin flush as if his touch had kindled a fire within her. She locked her hands around the back of his neck and pulled him down beside her. His lips covered hers, and she felt the softness of her body contrast against his taut, hard muscles. My Greek athlete! she thought. My Roman noble!

She surrendered herself to her love with a sigh.


Maggie kept the affair a secret from Pascal, but she never let Bryan interfere in her relationship with the older man. She still entertained him whenever he was free to come to the Place de Furstemberg. They dined and played chess as happily as before, and Pascal continued to present her with his "little surprises"—the latest, not a trip to the bottom of the sea, but a sable coat that reached to Maggie's ankles.

Nor did Maggie abandon her trips to the Père Lachaise Cemetery. Regularly, once a week, she rode alone through Paris and laid a bouquet of flowers at the foot of the cherub.

Then, in late autumn, Bryan's father died, and Bryan

became the sixth Lord Carrington. He traveled to London for the funeral and was back at Maggie's side within a week.

"My days in Paris are over," he said. They were sitting in her parlor looking out on the little square, so lovely in the spring and summer, now almost sinister with the leafless paulownia trees standing like black skeletons in the cold autumn rain. "I have to go back to England and take over my father's business."

Maggie sat silently.

Bryan stared at her intently. "Maggie . . . will you come with me?"

She had dreaded this question. She had known it would eventually be asked and had wondered a thousand times what her answer would be. Now . . . she knew.

"No, Bryan. I can't."

He didn't realize what she was saying. "I don't mean as my mistress, Maggie, or as a lover. I mean as my wife. I want to marry you."

She nodded. "I understood that, Bryan. But I can't. At least, not now."

His heart sank. He hadn't anticipated this, couldn't comprehend her rejection. He knew she loved him, for she'd told him so many times. "Why, Maggie?"

"It's Pascal," she said quietly. "I know I can't expect you to understand this, Bryan, but I can't leave him . . . not now. He's old, you see, and in his own way, he loves me very much . . . and needs me."

"No, I don't understand," Bryan said, "and for the very same reasons . . . looked at in another way. We're young, with our whole lives ahead of us. And *we* love and need each other very much."

Maggie forced herself to remain dry-eyed, although the ache in her heart was excruciating. "That's all very true, Bryan. But still . . . I can't walk away from Pascal, and in a strange way that has nothing to do with my feelings for you, I don't want to. I had hoped that I wouldn't have to make the choice, but now that I must, I know I have to remain here with him. I owe him that, Bryan . . . and more, so much more. He has been like a father to me."

Bryan shook his head in bewilderment and pain. "But women have been leaving their fathers to go with their lovers ever since the world began."

"I realize that . . . but I can't. I simply can't. I left my real father once for a man I loved. I just can't do it again."

Bryan rose, sighing with frustration and unhappiness. He paused at the door. "Maggie, this is not an ultimatum. Don't take it that way. But I'm leaving Paris on Friday. I'll have two tickets for the train and the ferry. If you decide to come with me, you have only to show up at the Gare du Nord at noon. I'll be there."

Soon after he left, the telephone rang and Maggie answered.

"Maggie, dear," Pascal said. "I'm not feeling well this evening and don't think I should go out in the rain. Could we cancel our dinner tonight?"

"Of course, Pascal. You must take care of yourself."

"I should be well in a day or two. What would you say to lunch? Friday, perhaps? Would that suit you?"

"Of course, Pascal. Friday."

"Good. I'll call for you at noon."

Maggie replaced the receiver and buried her face in her hands.

# 18

Dos and Lorna hadn't left San Francisco empty-handed. Before they set off in their car, he cleaned out his safe, taking with him more than eight thousand dollars in cash. Knowing the Oldsmobile would give them away, Dos quickly sold it in San Jose, and they traveled by train to Salt Lake City.

By then, Lorna knew she was pregnant, but she refrained from telling Dos right away, thinking he had worries enough, not wanting to burden him further.

But because she was small and naturally thin, she couldn't keep her condition a secret for long. They were lying in bed at their hotel room, and she felt Dos place his hand gently on her belly.

"How far along are you?" he asked quietly.

"Four months." She wished she could see his expression in the darkness. "Are you angry?"

"No."

She sighed with relief. For her part, she was ecstatic. Knowing she was carrying his child had dispelled any sorrow she had felt over losing the home she had always dreamed of.

She felt him push back the covers and leave the bed, and watched his silhouette pace the floor in front of the windows.

She let him think in silence. At last, he said, "That means if we're going to leave here, we'd better do it soon, while you're still able to travel."

"Where do you want to go?"

"Anywhere but here. I hate this place."

He passed by the bed and she reached out and grabbed his hand, pulling him down beside her. "Let's go to Denver, then. I lived there before when I was a girl. It's a big town. You'll find something to do."

He buried his face in his pillow, and when he spoke he sounded tired. "A big town could be dangerous for us. There's a warrant out. They'll have pictures. Some one'll spot us eventually."

She stroked his hair. "Grow your beard back. It makes you look different . . . all wild and woolly."

"And what about you?"

"I'll stay out of the way."

"You can't hide forever."

"We can't run forever, either," she said. "Let's sleep on it. We can decide in the morning."

By noon the next day, they were on the train for Denver. But Dos was jittery. He took them off the train at Grand Junction, and they stayed there for two months until his beard was thick. The day before they were to leave for Denver, he went to the depot, bought their tickets, and came back to the hotel to Lorna.

Lorna was sitting on the bed, letting out the waist

277

of a blue worsted skirt when he came in. He looked somber and mysterious.

"What is it, Dos?"

He sat down beside her. "I've been thinking, Lorna . . . about you, me, and the baby."

She held her breath.

"I know what it's like to be a bastard son. I don't want that to happen to our child. Don't you think . . . I mean, what do you say we get married?"

Lorna dropped her sewing and hugged him tightly. "Oh, Dos! Dos! I . . ." She almost said I love you, but the words caught in her throat. "I'm so happy!"

The justice of the peace politely ignored Lorna's condition, and an hour later, with the clerk down the hall as their witness, Dos and Lorna became man and wife.

"I'm sorry about the wedding ring," Dos said as they stepped from the courthouse into the bright afternoon sunlight. "It was the best I could find in Grand Junction. When we get to Denver, I'll buy you a real one . . . one with diamonds."

"I don't need diamonds," Lorna said, holding out her hand and joyously admiring the plain gold band. "This one's good enough for me . . . and I'll wear it till the day I die."

Dos smiled and bent to kiss her. "Lorna, you're better to me than I deserve. I've made a mess of so much of my life, but it's worth it because I found you."

"I found *you*, Dos . . . if you remember correctly."

He laughed and, holding out his arm, escorted her down the steps.


In Denver, they rented a small house on the edge of town where they had a view of the mountains to the west, and Lorna settled in, waiting for the baby.

But Dos was restless and even more unhappy than he'd been in Salt Lake City. He seemed nervous and on edge, and although Lorna often persuaded him to go out alone, he would return early, and she would hear him pacing the floor late into the night like a wild animal that had just been caged.

She began to fear that he felt trapped by the marriage, and one evening about two months after they moved into the little house, when she could stand the sound of his footsteps no longer, she forced herself to ask him if this were the case.

He looked surprised, stopped his pacing, and knelt beside her chair. "No, Lorna, no. That's not it at all. I'm sorry you even thought such a thing."

"Then what is it, Dos? What's troubling you so much?"

"I'm not sure I even know myself. I think it's all this running . . . this hiding out, changing our names everywhere we go, always looking over our shoulders, never being able to settle in one place. For a while I really thought we had it made in San Francisco. We had a house, Pandora's was bringing us in a pile of money, and nobody knew who we really were—nobody except that goddamned Malloy. We could have kept it all if I hadn't gone and shot off my mouth. God, I was a cocky sonofabitch!"

Lorna stroked his hair gently.

"Now we're twelve hundred miles away from there, and I still can't walk down the street without worrying that somebody's gonna spot me, put two and two together, and figure out who I am." He paused and looked up. "It's getting to me at last, Lorna."

She pitied him and wished desperately there were

something she could do to ease his misery, but she had no answers.

He lay awake all night, and when Lorna got up in the morning, she found him sitting haggard at the kitchen table.

"I've made a decision, Lorna . . . that is, if it's all right with you."

"Tell me, Dos."

"I want to go back home."

"To Texas?"

He nodded. "To the Lantana. It's not going to be easy. We could probably hide out on the ranch forever —it's such a goddamned big place. But like I said last night, I'm sick to death of hiding. It used to seem like a game. You know—catch-me-if-you-can. But I guess I've gotten too old for games, and I know nobody's going to call out, 'Olly-olly oxen, all home free.' "

"Peter Stark will come after you."

"I know he will. He'll put me up on murder charges. But I'll just have to face that. If I can track down any of those people in the saloon that night, I might be able to make a case for self-defense."

Suddenly Lorna felt terribly afraid. "But, Dos! What if you can't? What if they hang you?"

He smiled sadly. "I've always been pretty lucky in the past. I feel like I've still got a little luck left. Maybe I ought to go ahead and use it up right now . . . before it's too late."

Lorna felt a strange foreboding—a premonition that the whole idea was wrong, that something they hadn't counted on would intervene and separate them forever. But she looked at Dos's tortured face and saw his longing for peace. "We'll do it if you really want to, Dos."

He heaved a weary sigh as if a terrible weight had been taken from his shoulders.

"When do you want to go?"

"If you think you can travel, I'd like to leave right away."

Lorna was in her eighth month, but she said, "I can travel."

Dos bought the train tickets that afternoon, and the next day, as snow began to fall, they climbed aboard and settled into their sleeping compartment.

"Ooh, it's cozy in here," Lorna said.

Dos shrugged off his overcoat. "I never want to see snow again. I never want to be cold again. It hardly ever snows on the Lantana."

The train gave a lurch and began to pull out of the depot. Dos sank back on the seat and closed his eyes. A look of contentment passed over his face, replacing the worried frown he'd worn too frequently for the last several months.

He's finding peace at last, Lorna thought. Peace within himself, which is what he needed all along. And she was happy for him, although she couldn't shake off her own nagging feeling of unease. She was certain that he would go to prison for a while—Peter Stark would see to that—and she didn't know how she would be able to live without him. Since fleeing Joelsboro, they had never spent even one night apart, and the thought of separation sent a dagger of pain through her heart.

She struggled to put aside her misgivings and tried to imagine what the rest of their life together would be like. He would come back to her eventually—she had to believe that—and they would live on the Lantana. She wanted them to have a lot of babies, but hoped especially that this first one would be a boy who looked exactly like Dos.

She reached out and took his hand. "Oh, Dos! We're going to be happy again, aren't we?"

He smiled at her. "I'm already happy. I know this is the right thing to do."

Lorna hoped so.

By the time the train left the city behind, the snow had increased tremendously, and the fields were already a blanket of white.

"It looks like a blizzard," Dos observed. "It's good we got out when we did."

Lorna sat, her face to the window, and watched the growing storm outside. After a while, darkness settled over the passing countryside, and a porter strolled through the car ringing the dinner chimes.

Dos and Lorna made their way to the dining car. The train was crowded, and they had to wait a while before being seated at a table across from a husky middle-aged man with a florid Irish face and a handsome auburn mustache.

He smiled convivially and introduced himself. "I'm Alfred Beaty from Dallas."

"I'm John Williams," Dos replied, picking the name out of a hat. "And this is my wife, Laura." As he spoke, Dos thought with relief: that's the last time I'll have to lie about our names.

"What is it you do, Mr. Williams?" Beaty asked. His eyes were steady and forthright, and Lorna thought he had the look of a gregarious salesman, a drummer who had learned to make friends of strangers to alleviate the loneliness of his journeys.

"I'm in the cattle business," Dos answered.

"A rancher?"

"Yes. I have a small spread down in South Texas."

Beaty shook his head. "I'm not familiar with that part of the world."

"It's God's own country," Dos said. "You'd never see a storm like this down there."

Beaty peered out of the window, but the darkness was pervasive, and slushy wet snow streaked across the glass.

"And what do you do, Mr. Beaty?" Lorna asked.

"I'm a traveling man, ma'am."

Lorna smiled smugly. She'd figured him out right away.

"Yep, I make this ride about twice a month," Beaty went on. "Travel Kansas and Oklahoma, too. But right now I'm on my way home for Christmas. Sure will be nice . . . to get home, I mean."

"It sure will," Dos agreed.

They spent the rest of the meal exchanging small talk, and when Dos and Lorna rose to return to their compartment, Beaty was still sipping his after-dinner coffee.

"Nosy sort," Dos said as they left the dining car.

"I thought he was nice. He's just lonesome—poor man, away from his family all the time."

Dos shook his head. "Something about him doesn't sit quite right. I mean, asking me right away what I did for a living."

"Oh, everybody does that, Dos. You're just jittery. Don't get yourself all worked up. We'll be home before you know it."

They settled back in their compartment and Dos read the news while Lorna sat beside the window and stared at the blizzard that still raged outside the train.

The next morning, she left the compartment to go to the ladies' lounge. On her way back she ran into Beaty in the corridor.

"Good morning, Mrs. uh-uh . . . I'm sorry, I have a terrible way with names."

Lorna was suddenly ruffled. What *had* Dos told him?

283

She hesitated a second, thought she remembered, and said, "Wilson . . . Mrs. Wilson."

"Of course," Beaty smiled. "Wilson. Well, Mrs. Wilson, we'll be pulling into Boise City soon. According to the conductor we're running late because of the snow."

"It is terrible, isn't it?" Lorna said, eager to get away, Dos's suspicions beginning to affect her own opinion of Beaty.

When she returned to the compartment, she closed the door behind her and asked, "Dos! What did you tell Mr. Beaty our name was?"

Dos looked up at her, a glint of alarm in his eyes. "Why?"

"Was it Wilson?"

"I told him Williams."

"Damn! I just saw him again and told him Wilson. It probably doesn't mean anything, but I thought he looked at me strangely."

"That settles it, Lorna. I've been suspicious of Beaty all along. I've got a sneaky feeling he's a railroad inspector, and I think he's on to us. We've got to get off this train."

"We're coming to Boise City soon."

"We'll leave then."

Lorna was quiet for a moment; then she said softly, "Dos, that means we'll be on the run again. I thought we were through with all that. I thought you were sick and tired of it. What's the difference whether we get caught now or later? Let's turn ourselves in to Mr. Beaty and be done with it."

"Don't you understand, Lorna? If Beaty picks us up, it'll be for robbery in California. That means you as well as me. If we can only make it across the Texas border, I'll surrender myself for killing Klaus in Joelsboro. You'll be home free and clear. We've got to do it that way—for your sake . . . and for the baby's."

Lorna saw at last what Dos's plan was. She embraced him gently, kissed him on the lips, and without thinking murmured, "Oh, Dos! Now I see why you're doing all this. Whatever happens, remember that I love you. I've loved you from the moment I first laid eyes on you . . . and I always will!"

The train had slowed and was creeping through the driving snow into the depot at Boise City. Through their window, they saw Beaty, bundled in his overcoat, jump from the still moving train and hurry across the platform to the telegraph office.

"When do we leave?" Lorna asked.

"Now's as good a time as any."

They abandoned their compartment and made their way toward the front of the train, as far from the telegraph office as they could go. When they reached the first car, a porter warned them: "Mighty cold out there, folks."

"My wife needs a little fresh air," Dos muttered nonchalantly, leading Lorna past the man.

They stepped onto the platform, and Dos's spirits soared. We've made it!

But Beaty's voice cut through the howling wind. "Hold it right there! Hands up! I've got you covered!"

Dos felt he was going to be sick. Lorna sensed him sag against her and slipped her arm quickly around his waist. They turned.

"Hands up, I said! That means you, too, ma'am!"

Beaty dominated the other end of the platform, his heavy coat flapping wildly in the wind, his Colt .32 leveled at them.

"The jig's up, Rivers! You and the little lady aren't going anywhere . . . except back to California."

"Beaty," Dos called, "I'll go with you. But let my wife travel on to Texas."

Beaty was grim-faced. "I've got orders to take you both in. Now, let's go." He waved his revolver toward the depot, and Dos and Lorna obeyed.

The waiting room was empty except for the three of them.

"Sit over there on that bench where I can keep an eye on you."

Outside, the whistle blared and the train chugged away from the depot.

"We almost made it," Dos murmured. "At least we tried."

Beaty stood against the wall, his Colt cocked, his gaze never leaving them. "There's a northbound coming through in half an hour. I telegraphed ahead for it to stop and pick us up."

"How did you figure us out?" Dos asked, his face white and haggard.

"We've had your pictures for some time. I've got to admit, your beard threw me . . . but I recognized your wife right away. At least, I was pretty sure. Then when she couldn't remember the name you told me, I knew I was right."

Lorna shook her head sorrowfully. "It's all my fault."

"No . . . it's mine," Dos said. "And it started a long time ago before I even met you. I guess I was always heading for something like this. Only I was too stupid to see."

The hands of the big clock on the depot wall moved slowly, and after what seemed like an eternity, they heard the whistle of the northbound train.

"All right, I don't want any funny stuff," Beaty warned. "I've got my weapon on you. We're going to go aboard and take our seats, and you're going to do exactly as I say."

The train stopped in Boise City for less than a minute, just time enough to pick up the trio, and with a shrill cry of the whistle, began to creep away from the depot.

Suddenly Lorna cried out and clutched her belly. "Oh, God! The baby! Joel! The baby's coming! Help me, Joel!"

Dos noticed—as Beaty could not have—that she called him Joel. And he saw the secret look in her eye. Beaty's jaw dropped. He suspected a trick, but Lorna's face contorted terribly and she screamed in pain.

"Do something!" Dos shouted at Beaty.

"Joel! Joel! Help me!"

"She's going to have the baby right here!" Dos yelled.

Beaty was on his feet. "Take her into the ladies' lounge. But remember . . . I'm right behind you."

With Lorna bent almost double, her hands holding her swollen belly, Dos half-carried, half-pushed her toward the rear of the car. A few curious passengers looked up from their seats.

Lorna whimpered, then cried out again.

The train was still crawling through town, but accelerating slowly. Dos knew they had to act quickly if they were going to succeed at all. The three of them were crowded into the narrow corridor. Suddenly Lorna stumbled and fell to her knees. Dos dropped down beside her, but not before he saw the position of Beaty's revolver.

He made a move as if he were reaching for Lorna, then, with the grace of a cat, he swiveled and slammed his big fist against Beaty's wrist. The Colt flew from the lawman's grip and skittered along the corridor. A woman shrieked behind them and cowered in her seat.

With surprising agility, Lorna sprang to her feet and ran for the gun. Beaty bellowed with rage and grappled with Dos. He was strong for a man his age and had nearly pinned Dos to the floor when Lorna's voice, cold as ice, brought the struggle to an end. "Let him go, you sonofabitch, or I'll blow your brains out."

Beaty saw the barrel pointed at his head. He threw his hands above his shoulders and scuttled backwards. Dos flew to Lorna's side and flung open the door. The train was clicking along the track, picking up speed. The five-foot snow drifts were beginning to pass in a blur.

Lorna looked out, her eyes filled with fright. "We've got to jump, Dos! It's now or never!"

Dos fired the Colt at the floor to keep Beaty at bay, and with the screams of the other passengers ringing in his ears, wrapped his arms around Lorna and threw themselves from the train.

The drifts cushioned their fall, but Lorna was wrenched from Dos's embrace. They rolled over and over with arms and legs flailing like limp rag dolls. Dos came to rest against the cold track, but Lorna had tumbled over the top of the drift and lay in the snow-carpeted field on the other side.

The train sped on for another minute, but as Dos picked himself up, he heard the squeal of its wheels as the emergency brake was pulled.

He clambered over the drift and helped Lorna to her feet. "Are you all right?"

She nodded jerkily and put her arm around Dos's waist for support.

"We've got to move! They're stopping the train. They'll be all over the place looking for us!"

They trudged through knee-deep snow, trying to

reach a stand of brush in the distance. The wind howled from the north, covering their footprints as quickly as they made them. Dos heard shouts behind him, but when he turned to look he could see nothing through the thick blowing veil of flakes swirling from the lowering clouds.

They reached the brush and kept moving, not daring to stop and rest although both were on the verge of exhaustion. Then Lorna fell and was unable to rise. Dos picked her up in his arms and pressed forward, staggering deeper into the brush. The wind screamed in his ears, and his breath froze on his beard.

At last, they came to a fence, and following it arrived at a little corral, nearly buried beneath the snow. But Dos spotted a dilapidated shack and headed for it. The door was wired shut, but he yanked it open, and they stumbled inside, out of the howling blizzard.

"This'll have to do," he muttered. "It's as safe as we can get. We'll have to hole up here till the storm blows over."

Lorna had slumped against the wall and was cradling her head in her crossed arms. Dos knelt beside her. "Lorna, are you all right?"

When she looked up at him, he knew she wasn't.

"Dos . . . Dos . . ." she whispered weakly. Her lips were white and her dark eyes were wide with fear. "I think I hurt myself . . . hurt myself bad!"

He saw her slip her hand beneath her dress, and when she pulled it back, it glistened with blood.

"Oh, my God!"

"The baby's coming," she breathed, her voice trembling. "This time it's real. And I hurt so bad, Dos!"

The shack had once been a tack house but had been stripped of all its gear except for a few rusty bits and a couple of strands of rotten rope. Dos stripped off his coat and spread it on the buckled floor for Lorna to lie on. But when he picked her up to move her, she screamed, and he saw bright drops of blood spatter between her feet.

Handling her gently, he stretched her out on the coat and pushed her skirt up around her waist. Her underclothing was soaked crimson. He cut it away with his knife and flung it to the side.

Lorna pressed her fists to her mouth and screamed again. Dos tried to wipe her thighs clean, but the flow of blood kept coming, more copiously than ever.

"Dos, I can't stand it!" she cried. "I think I'm going to die!"

"No, Lorna! No, you're not! It's just the baby! It'll be over in a minute!"

But he wondered how much blood she could lose and remain alive. The crown of the baby's head had appeared, and he knew the moment was at hand.

He had never witnessed a human birth, but now he thanked God that he'd lived around animals all his life, because he knew he would be able to handle it.

Lorna writhed on the coat and screamed out from time to time, but each cry was weaker than the last.

Then suddenly the baby's head was free, then its narrow shoulders, and a few seconds later, Dos held it in his hands. He pulled out his shirttail and wiped the sticky blood from its face. The baby seemed to gasp; its little chest heaved, and the shack filled with the sound of its first cry.

Dos cut the cord and tied it with a strip torn from Lorna's petticoat. "It's over, Lorna. You've done it. We've got a baby boy!"

She lay quite still, her face white, her eyes glazed. But he heard her breathe softly and saw her lips form a feeble smile.

"Take him, Lorna. Hold him next to you. Keep him warm," Dos said gently, laying the baby against her breast. Her arms enfolded the infant, and she whispered, "My baby . . . my baby."

Dos saw that she was bleeding worse than before. Taking his knife he cut away her petticoat and pressed it between her legs.

"Am I still losing blood?"

"Not as much as before," Dos lied. "Don't worry. Everything will be all right."

He stretched out beside her, the baby lying in the cradle formed by their touching bodies.

"He's beautiful, isn't he, Dos?"

Dos tried to look at the baby, but hot tears blurred his vision.

Suddenly Lorna cried out again. "Oh, Dos! The pain! It's still there!"

He sat up and saw that the petticoat was saturated with blood and knew she was dying. He was helpless to save her. Strangely, a great calm came over him or perhaps it was numbness—from the realization that Lorna was lost to him. He lay back down beside her, his arm over the baby to keep him warm, the palm of his hand caressing Lorna's cheek.

"It's all going to be all right, Lorna. There's nothing to worry about. You're doing just fine."

"But the pain . . . !"

"Shh . . . it'll go away in a minute or two. Just wait. You'll see."

They lay quietly for a moment, the silence broken by the newborn child's soft whimpering. Then Lorna said, "You're right, Dos. It is going away. I don't feel it near as bad now."

Dos had to bite his lip to keep from crying out. "You see . . . you see. Everything's going to turn out fine."

"I'm sleepy, Dos."

"Then sleep . . . I'll watch over you and the baby."

She raised her lids and looked at him. "Don't ever shave your beard again, Dos. It . . . it makes you look so . . ." Her voice was growing faint.

"I'll keep it forever, Lorna," he whispered. "For you."

"Dos?"

"What?"

It took her a moment to gather the strength to speak again. "Will you tell him that his mama got to see him? That she got to hold him? And that she thought he was the most beautiful baby in the world?"

"Hush, Lorna . . . hush! Don't talk like that!"

"I'm dying, Dos. I can feel it. . . ."

*"No!"* he bellowed, tilting his head toward the ceiling. "You can't die! You can't leave me! How am I going to live without you? Lorna! Lorna!"

She seemed to drift off to sleep.

"Lorna! Don't leave me! I need you! I love you!"

She heard the words as an echo that resounded over and over again in her mind. I love you . . . I love you . . . I love you. . . .

# 19

Through her brass army telescope aimed from one of the turret windows, Anne spotted the man with a bundle in his arms headed for the house. He looked like a hobo with a grizzly beard and a filthy greatcoat, and the nag he was riding seemed about to drop from exhaustion.

She knew it wasn't one of her men, and it puzzled her how the stranger had managed to get past the gate guard.

She hurried down the spiral stairs, took a loaded double-barreled shotgun from a case in the foyer, and threw open the front doors.

There was a chill in the air, the remains of last week's norther, but the sun was bright and there was no wind.

"Who are you and what do you want?" Anne shouted to the rider.

He made no attempt to answer, but continued on his plodding horse toward the house.

"What's your business on my place? Stop right there and identify yourself, or you'll get a chestful of buckshot."

The man reined his horse and muttered something.

"Speak up, mister! I don't hear as well as I used to."

She squinted through the glaring sunlight. The man's face was shaded by his hat, but something about the way he sat his horse stirred a memory within her.

"Do I know you?" she called out.

To her surprise, she heard the sudden sound of a baby's cry, and the man glanced down at the bundle in his arm.

She felt a tingle up her spine, and the shotgun trembled in her hand.

Then the man lifted his head and looked at her. "I'm home, Ma."

Anne recognized the voice instantly, but her face paled with disbelief.

"Put the gun away, Ma . . . unless you aim to use it."

Anne raised it to the sky and fired off both barrels. Then flinging the gun aside, she ran, arms outstretched, tears of joy streaming down her cheeks, toward her son.

Dos swung down from his horse just as Anne reached him. Anne threw herself against him and hugged him, weeping too hard to speak.

"Careful, Ma," Dos said, his voice shaking with emotion. "That's my son you're about to smother . . . your grandson."

"Oh, my God! I can't believe it! This can't be true! It's not real . . . it's not happening!" Her hands reached up and she touched Dos's face with trembling fingers. "It's you, Dos! It *is* you!"

He tried to smile, but broke into sobs instead. "Oh,

Ma! Will you have me back? Can you ever forgive me?"

"Oh, Dos! You *know* I'll have you back! I was so afraid all these years I'd get you back in a pine box . . . *if* I ever got you back at all! My son . . . my son, it's so good to have you home!"

The baby was squalling between them.

Dos lifted the blanket from the infant's face. "You're going to have to help me raise him. He's a little dogie. His . . . his mama died."

Anne took the child in her arms, blinking back tears so she could study him. "He looks just like you, Dos."

"That's what his mama wanted."


Dos and Anne sat up late into the night trying to bridge the ten years they'd been apart. Their conversation caused more tears than joy. The news of Carlos's death affected Dos badly, and the story Anne pieced together about Maggie left him full of sorrow and pity, but he couldn't feel the rancor for his sister that Anne did. He wished he could write to her, but when he asked where Maggie lived, Anne told him she had no idea—nor did she seem to care.

The next morning they had breakfast together, and Anne fed the baby from a nursing bottle.

"What shall we call your grandson?" Dos asked.

"We could call him after you."

"I'd rather not. I'd like to see him have a fresh start."

Anne understood. "But it would be nice to give him a name that has some continuity . . . that means something to the family."

Dos thought for a moment, then said, "Let's call him Trevor."

Anne smiled. "Trevor . . . that sounds nice. And, of course, I like it." She bent and kissed the baby, her heart full of love for him, the first of a new generation, the promise that their line would abide. "Trevor Cameron . . . *Mister* Trevor Cameron of the Lantana!"

Later, she and Dos rode out in her buggy to the graveyard. It was Christmas Eve, but a southeast wind off the Gulf blew warmly over the dry brown grass, and the sky was clear and deep blue.

Anne looked out over the markers. "I was twelve when we buried Mama here. This was hard country back then—grass, sky, and wild cows for as far as the eye could see. Her grave seemed so lonely . . . then Papa joined her here. Then those six poor maids who died when the hacienda burned . . ." Her voice trailed off, but her eyes moved from stone to stone, reading off the other names, Sofia, Ramiro Rivas, Carlos . . . and Alex.

She sighed. "It's getting crowded here now. Do you reckon there'll be room for me?"

"No time soon, I hope," Dos said somberly.

Anne turned, having drunk more than her fill of remembered grief. "Let's go home, Dos, and leave these good people in peace. After all, we're still part of the living . . . and we've got Trevor to take care of."

"That's a job you'll have to handle on your own for a while, Ma," Dos said.

Anne's eyes searched her son's face. She knew what he meant. "When do you aim to do it?"

"I thought I'd ride into Joelsboro this afternoon."

Anne bit her bottom lip to keep it from trembling. "So soon? Can't you wait a while?"

"Peter Stark'll find out I'm back and come looking for me. I think it'll be easier if I turn myself in."

Anne knew he was right, but her heart ached at the thought of losing him again.

"I'm tired of running . . . tired of hiding. All I want to do now is get this over with."

Anne nodded silently. Dos helped her onto the buggy and climbed up beside her. He slapped the reins and they headed down the road toward the big house.

"Maybe I'll get lucky," he said, forcing a note of brightness into his voice. "Maybe they'll only give me a couple of years. That'll pass in no time."

"However long it is, Dos, just remember this . . . Trev and I'll be here waiting when you come back home again."

# 1907

# 20

From time to time, when passing a *tabac* that sold foreign newspapers, Maggie would pick up a copy of the London *Times* and, on occasion, would come across mention of Bryan Carrington.

In 1904, the paper reported that he gave his maiden speech in the House of Lords. The following year, his thoroughbreds won a number of races at Ascot; the Court Circular noted that the King and Queen spent a hunting weekend in Sussex at Carrington Manor; and once, Maggie read that Bryan had been fined five pounds for driving a motor car at excessive speed along the Brighton Road.

In early 1907, Pascal's health began to fail, and from the beginning of spring to the middle of summer, he managed to visit Maggie only twice at the Place de Furstemberg. But he telephoned almost every day, and

Maggie could tell by the sound of his steadily weakening voice that his condition was growing worse. Then, toward the end of July, a week passed when the telephone didn't ring at all.

Maggie waited, fraught with worry, wishing she could go to Pascal's side but realizing that such a brazen act would outrage his family.

Then, one weekday afternoon, Marie Dollois arrived at Maggie's townhouse.

"Marie!" Maggie said, welcoming her into her salon. "It's been so long. What brings you here?"

Marie reached out and gently patted Maggie's arm. "My dear, I wish our reunion could be happier, but I'm afraid I bring bad news."

"Pascal?"

Marie Dollois nodded. "I've been informed that he passed away peacefully in the middle of the night."

Maggie's eyes misted with sorrow, but she took the news calmly, having expected it for some time. Still, it was a blow, and she sank onto the sofa hugging herself as if she had suddenly taken a chill. "He was so good to me, Marie."

"I know, my dear."

"I'm going to miss him."

"*Hélas,* I'm afraid that, too, is true." Marie's tone carried more meaning than her words, and Maggie looked up inquiringly.

"Despite your sorrow, *chérie,*" Marie went on, "you must face up to . . . to certain practical matters. Pascal was your benefactor. Now that he is gone, you will have no means to maintain your way in the world."

"Oh, Marie, I can't think of such things at a time like this!"

"But you must!"

"Not now, Marie! Next week, perhaps."

Marie Dollois smiled kindly. "I understand, *chérie*. I sympathize with you. However . . . if you wish, I can take the matter off your shoulders. Just as I brought you and Pascal together, I could arrange a meeting between you and another man of means who, I am sure, would be amenable to keeping you here in your lovely home. It would be a pity to leave all this for something . . . less."

"Perhaps Pascal provided for me. He loved me like a daughter. Maybe he left a legacy in my behalf."

"Oh, my dear, don't even dare hope for such a thing! It's simply not done. And if it were, don't for a moment think that Pascal's family would let you receive as much as a *sou*." She rose to leave and made her way to the door. "No . . . I'm afraid you find yourself penniless at the moment. If you decide to set out on your own, let me wish you the best of good fortune. However, if you would like me to take matters in hand, I would be most pleased to do so."

"Marie, it's just that I'm tired of this life in the demimonde. I want to be something other than a kept woman. I would like some respectability at last."

Marie arched her eyebrows in surprise. "But, my dear! You're *not* respectable! You have a past."

Maggie's shoulders sagged. Marie was right, of course, and Maggie suddenly understood that it was always going to be this way. "Please, Marie, you must excuse me. I'd like to be alone at the moment. I'll talk with you later."

"*Entendu, chérie*," Marie said, opening the door. "You know where to reach me."

Left by herself with only her thoughts, Maggie couldn't help but remember Bryan. He had wanted to marry her—had offered her the opportunity to leave the demimonde behind and take up a new life. If she had only joined him at the Gare du Nord that Friday noon four years ago, how different her life would be now—Lady Carrington, living in London, chatelaine of Carrington Manor.

But her loyalty to Pascal had come first. Her heart had always regretted the decision, but she knew she had done the right thing. Her sacrifice had meant a few more years of happiness and pleasure for Pascal, and she believed she owed her kindly benefactor at least that much.

But now that she was free to pursue her love, she realized she had no right to do so. In allowing Bryan to leave Paris without her, she had made her choice. She couldn't go running to him now—not after all these years of silence between them. How could she be sure he still loved her, still wanted her? She was all too aware of the possibility that he had given his heart to another.

She buried her face in her hands and accepted the inevitable. Tomorrow morning she would go to Marie Dollois.

Marie was delighted. "My dear, I'll find you the most generous man in Paris. I promise that. In fact, I have my eye on several already. But we haven't much time. Before too long, creditors will be gathering like wolves at your door."

Her prophecy was only too true. First there was the dressmaker politely demanding two thousand francs. Then the butcher—in less polite terms—presented his bill, and the rent on the townhouse came due at the same time the servants and the coachman expected their wages.

So, by the time Marie Dollois arranged a rendezvous between Maggie and Jerome Louvet, Maggie had no choice but to accept. They met at the *Maison* Dollois, and after sharing a glass of champagne with them, Marie discreetly withdrew.

Jerome was in his early fifties, a prosperous silk merchant whose business kept him in Paris much of the time while his family stayed behind in Toulouse.

"So, fortunately," he declared as soon as they were alone, "we shall be able to be together without encumbrance."

Maggie tried to smile, but it was the last thing in the world she felt like doing. Jerome Louvet filled her with utter revulsion. He was obese, with a heavy paunch that strained the buttons of his waistcoat. His piggish black eyes regarded her hungrily, as if she were a next meal, and his bulbous nose was purpled with a network of broken blood vessels. His teeth were badly yellowed, and Maggie noticed his fingernails were as dirty as a common laborer's. And over his pate he had arranged a few lank strands of thickly pomaded hair in a vain attempt to hide his baldness.

He helped himself to more champagne, drinking noisily and wiping his wet lips with the back of his hand.

Before Maggie could fend him off, he reached across and laid a beefy palm on her knee. *"Mon dieu,* but you're a fine-looking woman! I'm most grateful to Marie Dollois for bringing us together. I shall make it very much worth her time and trouble."

Maggie recoiled at his touch, but Jerome seemed not to notice. "Marie has explained your former situation," he went on, refilling his glass. "Rest assured that nothing need change. You may keep the house in the Place de Furstemberg—I rather like that little square—and if you will turn over your bills to me, I'll see to it that all your creditors are paid."

Maggie listened to him with growing horror. She felt

certain that Marie Dollois had lost her mind to think that Maggie would allow herself to become involved with a man like Jerome Louvet. Never! She would sooner starve!

"Monsieur Louvet," she said, rising, "I'm sorry to cut this interview short, but I have pressing errands and must be on my way."

He looked surprised, then dejected, but he did not attempt to detain her. She picked up her coat and hurried from the salon.

A moment later, Marie Dollois entered through the other door. "And where is my little protégée?"

Jerome drained his glass and said between belches, "She had to run . . . she had things to do . . . but I shall see her later."

"But she suits you?"

He opened his tiny eyes as widely as he could. "Indeed she does! Perfect . . . perfect in every way!"

Marie smiled warmly. "Well, then, *mon vieux,* there's just one additional matter to take care of. . . ."

"Ah, yes," he said expansively, reaching into his breast pocket for his wallet. "I know we agreed upon the fee, but the girl is so delightful I'm going to give you a little more—a gift of appreciation."

Marie Dollois watched him count out the banknotes. *"Monsieur,* there's nothing finer than a generous man."


Maggie hurried home and secluded herself in her bedroom. She shuddered every time she thought of Jerome's hand resting on her knee, and the idea of him in her townhouse—much less in her bed—made her want to retch.

I won't have it! I'd rather die first! If I sell some of the things Pascal gave me, I can easily pay off all my debts. Then I'll find a job. . . . there's bound to be something I can do. I'd sooner be a servant than Jerome Louvet's mistress!

Going to her dresser, she opened her jewel box and took inventory of her possessions. There was the pair of diamond ear-studs that alone would bring enough— Maggie felt certain—to pay the dressmaker, and then there was the sapphire ring and the double strand of pearls. . . .

A knock at the door interrupted her. It was her maid announcing that Jerome Louvet was waiting downstairs.

"Tell him I'm not in," Maggie said. "Send him away."

The maid left, but a moment later Maggie heard Jerome's heavy footsteps on the stairs. She jumped up from her dresser, heading for the door to turn the bolt, but Jerome was already there. His corpulent body filled the frame; he was frowning and his close-set eyes glittered like two jet beads.

"I don't understand, *ma chère*," he said.

That he dared enter her bedroom outraged Maggie. "I'm not your *chère!* I'm not your anything! Now please do me the favor of leaving."

Jerome looked bewildered for an instant, then broke into a grin, showing his yellowed teeth. "Oh, now I see! You go in for games . . . a little struggle perhaps. . . ."

"Not in the least, *monsieur*. I don't want you here, and I don't choose to have a relationship with you."

Jerome was slow, but he was not stupid, and a flash of anger brought color to his otherwise sallow face. "I don't see that you have any choice, my dear. The arrangement has already been made. I've paid Marie handsomely."

"That's your problem, *monsieur*. Take it up with her." She reached for the door and tried to close it in his face, but he pushed through and shut it behind him, tripping the bolt.

"I've come to collect what I paid for."

Maggie backed up, frightened. He was huge, and she knew she would never be able to struggle against him. He caught her by the arm and twisted it violently behind her back.

"Let me go!" she screamed.

But Jerome held her even more tightly, a low laugh rumbling in his throat. "Oh, a little fire! I like that in a woman!"

He forced Maggie to the bed and threw her against the pillows. She tried to rise, but his hand, big as a bear's paw, covered her breast and held her down. Then the other took hold of her blouse at the collar and yanked, tearing the buttons from their holes. Maggie kicked, but he had fallen on top of her, pushing her against the bed with his enormous weight, and when she tried to scream again, his greedy lips covered her mouth. Helpless to move, she felt his hand fumble between them, freeing the buttons of his trousers and pushing her skirt up around her waist. Then his knees pried her legs apart and he tried to settle between them.

Maggie was suffocating beneath his bulk, and the foul odor of his breath caused her to gag. She looked about wildly, horrified at what was about to happen, and managed to free one arm. Flailing in desperation, she grabbed for the night table, and her fingers brushed against the heavy brass lamp, which wobbled and fell onto the pillow beside her head. She closed her hand around the base, raised it into the air, and brought it down crashing against the base of Jerome's skull.

He gave a surprised gasp, then shuddered and became dead weight on top of her. With the last of her strength, Maggie managed to roll him to the side and staggered from the bed. Every fiber of her body screamed with pain and exhaustion, but she stumbled across the carpet, grabbed her coat, and fled from the room.

The servants were at the back of the house and when they heard the front door slam, assumed that the gentleman caller had departed.

Only later, when the maid went upstairs with fresh towels for the bathroom, did she discover Jerome lying unconscious on Maggie's bed. Thinking he was dead, she picked up the telephone and called the police.

# 21

Having fled the house without a *sou,* Maggie hurried through the streets heading for Montmartre, where she hoped to find a friend among the artists she knew.

She looked in at bars and cafés that they frequented until she ran into a young man named Alphonse whose painting of the beach at Deauville she had bought the year before.

*"Mon dieu,* Maggie!" he said, rising from his table and staring at her in alarm. "You look as if you've been run down by an omnibus!"

"Alphonse, you must help me! I'm in terrible trouble!"

"Here," he said, passing his glass of wine across to her, "drink this and tell me what's happened."

Maggie swallowed the wine gratefully, then brushing back her disheveled hair from her forehead, she told him the story. "I think I killed him," she concluded. "I don't know. But if he isn't dead, I wish he were."

"No matter," Alphonse said decisively. "You've got to hide. The police will be looking for you in any case. We'll go to my place at once."

He lived in a stifling apartment not far away, but Maggie slumped in a chair by a dormer window and thanked him for his help.

That night, Alphonse gave her his bed—in actuality a hard mattress in the corner. Maggie didn't protest . . . she was too distraught to realize that he would have to spend the night on a blanket on the floor.

But the next day, looking haggard and tired, she collected her wits. "I've got to leave Paris, of course."

"But where will you go?" Alphonse had brewed a pot of strong, dark coffee and served Maggie a cup.

"I've been thinking of that . . . and it seems I have no choice. Could you give me some note paper and an envelope?"

"Would a sheet from my sketch pad do?"

Maggie smiled warmly. "It will do perfectly!"

Then, taking a pen dipped in his India ink, she scratched out a letter to Bryan.

Five days later she received his reply.

Here is money to cover your fare to London, and I'm enclosing a key to a house at No. 83 Hedlington Row in Hampstead. Go there and make yourself at home. I will come to you.

Maggie stared at the brass key in her palm, then, with a sigh of relief, closed her fist around it.

It was late evening the next day before Maggie reached London. She hired a hack and went directly to the address in Hampstead. Even in the darkness she could see that it was a charming house, set back from the street, with a tiny front garden from which she detected the sweet fragrance of roses.

She half-expected Bryan to be there—had prepared herself for their meeting—but when she let herself in, she found the house vacant. She explored the place, tiptoeing from room to room, feeling almost as if she were an intruder, for the house looked as though its occupants had just stepped out. It was fully furnished, and in every room bouquets of flowers graced the tables. The living room was lovely and cozy, and when she made her way to the kitchen she found that the cupboards were stocked with food and wine. Then, turning, she spotted a note from Bryan lying on the table.

"My Dearest," it read, "I will come to you as soon as I can. In the meantime, remember: I love you."

Maggie's spirits soared. She hugged herself and danced around the kitchen. Bryan loved her! Loved her still! Oh! My life is going to be all right after all! Bryan! Bryan! Hurry to me!

The next morning, just before eleven, she heard a motorcar pull up outside the house, followed by the creaking of the iron gate and footsteps on the garden walk. She flew to the door and threw it open, and Bryan caught her up in his arms. As their lips met, she felt a tremendous relief. Merely being near Bryan was enough to smooth over all her troubles, erase every worry.

She stood back and looked at him. He was tanned from a summer in the sun and more handsome than she ever remembered. She couldn't resist lifting a hand to trace the classic contours of his face. But as if he couldn't stand being separated from her, even by a few

312

inches, he pulled her back against him and held her tightly while they kissed.

"I never thought I'd see you again, Maggie. It's been so terribly long."

"Too long Bryan . . . I never want to be apart from you again."

She buried her face against his lapel, and they stood in silence, clinging to each other for a long time before entering the house together.

She wanted him to make love to her, hoped he would take her by the hand and lead her up the stairs. Instead, he opened the door to the parlor and crossed the room to a cabinet containing a decanter of sherry. He poured drinks for the two of them and settled on a sofa. Maggie sat on the floor at his feet, her elbow resting on his knee.

"Do you like the house?" he asked.

"It's lovely, Bryan."

"I rented it as soon as I heard from you. It's yours for as long as you want it."

"How can I thank you?"

"There's no need . . . it's my pleasure."

She took his hand and pressed his fingers to her lips. "Bryan, I love you so."

"And you know I love you, Maggie. But things aren't simple any more."

She looked up, feeling a premonition of dread.

"I could tell by your letter . . . " he began. "I can see just by looking at you now that you don't know."

"Don't know what, Bryan?"

He took a deep breath. "I'm married, Maggie. I have been for a little over a year."

The news struck her strangely. A feeling of giddiness swept over her. She thought she was going to burst into hysterical laughter and had to bite her lip to control herself. She struggled to her feet, pressing her palms against her forehead, and paced the floor a couple of times before she trusted herself to speak.

"No . . . of course I didn't know, or else I wouldn't have written. But I should have suspected. After all, it's been four years. . . ."

Bryan had rushed to her side.

"This seems to be my fate with men," she went on. "First Victor . . . now you. I wonder what it is that leads me to make the same mistake again and again."

"It's not your fault, Maggie."

"Oh, but it is! I should have left Paris with you when you asked me to."

"You only did what you thought was right. I understood your loyalty to Pascal. But let me confess that when I learned of his death, I hoped I would hear from you. And had you not written when you did, I would have sent a letter to you."

"But Bryan . . . for what purpose? You're married now."

"I don't love my wife. I never have. You're the only one I've ever given my heart to, Maggie, and you own it completely and for all time. Do you believe that?"

"Yes, Bryan."

"As I told you, I had no real hope of ever seeing you again. How was I to know that you would come to me eventually? I waited three years, and then I met Germaine."

"Germaine?"

"Yes . . . she's Belgian. Her father is a banker in Brussels."

"So it was business."

"Only partly . . . it was loneliness, too."

He took her in his arms again.

"Oh, my darling," she said. "I'm so sorry."

"I am, too, my love."

"So what's to become of us?" she asked.

"That's up to you, Maggie. I have no right to ask anything of you."

"You have every right, Bryan . . . at least as far as I'm concerned. When Pascal died, I wanted nothing more than to go to you, but I didn't see how I could after having turned you down in Paris. And because of foolish pride and false propriety, I probably never would have, had it not been for . . ."

She closed her eyes and tried to erase the memory of Jerome Louvet.

"Pride . . . propriety," Bryan murmured. "What a topsy-turvy world we live in!"

"We make it that way ourselves, I'm afraid," Maggie said bitterly. "Stupid as they are, they're our own rules . . . as confining as the corsets we women force ourselves to wear, as pointless as the cravats you men wrap around your necks. What sheep we humans are!"

Bryan smiled ruefully. "And would you be willing to go without a corset? And could I appear in public without a cravat?"

Maggie sighed. "I don't think so, Bryan. We're not strong enough for that."

"No . . . I suppose we're not."

"So . . ." Maggie said, breaking away and moving to the window that overlooked the rose garden. "If I stay here, Bryan, it will have to be as your mistress. Our relationship would have to be clandestine, meeting only when you aren't required elsewhere, having you come to me in the evening but knowing you won't be by my side when I wake up in the morning, never appearing in public together."

Bryan nodded miserably.

Maggie took a deep breath and turned to face him.

"Well, if that's the case, I accept! I've made a botch of my past, and what's gone by can't be undone. But I'll be damned if I'll throw away my future, too! I absolutely refuse to spend the rest of my life separated from the man I love!"

Bryan's heart brimmed with happiness. He held out his arms and took her to him. Maggie's eyes misted with tears of joy, for although she knew that she was not entirely free—perhaps never would be—she had by her decision managed to crack the door of her prison. And the light that streamed in filled her soul.

She tilted her head to Bryan. "Now," she whispered. "Now that we've made this commitment, kiss me . . . and then let's go upstairs to bed."


It was the week before Christmas, and Maggie was browsing in the Burlington Arcade looking for a gift for Bryan. She wanted something unique, yet modest, so as not to arouse Germaine's suspicions.

The two women had not yet met, although Bryan had casually mentioned Maggie to Germaine, saying only that an old friend from Paris had recently moved to London and suggested, with an offhand manner, that Germaine invite Maggie to a party if the occasion should arise. Germaine had only half-listened, then promptly forgot all about it. And now, five months later, Maggie had yet to see Bryan's London home or his estate in Berkshire.

She didn't really care—other than for a mild curiosity—for she considered the cottage in Hampstead to be *their* home; and for the moment, that was enough.

The Arcade was bustling with Christmas shoppers, and Maggie almost missed the little crystal paperweight sitting on a velvet cushion at the front of a store window.

She hurried inside and asked to see it; then, turning

it over and over in her hand, she murmured to herself, "This is perfect . . . absolutely perfect."

It was a polished ball, and floating in its center—how it got there, she couldn't imagine—was a tiny balloon cast in gold, precise in every detail, exactly like the one that had carried her and Bryan over the rooftops of Paris the day they first met.

She bought it, her heart singing, certain she couldn't have found anything that would please Bryan more. The clerk put the paperweight in a silk-lined box, wrapped it up, and tied it with a ribbon.

With her purchase tucked beneath her arm, Maggie bade the man "Happy Christmas" and fairly danced out into the Arcade. She had gone only a few feet when she was brought up short by the sight of Bryan heading in her direction. She almost called out to him, but caught herself in time when she noticed the woman walking at his side.

She had no time to turn away, for Bryan had already spotted her. She saw him smile and heard her name.

Well, it had to happen sooner or later, Maggie thought. We had to meet at some time. Better here in the midst of a crowd than at a small, intimate party.

"Maggie! Maggie Cameron," Bryan said with studied formality. Then turning to Germaine, "My dear, I'd like you to meet a friend of mine, Miss Maggie Cameron. Maggie, this is my wife."

Maggie's face was composed, and she arranged a smile. "It's a pleasure meeting you, Lady Carrington."

Germaine returned the pleasantry, then paused for a moment before asking, "But haven't we met before, Miss Cameron?"

"I don't believe so, my lady. I haven't been in London long."

Germaine frowned. "Yet you look so familiar."

"I'm sure we haven't met."

Maggie would have remembered. Although not beautiful, Germaine was nonetheless striking, looking as if she could have been a model for Renoir with hair a shining russet-gold and a complexion the color of pink roses and cream.

"Christmas shopping?" Bryan asked.

"Oh, just picking up a few things here and there. And you?"

"We've just finished," Germaine said. "A sweet little music box for my mother."

"We're off to Carrington Manor tomorrow," Bryan added. "The whole family's meeting there . . . Germaine's too."

"It's going to be a madhouse."

"You won't have to lift a finger."

"That's what you promised last year," Germaine laughed happily, "and yet, I nearly worked myself to death. You see, Miss Cameron, there are only three in my family, and the Carringtons seem to go on endlessly."

Maggie's smile was genuine. She liked the woman. She had always hoped she wouldn't—that would have made things easier—but she was as captivated by Germaine's friendly warmth as she was by her looks.

"Well, I won't detain you any longer," Maggie said. "Have a happy holiday . . . both of you."

"You must call on us," Germaine said as they prepared to part. "I'll send a note around when we come back up to London."

"I would like that very much, Lady Carrington,"

Bryan and Germaine moved off down the Arcade.

"She's a lovely woman," Germaine said as they reached the street. "I liked her."

318

"I told you about her before."

"You did? I don't remember. But I *still* say we've met. Otherwise, why would she seem so familiar?"

Bryan knew, but he said nothing.


That evening at five, he came to the cottage in Hampstead. Maggie was waiting for him. There was a fire in the fireplace and champagne on ice in the parlor. It was to be their last meeting for a fortnight.

"She liked you, Maggie."

"I liked her, too. But I don't feel sorry for her. She has you in a way that I never can."

Bryan kissed her gently. "Yet *you* have me in a way that *she* never can."

Maggie nodded. "If I had to make a choice, I wouldn't change a thing. Your love means more to me than your name."

"Yet, I know how hard it is on you, Maggie. Here it is Christmas, when lovers should be together, and I'm off for Carrington Manor while you have to stay here by yourself."

"I won't mind. We'll have our Christmas tonight. After all, what's a mere date on the calendar?"

"And we'll celebrate New Year's when I return."

"Hogmanay, my father always called it," Maggie said, remembering. "In our house, it was more of a holiday than Christmas itself."

"As it is with all the Scots," Bryan said.

They toasted the season with champagne, made warm, exciting love in Maggie's darkened bedroom, then dressed and exchanged gifts.

Maggie opened hers first. It was a bracelet of Florentine gold set with perfectly matched diamonds, and on

319

the inside was engraved: "They that love beyond the world cannot be separated by it."

"Bryan . . . how beautiful!"

"William Penn gave that as advice to his children. I think it's worthy to remember."

"I'll always remember."

She leaned across and kissed him, then handed him his gift. His face lit up when he saw it. He held the gleaming ball in his hand turning it this way and that, letting the light catch the little balloon floating forever in its atmosphere of crystal. As delighted as a child with a treasured toy, he cried out with pleasure, "I love it, Maggie. It's perfection!" He brought it close to his eye, squinting at the tiny basket suspended beneath the golden balloon. "Are we in there? Can I see us floating over Paris?"

"No, I couldn't manage that," Maggie said laughing.

"No matter," Bryan said, pulling her to him. "I see it in my mind's eye, and that's good enough for me."

They embraced and sank onto the floor in front of the blazing hearth. Bryan kissed her until she gasped for breath, and he felt her body burn more warmly than the fire. They made love again, gently, slowly, prolonging each caress, spinning out time as slowly as they could, wishing in fact that they could halt the hands of the clock and remain in each other's arms, suspended for eternity like the golden balloon.

But after a while, as they lay together happy and satisfied in front of the glowing coals, the chimes on the mantel rang nine o'clock. Bryan groaned at the reminder that he had to leave and go back to Germaine. But Maggie kissed him one last time and said, "It won't be for long, my darling. We endured four years apart . . . two weeks will pass in a wink."

"But I'll miss you every instant."

They embraced at the door and said goodbye, and a moment later Maggie heard his motorcar sputter and drive off down the street.

She moved about the house, turning off the electric lights. Then she went upstairs alone to her bedroom. The pillow still held the impression where Bryan's head so recently lay. She stretched out on the bed, took his pillow in her arms, and brought it gently to her lips.

Closing her eyes, she smiled happily, her heart full of joy; and remembering the inscription on the bracelet Bryan had given her, she whispered, "They that love beyond the world cannot be separated by it. . . ."

# 1908

# 22

Of all the possessions Maggie left behind in Paris, the only ones she truly cared about were the paintings that once covered the walls of the townhouse in the Place de Furstemberg. She had corresponded with her artist friend Alphonse, asking if he could manage to have them returned to her, but he wrote back that when he called on the new tenants, they had been unable to give him a clue as to where the pictures had been taken.

She had bemoaned their loss to Bryan. "It's not that they're worth anything—I paid less than a hundred francs for some—but I liked them so much. And they were painted by my friends."

Bryan listened sympathetically, and the subject was dropped, with Maggie believing she would never see her pictures again.

Then, a few weeks later, Bryan drove up to the cottage followed by a horse-drawn delivery van. Maggie watched, puzzled, as two workmen began unloading a dozen wooden crates onto the pavement.

"What in the world. . . ?"

"Your treasures, Maggie," Bryan said, beaming.

The first of the crates was brought into the house, and Bryan pried it open with a claw hammer. Maggie whooped with joy as she recognized a small portrait of a young girl, painted by Renoir; and behind it was a favorite poster by Lautrec.

"My pictures!" she cried. "Oh, Bryan! How did you manage?"

"It wasn't easy, my dear," he said, stepping back so the workmen could carry in another crate. "But when I went to Paris on business last week, I thought I would try to track them down. It seems that everything you owned was sold to pay your debts, and I finally found a dealer in Montmartre who had bought your collection. I'm afraid he'd sold a great many paintings before I got to him, but at least you have some of them back. And I assure you, there isn't a one in the lot that can be bought at this time for less than a hundred francs . . . nor a thousand! It seems you've unwittingly amassed quite a valuable collection."

"An unfailing eye, Bryan, my dear!" Maggie laughed, hugging him happily. She seized the Renoir and propped it on the mantel. "Look! Isn't it beautiful there!"

Later, when all the crates were unpacked and the pictures lined up against the wall, Maggie danced around the room, glancing from one to another, as if she'd suddenly been visited by a group of old friends and didn't know whom to greet first.

She judged that perhaps half had been sold, including some of her very favorites; but she calculated that there were almost a hundred left—and among them was her portrait by Bonnard.

Bryan delighted in her pleasure, and when she calmed down and apologized for the expense he'd undergone, he took her in his arms and said, "Your happiness is worth every penny . . . even more."

But the paintings were not all that eventually caught up with Maggie. She had known far too many Englishmen during her years in Paris for her past to remain a closed book; and it wasn't long before Germaine was told.

She was taking tea with Ivy Wingate, an inveterate gossip who would rather die than keep a secret under her hat. Germaine listened with a doubting ear, for Ivy wasn't known as a great respecter of truth.

"My sources are impeccable," Ivy averred, sitting back, a bit put out with Germaine's skepticism. "She was a kept woman for years."

"Well, no matter," Germaine said, reaching for a watercress sandwich. "A person can't help one's past. That's over and done with. It's the present and future that count. I've met her and I like her, and I shall continue to invite her to my house. If a person were to be shunned for former peccadillos, the poor King would be banished to Windsor."

"But *he's* the sovereign!" Ivy said, unhappy that her news had not shocked Germaine.

"And he sets the temper of the times. After all, this is the twentieth century! We're not hidebound as we were in the days of the old queen. Besides, Maggie Cameron is a longtime friend of Bryan's."

Ivy had waited eagerly for this moment. She leaned forward, her black eyes flashing with unconcealed pleasure. "It's obvious, my dear, you have no idea how good a friend she was."

"What do you mean?"

Ivy prolonged the suspense by pouring another cup of tea and tasting it before going on. "Well, according to . . . rumor, Bryan and Miss Cameron had a relationship in Paris."

Germaine's lips compressed only slightly, but she heard a roar of thunder in her ears. "Go on. . . ."

Ivy shrugged. "Well, that's all there is to it. A thing of the past, no doubt . . . all long before Bryan met you."

Bryan and Maggie! Germaine thought. Then suddenly the puzzle that had troubled her for months was solved. She had never been able to shake the belief that she had met Maggie before; she seemed too familiar. Now she remembered! It was the portrait that Bryan had hanging in his bachelor flat before they married, the picture of the nude on the Récamier divan. Of course, of course! That was Maggie!

Germaine controlled her expression, unwilling to add grist to Ivy's gossip mill. "Rumors . . . rumors," she said. "What enemies Bryan must have to spread such tales!"

Ivy shook her head. "Enemies don't spread rumors, my dear . . . friends do."

Germaine smiled sardonically. "How true, Ivy . . . how very true."

The following week, Germaine gave a dinner party and invited Maggie as a partner for one of her cousins visiting from Brussels. Maggie looked ravishing in a spring gown of sea-blue silk worn off the shoulders, and a choker of matching sapphires glittered around her neck. She was easily the most beautiful woman in attendance and could have had the attention of any man

328

present, but she stayed close to the cousin, a shy bachelor, and charmed him by carrying on their conversation in French.

Throughout the evening, Germaine observed Maggie unobtrusively, looking for any sign of private communication between her and Bryan. But Maggie played her role to perfection, and as the time came for the guests to depart, Germaine heaved a sigh of relief. Even if Ivy's malicious prattle were true about Maggie and Bryan in Paris, Germaine felt certain that there was nothing between them now. A cold ember, Germaine thought to herself happily. A fling, long over and done with. And as long as that's all there was to it, she had absolutely no objections to their continued friendship.

As Maggie prepared to leave, Germaine drew her aside. "Bryan and I are going to Carrington Manor next week. It would please me very much if you could come, too."

Maggie smiled. "Thank you, Germaine. May I let you know tomorrow after I've checked my engagement book?"

"Of course, dear." Germaine leaned forward and kissed Maggie's cheek.

The next day, Bryan called at Maggie's cottage for luncheon. "Are you coming with us to Carrington Manor?"

"I wanted to discuss it with you first," Maggie said. "Do you think I should?"

"I don't see why not. In fact, if you turn Germaine down, it might cause her to wonder."

"Good," Maggie said. "I've always wanted to see your estate. I just thought perhaps there might be . . . problems. There are stories all over London."

"You've heard them, too?"

"From all quarters. God! What gossips we have around us!"

"But it's all old news . . . at least as far as I've heard. Just stories about us in Paris. Even Germaine is aware. It seems that Ivy Wingate came to tea the other day."

"Ivy Wingate! Well, I'm not worried about her. She has a reputation for being totally inaccurate."

"Still . . ." Bryan said. "I suppose we ought to be careful."

Maggie held her forefinger to her lips. "The soul of discretion."

The day they left for Carrington Manor was one of the loveliest that spring, cool, crisp, with a dazzling sun in a cloudless sky.

Maggie's heart sang. Carrington Manor! At last, she would see it! No matter that she was paired with the shy cousin from Brussels. He was nice enough. And it meant an entire week in Bryan's company—every morning, every meal, every evening, not just bits and pieces of time like their life in London. Of course they would never be alone together, and she would have to watch as Bryan and Germaine retired to their bedroom. But she didn't care. She had his love, and she was as sure of it as she was of her own for him.

The estate was spectacular, far exceeding Maggie's expectations. The old house dated from the thirteenth century, the main structure having been a priory before Henry VIII confiscated the monasteries. It was made of stone, mellow with age, and sat grandly amidst holly trees and oak.

Germaine herself showed Maggie to her room, leading her into a spacious chamber with a high vaulted ceiling painted blue and spangled with silver stars. "This is the King James room," Germaine told her.

"He must have spent the night here at one time or another. The place positively reeks of history . . . and mystery. There's even a story that a wicked nun is sealed up in one of the walls downstairs."

"How frightening!"

"Even more so, dear! It's said that she haunts the place . . . although I must admit I've never seen her. Ask Bryan. He'll tell you all about it."

And when she did ask Bryan after dinner that night, he laughed and offered to show Maggie about the place. They entered the ballroom, a vast, long hall lined with trefoil windows.

"Can you see it?" Bryan asked. "Count the windows."

Maggie glanced from left to right. "There are seven on one side of the main door, and only six on the other."

"Exactly . . . now, let's step outside."

They strolled into the front garden and turned around.

"Now, count," Bryan said.

"There are seven on each side. Oh, Bryan, one of them is fake."

"Sealed up, Maggie! That's where poor Mother Angelica—at least, that's what she's called—is entombed."

"Oh, God, Bryan, is it true?"

He laughed. "No . . . of course not! But a hundred years ago, every castle had to have its ghost. I suspect my grandfather or my great grandfather was simply having his little joke."

"Mother Angelica . . ." Maggie whispered. "Walled up because she was a bad woman. I hope it's not true, Bryan. I'd hate to see what they would do to me."

His hand sought hers in the darkness, but she pulled

it free. "No, Bryan! Let's not tempt fate. And besides, I would hate myself if I ever hurt Germaine."

Bryan nodded, and she could hear him sigh.

"No, Maggie, you're right," he said. "I shouldn't want to hurt her, either."

"She doesn't deserve it, Bryan. She's as good and kind to me as any person could possibly be. I like her. Much as I wish I didn't, I can't deny it. And I won't ever harm her intentionally."

Bryan turned and sought Maggie's eyes in the darkness. "But it's bound to happen sooner or later. One day we'll make a mistake, and she'll find out. We can't be lucky forever."

"Don't say that, Bryan! Because if I believed that, I'd leave right now."

"I wouldn't let you . . . and even if you did, I'd follow you."

Maggie smiled sadly. "No . . . no, you wouldn't."

"I swear it."

Maggie wanted to burst into tears. Her love for him seemed to explode like fireworks within her soul. She had to fight herself to keep from collapsing into his arms.

Oh, God! she thought. A week of this! I won't be able to stand it! Why did I ever agree to come?

Germaine watched from a ballroom window. They started back toward the house, betraying no sign of intimacy, no indication of closeness. As they neared the door, Germaine turned and hurried from the great hall, her spirits buoyed. Any suspicions she may have harbored, were now totally erased. Ivy Wingate is merely a gossip!

But at the door, unseen by anyone, Bryan caught Maggie up in his arms and kissed her. "Oh, how I love you!"

His warm lips brushed her cheek and caressed her ear. They clung to each other for a brief, desperate moment, then went back inside and rejoined the others.

Although Maggie had eagerly anticipated her visit to Carrington Manor, now she was just as impatient for the week to be over so she could go back up to London. It was simply too difficult being around Bryan with Germaine always present. Maggie would have left early had she been able to come up with a plausible excuse. As it was, she endured the rest of the stay, walking on eggs, taking pains that nothing in her manner reveal her true feelings.

When at last she arrived back at her house in Hampstead, she heaved a sigh of relief. Finally, I can be myself again! I've felt like a prisoner in my own body. God, how I hate deception! . . . and I've had to live that way for so long!

And even as she thought this, she realized that she could see no end to it. Behind the closed door of her cottage, she *was* herself; but the moment she stepped out onto the street, she was forced to live a lie. The mysterious Maggie Cameron, the woman with a past, the woman whose present was carefully veiled.

She wondered what was being spoken behind her back. Surely there were those like the meddlesome Ivy Wingate who were at this very instant seeking to lift the veil and discover the truth.

Well, I won't let them! Maggie decided. I won't give them the opportunity!

So, when Bryan came to see her the next day, Maggie told him she was going away for a while. "Not long, my darling . . . but just long enough to throw those biddies off my trail."

"But where, Maggie?"

She shrugged. "I hadn't really thought about it. Maybe I will go to Scotland and see if there are any Camerons left up there."

"I could join you . . . we could meet in Edinburgh."

"No, Bryan. The whole idea is to separate us for a while . . . not that I want to be away from you for a moment, but if I seem to move independently, there will be less chance that anyone will make the connection between us two."

"You are a strong woman, Maggie."

She smiled thoughtfully. "Hmm . . . that's what everyone used to say about my mother. But it's not true of me. A strong woman would stay here and risk the brickbats. No . . . I'm running, as I've done in the past. Running and hiding."

Bryan frowned with worry and unhappiness. "Is it too much for you, Maggie? Would you be better off without me?"

"Oh! No! Never think that. It's you I live for! The fault's within me, Bryan, and I must work it out in my own way."

"Then you're determined to go?"

"Yes, my love, but not for long."

"I shall miss you," he said, taking her into his arms. "While you're gone, I know I'll come to this empty house and wander like a lost child from room to room, trying to find some evidence of you left behind . . . an earring, a scarf, a handkerchief that still holds the fragrance of your perfume."

"Bryan? Have two people ever loved as ardently as we?"

"If they have, Maggie . . . I hope they found it easier."

The following week, Maggie left by train for Scotland and put up in a suite at the George Hotel in Edinburgh. For the first few days, she explored the city alone, finding it a lovely town, strolling through the rose gardens below Prince's Street, turning to see the soot-darkened castle atop the Mound, following the Royal Mile down to Holyrood House, and hearing in the rolling brogue of each friendly Scot an echo of her father's voice.

At last, she made the effort to locate her Scottish family. She wrote a letter and within three days received a reply from another Margaret Cameron inviting her to the ancestral home in the Highlands.

She left Edinburgh on a Friday morning and arrived that evening, met at the station by Margaret and Ian Cameron. They kissed her and welcomed her with such warmth that she felt she had known them all her life, and when she arrived at the house, sitting alone on a barren hill, she saw that every window glowed with cozy friendship and love.

It looked as though every Cameron in Scotland had gathered to greet her, and Maggie was led around from one group to another before they sat down to a banquet in her honor complete with entertainment by kilted pipers and Highland dancers. And when the meal was finished, Ian Cameron rose to speak.

"We're a happy clan," he began, "made even more happy by this visit from our American cousin."

Maggie smiled with pleasure, her heart full of love.

"There are many here who remember Maggie's father. Alex Cameron was the bravest of us all. He set out on a venture to confront the New World, stopping not in New York or Boston where life was easy, but journeying on to the wilderness of Texas. . . ."

Maggie grinned at the choice of words.

335

"And Alex went on to conquer that wild and savage place, becoming the greatest cattle baron that country has ever known. Ach, he was a braw man, he was . . . the finest you'd ever hope to meet! And our only regret is that he didn't live long enough to visit us once again."

Maggie's smile froze on her lips; her blood turned to ice. What? Not live long enough? Papa! Papa! She felt her brain begin to spin. She reached out to the table for support as blackness overtook her, then slumped sideways in a faint.

When she came to, she was in her bedroom being watched over by Margaret Cameron. She opened her eyes woozily, unsure for a moment where she was. Then the memory of Ian's words swept over her in a rush, and she broke into sobs. She cried for her father, whose heart she knew she broke; she cried for her mother, whose cold fury she could feel even today. And she cried, for the first time in years for the Lantana— her home—that she knew she'd never see again.

Margaret took her in her arms and comforted her, still unaware of the reason for Maggie's sudden faint.

"I didn't know," Maggie moaned, burying her face against the older woman's bosom. "I've been gone so long . . . I didn't know that Papa . . ."

"Oh, my dear," Margaret said, understanding at last.

"When was it?" Maggie asked.

"Several years now," Margaret whispered, rocking Maggie in her arms. "Four or five. We received a letter from your mother. But how is it, Maggie, that you didn't know?"

Maggie shook her head and wept more bitterly than before. It was impossible to explain.

How could you tell someone, even a relative, that your mother sent back your letters still sealed; that you

336

were responsible for the death of a beloved uncle and friend, that your past and present made you a scarlet woman?

The next day, despite pleas from her relatives to stay, Maggie packed up and set out for London. The long train ride gave her time to think, to accept in her own mind that Alex was dead, and when she arrived at home, she realized that the only man left in her life was Bryan . . . yet he was only half hers.

He came to the house the next day and was surprised to find her already back in London.

"It was a mistake to go," she said simply, lacking the heart to tell him what she had learned.

"I'm glad you're back."

"I'll never leave you again."

"I never want you to."

She sank gratefully into his arms and let him kiss her.

"Hold me, Bryan," she said, shuddering. "Hold me tightly. I need you."

Later, as they lay in bed together, he said, "I have good news. Germaine is going to Brussels for a month. I was thinking we could go down to Carrington Manor and be alone together at last."

"But, Bryan, what about the servants? Won't that be risky?"

"There's no one there now but the caretaker and his wife . . . besides, I hadn't intended that we stay at the manor itself. There's a small cottage where the gamekeeper used to live. It's deserted now, but still in good repair, a cozy little retreat, very secluded. There would be no one around to disturb us. Say you'll come, Maggie."

She rolled over and draped her arm across his chest.

"Of course, I'll come, Bryan! It'll be wonderful having you all to myself—even for a little while."

The day after Germaine left for Belgium, Bryan called for Maggie and they set off in his Daimler for the Berkshire estate. They stopped along the way and had sandwiches and beer at a country pub, and at Reading they shopped for provisions, packing the groceries into two large wicker baskets Bryan had brought along.

With each passing mile that led them farther from London, Maggie's heart grew lighter, until at midafternoon, when they reached the estate, she was almost beside herself with happiness . . . and not a little relieved, for Bryan was still very much a daredevil fascinated by speed, and time and again, as they flew along the road, Maggie had had to beg him to slow down.

"But, Maggie, darling," Bryan had objected, reveling in the control he had over the Daimler, "what's the use of having a motorcar if not to get to your destination in a hurry?"

"I would think the first consideration is to get there all in one piece! Besides, I've heard that if a person goes too fast, the wind will suck the breath from his body!"

Bryan had laughed heartily, but for Maggie's sake he slowed down to what he considered a crawl, although Maggie still tightly gripped the edge of her seat and watched the road carefully through her goggles.

So when they reached the abandoned gamekeeper's cottage, she was doubly thankful. They had arrived safely . . . and they were alone together away from prying eyes and snooping gossips.

The cottage delighted her. Built of stone, it sat snugly in a grove of shady oaks with tangles of ivy clinging to its walls. Wild roses bloomed along the path leading to the door, and beneath her feet was a carpet of fine green grass.

She hurried ahead of Bryan and explored the little house. There was a bedroom with a low, slanted ceiling, a long, narrow living room, and a bright, cheery kitchen with an open hearth and four large windows overlooking a lively brook that raced over smooth white stones just behind the cottage.

"It's beautiful, Bryan. I love it! I could live here forever . . . as long as you were with me."

He smiled happily, and they spent the next hour unloading the car and making the house ready. Then Maggie went outside and returned with an armful of roses which she arranged in clay pots and placed on tables in each room.

While Bryan sipped wine and read that morning's edition of the *Times,* Maggie bustled about the kitchen preparing supper, and as she worked she could almost pretend that they were husband and wife, that this was their home, and that this idyllic moment would go on forever.

They went to bed early that night; and when Maggie opened her eyes at first light the next morning, she found Bryan already awake, propped up on one elbow next to her, staring at her.

"Do you realize," he asked, kissing her lightly between words, "that this is the first time we have spent all night together?"

Maggie smiled with perfect contentment, stretched, then put her arms around his bare back and pulled him back to her.

# 23

They had been at the cottage for about a week when Bryan suggested they drive into Newbury. He wanted some tobacco and the latest newspapers. They set out in the morning, motoring beneath clear, fresh skies, dawdled over lunch at a little restaurant, shopped and browsed until mid-afternoon, then prepared to head for home.

The day had grown dark with dismal gray clouds rolling in from the west, and as the Daimler sped out of town, the first raindrops spattered against the wind-screen. After a few more miles, the heavens opened up, with rain falling so heavily that Bryan was unable to see the road ahead.

He parked on the verge beneath the sheltering arms of an oak, and they waited there for an hour, nibbling on bread and cheese, until the sudden storm passed.

Then Bryan restarted the car and pulled back onto the road.

The skies had still not cleared, and it was darker than twilight with the road winding like a ribbon of wet silk ahead of them. Maggie tried not to show her apprehension as the Daimler careened through curves and the rain-soaked vegetation on the verge rushed madly past them.

The road wound around the foot of a wooded hill, then dropped away into a narrow valley before bending sharply to the right. Maggie thought they were approaching the curve too quickly and started to say something when she heard Bryan's sharp intake of breath and his muttered, "Oh, oh. . . !"

It all happened so quickly. The car skidded, slewing about as its tires locked and slid on the slippery surface. Then suddenly they left the road, the trees ahead rushing up to meet them, and as Maggie felt the car beginning to pitch over, she held on tight and screamed.

Less than five minutes later, a farmer and his son, returning from the fields, came upon the unconscious forms of Bryan and Maggie lying on the roadside, a short distance from the overturned car.

The farmer bent over Bryan and recognized him, having seen him at a fair three years before. "It's the lord," he called to his son. "Alive but pretty well banged about. How about her ladyship?" He moved to join his son.

"Breathing . . ." the boy replied. "But knocked out cold."

The farmer nodded, checking Maggie over. "And from the looks of her, she's got some broken bones. Well, come on, lad, let's put them in the wagon and take them into town. Careful, now . . . gentle, there . . . we don't want to do them another injury."

Neither Bryan nor Maggie regained consciousness until the next day, and as soon as his head cleared, Bryan summoned the physician and said, "There must be no publicity about this whatsoever."

"I'm afraid it's too late for that, my lord," the doctor replied. "The morning papers have already reported that you and Lady Carrington were injured in a motor accident."

Bryan closed his eyes. The mischief was afoot; there was no stopping it now. Their secret would be out, and Germaine would know. Although his body was racked with pain, he felt a greater ache for his wife, for he knew how much she loved him, and he despised himself for the embarrassment and grief she was about to suffer.

When Maggie came to, she found both arms in casts, and her befuddled brain could not comprehend why the sisters kept referring to her as "my lady."

But when her mind was finally lucid, she realized with horror the greater tragedy of the accident. "No, don't call me that," she murmured weakly to one of the sisters. "I'm not Lady Carrington."

The sister looked surprised and said, "I'm terribly sorry, ma'am. Everybody assumed you were."

Germaine arrived the next afternoon. Going directly to Bryan, she stood by his side, her face ravaged with hurt and betrayal. "So . . . it was true, after all!"

"Germaine, let me explain."

"I see no need for it."

"Please . . ."

"There's nothing for you to say. It's plain as day. I won't divorce you, Bryan . . . and you've no grounds to do away with me. I've been a true and faithful spouse, even as you haven't. But I like being Lady Carrington, and I shall remain so. Henceforth, what-

342

ever you do with your life, whomever you choose to bed with, is of no concern to me. Do as you wish. Just leave me alone."

She turned, fighting back tears, and left the room. On her way out, she stopped at Maggie's room and looked in from the doorway.

Maggie felt her heart stop, her shame burning across her face.

Germaine looked at her silently for a moment, then with lips curling in hate, said, "You were my friend . . . now you're Judas! I wish you had been killed!"

Maggie lay on her bed and wept, hot tears streaming down her face and staining the pillow beneath her head.

A week later, Maggie and Bryan left the hospital and returned to her cottage in Hampstead. Bryan, who had suffered no broken bones, helped Maggie inside and settled her in a chair in the parlor.

They had spoken little during their trip up from Berkshire, and now alone at Maggie's house, they both realized they had to discuss the future.

"So, what's to happen to us, Maggie?" Bryan asked. "You once said you'd leave me before you would hurt Germaine. However, that's already been done. What now?"

"I've thought about it, Bryan," she said softly. "As a matter of fact, I've thought of nothing else. I was sincere when I said that. I cared for Germaine and never wanted to hurt her. But, now, there's no going back. And in a way, what's happened made up my mind for me. I couldn't stand the thought of leaving you. I would rather die first. We'll be a scandal . . . indeed, we already are. And if that be the case . . . well, I'm willing to live with it. I'm willing to endure anything as long as it means sharing my life with you." She paused, then added, "But only if that's what you want."

He knelt at her feet. "My darling!"

"I no longer care what others think or say. I'm finished with deception. I've lived with it too long. I'm going to hold up my head with pride at being your mistress. And if the idea troubles anyone, let them go to hell. I don't need them. I don't need anyone but you. If it means living beyond the edge of society, I'll live there happily. If it means being excluded from the Royal Enclosure, I'll be content to watch the races with the public . . . anything, as long as you are by my side."

"And I shall always be there." He bent forward and kissed her gently. "I love you, Maggie."

She smiled, her lips trembling. "Love beyond the world . . ."

"Beyond the world," he repeated and kissed her again.

The scandal titillated London for a while, first with the news that Germaine was estranged from Bryan, then that Bryan had moved into the Hampstead house and was living openly with Maggie. Initially, most of Bryan's old friends kept their distance, although if they chanced to meet at the theater or the racetrack, heads were politely nodded and brief pleasantries exchanged; and eyes studying Maggie's face for a hint of shame received a bold, self-assured gaze in return. As Ivy Wingate put it, "It's almost as if she were proud, the hussy!"

But before long, the more liberal-minded Continental financiers with whom Bryan dealt in the City began calling at Hampstead and inviting the couple to their homes. And then, at Cowes Regatta, the King, who despite his advancing age still had a keen eye for lovely women, noticed Maggie and remembered meeting her years before on a night out in Montmartre. Soon afterwards, it was buzzed about London that His Majesty had visited Bryan and Maggie for an evening of bridge and drinking, and that when he left, well after midnight, he had invited the couple up to Balmoral for shooting later that year.

With the King's blessing, the cloud of scandal evaporated, and Bryan's old friends returned as if nothing untoward had ever happened. And it wasn't long before Maggie received a note from Ivy Wingate requesting "the honor of your presence, along with Lord Carrington's, at my annual garden party."

Maggie had laughed and shown it to Bryan. "Well, it looks as if all is forgiven."

"Shall we go?" he asked.

"Of course we'll go, my love. I imagine we'll be the main attraction. It would break the old busybody's heart if we turned her down!"

# 1915

# 24

Despite his hopes, Dos's luck had not held during his trial, and he was sentenced to twenty years at the prison in Huntsville. Once a month, for over a decade, Anne made the trip from the Lantana to visit him, although now, nearing her sixty-seventh birthday, she found the journey growing arduous and exhausting.

She brought Dos food, books, magazines, and, of course, the latest Kodak snapshots of Trev. She knew it broke Dos's heart that his son was growing up without him, but Dos was adamant that the boy should never see him in prison. "I'll get out of here eventually," he would tell Anne, "and then Trev can meet his papa . . . but not before."

"He misses you."

"I miss him, too. Funny . . . how you can miss someone you don't even know."

"You'll like him, Dos. He's big and strong . . . and he's got a stubborn streak like you."

"I hope he's smarter."

Anne smiled wryly. "He is . . . I guarantee you that."

And Anne, too, was as wise as she'd ever been. During the gubernatorial campaign of the year before she had sagely donated an immense amount of money to the campaign of James Ferguson, and now that her candidate was solidly ensconced in the Executive Mansion in Austin, she was waiting impatiently for her due reward. It came less than a month after "Pa" Ferguson took office: a pardon for Dos. He would be home by the first of March!

As Dos walked out of the prison gates, a group of reporters surrounded him.

"How 'bout a few words, Mr. Cameron?"

"What's your plans, Mr. Cameron? Going back to the ranch?"

"I've got nothing to say," he murmured, trying to brush past them.

"Mr. Cameron?" came another voice just outside the group.

"I said I don't have any statement to make."

The man pushed into the circle. "I'm not a reporter. I'm Jim Watts. I sell cars."

Dos looked at him, puzzled. Then Jim Watts held out his hand, dangling a set of keys. "See that automobile across the street? It's all yours. A gift from Mrs. Anne Cameron. She called me this morning and arranged it."

Without a word, Dos accepted the keys, left the reporters behind, and took his seat in the brand new, bright red Packard. On the dash was a note, in Jim

350

Watts's handwriting, but in Anne's words. "Hurry home. Drive all night if you have to. I love you. Mama."

It was two in the morning before Dos turned in at the Lantana gate. The guard snapped to attention and waved him through.

He was expected.

The road to the big house was paved now, a wide arrow-straight boulevard lined with palm trees and cenizo. Dos sped along, straining for the first glimpse of home. Then all at once, he saw it. The house was still five miles away, but every window was blazing with light. He pressed on the accelerator and hurtled on down the road until at last he swung onto the curving driveway that swept up to the house.

He heard music, then saw that a crowd of ranch hands was gathered on the porch and in the yard. Anne had arranged a band: accordions, guitars, and trumpets playing a lively Mexican tune. And there she was, surrounded by her people, but standing taller than all the rest, her arms outstretched in welcome, tears of happiness streaming down her cheeks.

And then a banner unfurled from the tower, reaching almost to the ground. It whipped in the wind, then settled back against the house, and down its length was written: WELCOME HOME, PAPA!

He looked up and saw a tow-headed boy waving from one of Anne's office windows.

Dos stood on the running board and waved back. "Trev! Trevor Cameron! Your daddy's home for good!"

Anne ran down the steps to hug her son, but all she could think of to say was, "God bless 'Pa' Ferguson! You're home at last!"

For a week, Dos did nothing but get to know Trev. He was astonished at how much the boy knew about the workings of the ranch and actually found himself learning from his son.

"So much has changed in twenty-two years," Dos remarked in wonder. "Do the hands still ride horses?"

"Sure, Pop," Trev answered, pleased with himself for being able to instruct his father. "But they drive cars and trucks, too."

"And you've got telephones. . . ."

"Aw, sure," Trev said, surprised that Dos would remark on something so ordinary. "We've got our own switchboard in the basement of the big house. They let me work it, sometimes. It's not hard. I'll show you how. You just have to know which plug goes into which hole. You know . . . like if somebody's calling from the Ebonal to the Casa Rosa. . ."

Dos smiled in wonder. Imagine! Calling from the Ebonal to the Casa Rosa! He remembered when it was a day's ride and more!

Dos and Trev took his Packard and drove out on the range, and Dos saw another sign of change. "Can't believe the way the mesquite has taken over!"

"Grandma says when she was a little girl, there were hardly any trees anywhere."

"There were hardly any when I was your age, either."

"Grandma says mesquites aren't any good. They use up so much water they keep the grass from growing high. She's got crews out cutting it all the time, but she says it grows back faster'n they can work. I heard her tell Anselmo Rivas . . ."

"Anselmo Rivas? Is he still foreman?"

"Sure . . . he's been around longer'n anybody . . . except Grandma. She's been here forever. Anyway, she told Anselmo that maybe the Lantana should quit raising cows and go into the wood business."

Dos laughed. "Well, that's something that'll never change. As long as there's the Lantana, we'll be raising cows."

And late one evening, after darkness had settled over the land, Dos sat alone with Trev on the porch of the big house. "I have to tell you something, son."

"What's that, Papa?"

"Something I promised your mother . . . she wanted you to know that she lived long enough to hold you in her arms and that she thought you were a fine-looking boy, the best in the world. And she wanted me to tell you that she loved you."

Trev squirmed uncomfortably, embarrassed. Dos understood and reached across to rumple his son's hair. "Now, off to bed. It's late, and we're driving into Joelsboro tomorrow to buy me some new duds. How am I gonna run this ranch without Levi's, boots, and a wide-brimmed Stetson?"

The next afternoon, when he returned from town and slipped into his new clothes, Anne took one look at him and laughed. "Now don't you look just like a dude!"

"Give me a week, Ma, and all this'll be broken in. These damn boots won't be creaking forever."

She kissed him on the cheek and said, "Let's go up to the grumble room."

*Grumble room!* Dos thought instantly of Maggie. "I don't suppose you ever heard from her."

Anne knew whom he meant, but pretended she didn't understand.

"I'm talking about Maggie, Ma. She's the one who always called your office the grumble room."

"No . . ." Anne said slowly. "I never heard a word."

353

They reached the spiral stairs that wound up the side of the house to the turret office. "I'd like to see her again," Dos said.

Anne spoke without turning around. "After all these years, I don't suppose . . ."

"Wouldn't *you* like to, Ma? Deep down in your heart?"

Now she turned. Her face was tragic. She looked her years. "I made a mistake with her, Dos. I always prided myself on not holding a grudge against those I love. But with Maggie, it was more than a grudge, I suppose. I actually hated her for what she did to Carlos . . . and to Alex. She broke his heart, you know, and he never recovered. I never wanted to see her again. But now, well, I suppose if I knew where she was, I'd go to her. But after all this time, I don't imagine she'd want to see me."

She trudged up the stairs . . . so slowly that Dos could see her age was weighing heavily on her.

They entered the little office, and he was surprised by how much smaller it was than it had seemed on the rare occasion when he was a child and was permitted a visit.

Anne waved him into a seat in front of the rolltop desk while she settled into her rocker. She reached into a silver box engraved with the Crown of Thorns and took out a slim, black cheroot. Then, scratching a kitchen match on the rocker arm, she fired it up, blowing a perfect smoke ring.

Dos smiled. "You never used to let us see you smoke."

"But you always knew I did, didn't you?"

He nodded.

She was amused. "And I drink, too."

"You never made a secret of that. . . ."

"I mean I drink up here sometimes. Now, don't get worried. I'm not a secret boozer. What I'm saying is that if you open that drawer by your knee you'll find a bottle of whiskey and a couple of glasses. Let's have a little toast. To welcome you home."

Dos poured two shots and passed a glass to Anne. She raised it toward her son. "To you . . . and the Lantana."

He looked at her strangely.

She tossed back the whiskey, then glancing at her watch, she picked up her silver cigar box and rose. "This is your office now, Dos. I'm handing it over to you. I've been in this business since I was a girl of twelve. Don't you think it's time I had a little rest?"

"Mama . . . I don't know the ropes. I can't handle it without you."

"Sure you can, Dos." She was moving toward the door. "Just start reading. Go through that desk from top to bottom . . . it'll take you weeks! When you finish, you'll know as much as I do."

She left the turret room and closed the door behind her. Although she had thought about this moment for years and had carefully planned every word she'd said, she hadn't realized how terribly it was going to affect her. She really wasn't tired . . . and she needed no rest. In fact, considering her age, she thought she felt marvelous. But standing at the top of the stairs, she knew that she would never enter that office again.

It was hard for her to believe that she no longer ran the Lantana.

The Lantana! It was more than just a part of her. It had been her very life . . . and how she loved it! But she loved Dos more! She loved him enough to make this sacrifice, and she realized that if she were ever going to hand him the reins, she would have to do

355

it quickly, cleanly. A long, gradual transition would cause confusion among the workers while it diluted both her authority and Dos's. No, this was the best way. There should never be any doubt in anyone's mind who was the boss.

She heard the telephone ring on the other side of the door, and she looked at her watch again. That would be Anselmo Rivas calling—right on time, just as she had instructed him to do.

"There you go, Dos," she whispered. "Get to work. You're on your own, now."

Inside the office, the telephone jangled again on the rolltop desk. Dos looked at it for a moment before answering and almost shouted after Anne; but then, he lifted the receiver and put it to his ear. "Dos Cameron. Who's calling?"

There was no hesitation or surprise in the voice on the other end. "Mr. Cameron. This is Anselmo Rivas."

"Hello, Anselmo! What's up?"

"I'm down on the Hallelujah. We got a problem."

"You think you need me?"

"Yes, sir, can you come over?"

"Be there in the morning."

*"Muy bien, adios, señor."*

Dos hung up and sat back in his swivel chair, staring up at the ceiling. Anselmo hadn't even asked for Anne. It dawned on Dos that the foreman must have known, even before he did, that Anne was putting him in charge. He faced the desk and pulled out the first stack of papers.

And if Anselmo knows, the word must already be out . . . all over the ranch. Dos Cameron was boss!

# 25

It took Dos a full three weeks to go through the papers in the desk. He was up before dawn, and the turret lights continued to burn well past midnight. He summoned the Lantana's lawyers and accountants from San Antonio and held long afternoon meetings around the massive oval table in the conference room on the mansion's first floor. And with Trev at his side, Dos drove his Packard to all parts of the ranch, getting to know the *caporales* and the hands, discussing their work, and examining the stock.

Finally, late one night, after he shoved the last of the morocco-bound ledgers back in place, he leaned back in the swivel chair and let out a long, low whistle in admiration and astonishment at the immense scope of the Lantana.

He went downstairs and found Anne still awake. He

poured drinks for the two of them, and they went out to the veranda and sat in rockers side by side.

"I knew we had money," he said, his voice quiet with awe. "Hell, you can't own this much land without being worth something. But I had no idea! Ma . . . we could buy and sell anyone in the state!"

Anne smiled in the darkness and let him continue.

"We've got banks stuffed with money in towns I never even heard of before."

"It comes in handy on rainy days," she said at last. "And believe me, we've had our share of rainy days . . . we're going through a bad period right now with the war cutting off our European markets. Lots of ranchers have already gone bankrupt. We'd be knee-deep in trouble, too, if it weren't for those reserves. Thank God we can wait it out. Soon as the war's over, the price of beef will be higher than a cat's back."

Dos agreed with her, but he thought for a while and said, "Well, as I see it, we've got more than enough to tide us over, and I'd like to use a little . . . really more of an investment than an expense."

"What's on your mind?"

"The place is running fine right now, but there's a helluva lot more we could be doing. I've been reading about irrigation. I'd like to call in some experts for their advice . . . see if we can make some grass grow down on the Piedras Blancas. I'm thinking about putting an office building, right here on the place, walking distance from the house, and bringing down some of those money men from San Antonio. I'd like to have them around me all the time so I can see them whenever I want to. And a laboratory . . . we could really use one, with our own vets and agronomists working full-time to develop better feed and finer cows. And those damned mesquite trees that are taking over the place! I bet there's some smart engineer somewhere who could rig up a machine that could rip 'em right out of the ground. Think of the labor we'd save!"

"But labor's your cheapest resource."

"I know that . . . but it won't always be."

Anne's heart filled with contentment. If she'd ever had any doubts about Dos, they were gone now. She could hear the pride and excitement in his voice, and every one of his plans appeared sound. She finished her drink and rose to reenter the house. At the door, she turned and said, "Do it, Dos! Do whatever you want . . . as long as it's good for the Lantana."

She left him there alone, and he sat for a long time watching the stars wheel across the sky, looking out across his land, and feeling the same love for this special place as his mother did.

And he had another plan . . . one he hadn't voiced to Anne but which he felt would also be good for the Lantana. It would probably be the most difficult to achieve, but he intended to act on it in the morning.

Up before dawn as usual, he wrote a letter to Elise in New Orleans. Earlier, he had asked Anne about her, and Anne had told him: "She never remarried. She's bitter and broken. For the longest time, I tried to get her to come back for a visit, but she never came. I never hear from her any more. Once a year I send her a full accounting and a check for her share . . . Carlos's share. But she's never cashed a one. I don't suppose she needs the money. It's obvious she doesn't want it."

Now, Dos waited for her reply to his letter. It came a week later.

. . . For the life of me, I can't understand why you or your mother would want to find Maggie

359

again. And it's beyond me why you think I can be of some help.

The last I saw of her was at the Ritz Hotel in Paris, in 1895. For all I know, she went back to that brothel called the *Maison* Dollois. If you're bound and determined to seek her out, you might start there. . . .

There was a final paragraph, stating that she was well taken care of, that Jeanette had died and left her with more than enough money to see her through the rest of her life. And, attached to the letter, was a document renouncing forever any and all claims Elise might have to the Lantana.

Dos filed the legal paper, then picked up the telephone and asked the switchboard to connect him with Peter Stark in Joelsboro.

"I read in the paper that you finally made it out," Peter said. He spoke calmly but couldn't mask his surprise at hearing from Dos.

"I did eleven years. I hope that's satisfactory with everyone."

"You've got nothing to worry about from my side, Dos."

"I'm glad to hear that." There was a pause; then Dos went on, "But I'm calling about a different matter, Peter . . . one I think you can help me with since it's sort of down your line of business. I want to know how to go about tracking down someone who's been missing for quite a number of years."

"And who might that be?"

"My sister Maggie . . . last we heard, she was in France."

"Be glad to help you, Dos," Peter said. "Why don't you drop by my office next day or so and fill me in on

360

the details? Then I'll get in touch with Pinkerton's. I've done some business with them in the past and imagine they'd be our best bet."

Because of the war in Europe, the information Dos requested didn't come until the end of summer. He read the report, memorized Maggie's address in London, then burned it. Late that night, after everyone else was asleep, he wrote to Maggie. Not wanting Anne to see the letter, he carried it into Joelsboro himself the next day and mailed it.

The year before, Maggie had watched the clouds of war gathering over Europe, and although she knew it was foolish and selfish, she felt the gods had sent them just for her—a calling-in of accounts for the past few years of the only true happiness she had ever known in her life.

And just as she'd expected, as soon as Britain declared war with Germany, Bryan volunteered, going quite naturally into the Royal Flying Corps. He underwent training at the central flying school on Salisbury plain, and while Maggie tried to uphold a brave front, he prepared to leave for France. Nevertheless, on their last night together before his squadron mobilized, she broke into tears and was inconsolable.

"Oh, Bryan, I'm so afraid for you!"

"Don't worry, Maggie. We'll push the Hun back to Berlin, and then I'll come back to you . . . all in one piece, I promise. And be glad I'll be serving with the R.F.C. If I were fighting in the trenches, they'd be shooting at me. As it is, I'll be safe and sound in the air. It's only reconnaissance . . . not dangerous at all."

But she couldn't be comforted and cried in his arms all night. The next day, not trusting herself to hold up in public, she told him goodbye at the door of their cottage. He bent to kiss her and whispered, "Keep a light in the window . . . I'll be back soon."

However, his squadron was gone more than six months, not returning to England until the summer of 1914, and only then to take possession of the new two-seater Vickers fighters armed with Lewis guns.

"So now it's no longer reconnaissance," she said. "You're shooting at each other in the air."

"The Vickers is as good a fighter as anybody has," he told her, trying to allay her fears. "I'll be perfectly safe." But he had already heard at the War Office of a new German machine, the Fokker monoplane that intelligence reports said was superior in every way to the British craft.

Left alone again, Maggie threw herself into hospital service. Although she detested it, hating the stench of gangrenous wounds and the pitiful sight of dying men —any one of whom could have been Bryan—it was a bribe on her part, a bargain with the gods, her time and effort to keep Bryan safe from harm. She was indefatigable, working double shifts without complaint, taking on the foulest of tasks, and earning the respect and admiration of the nursing sisters around her.

But it wasn't their respect she desired; it was the attention of the gods. As she cleansed a festering wound or read a letter to a blinded soldier, she would send up a silent challenge. "For each one of these I help, you owe me another day of safety for Bryan!"

It seemed her belligerent prayer was answered, for at the end of August, Bryan returned unexpectedly to London.

"Say you don't have to go back!" she wept in his arms. "Say you don't *ever* have to go back!"

He held her tightly. "At least, not for a little while. I'm being sent to Washington. The American army has requested a briefing on aerial warfare. The War Office has chosen me."

"When do you go?"

"In two weeks."

"Take me with you, Bryan!"

He drew back. "The Atlantic's a dangerous place, Maggie. The U-boats . . ."

Maggie was aware of that, for the *Lusitania* had been torpedoed only three months before. "I don't care, Bryan. I want to go with you anyway."

"You're not afraid?"

"Not with you."

He smiled and took her back into his arms. "I was hoping you'd want to go. I can't tell you how much I hate being apart from you."

Maggie took leave from the hospital and got ready for the voyage while Bryan worked day and night at the War Office preparing the briefing for the American generals.

In the middle of September, they boarded a steamship in Liverpool and sailed for New York. The next day, the letter from Dos arrived at the Hampstead cottage.

The United States was a foreign country to Maggie. The flat American accent sounded strange to her ears, and she was amazed at how modern her homeland had become. The streets of Washington were choked with automobiles, even more than they were in London, and the noise on the streets was deafening.

Prosperity was everywhere, or so it seemed, for the war in Europe had meant a boost to the American economy. While Bryan met with the Americans, Maggie browsed in the stores, marveling at the abundance, intrigued by every new item she found, spending far more than she had planned on gadgets that no one in England had ever seen before.

And she fell in love with the city, thinking: If I didn't live in London, I could easily live here.

The buildings looked new and clean, dazzling white in the autumn sun, and the wide boulevards reminded her of Paris. She toured the capitol, the Washington Monument, and the Lincoln Memorial; and she spent two days in the Smithsonian Institution.

And then, after they had been there for a week, she met President Wilson at a reception at the British Embassy.

The next morning, as Bryan was dressing, she lay in bed reading the *Post*. "Oh, listen, Bryan!" she called to him. "I'm in the paper . . . 'attending the function was Miss Maggie Cameron of London,' and then they list some of the others who were there."

"Did they mention me?" he asked, buttoning his coat.

"Oh, don't worry . . . you made the first paragraph. But how in the world do you suppose they got my name?"

"The embassy supplied a list. They always do."

That same morning at the Lantana's big house, Anne went downstairs to breakfast. Dos was just finishing as she entered, and Trev sat hunched at the table ignoring his plate of *huevos rancheros* in favor of the *Corpus Christi Caller*.

"Eat your breakfast, Trev. You'll be late for school," she admonished, reaching for her coffee cup. "Anyway, what are you doing reading the paper? A child your age shouldn't worry himself with all the commotion going on on earth."

"I like reading about the war. I hate the Huns, Grandma."

She smiled. "Your grandpa would have been glad to hear it."

"I know, because he was British."

"He *was* British . . . he *became* Texan, just like you and me. Now, hand me the front page, and you get to work on your eggs."

Reluctantly, Trev passed the newspaper across to Anne and picked without interest at his breakfast. Anne propped the *Caller* against a silver candlestick, adjusted her glasses, and began to skim the headlines.

"Trev," she said after a moment.

"Yes, Grandma."

"It says here there's another outbreak of influenza. Be sure and wear your coat today."

"But, Grandma! It's hotter'n spit outside."

She peered at him over her spectacles. "Hmm . . . now isn't that a nice expression! Well, take your coat with you anyway, just in case we have a norther. You don't want to go catching the flu. It can be a killer, you know."

"Oh, Grandma . . ."

Anne turned back to the paper, and an instant later, Trev heard her gasp suddenly. "What's wrong, Grandma?"

She had gone quite pale.

"Pop!" Trev called, but his voice was drowned out by Anne's, shouting, "Dos! Dos! Come here quick!"

Dos was at the front door. He turned and ran back to the breakfast room.

Anne had the paper in her hands now, nearly crushing it between her fists. "Look! Look! Read it! There!"

Her finger shook as it pointed out the name Maggie Cameron.

365

"Oh, Dos! Do you suppose . . . ?"

Dos's eyes ran down the article . . . "a reception for the president at the British Embassy . . . Lord Carrington, colonel in the Royal Flying Corps . . . among those present, Miss Maggie Cameron . . ."

He remembered the Pinkerton report which had said, ". . . at this time, Miss Cameron is closely associated with a member of the British peerage, Lord Bryan Carrington of Berkshire."

Dos looked at Anne. Her face was upturned, her eyes imploring. "Yes, Ma . . . that's Maggie."

"I'm going to her," Anne said. She was in her bedroom throwing clothes into a trunk.

"Let me write to her first," Dos said. "Let me call her. I can find out where she's staying from the British Embassy."

"She's liable to turn tail and run," Anne said, tossing a handful of stockings into the trunk. "I can find out for myself when I get to Washington. Let's not take a chance, Dos. I've got to see her."

"Then, let me go with you."

"No, so much has happened between the two of us, I think it'd be best if we met alone. You know, so much of what took place was my fault. I didn't show her the same affection I showed you. She was Alex's, you see . . . she was his baby. I kind of left her to him. And all the while, she needed me, and I was too blind to see. I've blamed myself all this time. All Maggie needed was a little direction, a little love . . . but I thought she got enough from Alex. She didn't need me . . . at least, I thought she didn't. And, because I was so worried about you, I gave you more. Poor Maggie! I'm afraid if I don't see her now, it will be too late. So, don't warn her, Dos. She might not see me if she has time to think

366

about it. Let me go to her in my own way. Let me try to make amends. I owe her that. If I don't explain to her, she'll never know."

Dos stood back and let his mother finish packing. At last, she closed her trunk and said, "Now, call Marquez and tell him to get the train fired up. I'll leave after lunch."


Bryan's work in Washington was finished, and he and Maggie planned to spend their remaining two days in America relaxing and enjoying themselves. Maggie took Bryan to Mount Vernon and as they strolled the grounds she asked, "What are the English taught in school about our revolution against the crown?"

Bryan smiled and said, "They say . . . that the rotten apple fell from the tree."

Maggie threw back her head and laughed. "They would . . . oh, they would!"

When they returned to the hotel, the desk clerk handed Maggie a telegram. She took it, puzzled, and ripped it open. Bryan saw her face go white. "What is it, Maggie?"

She handed it to him without a word, but her hand was trembling.


MAMA COMING TO SEE YOU STOP PLEASE DONT LEAVE STOP DONT TELL HER I WIRED STOP LOVE

DOS

Bryan looked at her and said, "You must stay."

"Oh, Bryan! And let you leave without me!"

"You can take the next boat . . . it will only be a matter of days."

"Can't you postpone . . . ?"

"I have to be back in London Monday week."

"But, Bryan . . ."

"Maggie, you can't be gone when she gets here."

"I'm afraid to see her."

"You shouldn't be. Somehow she learned you were in this country, and she's coming to see you. Maggie, it must be because she wants to heal the wound between the two of you."

Maggie sank onto the sofa and held her face in her hands. "I haven't seen her in twenty years. I was a child then. Now I'm grown, and she's an old woman . . . oh, Bryan! I can't even imagine her old! She was the most beautiful . . ."

The words caught in Maggie's throat, and her shoulders shook with sobs. Bryan dropped to her side and held her.

"Be kind, Maggie . . . be generous. Stay here and meet with her. It will gladden both your hearts. It's time you made peace with each other."

Maggie struggled with herself and finally gave in. "All right . . . I'll stay. For a few days. But I won't go back to Texas with her. I'll take the next boat leaving for England. I want to be with you again before you return to France."

"I'll be waiting for you." He kissed her and wiped the tears from her eyes.

# 26

Bryan departed for New York the next afternoon, leaving Maggie at the Willard Hotel to wait nervously for Anne's arrival. She slept fitfully that night and, in the morning, would have packed her bags and followed Bryan if she thought she had a chance of reaching New York City before his boat sailed.

She got through the long hours of the day by taking a walk that led her to Georgetown and back, scarcely noting what she passed, paying little attention to where she wandered; and all the while, she kept thinking: How am I going to face her? What am I going to say?

And she could imagine the two of them sitting, facing each other in silence, separated by too many years and too many painful memories for any bond to remain between them. I wish she weren't coming! I wish I had never left England!

The bright autumn sun was setting now, and the afternoon was turning cold. Shivering, Maggie stood on a curb and hailed a taxi to take her back to the hotel. There was a note in her box at the reception desk. She waited until she reached her room before reading it.

Maggie dearest,
  I am in Washington and want desperately to see you. I could meet you any time and any place you wish. Or, if you'd prefer, you could come to my suite at the Mayflower Hotel tonight at nine.

Love,
Mama

Now it was too late to run. Maggie sat on the edge of the bed with the note in her hands and decided she would go to Anne that night.

Suddenly, an old panic seized her. She jumped up from the bed and ran to the mirror to examine her face. She ran her fingers through her hair, wishing she had thought to have it done that afternoon. And what would she wear? She threw open the closet door and fanned through her dresses. Maybe the blue . . . but I don't like the hat! The gray is pretty . . . or the brown!

Unable to decide, she abandoned the closet and filled the bathtub. An hour later, dressed in the gray with a rope of pearls wrapped around her neck and her sable coat lying on the bed, she sat at her dressing table putting the last touches on her face. She dabbed perfume behind each ear, patted her coiffure carefully, and pinned on a smart new hat she'd bought a few days before.

"Not bad!" she breathed, eyeing her reflection critically. Then she snapped her gold bracelet onto her right wrist and reached for her watch.

Seven-thirty!

"My God! I'm early for the first time in my life! Well, if nothing else comes out of the reunion, Mama's visit has achieved the impossible!" She laughed at herself, and for a moment the tension within her was broken.

But as the minutes ticked by, she grew apprehensive again. She called room service for a bottle of champagne and drank three glasses as she paced the floor, leaving the rest only because she felt herself growing tipsy. At last, unable to remain in the room any longer, she slipped into her coat and went downstairs.

Dare I be early? She looked at her watch. It was only eight-thirty, but the champagne had given her courage. She walked out onto the street and asked the doorman to summon a taxi.

Anne's maid answered Maggie's knock at the door. She was a pretty girl with sleek black hair tied in a single thick braid that reached to her waist.

"Is my mother in?" Maggie asked, her voice quiet and tremulous.

The maid smiled. *"Sí, señorita Cameron. Pase Usted, por favor."*

She led Maggie into the sitting room of the suite and with a graceful wave of her hand indicated a buffet that had been laid out—cold chicken and lobster, sandwiches and petit fours, a choice of wines and two bottles of Dom Pérignon chilling in silver buckets.

Maggie smiled. So! You knew I'd come tonight after all. The maid had left the room, and Maggie was reaching for a wineglass when she heard a door opening behind her. A tingle raced up her spine, and she took a deep breath before turning.

Anne stood just inside the room. She was dressed in green, looking tall and regal, with her hair piled softly

371

atop her head and a choker of diamonds and emeralds around her neck.

For a moment, neither woman spoke, the tension crackling like electricity between them. Then Anne smiled and said, "Do you recognize your old mother?"

A dam burst within Maggie. She ran across the room, and Anne held out her arms to receive her. They hugged each other tightly, their sudden tears dampening each other's cheeks.

"Mama! Oh, Mama!"

"Maggie . . . my darling! It's been too long!"

It was half an hour before they settled down enough to say anything of consequence. Maggie opened a bottle of champagne, and they sat together on the sofa.

"Mama, I'm glad you came. And you achieved the impossible—I'm early!"

Anne laughed. "I'm glad I came, too, Maggie dear." She was unable to take her eyes off Maggie. She reached up and touched Maggie's cheek. "You know, my dear, that photographer Elmendorf was only half-right. He said you would be beautiful. But he failed to predict that you would also be magnificent!"

The lavish buffet remained untouched, neither woman feeling the slightest hunger. But they finished the bottle of champagne, and Maggie opened the other.

By unspoken consent, the past that tore them apart for so many years was never mentioned. There seemed no need for it. But Maggie did tell Anne that she was living in London and was in love with a wonderful man.

And Anne talked of Dos and Trev.

"So, I have a nephew!"

"He's a fine boy, Maggie. You'd like him."

"I'm sure I'd love him."

"You could get to know him, Maggie . . . if you'd come back to the Lantana with me."

Maggie knew that was coming, and she saw the glimmer of hope in Anne's eyes. She reached out and clasped her mother's hand. "I can't just now. I have to go back to Bryan. He's fighting in France, and . . . well, things are so uncertain. Each time I see him could be the last."

"I understand, dear. I'd do the same thing."

"Maybe next year . . . if the war is over by then."

"Yes . . . let's wait till the war is over. It frightens me to think of you crossing the Atlantic."

They sat in silence for a moment; then Anne rose. "Well, my darling, it's getting late. I'm a country woman, used to going to bed with the chickens. Let's meet in the morning. Will you take me shopping? There are a few things I'd like to buy . . . presents for Dos and Trev."

"I'd love to, Mama."

"And I have something for you. I'll give it to you tomorrow."

They met the next day at ten, and Maggie astonished herself by being early again. They shopped, lingered over lunch at a fashionable restaurant, then visited several more stores, and when they arrived back at Anne's hotel, it took four bellboys to carry up her packages.

"You said you wanted to buy a few things," Maggie laughed as the pile of parcels grew in the sitting room. "You didn't say you intended to take half of Washington back with you!"

"I just couldn't resist," Anne said happily. She looked more relaxed and less her age than she had in years. "Tomorrow, I'll have all this carted off to the train. Then, I'll be going. I don't like to leave Trev for too long."

"Then, I'll be going, too," Maggie said. "I'll take the next boat sailing for England."

Anne embraced Maggie and murmured, "My darling . . . I can't tell you how happy I am that we've seen each other again."

"Oh, Mama! I was so afraid . . . I was so worried that . . ."

"Shh," Anne whispered. "It's all over and done with, Maggie. There's no need to look back."

"Thank you, Mama. Thank you for being so good to me."

They kissed gently and put the past, once and for always, behind them.

Then Anne said, "I told you I had something for you. Wait here. I'll be right back."

She went to her bedroom and returned with a little black velvet box in her hand. "I always intended that you should have this. It's just taken a little longer than I planned."

Maggie received the box and opened it. Inside lay Anne's garnet necklace with its golden chain.

Maggie trembled with emotion. "Mama! Your lavaliere!"

"Yours, now, my darling."

Maggie had to blink back the tears. "Whenever I think of you, Mama, I picture you wearing it. You had it on in that old family photograph."

"I always wore it on special occasions. It meant so much to me. It belonged to my grandmother—whom I never even knew—and she gave it to my mother when she married. And the night my mother died, she gave it to me. So, you see, it's very old and has shared a lot of memories. Now . . . you're the fourth to have it."

"I'll treasure it always."

"Put it on, dear. Let me see it around your neck."

374

Maggie opened the tiny clasp and fastened it behind her. The garnet glowed like a blood drop on her breast.

Anne spoke softly. "If you ever have a daughter, promise you'll pass it on to her."

Maggie's lip trembled. She thought of the little grave beneath the stone cherub at Père Lachaise. "Oh, Mama . . . oh, Mama!"

Anne hugged her tenderly and rocked her back and forth just as she used to do when Maggie was a child.

The next day at noon, they said farewell at the station. The Lantana train that Maggie remembered from her childhood had been replaced by a newer locomotive and by sleeker, more comfortable cars, although they were painted the same midnight blue and bore the Crown of Thorns in gilt on their sides.

The engineer told Anne that they were ready to leave. She turned, and Maggie thought her face looked pale and strained. "Are you all right, Mama?"

Anne nodded quickly, but despite the autumn chill, beads of perspiration had broken out on her brow. Maggie touched her cheek. "You feel warm."

"I'm fine, Maggie. I suppose I'm just tired. It's hard traveling at my age. If I'm feverish, it's only from excitement and happiness."

They embraced.

"Well, I'm off, dear," Anne said, climbing into her parlor car. She searched Maggie's face as if memorizing every feature. Her eyes seemed to blaze, and her cheeks were as white as the lace collar that encircled her neck. The locomotive whistled and the train inched forward. Anne leaned from the doorway and waved.

Maggie stood on the platform watching until the train was out of sight; then she went back to the Willard,

375

took dinner in her room, and stretched out on the bed. She felt an immense gratitude toward Anne, for her graciousness and kindness. Whatever Maggie's sins, clearly Anne had forgiven them. As she had said, "There's no need to look back."

Maggie's fingers found the garnet lavaliere around her neck. She realized it was the most precious jewel she owned. She brought it to her lips and kissed it.

Shortly after midnight, the strident ringing of her bedside telephone yanked Maggie from a deep sleep. She fumbled in the darkness for the receiver and mumbled a hello.

"This is John Gregory, engineer on the Lantana train."

Maggie's sleepiness disappeared instantly, and she sat up quickly. "What's happened? Has there been an accident?"

"No, ma'am . . . no accident. But it's your ma. She's taken sick . . . bad sick. I thought I oughta call."

"Where are you?"

"Cincinnati."

"What's wrong with her?"

"I don't rightly know. We called a doctor soon as we pulled in. He's with her now."

"Go get him. I want to talk to him."

There was a long wait, and then the engineer came back on the line. "Sorry, ma'am, but the doc says he don't have time to come to the phone. He says if he was you he'd get here as quick as possible."

Maggie threw back the covers. "I'm coming . . . on the first train out. Meet me at the station."

She got no more sleep that night. She packed a bag and went to the depot only to find that the next train didn't leave until early morning. She sat on a hard bench in the waiting room, watching the hands on the big clock creep slowly around the dial.

The trip to Cincinnati seemed interminable. It was night when they finally pulled in, and Maggie hurried from her compartment and searched the station until she found the midnight blue Lantana train. Gregory, the engineer, was sitting on one of the steps.

"How is my mother?" she shouted as she ran up to him.

He stood up and took her suitcase. "They carried her off to the hospital. Come on with me. I'll get you a taxi."

When Maggie arrived at Anne's room, she found the maid weeping in the corridor outside the door. "How's the *señora?*"

The maid looked at her, eyes red with tears. *"Muy mala! Muy mala!"*

Maggie rushed past her and entered the room. Anne lay on a narrow bed, her face white as death. A nurse had just finished putting a fresh, cool compress on her forehead.

"I'm her daughter. What's wrong with her?"

"It's influenza, I'm afraid," the nurse said softly.

Maggie's soul filled with dread. "How . . . how bad?"

The nurse looked away.

"Tell me!" Maggie pleaded.

"It's good you got here when you did."

Maggie stifled a cry. She dropped into the chair beside Anne's bed and took her hand in hers. It felt hot and dry in her palm. Other than for Anne's shallow, ragged breathing, there seemed to be no spark of life left in her. Her hair fanned out in a lank mass about her waxen face, her eyelids were closed, and her cheeks were thin and hollow.

377

"Mama," Maggie whispered, bringing her lips close to Anne's ear. "Mama . . . it's Maggie. I'm here."

She felt her mother's fingers move within her clasp.

"Mama . . . Mama!" She rose from the chair and bent over Anne. Anne's eyelids fluttered and slowly opened.

"It's me, Mama . . . Maggie."

She saw through the tears cascading down her cheeks that Anne was trying to smile.

"I'm here. I'm here, Mama. Everything's going to be all right."

She felt Anne pull her hand from hers. Then she reached up and touched the garnet lavaliere that dangled from Maggie's neck. Now she did smile. And she whispered, "Maggie! Maggie! I love you."

Then her hand fell across her breast.

"Mama!" Maggie cried, sobbing uncontrollably.

But Anne could no longer hear. Her eyes had closed, and her labored breathing ceased.

# 27

Dos was at the siding when the Lantana train pulled in. Standing beside him, fighting back tears, was Trev. When the train stopped, Maggie stepped onto the platform.

Home! Home at last after all these years! But on such a painfully sad mission! She looked about, squinting in the bright fall sunshine. The wind off the *brasada* was warmer than England in summer, and the land was as flat as the sea. The Lantana! She had thought she would never see it again.

Dos came up to her. "You must be Maggie."

She fell into his arms. "Oh, Dos! I'd know *you* anywhere!"

"You're all grown up, Maggie. You're not the little girl I remember."

She shook her head. "No . . . not any more. Not at all."

"This is my son, Trev."

She bent and kissed the boy's cheek.

Behind them, four vaqueros were unloading Anne's bronze casket.

Both Dos and Maggie glanced at it, then looked quickly away.

"Did she suffer?" asked Dos.

"She died with a smile. I know people always say that, but this time it was true."

Dos didn't attempt to stop his tears. He hugged Maggie, and they wept together.

"I'm glad you two got together again."

Maggie looked up at Dos. "You and I weren't the best children, were we?"

"No. She deserved better."

"But I think in the end, she was happy with us."

"I hope so," he said.

"Yes . . . I think she was." Maggie's hand went automatically to the lavaliere around her neck.

Then she broke down completely and clung to her brother to keep from collapsing. "Oh, God, Dos! Oh, God! We're all there is left!"

"No," he said gently. "No . . . there's Trev."

Maggie blinked back her tears and looked at her nephew. "Yes," she said reaching for his hand. "Trev . . . and the Lantana!"


The next morning the three surviving Camerons laid Anne to rest in the land she had loved so much. Mourners came on horseback, in buggies, and by automobile. Newspapers across the state carried her story on the front page. Telegrams and letters of condolence piled up on the oval table in the conference room. Flags in every county south of the Nueces flew at half-mast. And in Austin, the Governor issued a proclamation, honoring Anne as "a woman of vision, a citizen of greatness, and a true pioneer of Texas."

As Dos and Maggie made their way from the graveyard to the car waiting to take them back to the big house, they heard an old man say to his grandson whom he held by the hand, "Remember this day, Jimmy. What you just saw is the passing of the old frontier. It ain't gonna come again."

Maggie bit her lip and burst into tears. Dos waited to cry until they were back at the house.

The next day a cable arrived from Bryan.

LEAVING FOR FRANCE TOMORROW STOP STAY IN AMERICA STOP NO REASON FOR YOU TO RISK ATLANTIC CROSSING STOP WILL CABLE WHEN I RETURN TO ENGLAND STOP UNTIL WE MEET AGAIN REMEMBER I LOVE YOU MORE THAN LIFE ITSELF STOP

BRYAN

Maggie didn't want to stay, but being in London would actually put her no closer to Bryan than she was on the Lantana. The war separated them as no ocean ever could. But she would have disobeyed him, would have chanced the U-boats and returned to London, if it hadn't been for Trev.

Without Anne, who had raised and loved him, he was lost, a pitiful, grieving boy who seemed to have abandoned interest in everything. Even Dos, whom he adored, couldn't dispell Trev's sorrow. And night after night, when Maggie heard him sobbing she would cross the hall and sit by his bed, murmuring softly, stroking his forehead, until he fell asleep again.

So in the end, it was Trev that kept her on the Lantana. She was afraid to leave him . . . afraid he would never recover from his sadness.

"Don't you think it's time to go back to school?" she asked him one morning at breakfast.

"I never want to go back. Everyone will know that Grandma died."

Maggie didn't understand. "Of course they know. Everybody knows."

"But I don't want them looking at me as if they knew."

Now Maggie understood. And she remembered how she once begged Anne and Alex not to send her back to school in Joelsboro. She rose and hugged Trev. "I see now. Don't worry. You don't have to go back until you want to."

He looked at her hopefully. "Is that true?"

"Trust me."

"Aunt Maggie, will you stay here forever?"

"I'll stay for a while, anyway. But someday, I'll have to go back to England."

"I don't want you to leave."

"Don't think about it now."

"Say you won't leave."

"Maybe I'll take you with me."

But later, as she stood on the veranda and looked out over the land she'd been born to, she thought how much she wished she had never returned . . . how each succeeding day made it more difficult to think of abandoning it once again.

What is it about the Lantana? she thought. Why does it compel us so? What is its secret? Why is it so powerful that I can feel it in my blood? Strange! she thought. How strongly one can love a bleak piece of earth! And she realized that only Bryan meant more to her than the Lantana.

And that day, drawn by forces she didn't understand, she saddled a horse and rode out alone to the cemetery.

Anne's grave was still a mound of raw earth, and would remain that way, a painful wound, until spring grass sprouted to cover it over. All the rest seemed settled, content in death, as if they had been there forever. Joel, Martha, Sofia . . . and Carlos.

Maggie's fingertips traced his name carved in marble. Carlos! If Mama forgave me, will you forgive me, too?

She heard the answer in her soul.

And when she turned to go back to her horse, she felt the first peace she had known in a long time.


A week later, Maggie went to Joelsboro on an errand for Dos. He was having a swimming pool built beside the big house, and she had promised she would go in to pick up the plans. She hadn't seen the town in over twenty years and took a stroll down Main Street, noting with interest how much it had grown. Many older buildings on the south side were familiar, but the north side, which had burned to the ground the night Dos killed Klaus Stark, was relatively new, and she walked slowly, looking at each one, peering in at the drugstore, the dress shop, the rebuilt saloon, and the offices of lawyers whose names she didn't recognize. Then at the corner of Main and Guadalupe she glanced up and thought she recognized Dos.

She called out to him. "What are you doing here? I thought you were down on the Casa Rosa?"

The man turned, and she realized her mistake. Yet he looked so much like Dos . . . burly, blond, just like her brother.

"Oh, I'm sorry!" she apologized. "I thought you were

someone else." She saw the silver sheriff's star on his lapel.

The man nodded and said, "How do you do? I'm Peter Stark."

Maggie froze. Of course . . . now she remembered! She started to turn away.

"Wait a minute," Peter said.

She stared out of the corner of her eye.

"Don't I know you?" he asked.

"I . . . I . . ."

"Wait . . . you're Maggie Cameron, aren't you?"

"You remember me."

"Hmm . . . it's your eyes. That blue. Just like your daddy's."

Maggie blinked.

"You've been gone a long time, haven't you, Miss Cameron . . . or is it Mrs. . . . ?"

"It's still Miss."

"Well, welcome back to Joelsboro." His warm and genuine smile relaxed her and swept away her reserve.

He sauntered over and his face grew serious. "May I say how sorry I am about your mother's passing? There's been bad blood between our families, as you know. But I had nothing but respect for your mother. I only wish I had gotten to know her better. You know I was born on the Lantana . . . just like you. But we left there when I was a kid. And I never really got to know Mrs. Cameron until years later . . . after the trouble."

Maggie lowered her eyes.

"Well, that's all over, isn't it? Dos did his time. We speak when we meet on the street. You can't ask more than that."

"No . . . I suppose not."

384

"Anyway," Peter Stark said, "it's good to see you again."

"Thank you, Mr. Stark."

"Call me Peter."

"If you'll call me Maggie."

He smiled again. "I'll be glad to."

She smiled back. "So, you're still sheriff."

"Gonna be mayor."

"Oh, really?"

"Least I will be after the election."

"You're pretty confident. You must have a lot of support."

Peter smiled. "We're having a rally in the plaza this Saturday night. Why don't you come with me and see for yourself?"

Maggie accepted, seeing no reason not to.

The next day, when Dos returned from the Casa Rosa, Maggie mentioned that she'd run into Peter Stark. "He says he's going to be the next mayor."

"I'm sure he will be. He and his brother Davey are building a pretty powerful political organization around here."

Maggie was surprised. "I can't imagine why they'd bother. I wouldn't think Zamora county was worth the trouble."

"Money . . ." Dos answered bluntly. "Davey's the commissioner, and with Peter as mayor, they'll be holding the purse strings. The area's growing, Maggie. Lots of business is coming in now, and there's talk of oil. They're building a new courthouse and laying roads all over the place. And besides . . . it's not just Zamora the Starks are dealing with. They've got their machine geared up in four or five other counties."

"I guess that means the Lantana will have to be dealing with them."

"Not right away, I wouldn't think," Dos replied. "For the time being, we're pretty much our own power. But eventually . . ."

"Funny . . . how the Starks and the Camerons keep getting involved with each other."

Dos looked up at her. "You know I'm one of them, don't you? By blood."

"I'd never thought about it, Dos . . . not until I mistook Peter for you on the street the other day."

"Then . . . you saw it?"

She nodded. "It was plain as day."

Dos smiled ruefully. "I was so blind, I had to be told."

"By Mama?"

"Uh-uh . . . by Klaus."

"Oh, Dos!"

"Well, it doesn't matter. I'm still a Cameron in my heart."


On Saturday, Maggie drove into Joelsboro and met Peter. He welcomed her into his big white stucco house, built in the Spanish style around a courtyard, with grill-work windows and a red-tiled roof.

"You're doing well for yourself, Peter," she said, looking around appreciatively, noting that the house was well staffed with servants and that the furniture, though not at all to her taste, was expensive and suited the rooms nicely.

He was obviously proud of the place. "Yep, I've come up in the world . . . and I aim to do better."

"Nothing wrong with that."

"I wouldn't think so."

They still had an hour before the rally, so he offered her a drink and they sat in wooden rockers on the veranda. Off to the side, a smaller house, built in the same style, was crowded with men, both Anglo and Mexican, talking excitedly in loud, confident voices. Maggie caught a word now and then and noticed that they used as much Spanish as English.

"Who are they?" she asked.

"Well, I call 'em my friends," Peter said slowly. "Other people refer to them as my cronies. All of 'em, in one way or another, help me with my work. Some go out and drum up the vote, see that poll taxes are paid on time, try to find out what the opponents are up to . . . that sort of thing. And three of 'em are body-guards."

"Bodyguards?"

He smiled. "We're still a rowdy bunch down here, Maggie."

Maggie sipped her drink. "You never married, did you, Peter?"

"Never had time. How about you?"

"I had time . . . I just missed the opportunity."

He hadn't needed to ask. He had read the Pinkerton report before turning it over to Dos, and he knew all there was to know about Maggie.

He sat in the rocker, one leg draped over the chair arm, and watched her over the rim of his glass. She was a damned good-looking woman, tall like her mother, but with Alex's strong, dark coloring. He wondered what it would be like to hold her in his arms and kiss her, and he tried to imagine how she would be in bed.

Maggie was used to the stares of men, and Peter's gaze didn't disconcert her. She smiled at him, her eyes level with his, and said, "Don't even *think* of it, Peter."

He grinned. "How do you know what I'm thinking?"

"It was so loud, I could hear it."

He laughed and got up out of his rocker. "Well, I

think it's time to go to the plaza. The crowd ought to be there by now." He tossed the rest of his drink over the veranda's railing and shouted to the little house. "Miguel! Roy! Sanchez! Let's drive on over!"

The sun had just set and the plaza was illuminated by hundreds of electric lights strung on lines from tree to tree. A band was playing a jaunty Mexican tune from a concrete pavilion. The park benches were already filled, and late-comers were settling themselves on blankets spread out on the grass. In the darkness beyond rose the half-completed courthouse.

Maggie was surprised to see the number of women in the crowd. "Why do they bother? They can't even vote."

"No . . . but they sure do spread the word," Peter answered. He started to lead her onto the pavilion, but Maggie held back.

"I think I'll just watch from here," she said.

"You mean I don't have the Lantana's endorsement?" His question was spoken lightly, almost jokingly, but it suddenly dawned on Maggie that he'd intended to use her. After all, the Lantana was a powerful force—everyone here in one way or another was affected by the ranch, and her presence at his side would be bound to carry weight.

"From what I hear," she said, "you don't need anybody's endorsement . . . except your own."

He laughed and started up the steps.

Maggie enjoyed the rally. It was a combination of raw politics, a rollicking fiesta, and Bible-thumping revivalism. The crowd had come for fun, and they got it. Maggie couldn't tell whether they believed the speeches, or even cared what they heard. But they cheered and applauded and let themselves be worked up into a near frenzy. And when it was all over, they picked themselves up off the grass and streamed away from the plaza, laughing and chattering in the best of moods.

"It looked like a great success," Maggie said when Peter rejoined her.

"Aw, it's just for show . . . to give them a good old time. It doesn't mean a damn thing. I'm going to win by a landslide. That's already been taken care of."

"You mean you've counted the votes before they've even been cast."

"That's the only way to be sure you're gonna win!"

Later that night, Maggie had a drink with Dos in the parlor of the big house.

"Well, I've just seen democracy in action," she announced.

"You mean you've seen South Texas democracy. That's a horse of a different color."

"I'll say. If I were a man, I'd run against Peter Stark just on principle."

"You'd lose."

"He's got the county tied up, has he?"

Dos nodded. "Seems to. But from what I hear, he wouldn't need to rig the elections. He and his crew would win anyway, fair and square. The people like them."

"But why?"

"Because they do a lot of good . . . especially for the poor. They're paving streets, putting in sewers, building a high school with a football field. So what if they're skimming off the top? It's no secret from anybody. The Starks consider it a commission, and so do the people. Besides, there's not a peon in Zamora county who can't walk right into Peter's house and touch him for a loan that'll never have to be repaid.

You'd be hard pressed to find a poor man around here who doesn't owe Peter something."

"So . . . he's a real *patrón*."

Dos nodded. "That's what they call him . . . *El Patrón*."

The election was held a week later, and Peter won, just as he'd predicted, by a landslide.

It was late in November. A norther had come and gone, and the weather had warmed up nicely, bringing one of those perfect autumn days that everyone on the Lantana wished could endure forever.

Maggie sat on the porch, a lap desk on her knees, writing a letter to Bryan.

I know there's no need to tell you how much I miss you, but I read the paper every day on the chance I will see something about the R.F.C. But most of the stories are about the men in the trenches—and hardly ever a word about fighting in the air.

Because you asked me not to in your last letter, I won't tell you how much I worry about you. (Please note how cleverly I managed to tell you nevertheless!)

Right now, I'm sitting on the porch watching a work crew digging an enormous hole off to the side of the house. Dos is building a swimming pool. He says it will be so much nicer than the old water hole at Bitter Creek, but, of course, it means we'll have to be quite proper and wear suits whenever we want to take a dip.

Trev is in the parlor, pumping away on the Pianola. A while ago, for my benefit, he put on "When You and I Were Young, Maggie" and that awful tune "Maggie Murphy's Home." And for the past half-hour, we've heard "St. Louis Blues" over and over. It's a catchy number, but I've heard it so many times, I'll be glad when the roll finally wears out.

He still won't go back to school, and I don't see any reason to press him. I met with his teacher and have begun to give him lessons here at home. Imagine me, a schoolmarm!

So, perhaps it is a good thing that I'm here after all and not in London where—even though we would still be apart—I would feel closer to you.

I agree with you that the Atlantic is growing more and more dangerous every day, but I would brave the torpedoes if I thought we could be together again. Yes, I'd take chances with the U-boats this very moment, but having crossed the Atlantic in winter one time, I think—on second thought— I'd wait till spring!

She didn't mean that last at all. She would have taken to the ocean on an open raft if there were a chance she could spend even one hour with Bryan.

Her pen hovered over the paper for a moment; then she added:

I miss you, my darling. I live for your letters— and for the time when we meet again. I love you.

Maggie

P.S. God! There goes "Maggie Murphy's Home" again!

# 1917

# 28

America entered the war at last. Maggie stood on the veranda gripping the railing as she watched an excited cowboy ring the big yard bell and announce the news she'd long been waiting for. At last! At last, the Yanks were going to join the fight—and she was convinced they would bring the war to an end. And then . . . then she could go home to Bryan!

"Thank God you're as old as you are," she said to Dos as he joined her. "I couldn't stand it if I had to worry about you, too."

Dos looked at her tenderly. "What's the latest from Bryan?"

"Nothing since that last letter two weeks ago. He said it was getting harder and harder to find time to write. I suppose I have to be patient, but it's driving me absolutely crazy."

"Still, you must be proud of him."

"Oh, Dos, I don't see any glory in war. Even when Bryan wrote and told me he'd become an ace, I couldn't find any joy in it."

Cheering and yelling, a host of cowboys streamed into the yard. There were shouts of "War!" "Let's git 'em!" and "We're gonna whup the Kaiser!"

And Trev, just barely thirteen, was right in the middle of them, waving his hat and stomping out an impromptu war dance.

Maggie sighed. "What is it that makes men so eager to fight? Just look at their faces! You'd think they're setting off for a rodeo."

The next day, there was a big enlistment rally in the plaza, and more than a hundred cowboys from the Lantana trekked into town to volunteer.

"They're our men," Maggie told Dos. "I want to go in with them to tell them goodbye."

The town's mood was festive. A band played in the plaza, and bunting fluttered from every storefront. Texans had long been eager for war; and a month ago, with the release of the Zimmermann telegram, their mood reached fever pitch. The message from Germany's Secretary of State for Foreign Affairs to its ambassador in Mexico proposed an alliance between the two countries and called for an invasion across the Rio Grande with the aim of returning Texas and the rest of the Southwest to Mexican control.

The diplomatic note revived old racial hatred and fears, and it suddenly became dangerous to have a Spanish—or even a German—surname. A thousand Rangers patrolled the valley, and the story went that they shot first and asked questions later. There were verified reports that hundreds of Mexicans, guilty of nothing more than carrying six-shooters, had been rounded up, led into the deep brush, and shot; and Dos sent a message to all his vaqueros to leave their weapons behind whenever they crossed the Lantana's fence.

Maggie joined the crowd jamming the plaza and pushed her way toward the pavilion. The band finished its tune and launched into a spirited rendition of "Over There."

Hearing her name called, she turned and saw Peter Stark making his way in her direction.

"What a turn-out!" he exclaimed as he reached her side. "It's bigger than we expected."

Maggie looked around her. "And what irony! Almost every man volunteering here is a Mexican, and the Rangers are down in the valley shooting their *compadres*."

A lieutenant, hastily dispatched from Fort Sam Houston, had set up a recruiting booth beside the pavilion and was swearing in men in groups of a dozen and more. As each man raised his hand and said, "I do," the band played a fanfare bringing cheers from the crowd.

"And how do you feel, Peter?" Maggie asked. "Your family's German. Have you had any trouble?"

"I'm an American, Maggie . . . second-generation Texan."

"So are the Koenigs . . . but his store windows get broken once a week, despite the flag he's got hanging out front."

"That'll pass," Peter said with confidence. Then, excusing himself, he made his way to the pavilion. The band fell silent, and Peter addressed the crowd.

"My friends! What a glorious day! All of Joelsboro is proud of her sons for stepping forward to defend democracy. The war in Europe has reached to our very doorstep. We are all aware of the nefarious plans to

397

wrest our beloved state from the Union and deliver it into the hands of our enemies—"

"You ought to know, Stark!" came a cry from the edge of the plaza.

Peter halted, and a stunned silence fell over the crowd. Maggie craned her neck to see who had spoken.

Then someone else shouted out, "Whose enemies are you talking about, Stark? Ours . . . or yours?"

An ominous rustle swept over the square.

"Now, wait a minute . . ." Peter began, forcing a smile and holding up his hands for quiet. But the mood was turning ugly, and he sensed he was losing control. "I'm an American . . . as patriotic as any man . . . born right here on the Lantana Ranch!"

For a moment, the crowd seemed to settle down, then another voice called out, "The Starks are Germans! Can we trust them?"

"Who said that?" Peter shouted, his face flushed with anger. "Come on up here! Tell that to me face to face."

Peter's bodyguards flew up the pavilion's steps and flanked him, making a point of showing their weapons.

"Hun!" someone yelled.

"Kill the Hun!"

Maggie had listened with mounting horror. She detected fright in Peter's eyes—and, worse, she saw his bodyguards falter and step back. He stood his ground, isolated and vulnerable. Maggie could hold back no longer. She shoved her way to the pavilion and strode to his side.

Silence again. Everyone in the crowd recognized her. She dominated the platform, standing taller than anyone, her head held high, her jaw set and determined.

"Listen to me!" she shouted, and her voice carried across the plaza. "You know me! And you all know the Lantana . . . and what it stands for. This town wouldn't be here if it weren't for the Lantana. Today, over a hundred of our men joined the service of our country . . . *our* country! The United States of America! Most of them were Mexican, a few were Anglos, and some of those bear German names. Who would call any one of them unpatriotic? Go ahead! Let me hear you!"

She paused and her stare dared the crowd. No one spoke. She couldn't suppress a sneer. "Where are the brave men who shouted out a minute before? Come on up here . . . let's talk about it!"

No one met her challenge.

Her voice trembled as she spoke again. "I'm proud of these men who volunteered today . . . and that's more than I can say for you cowards who hide in the crowd and imply that Peter Stark has ties with the enemy. Let me assure you that Peter Stark is as true an American as I am . . . as you are! And you know it in your hearts!"

A low muttering filled the plaza. She had defused the gathering, and they looked to one another sheepishly. The men who had cried out kept silent and tried to lose themselves in the crowd.

Maggie pointed to the band director, and the musicians launched into another number. She turned about and saw the look of gratitude in Peter Stark's eyes. Only then did she feel her legs begin to shake. All at once, she realized where she was and what she had done. She felt the panic of stagefright, but it was too late. It was all over. She leaned against a pillar on the pavilion and tried to catch her breath.

Peter came up to her. "Maggie . . . thank you."

She smiled weakly. "Don't thank me. I didn't even know what I was doing. Something came over me. . . . I couldn't help it. If I had planned it, I wouldn't have

399

been able to get a word out . . . much less make a speech."

"May I take you home?"

"I've got Dos's car. But let's leave here together so everyone can see that I meant what I said."

But despite her words, and her appeal to the crowd using the prestige of the Lantana as support, Peter Stark was awakened that night by the sound of a car pulling up outside. He hurried from his bed and reached the window in time to see a band of men, dressed in white robes, clamber from the vehicle and gather quickly on the sidewalk.

Before he had time to reach for his gun or shout out for help they had set fire to rags stuffed in bottles filled with gasoline and hurled them at the house. There was the sound of breaking glass and an ominous whoosh as the gasoline exploded.

Peter spun about, grabbed his revolver, and fought his way past the spreading blaze, but by the time he got to the sidewalk, the car was speeding off and squealing around the corner. He squeezed off a shot, but it was useless. Behind him, the fire was already raging, yellow flames filling the rooms and roaring through the iron-barred windows.

Peter shook with fright and rage, for he saw in the holocaust a challenge to his power and a threat to the empire he had so carefully built. He stood on the curb and watched as the house burned to the ground.

The next day, when Maggie heard the news, she went to Dos. "Will you go into town with me . . . to call on Peter?"

Dos turned away. "Don't ask me for that, Maggie."

She moved across the room to face him. "Please! It's obvious I don't carry enough weight. But you,

Dos . . . you're the Lantana. People will take notice."

"Why should I want to help Peter Stark?"

"It's not Peter you'll be helping . . . it's us, all of us. There's a hateful poison in Joelsboro, and it'll destroy us all if it's not stopped now."

"You really believe that?"

"Dos, if you'd only seen the crowd . . ."

He sighed, and she knew she'd won.

Peter Stark had taken shelter in the little house beside the still smouldering ruins of his home. A gawking crowd outside witnessed the arrival of Dos and Maggie and saw Peter cross the rubble-strewn yard to greet them. And just as Maggie had calculated, the onlookers were impressed.

Peter shook hands with Dos.

Maggie said, "When you ran for mayor, you wanted the Lantana's endorsement. I hope this is good enough."

Peter nodded. His face was still white with shock. "This is even more important . . . thank you, Dos."

The meeting lasted less than half an hour, but when Dos and Maggie returned to their car, Maggie could see on the faces of the people standing at the curb that their visit had succeeded.

On the drive back to the ranch, she reached across and touched her brother's arm. "We did the right thing, Dos."

He spoke without taking his eyes off the road. "Peter's grateful now. In some strange, peculiar way that wasn't any of his doing, he's managed to get us where he's always wanted."

Maggie removed her hand and sat back. "Well, whatever . . . we did what we had to do. At least we can hold our heads up high."

Now Dos looked at her, a sense of wonder and

respect in his heart. "Maggie, you're an amazing woman. You're strong . . . like Mama was."

"I'm not strong, Dos. It's just that I know what it's like to be a prisoner of other people's opinion. I can't stand to see it happen to anybody else."

They drove for a moment in silence, and as they reached the outskirts of Joelsboro, Dos said, "Look at the horizon, Maggie. There's a storm coming out of the west."

A violet line, barely perceptible, marked the horizon, but before they'd gone another five miles it covered a quarter of the sky.

"It's moving fast," Dos observed. "It's going to be bad. I bet we don't make it home before it hits."

"Mama always said storms out of the west were the worst."

It struck just as they wheeled into the main gate. The day had gone dark as midnight, and great flashes of lightning turned the landscape into silver, while thunder rolled across the prairie.

The cook and her nieces were standing in the driveway, wielding knives, making slashes at the turbulent sky, enacting their old superstition that they could cut the clouds and dissipate the storm.

"Get inside!" Dos shouted above the howling wind. "Lightning will strike you! Get inside!"

They obeyed reluctantly, grudgingly abandoning their magic. And by the time Dos and Maggie dashed from their car into the big house, they were drenched through.

Trev was waiting for them.

"Run upstairs," Dos ordered. "Pull all the shutters."

Trev turned and took the steps two by two. Maggie raced around the ground floor, slamming shutters and turning on lights.

The wind howled like a thousand demons, and every

minute or two, the electric bulbs flickered and dimmed.

Dos had hurried up to his office and was pulling down the windows when he spotted a car's headlamps bobbing up the drive. He closed the last shutter and went back down the spiral staircase, wondering who would be arriving in the middle of such a storm.

By the time he reached the foyer, Maggie had already answered the door. He recognized the man on the threshold, the messenger from Western Union.

"I tried calling," the man said, "but the lines are down. I thought I ought to deliver this right away."

Maggie stared at him oddly, looking at the yellow envelope in his hand.

"If you'll just sign here," he said, holding out his clipboard.

"No," Maggie whispered, backing away.

The man spotted Dos and looked him inquiringly. "It's gotta be signed for."

Dos scratched his name on the ledger and took the telegram.

"No," Maggie murmured again. "No, don't accept it. I know what it says."

Dos suddenly shared her fear.

"Don't open it! Don't read it!"

Trev appeared in the foyer and was frightened by the look on Maggie's face. She lunged at Dos and tried to rip the telegram from his hands. "I said don't take it! You know what it's going to say!"

The Western Union man backed through the door and hurried to his car.

"Maggie! Maggie!" Dos said, trying to calm her. "Get hold of yourself! It's only a wire!"

"Oh, no! It's more than that!" Her voice trembled and broke.

Dos tore open the envelope. What he read turned his

stomach. He looked away, lacking the heart to face Maggie.

Seeing his reaction, she backed up, her hands covering her mouth, stifling her scream, and before Dos or Trev could react, she had bolted from the house.

"Pop!" Trev hollered. "What is it?"

"It's Bryan . . . he was killed in France." Dos crumpled the telegram in his fist.

"How does Aunt Maggie know?"

"She just does . . . sometimes you just know these things without being told."

Maggie had dashed into the yard. She stood in the pelting rain, her dark hair plastered to her neck and shoulders, her voice raised in a wail louder than the wind.

She lifted her arms and tilted her face toward the sky; then she screamed in defiance to the gods who had hounded her all her life. "I knew you would do it! You couldn't leave me alone! You couldn't let me be happy! You've beat me again! Now finish it off! Take me, too! I dare you!"

Lightning crackled from the clouds, a blinding-white bolt that struck the yard bell, causing it to moan eerily as the thunderclap shook the ground beneath her feet.

"Pop! Go get her!" Trev cried.

But Dos watched transfixed, unable to move. The expression on Maggie's face was the most tragic he'd ever seen in his life.

Trev started to run to his aunt, but Dos grabbed him and held him back. "No! Let her be! She's got to do this!"

The boy started to cry and clung to his father.

Maggie shook her clenched fists at the heavens. "Come on! Hit me! I dare you!"

Lightning flashed again, twin forks splitting the air,

exploding a tree and setting it ablaze, then striking a wire fence causing it to zing as sparks shimmered along its length.

The palms lining the drive bent and groaned before the howling wind; thunder roared continuously; and the clouds let loose bolt after bolt of lightning, transforming the stormy darkness into blue-white day.

Maggie's knees buckled and she slumped to the ground. Tears, mingling with rain, streamed down her cheeks, and her eyes were as wild as the heavens. "Kill me!" she screamed again. "Just try!"

She pitched forward and lay face down in the mud. At last, Dos broke from the doorway and ran out into the storm. He put his arm around her and pulled her up. She was trembling violently. Wet earth clung to her hair and caked her clothes. He carried her up the steps and into the parlor, where he stretched her out on a leather sofa. Trev knelt beside her, so filled with horror at what he had just witnessed he was unable to speak.

Maggie's shoulders shook with silent sobs, and tears made rivers through the mud that covered her cheeks.

Dos held her hand tightly. She was trying to say something, and he had to bend close to her lips in order to hear.

"I beat them, Dos! I gave them their chance, and they didn't . . . they couldn't . . ." She exhaled—a long desolate sigh—but Dos thought he saw a look of victory cross her ravaged features. "They had their opportunity . . . and they failed. I'm not afraid of them any more. They'll never get me now!"

# 29

For a long time, Dos feared that Bryan's death had taken the life from Maggie, too. She sequestered herself in her room, and on the rare occasions when she came downstairs, she moved about like a pale spectre. Dos left her alone, feeling helpless in not knowing how to comfort her. But in the end, it was Trev who finally brought her back into the world.

One afternoon, he knocked at Maggie's door and found her sitting at her dressing table, listlessly brushing her hair. He crossed the floor and stood behind her, staring at her reflection in the mirror.

"Are you going to stay in here forever?" he asked simply.

She lowered her eyes and set the brush carefully down next to the comb.

"You're still alive, Aunt Maggie. Why do you want to seal yourself up?"

Her thoughts flew back to Carrington Manor, to the missing window where the nun was supposedly entombed.

"I know you're sad," he said bluntly, "just like I was after Grandma died. You helped me then . . . and I'd like to help you now. Besides . . . I'm lonesome, Aunt Maggie, and I miss you."

She felt his hand rest gently on her shoulder and thought, My God! He's right! I didn't escape the prisons of my past only to wall myself up again!

Tentatively, she reached up and covered his hand with hers. "Oh, Trev! Be my strength! I don't want to go on like this!"

She felt him tug at her hand and lift her from the chair. "Come on, Aunt Maggie. Let's get out of here. We'll take Pop's car and go for a drive. Come on . . . come on." He was leading her toward the door. "Let's see what's happening outside."

They drove all afternoon. It was late summer, blazing hot, but Maggie thought she had never felt a more refreshing breeze as Trev drove her all around the Lantana. And when they came back to the ranch house, just as evening began to creep across their land, Dos watched from the turret window. He saw Maggie climb out of the car and noticed a new lightness in her walk. Then Trev said something to her, and Dos heard Maggie laugh. He had no idea what his son had done to break the tragic spell that had held her for so long, but he was grateful and relieved that she was back with them after so long.

Maggie began to give Trev his lessons again—as much to occupy herself as to educate him—for she found that as long as she kept busy she was able to hold her sorrow at bay.

She bought a car of her own, a shiny green Buick,

and began to travel around the county, visiting little settlements she had never seen before, taking the time to stop and talk with farmers and Mexican laborers and to call on their wives in their poor, tarpaper shacks. She realized they thought she was crazy. Never before had anyone from the Lantana bothered to inquire about their lives, and she sensed, despite their shy graciousness, that her presence in their homes made them uncomfortable. But, in time, they grew used to her visits and were no longer ashamed to serve her hot sweet coffee in chipped, unmatched cups or to offer her a plate of *pan dulce* they had baked that morning. And they were pleased when she admired their fat-bellied babies and cuddled them on her lap.

They called her *Doña* and began to listen eagerly for the roar of her car. She never arrived empty-handed, but learned how to give food, cloth, and even money without making it seem like charity. With the children, it was another matter. Too innocent to be burdened with pride, they would throw down their hoes and run from the fields, hands outstretched for the loose change she distributed among them.

"Why aren't these children in school?" she asked one of their mothers.

"There is no school, *Doña*."

"No school?"

"Not here in Rincon . . . and Joelsboro is too far away."

Maggie stood by her car and watched for a while as the children rejoined their parents in the field. Then she climbed behind the wheel and drove back to the ranch.

"I want some money," she told Dos later that evening. "I'm going to build a school over at Rincon."

"What for?" Dos asked.

408

His question shocked Maggie. "Those children are growing up ignorant. They've never been inside a class-room. I bet none of them can read or write."

"They don't have a need to."

She heaved an exasperated sigh. "Now that's what I call a vicious circle, Dos. Keep them illiterate and they'll stay in the fields—keep them in the fields and . . ."

"But, Maggie, it's always been that way."

"That's the same tune I get from Peter Stark."

Dos looked up. "And speaking of Peter, if you go around building schools, you'll be trespassing on his bailiwick. He won't take kindly to it."

"Then I'll go to the priest at Rincon, and we'll build a parochial school. It won't have anything to do with the county. Peter can't possibly object."

"Try it and see."

"Then I can have the money?"

"You never have to ask me that, Maggie. The Lantana's half yours. You can do anything you want with your share."

"Good," she said decisively. "I'm going to build a school . . . just like Mama did in Joelsboro. You know, we've taken so much from this land, it's time we started to pay for it."

The next morning, Maggie hired a contractor, and within a week, work began on an acre of land she had bought and donated to the church. She visited the site every day, measuring the progress; and she estimated that by the end of November, the children of Rincon would be in class. But one morning she arrived to find the half-completed building deserted. She got out of her car and walked through the construction, noticing that the workmen had packed up their tools and quit in mid-job.

She frowned, puzzled, not knowing what to make of the scene. Then, hearing a car drive up, she went to the door and spotted Peter Stark. He slid from behind the wheel and touched his hat brim as he made his way toward her. Maggie narrowed her eyes, sensing that his arrival was not accidental.

"Morning, Maggie," he called. "How are you today?"

She ignored the question. "Peter, are you behind this?"

He smiled broadly. "Now, don't get your back up. You ought to thank me. I'm just trying to save you a little money."

She had her hands on her hips and stared at him suspiciously. "Oh . . . ? Maybe you'd like to tell me how."

He swaggered up, trying to appear nonchalant. Actually, his pulse had quickened as it always did when he saw her. Lately, he hadn't been able to get her out of his mind. She was the most beautiful woman he'd ever known—and the most worldly, by far. He couldn't shake the fantasy of holding her in his arms and kissing her. And he never doubted for a moment that he would be able to take her to bed. Nor could he avoid thinking what a match they would make. By God, they would be damned near invincible! His power and the Lantana's wealth; together they would possess the state.

"I heard about the school," he said as he drew near. "And I didn't see any reason why you should foot the bill. After all, it's the county's place to educate these kids."

"Well, it's been doing a damned poor job. . . ."

"I've taken steps to remedy that."

"What do you mean?" Maggie asked.

Peter smiled again and shrugged. "My brother Davey and I met with the padre and persuaded him to sell the

410

school to us . . . to the county, I mean. We're going to finish the building, and it won't cost you another penny."

"You had no right!"

He pretended to look surprised. "But it's better for everyone! You don't have to spend any more money, the church won't have to support it, and the kids will have a school."

"And you and Davey will make a handsome profit on every nail and two-by-four that goes into the building."

He kept his expression blank. "I didn't mean to rile you, Maggie. I was only thinking of the expense you were incurring. I didn't see any reason . . ."

"I don't believe you, Peter."

He backed off, wary of her anger, and decided to try another tack. "Well, I really didn't know how you felt about it, Maggie. If I had realized you were building this school out of pride—"

"Out of pride!" Her cheeks flushed suddenly. "Hardly! More out of a sense of obligation!" She stopped, ashamed of how she sounded—the feudal ruler distributing largesse among her people as balm to soothe her guilty conscience. When she spoke again, her voice was barely audible. "I've driven around, visiting all the little towns in the county, and . . . Peter, I've never seen such horrible poverty . . . not even in the slums of London."

Peter felt on surer ground. He raised his eyebrows and shrugged. "It's always been this way, Maggie . . . at least, down here. There's the handful of wealthy, and then there're the peons—with nothing in between."

"I suppose what they say is true . . . this is the part of Mexico that just happens to belong to Texas."

He nodded.

"Well, Peter . . . why does it have to be that way?"

411

"Because people like you own all the land . . . and people like me control the government."

"It'll change one of these days."

"We won't live to see it."

"I wonder . . ." Maggie murmured, pulling her coat closer around her, for a cool north wind whipped across the dusty fields, catching her hair, lifting it away from her face, revealing the high, sculptured curve of her cheek. Sunlight glinted off her lashes, and her eyes matched the clear blue sky above.

Peter reached out impulsively, took Maggie's arm, and pulled her to him. Before she could react, his lips covered hers, and he kissed her hungrily.

Maggie jerked her head to the side and pushed him away with her palms against his chest.

"Please, Maggie!" he whispered, reaching for her again.

She covered her mouth with her fist and backed up against the schoolhouse wall. "Stop it, Peter! Don't ever do that again!"

He stared at her, his chest heaving, his lips still trembling from the kiss. "Maggie, I want you. Can't you see that?"

She had experienced a moment of fleeting fear, but that quickly gave way to a feeling of outrage and violation.

"I want you, Maggie," he repeated.

"I'm something you can't have, Peter. You've taken my school, but you won't take me."

Suddenly his shoulders sagged. He shook his head as if he had been under a spell and was attempting to clear his brain. He took a deep breath and ran his hand over his forehead. "Maggie, forgive me! I don't know what came over me!"

She eyed him warily.

"I'm sorry," he said huskily.

"Then let's forget it ever happened." She left the wall and headed for her car. He caught up with her just as she climbed in and closed the door.

"Maggie, I'm . . ."

"I said forget it, Peter!" Her face was cold and angry, and she had to grip the wheel to keep her hands from trembling. "Now, if you'll move away from my car, I'll be going."

He backed up and watched as she sped off in a cloud of dust. His fingertips went to his lips. He could still feel the touch of her mouth on his, still smell the elusive fragrance of her perfume—and he knew that it hadn't been enough, that he wanted more, that he would do anything to get it.

Her car vanished on the horizon, leaving a smudge of dust against the sky, and Peter still stood watching in the road. Then he cursed himself for losing control, for acting like a schoolboy stealing a kiss. He knew Maggie was not that kind of woman. She would have to be played carefully, wooed before she was won. And he was afraid now that he had spoiled everything.

But I know about you, Maggie Cameron, he thought. I read the investigator's report about your past. I know you had a lover in France . . . and another in England. You're still young, and you're bound to be a lusty woman. Before long you'll want a man to take you in his arms again and make love to you. Why not me?

He threw back his head and shouted down the empty road. "Why not *me*?"

Maggie made no special effort to avoid Peter, and they met from time to time on the streets of Joelsboro or at an occasional party. He was careful to be perfectly polite and never referred to the incident at the schoolhouse. And after a while, she found it easy to forget that it had even taken place.

She couldn't deny to herself that he held a certain fascination, for she was intrigued by his amorality and by the methods he used to maintain his power. Once, at a Christmas party at a nearby ranch, after he boasted about a kickback he'd received from a construction firm doing county work, she asked him, "Why are you so open with me, Peter? Why do you tell me about all your shady deals? Aren't you afraid I might hold them against you someday?"

"Why would you? After all, we're two of a kind. It's us against them."

She resented the implication, but said nothing, letting him continue.

"You once said that this land south of the Nueces is just a part of Mexico that *happens* to belong to Texas. Well, that's not quite right. It's not Mexico at all. It's more like medieval Spain . . . and we're its feudal rulers. You've got your duchy, and I've got mine. You can see yours—that two and a half million acres behind barbed wire. Mine's invisible . . . but it's there all the same. And just as powerful! So, you see, we're equals, Maggie. Both rulers in our own way. Why shouldn't we talk freely to each other? It keeps us out of trouble. You stay in your duchy . . . I'll stay in mine."

She understood his point, but he went on. "Let me give you an example. There's been some pressure to put a direct road from Joelsboro to Agua Blanca, but it would mean cutting right across the Lantana. Now, I know that would rile Dos, and there's no sense causing another fight between the Starks and the Camerons. So, my brother and I have seen to it that the road will bend a little this way and a little that way, skirting your ranch. Oh . . . it'll cost a little more, but it works out

fine for both our families. Davey and I'll take our cut
. . . and the Lantana stays whole."

He smiled at the simplicity of the scheme.

"Besides, Maggie," he went on, "I never tell anybody
anything unless I've got twice as much on them."

She looked at him obliquely, wondering what he
meant, not knowing that he had any inkling of what
her former life had been.

Peter smiled broadly again, wished her a merry
Christmas, and drifted off into the crowd. Throughout
the rest of the evening, she couldn't shake the impression that he had issued her a warning . . . even a threat.
Nor could she ignore the feeling that Peter was watching her. But no matter how stealthily she turned and
glanced across the room, she was never able to catch
his eyes on her.

# 1919–1922

# 30

The summer after the Armistice, Maggie returned to England and took Trev with her. She was in London for more than a week, occupying a suite at the Savoy, before she could bring herself to go to the cottage at Hampstead.

"This is where I used to live," she told Trev as they alighted from a taxi. The once lovely little rose garden had gone to weed, rust covered the iron gate, and the tightly curtained windows were soot-smeared.

She paused in a moment of uncertainty on the step before taking the brass key and unlocking the door. Inside, everything was just as she had left it three years before, but to Maggie it was a ghost house—hollow and dead.

She walked through the rooms, keeping her silence, taking one final look. The auctioneers she had employed had already tagged the furnishings, for she intended to keep nothing except her paintings. They were already crated and stacked in the center of the living room.

Maggie remained at the house for less than ten minutes, and when she told Trev that it was time to go, he hung back and asked, "Aunt Maggie? Would you let me have this?"

"What is it, dear?"

He held out his hand and showed her the crystal paperweight with the golden balloon. The room dimmed with memories for a moment, but she caught her breath and managed to keep her voice steady. "Of course you may . . . I'd like for you to have it, Trev."

He grinned happily and held on tightly to his treasure. Together, they went outside. Maggie pulled the door shut, locked it, then climbed into the waiting taxi and drove off without looking back.

She and Trev stayed another month, visiting Oxford, Cambridge, the Lake Country, and Edinburgh before sailing for New York.

As their ship left Southampton, Trev stayed on deck until the last bit of land disappeared beneath the horizon. Then, catching up with Maggie in the main salon, he perched on the arm of her chair and said, "I really liked England, Aunt Maggie. Do you think I could go back someday?"

"I don't see any reason why not," she replied, brushing his windblown hair away from his forehead. How like Dos he looks! Exactly like Dos! "Maybe you'd like to go to school there . . . to Cambridge where your grandfather studied."

His eyes lighted up. "Yes! Cambridge was swell. I liked punting on the river."

"Then you'll have to go back to school this fall . . .

and study as hard as you can, because you'll be doing more at Cambridge than just boating on the Cam."

"Can't you keep on teaching me?"

She laughed and hugged him close. "Lord, no! I never even finished high school!"

He looked at her in amazement. "Ha! And I always thought you were smart!"

"Street-smart, dear! And that's not such a bad thing, either!"

When they reached the ranch two weeks later, Maggie found that her paintings had already arrived. She had them uncrated and began hanging them on the down-stairs walls.

"You paid good money for these?" Dos asked incredulously as each new picture was brought forth.

"That shows how much you know," Maggie countered. "I picked them up for nothing. They're worth a fortune now."

"Amazing . . . absolutely amazing!" He shook his head in wonder and tried to make sense of a broken guitar, a few splotches of color, and some discordant stripes zigzagging through the middle of the canvas.

Then the last crate was pried open and Maggie raised her eyebrows, murmuring, "Oh, my! I forgot about that one!"

It was the portrait of Maggie nude on the divan.

"Aunt Maggie!" Trev asked. "Is that *you?*"

"Really, Maggie!" Dos said. "You can't mean to hang that!"

She smiled. Gone was all bitterness and hate. She looked at the picture of the young girl with the lovely body and clear innocent blue eyes as if it were the image of someone she had never even known. "Of course, I mean to hang it . . . right over the fireplace!"

"But people will see it!"

421

"I want them to. I want them to see how beautiful I was."

"You're still beautiful, Aunt Maggie."

"Hmm," Maggie said, unconvinced. "No, I used to be. Now, I'm at the age where I'm called handsome. Handsome!" She wrinkled up her nose. "What a tacky word for a woman!"

So the painting was placed above the fireplace in full view of everyone, and everytime a visitor saw it for the first time and reacted by glancing back and forth from the picture to Maggie, she felt a thrill and realized that at last she was utterly released from the prison of her past.

The visit to England had set a goal for Trev—he was determined to return to Cambridge and study where Alex had. He applied himself at school with a vigor that surprised and pleased Dos and Maggie, earning marks that sent him to the head of his class. He played football and baseball, and went out for track. Although he'd always been strong, athletics added weight and even more muscle, and by the time he graduated in May, 1921, he was as big and burly as Dos—and easily as handsome.

Knowing the little school in Joelsboro hadn't properly prepared him for Cambridge, he planned to spend two years at the University of Texas before heading for England. Dos argued that A&M would be more appropriate for a rancher, but Trev declared, "I know plenty about cows and horses. I think I ought to learn about something else."

Maggie backed his decision and calmed Dos when Trev informed him that he intended to major in history.

"It's important to know the story of the land you own. It'll be good for Trev. Let him do it."

Dos acquiesced, but as Trev threw his suitcases into the back of his Ford and prepared to leave for Austin, Dos gripped his son's shoulder and said, "I hope you're not leaving us for good."

Trev smiled. "Don't worry, Pop. I love this place. I've got the Lantana in my blood . . . got it bad."

"That's what Maggie and I thought when we were your age. Then we went away and almost never got back."

"Maybe you didn't love it as much as I do."

Dos stared intently at his son. His heart was bursting with pride and affection. "You're probably right, Trev . . . yes, I think you are."

He wanted to reach out and embrace his son, yet was too shy and embarrassed to make the first move. But Trev opened his arms and hugged his father. "Bye, Pop. I'll write."

For the instant that they held each other close, Dos found himself wishing that Lorna were there. She would have been so proud! Then Trev broke away, jumped into the car, and sped off down the curving drive.

Maggie had watched it all. She moved quickly to Dos, linked her arm in his, and said, "He's a damn sight better than we were, isn't he!"

Dos was too choked up to reply.

Together they turned and reentered the big house. They ended up in the parlor, studying the photographs that had been taken of them when they were children.

"Look at us, Dos. Weren't we young? Weren't we innocent?"

"We had the whole world at our feet."

"Well, between you and me, we covered a good part of it."

"And we ended up back here."

"I'm glad."

He looked into his sister's eyes. "Are you, Maggie? No regrets?"

"None. I'll never get over Bryan. I never want to. But I can go on living."

"I suppose we have no choice."

She read his mind. "You're thinking about Lorna, aren't you?"

He nodded.

"I wish I had known her."

"You would have loved each other."

"I'm sorry you don't have a picture."

He looked strange for a moment, then said almost shyly, "But I do."

"Oh, Dos! Let me see it!"

He hesitated a second before saying, "Come with me."

He led her up the spiral stairs to the grumble room, and going to his desk, he unlocked a drawer and took out a sheet of stiff pasteboard which he handed across to Maggie. "This is the only picture I have."

At first, all Maggie saw were the bold black letters spelling out: WANTED FOR ROBBERY.

"Oh, my God!" she cried out despite herself.

"Isn't it awful?" Dos said. "My wife . . . Trev's mother! And our only photograph is a wanted poster!"

Maggie clapped her hand over her mouth. "Dos! Forgive me, but I can't help laughing! A wanted poster! That's awful! It really is!"

Now he was laughing, too.

"But she's beautiful, Dos! Even in this horrid picture you can see how beautiful she was!"

"Oh, God!" he said, unable to stop his laughter. "This is the sort of thing that Lorna would have loved! She would be laughing harder than the two of us!"

"Oh, Dos! Don't hide this away! If I can hang that

naked picture of me above the mantel, you can frame this poster and put it in the parlor. I don't think Lorna would be ashamed of her past . . . any more than I am."

He wiped his eyes with the back of his hand. "You're right. Lorna would have hung it a long time ago."

"Then you'll put it up?"

"Why not? What the hell do we care what other people think?"

"Not a thing, Dos! No more! No more!"

So, Lorna's picture took its proud place with the other family photographs, and forever after, when Dos saw a guest spot it for the first time, he could almost hear Lorna's laughter echo through the room.

Peter Stark had not given up on Maggie. From time to time he called on her, or invited her into town to attend a party at his side. She went gladly, freely admitting that she enjoyed his company, even though Dos warned her that Peter almost certainly had hidden motives.

"I *know* he does, but I can take care of myself," Maggie assured her brother one evening as she prepared to attend a function Peter was giving in honor of his handpicked candidate for Congress. "We have an understanding."

"I hope Peter knows it."

"He ought to by now."

Waving goodbye to Dos, she set off for Joelsboro and arrived to find a huge crowd already in attendance at Peter's beautifully rebuilt house.

An armed guard checked each arrival's invitation before swinging back the heavy iron gate, but when Maggie appeared, he smiled broadly and addressed her as *"Doña."*

"Hello, Ricardo. *Cómo está?*" She reached out and shook the guard's hand.

*"Muy bien, Doña."*

"And how is your wife?"

"Much better, *Doña*. She told me to thank you for driving her to the doctor last week."

*"De nada,* Ricardo. I happened to be passing by and one of your neighbors told me that Maria was sick. I'm glad to hear she's getting well."

"She said she would like to do something for you, *Doña*. If you have sewing or ironing . . ."

"Well, I have women who do that for me out on the ranch. But I'll tell you what, Ricardo. Tell Maria that next Christmas I would love for her to make me some of her sweet tamales. Hers are the best I've ever tasted."

He smiled again, happily.

Maggie shook his hand again and said, as she moved on, "I'll drop by your house in a day or so to check on Maria."

*"Gracias, Doña."*

Maggie threaded her way through the crowd toward the bar set up in the patio and joined Jack Kendall from the Agarita Ranch.

"Howdy, Maggie," he said, touching the brim of his white Stetson. "How's it going over on the Lantana?"

"Middling," she said, following the unwritten code in those parts never to admit that business was going well.

"Yeah," he agreed, playing along. "Couple of years like the last one and we'll both be in the Mexican poorhouse."

Maggie's eyes swept the accumulation of liquor bottles arranged on the bar. "Look at all that booze! You'd never know there was such a thing as Prohibition."

"Hell, Congress don't make laws for Peter Stark! If

426

the Starks had been around in the time of Moses, God would've checked with Peter before he handed down the Ten Commandments."

Maggie laughed, knowing Jack Kendall had no use for the Stark political machine. "Especially 'Thou shalt not steal.' "

Kendall nodded. "Yep. I reckon that particular one would have said, 'Thou shalt not steal except from the county coffers.' Hell, Maggie, take a gander at this goddamned house . . . big as a castle, fortified like one. And taxpayers like you and me paid for it."

"I imagine we bought a couple of rooms each," she agreed.

"More like the whole downstairs."

Maggie accepted her drink from one of the bartenders. "I suppose it's bad manners to be talking about our host like this."

"I wouldn't be here at all, except I want to meet that fellow he's sending to Congress," Kendall grumbled.

"Who is he, anyway? I never heard of him."

"Name's Curtis Hankins. He's a nobody, a history teacher over at that Presbyterian college, but he's got an ambitious wife and a bend-over-backwards attitude toward Peter Stark. He'll be a manageable puppet." Kendall glanced up. "And speak of the devil—or *both* devils—here they come now, him and Peter."

Maggie turned and saw Peter ushering Curtis Hankins in her direction. The candidate was tall and thin with a shock of coarse black hair that fell across his forehead, presenting a vague carbon copy of Abraham Lincoln. Hankins's rumpled blue serge suit looked awful. Peter, by contrast, was meticulously dressed in pale gray wool with a rich burgundy tie fixed to his shirt by a diamond pin too big to be real—only Maggie knew it was.

Peter was beaming, at the top of his form, the king-maker, the power behind the throne. Hankins followed behind like a lanky, trailing shadow.

"Meet our new congressman," Peter said as he reached the bar.

Maggie smiled politely, but said, "Oh, have we already had the election?"

Hankins looked disconcerted, but Peter merely laughed. "He's got my vote . . . and that's the one that really counts."

"How do you do, Mr. Hankins. I'm Maggie Cameron, and this is Jack Kendall."

"Together these two own most of South Texas," Peter informed his candidate, but his description was unnecessary, for Hankins was well aware who they were. His eyes brightened, and he shook their hands with gusto.

Kendall hung around only long enough to avoid appearing rude, but Maggie stayed at the bar, talking to Hankins, sounding him out. She concluded that he was pleasant enough, almost childlike in his eagerness to please, malleable of course, and for the moment, probably honest. She wondered how soon that would change. It would have to . . . with Peter at his side.

After a while, Maggie started to excuse herself, but Peter held her back. "Don't run off. Let me turn Curtis over to some people I want him to meet, then I'll be back."

He was gone only a moment, and when he returned, he ordered a new drink for Maggie and invited her into his study. He closed the door behind them, shutting out the noisy hubbub of the party. The room was dimly lit —small and cozy with a beamed ceiling, a D'Hanis tile floor, and white plaster walls covered with maps of the five counties Peter controlled.

Maggie waited a minute for him to speak, and when

he remained silent, she asked, "Why the private interview?"

"I just wanted to visit with you alone," he said. "It seems we never see each other any more except in large crowds."

"It's safer that way," Maggie said. Her voice was studiedly casual, but he knew she meant it.

She glided across the floor and sank onto the sofa, arranging a pillow behind her back. "This is good Scotch," she commented, taking a sip. "Who's your bootlegger?"

"I have it brought across the border. Would you like a case? Scotch? Or how about rum or brandy? Whatever you want."

Maggie raised an eyebrow. "As easily as that? We've been making do with bathtub gin and an occasional pint of Four Roses whenever we can get Doc Rogers to prescribe it . . . for medicinal purposes, of course."

"Of course," Peter said, smiling. "Well, there are some things I can arrange better than the Camerons."

All this while, he had been standing by the door. But now he moved and joined her on the sofa. It was dark outside, but a streetlamp cast its slanting rays through the barred window creating highlights in Maggie's dark hair and accentuating the fine curve of her cheeks.

Peter gulped his drink, but his lips and throat remained dry, and he felt an odd flutter in his heart.

A cooing whitewing on the roof distracted Maggie and she glanced into the darkness, but she heard the clink of Peter's glass as he set it down heavily on the marble table and moved closer, trapping her in her corner of the sofa.

"Maggie, I'm nearly fifty. Time seems to fly faster and faster, and every day I get more and more impatient. I don't like to have to wait for what I want, and it's finally dawning on me that tomorrow may be too late."

"Too late for what, Peter?" she asked, although she knew exactly what he meant.

He took her hand. "For us, Maggie. I love you, you know."

His words threw her. She was prepared to hear him say that he wanted her, needed her, desired her. But not love! She hadn't expected that.

So when he moved even closer to her and took her face between his hands, she was still too surprised to resist. And when he pressed her back against the pillow and kissed her, she didn't react. She felt strangely detached, as if she were an invisible observer watching this burly, handsome man slip his arms around someone else's body and kiss her lips before burying his face into the soft curve of her neck and shoulder. She was scarcely aware of his weight against her and never heard him softly murmur her name over and over again.

Then suddenly she snapped back to reality. His attentions had stirred nothing within her, neither passion nor revulsion, and all she could think of was that she wished he wouldn't lean on her so, wouldn't crowd her.

She put her hand on his chest and pushed him away. He opened his eyes and looked at her in bewilderment. He had misunderstood, believing she had acquiesced at last, and his passions were aroused.

She managed to slip from beneath him and stood up, smoothing her skirt. She had no desire to hurt him—or embarrass him; so she smiled and tried to make light of the incident. "Now what if someone had popped in and caught us thrashing around on the sofa? Wouldn't that do wonders for our reputations?"

But her attempt at levity was lost on Peter. All he

knew was that she had rejected him once again, and this time he sensed it was for good. She'd let him take her in his arms and kiss her—and tell her that he loved her. And then she had pushed him away with a joke and left him sitting on the sofa like a thwarted, love-sick boy.

Angry, feeling he'd been made a fool of, he jumped up and grabbed her by the wrists. "What do you mean, 'reputation'?"

She tried to twist free, but he held her fast.

"I don't give a damn about mine," he murmured, his voice a low menacing hiss. "And I know all about yours!"

Her eyes flashed as she looked into his face and saw that he was telling the truth.

"You slept around all over Paris and London. And now you come back to this little hick town and try to pretend you're a lady. You can't fool me, Maggie. I know what you were."

She wrenched her hand free and brought it cracking against his cheek. "You bastard!"

Then, turning, she raced for the door, but he caught up with her, blocking her way. "Maggie, no! Wait! I didn't mean what I said!" His tone had changed. Now he was pleading, contrite. "I love you. I really do. Marry me, Maggie. I'll give you anything you want. If you don't like this house, I'll build you another. If you want to travel, we'll go anywhere. . . ."

She listened impassively, staring blankly over his shoulder. Her mind was full of thoughts of Pascal and Bryan. How could this lecherous, shady-dealing, two-bit politician ever hope to compare himself with those two men? Oh, Pascal! You were in government, too . . . and how gracefully you used your power! And with

431

what sweet elegance you showed your affection for me! And Bryan! My noble love!

Her hand touched the gold bracelet that never left her wrist, and she remembered the words engraved inside it.

"Bryan! Bryan!" She was murmuring his name without knowing it.

But Peter heard and fell silent. At last, her eyes met his. "Move away from the door, Peter. I want to go home."

He knew he had lost her—forever—the first thing in his life that he had wanted and couldn't have. He stared in disbelief. It just wasn't possible. He was Peter Stark. He ran this part of the world!

Her face was hard as stone. "I said, move away!"

He stepped aside, but anger rose in him again, and as she slipped quickly through the door, she heard him whisper, "You're still a whore, Maggie! And you'll be sorry you turned me down!"

She rushed through the house, her face composed, her chin held high, but her entire body vibrated with fury.

At the iron gate, Ricardo, the guard, brightened when he saw her. *"Buenas noches, Doña!"*

"Good night, Ricardo." She headed outside, then remembering, looked back over her shoulder and said, "Don't forget. Tell Maria I'm coming to see her."

"You honor us with your visits."

She turned and strode briskly toward her car, unable to ignore the irony. *El patrón* had called her a whore and tried to maul her, while his peon treated her with respect and friendship that cut cleanly across class and wealth.

Peter's parting insult rang in her ears and mingled

with his final threat. "You'll be sorry," he had said. "You'll be sorry. . ."

Maggie climbed behind the wheel and mashed savagely on the starter. The car roared into life and shot off down the street while Peter watched from his office window.

There was a knock at the door behind him. "Boss?" He recognized the voice of one of his cronies.

"Boss?"

He opened the door.

"Better get out here," the man said. "Jack Kendall's talking to Hankins, and . . . well, our boy ain't making too good a showing. In fact, he's sounding like a damn idiot. And everybody's listening. I think he needs you by his side."

Peter straightened his tie, smoothed back his hair with a swipe of his hand, and headed back to the party.

Her mind flashing with anger and vengeance, Maggie flew down the highway. As she approached the Lantana's gate, she flashed her headlights and barreled past the guardhouse. From his turret window, Dos saw her hurtling down the dark road between the rows of silhouetted palms. He slammed the rolltop desk shut and hurried down the spiral stairs to meet her, reaching the foyer just as she burst through the front door. With windblown hair and color blazing on her cheeks she looked as if she'd just come in off the range after a wild gallop on a spirited stallion.

"What's up?" he asked. "The way you were speeding past those trees, you must've been driving eighty."

She hadn't intended to tell him, but now that he knew something was wrong, she saw no way to hide it.

"It's Peter Stark," she said simply.

Dos's jaws tightened. "What did he do to you?"

"It's not what he did . . . it's what he said."

433

"Tell me!"

"He knows all about me, Dos. All about Paris and London. He called me a whore."

"That goddamned sonofabitch!"

Maggie grabbed Dos's arm. "Cool down! It doesn't concern you. I can take care of myself."

"I'll get the bastard!"

"Dos! Leave it alone!"

"Did he try something with you?"

"It doesn't matter!"

That told Dos everything. He tried to get past her, but she held on to him and pulled him back.

"Let me go, Maggie! I'll put him in his place once and for all!"

"No, Dos! You've had enough trouble because of the Starks! Don't let it happen again! Besides, this is my affair!"

"You don't expect me just to let it pass, do you?"

"Yes! Yes, I do! Peter won't stand for any trouble from you, and . . ." She lowered her eyes and appeared to sag. "And we've already buried Carlos because of me. I won't have you lying beside him!"

Dos quit struggling with her. He heard the pain and fear in her voice and realized he didn't dare be the cause of further grief.

Maggie pressed a hand to her breast and forced herself to breath calmly. She slipped her arm around Dos's waist and said, "I need a drink, Dos. Will you join me?"

Together they went to the parlor. Dos filled two glasses with straight whiskey and leaned against the mantel while Maggie paced the carpet.

"He asked me to marry him, and when I turned him down, he got angry. That's when he said what he did. And then, he threatened me. He said I'd be sorry."

"You won't be."

434

"Of course I won't be," she said with resolve, "but as I told you, I can take care of myself. And I'm not going to let that challenge pass. I'm going to take on Peter Stark and beat him at his own game! It's about time someone shows him he can't have everything he wants."

She tilted her glass and took a swallow. The moonshine tasted raw and burned her throat. "You've got to fire that bootlegger, Dos. This stuff would kill a horse."

She smiled suddenly, almost ruefully, but Dos could detect mischief in her eyes. "I think I turned Peter down too soon. He offered me a case of Scotch."

Dos relaxed, seeing that her tension was dissipating.

Maggie had ceased her pacing. She was looking over his shoulder at her portrait hanging above the mantel.

"What do you think that picture of me would look like on a poster?" she asked, a sly smile playing across her lips.

"What do you mean?"

"No . . . no, I don't suppose it'd do at all."

"What are you talking about, Maggie?"

She had stopped by the sofa. Suddenly she reached down and picked up the telephone. The switchboard in the basement answered immediately. "Connect me with the *Joelsboro Journal*," she said.

"What are you doing, Maggie?"

She winked across at Dos while the phone rang and held up her finger, telling him to wait. "Hello . . . hello. This is Maggie Cameron. Would you send a reporter to the Lantana tomorrow morning? I want to announce my candidacy for the U.S. Congress."

# 31

Peter Stark was still in bed, sipping his morning coffee, when Curtis Hankins burst in with the newspaper. Peter glanced at the headlines, then tossed the paper to the side.

"I've already heard about it through the grapevine."

"What do you think it means?" Hankins demanded, his brow furrowed with worry.

"It means . . . that Maggie Cameron is trying to beat you out of a job."

"Does she have a chance?"

Peter smiled. "Simmer down, boy. Reach over there and pour yourself a cup of coffee. You look nervous as a long-tail cat in a rocking chair factory."

"But I thought it was going to be a sure thing . . . no competition. That's what you said."

"She won't be any competition. Don't get all worked

up over that. Who in the hell's going to send a woman to Congress?"

"There was that Jeannette Rankin from Montana . . ."

"Aw, that was a fluke . . . and she only lasted one term."

". . . and Alice Robertson from Oklahoma."

"Can't imagine what came over those Okies . . . anyway, Maggie Cameron doesn't have a platform to stand on, and besides, the men of South Texas would sooner elect a monkey than a woman. They've got too much sense to have some female represent 'em."

His assurances mollified Hankins somewhat, and the former schoolteacher took a seat and helped himself to coffee. "She's got all the money in the world to finance her campaign."

"How much does a person need?" Peter asked. "A hundred bucks for posters, a few dollars to rent a hall here and there, some gasoline . . . it doesn't take a lot."

"What about poll taxes?"

Peter leaned forward in his bed and wagged a finger at Hankins. "Now, Curtis, you're worrying about things that have already been taken care of. My people got hold of the rolls, like they always do, and paid the poll tax for all those who won't or can't. And, just before election day, we'll pass out sample ballots with an $X$ by your name so even those who can't read will know who to vote for."

Hankins nodded, relieved, and his shock of lank black hair fell across his forehead, obscuring his eyes. "I wonder why she did it . . . why she decided to run."

Peter sank back against his pillow and sighed. "There's no accounting for what a woman's going to do next. Just when you think you've got them figured out, they turn the tables on you. Hell, if I'd known Maggie was fired up to go to Washington, I'd've made her a senator."

Hankins brushed his hair out of his eyes and looked up. "You're kidding, aren't you?"

Peter smiled wryly. "Sure . . . I'm kidding, just kidding."


As soon as Trev heard the news of Maggie's candidacy, he withdrew from the University, threw his bags into his car, and headed home. His brain buzzed with visions of a wild, woolly campaign with noisy rallies in the plaza, a brass band playing from the back of a flatbed truck, and heated debates between Maggie and Curtis Hankins. But when he reached the Lantana he found that Maggie had other ideas.

"I'm not going to make any speeches," she declared. "Especially not in the plaza. I still shudder when I remember the time I spoke out for Peter. It scared the daylights out of me. After it was over, I was so nervous I could hardly stand up."

"But you've got to have some publicity," Trev argued, unable to hide his disappointment at being denied a good time. "Nobody's going to vote for you if they don't know who you are."

She looked at him with amusement. "Trev, honey, people on two continents know who I am."

"Well, at least, put up some posters," he offered lamely.

She nodded in agreement. "I'll let you take charge of that."

"Swell!" he said, jumping up. "I'll get hold of a printer right away."

"Just one thing," she said, calling him back. "Make the posters simple and plain . . . and not too many of them, either. I don't want anyone saying Maggie Cameron bought her way to Washington."

Trev looked at her in silence for a moment, then asked softly, "Do you really think you'll win, Aunt Maggie?"

She shrugged, but her face was serene. "I think I'll give Peter Stark a good race. After all, he's the one I'm really running against . . . not Hankins."

"Sure wish I was old enough to vote."

"So do I," she said. "As it is, I can only count on two . . . Dos's and mine."

After Trev left for town to find a printer, Maggie climbed into her car and began the most peculiar campaign the district had ever known. She drove over to the village of Rincon and called on Maria, the wife of Peter's bodyguard.

The woman was delighted to see her and served her coffee as they sat together at the kitchen table.

"I'm running for Congress," Maggie said.

Maria nodded. "Ricardo told me, but he says *el Patrón* is telling everyone you don't have a chance."

"I probably don't, but I'm going to try, anyway."

Maria lowered her eyes and said quietly, "If you won't tell anyone, I promise to vote for you."

Maggie reached across the table and clasped the woman's hand. "That's brave of you, Maria."

"You were good to me when I was sick, *Doña*."

"I was only helping a neighbor."

"Then I shall help you in return."

"*Gracias,* Maria."

"And . . ." Maria spoke in a whisper as if she were afraid of being overheard. "And you have Ricardo's vote, too. He says *el Patrón* may pay our poll tax, but he can't see what we do inside the booth."

Later, Maggie visited each house in Rincon, spreading the word, asking for support, and in the days that followed she became a common sight speeding along county roads alone behind the wheel of her dusty green Buick. She stopped at every dwelling, chatting in Spanish, rocking babies in her arms, and drinking so much coffee that she found it next to impossible to fall asleep at night.

Her quiet—nearly invisible—campaign lulled Peter, and he commented to Hankins, "She must have come to her senses and realized it's useless to waste her time. She's going to be mighty ashamed of her showing come election day."

His confidence spread to Hankins, and neither saw any reason to intensify their efforts, even though every telephone pole in the district now bore a poster imprinted with Maggie's picture.

Trev did his best to persuade Maggie to hold a rally, but she absolutely refused.

"I like doing it my way," she declared after returning from a long day in the neighboring county.

"But you're wearing yourself out. You can't hope to visit every house in the district."

"I'm going to try."

Dos had been listening silently. Finally, he spoke up. "Where are you off to tomorrow?"

She heaved a weary sigh. "Carmelo."

"Long drive."

"You bet. It'll take all day just to drive there and back."

He nodded thoughtfully and, after a while, excused himself and left the room. The next morning, when Dos came to the breakfast table, Trev noticed an odd expression on his father's face. It was as if he had a secret that pleased him immensely and he couldn't wait to tell it.

Maggie was too preoccupied to notice, already fretting because she was half an hour behind schedule and wouldn't reach Carmelo until noon. She shuddered as the cook tried to fill her cup with coffee. "Please, no! I'll probably drink gallons before I get back home tonight!"

She barely touched her breakfast, taking a bite or two of bacon, nibbling a corner from a piece of toast, and ignoring completely her scrambled eggs. She tossed her napkin beside her plate and stood up. "Well, I'd better hit the road. If I don't get going now, I won't be back till midnight."

"Wait a minute," Dos urged. "Let's all finish breakfast together."

"I'm already late . . . and you know how long that drive is."

Trev watched his father and saw a sly smile play across his lips.

"But I've got a surprise for you, Maggie."

Standing in the doorway, purse in hand, she looked at Dos expectantly, but he waved her back to her seat.

"It'll be along directly."

"Oh, Dos. Can't it keep till tonight?"

He shook his head. "Just hold your horses, Maggie. And finish your breakfast. You have time . . . believe me."

Mystified she returned to her meal. She really was hungry, and she knew the day ahead promised to be grueling. She was the last to become aware of a low drone that drifted through the open windows.

"What's that?" Trev asked.

Dos smiled again. "That must be my surprise."

Maggie glanced up, her ears catching the sound.

441

"Come on, Maggie," Dos said, pulling back her chair. "Let's go outside."

"What's that noise?" she asked.

The drone grew louder. Dos slipped an arm around Maggie's waist and led her from the room with Trev hurrying after them.

They reached the porch just as a crimson biplane swooped from the sky and buzzed the turret, missing the mansard roof by inches. The engine's roar was deafening, causing Maggie to clap her hands over her ears. The plane swept by so low that Trev felt he could have reached out and grabbed it. Then it pulled up swiftly, steeply, and seemed to hang in the sky for an instant before rolling quickly over into a graceful loop.

"Oh, my God!" Maggie cried, certain it was going to crash, but the pilot leveled off just feet above the ground, circled the big house once, and landed in the pasture with scarcely a bounce.

"Wings, Maggie!" Dos shouted. "I've bought you a set of wings to fly you wherever you want to go! That's my surprise."

"Oh, Dos!" she exclaimed, hugging him tightly, thinking of Pascal and his little surprises. Then she backed away. "Oh, Lord!" she said. "I've never been in an airplane!"

"If you can sail across Paris in a balloon, you can do anything," Dos promised. "You're going to love this, Maggie. It's just your style."

Maggie wasn't so sure. She watched warily as the crimson craft came to a halt. When the pillot killed the engine, he climbed from the cockpit and jogged over to them.

Dos greeted him with a handshake. "Howdy, Mr. Porter. This is my sister Maggie and my son Trev."

But Trev had already left Dos's side and was exploring the plane.

Porter perfectly suited the image of a barnstormer—young and dashing, wearing a light leather jacket with a white silk scarf wrapped around his neck. His goggles were pushed up onto his forehead, and his sandy hair looked like a haystack whipped by a storm.

"So you're my passenger," he said to Maggie.

"I'm afraid so," she replied, glancing apprehensively over his shoulder at the plane.

"Well, if you're ready, we might as well be off. You want to go to Carmelo, right?"

"Yes, Carmelo, first. Then down to Ochoa. And then, I thought if we had time we could drop in at Madison."

"Oh, we'll have time. We'll be in Carmelo in less than an hour."

"Imagine, Dos!" Maggie said, turning to her brother. "Less than an hour to Carmelo!"

Porter reached into one of the cockpits and handed Maggie a pair of goggles. "Better put these on. It gets pretty windy up there."

She did as she was told and let him help her into the plane. When he had seated himself behind his controls, he called out to Trev to give the propeller a yank.

"You be careful, Trev!" Maggie shouted, but Trev did his job perfectly. The engine caught and the propeller began to spin.

Trev sprinted over to Dos's side, and as the little biplane began to roll, they heard Maggie yelling over the motor's roar. "Now, please be careful, Mr. Porter. No stunts! No loop-the-loops! No flying upside down. . . ."

The plane bounced across the field, then rose into the air like a leaf carried aloft by a gust of autumn wind.

Porter steered the aircraft into a gentle bank, and Maggie held her breath until they straightened out again. Only then did she dare look over the side, and she found herself just as enchanted by the view as she'd been the morning Bryan took her up in the balloon.

The big house, looking very small, was off to the left, and she could see the blue swimming pool sparkling in the sunshine. Dos and Trev were still standing together, waving, and Maggie would have waved back if she could have pried her fingers free from the sides of the cockpit.

In the distance, she caught sight of a herd of grazing cattle and wondered if someday the Lantana's cowboys would use airplanes for roundup. Why, one man in a plane could do the work of ten on the ground—and a lot faster, too! But then, deciding that the engine's roar would spook the cattle, she dismissed the idea as foolish and sat back, resolving to enjoy the trip.

How different it was from ballooning! That time, so long ago, she had clung to a fragile soap bubble drifting with the wind. But the airplane was harnessed to power; its propeller chewed its way through the sky, and rather than relying on the capricious breeze, she and Porter were its masters. Her pulse fluttered, her cheeks glowed, and she felt her entire body sharing the tremendous energy.

She released her grip on the cockpit's sides and relaxed. This wasn't so frightening after all; in fact, she might even call it enjoyable. And she wasn't at all sure that she would object if Mr. Porter forgot her orders and flipped the plane through a dizzying loop.

Almost before she knew it, they were buzzing Carmelo, bringing women streaming from their houses and causing a stir among the workers in the fields as the aircraft skimmed along tree-top high circling the town. They dropped into a pasture, and before the propeller spun to a stop, a crowd had surrounded the plane.

Trev would have been happy, for Maggie's novel arrival forced her to make a speech. The crowd demanded it, and she was surprised at how easy it was, after all. Perhaps the excitement of the flight had cured her stagefright, or maybe it was the throng's enthusiastic welcome—but she found herself standing on a wing, waving both hands above her head, shouting: *"Buenos días, señoras y señores! Me llamo Maggie Cameron del rancho Lantana!"*

There was a cheer that rattled her for a moment, but she regained her composure quickly and went on, telling them about her candidacy, asking for their support, and when she finished, she heard a young boy call out: *"Viva la Doña Águila!"* Long Live Lady Eagle!

The nickname caught on, spreading from village to village, faster than she could fly, and in the days to come, whenever she landed, she was greeted by chants of *"Águila! Águila! Águila! Eagle! Eagle! Eagle!"*

Suddenly, Peter Stark was worried. Maggie and her biplane had captured the people's imagination, and everywhere he went he heard the word Eagle.

"She's going to beat us with a slogan," he told his brother Davey. "Hankins is a good man, but he's dull. The crowd'll vote for excitement every time. I think I've made a mistake."

He stewed for a day or two, then put in a call for Maggie, leaving a message with the switchboard at the Lantana. When she flew in that evening and learned he'd tried to reach her, she considered ignoring him, but her curiosity got the best of her and after supper,

445

she picked up the phone and asked for his number.

"What do you want, Peter?" she asked when he answered.

"Can you meet with me?"

"Whatever for?"

"I need to talk to you."

"We're talking now."

"Not on the phone," he said. "Why don't you come here?"

"I'd rather not."

There was a moment's silence at his end. Then he said, "How about the Palace Café? I'll buy you a cup of coffee."

Maggie rolled her eyes at the mention of coffee, but she agreed. "All right, I'll be there at eight."

The Palace Café didn't live up to its name—it was a dingy establishment a mile out on the highway leading south from Joelsboro and not the sort of place where a woman went alone; but when Maggie arrived she recognized Peter's black Packard parked in front. His windows were tinted deep blue, making it impossible to see inside, but when she climbed out of her car, his door opened and he beckoned her over. She crossed the parking lot and slid into the passenger seat. Peter was alone.

"Thanks for coming," he said.

She kept her voice cool and aloof. "What do we have to discuss?"

"I want to make you an offer."

She waited.

He reached behind him and brought forth a flask and two glasses. "Let's have a little drink."

"That sounds fun," Maggie said without enthusiasm.

He ignored her tone and splashed the liquor into

the glasses. "I've got a proposition that I hope you'll accept."

"I'm all ears."

Again he ignored her sarcasm. "You've whipped up a little excitement around here . . . more than I would have thought. Now, I still don't think you can win, but you're probably going to give Curtis a run for his money."

*"Whose* money?"

He let that pass. "That bit about the Eagle was pretty clever."

"It wasn't my idea."

"It doesn't matter . . . people like sideshows, and you're giving them one."

Maggie smiled in the darkness and took a sip of Peter's excellent Scotch. "If you've got any extra bottles of this lying around, I'd appreciate it if you'd send them out to the ranch."

"I'll give you anything you want, Maggie . . . in fact, I'm willing to give you the election!"

She looked at his shadowy form over the rim of her glass. "Thanks, Peter. I appreciate it. This campaigning has begun to get me down. Now I can relax."

"Wait a minute . . . it isn't for free!"

"I didn't think it was." She laughed softly.

"Maggie, forget the past! Forget what happened between us! I'm trying to make you a deal."

"Go on."

"You can win, you know. I can see to that."

"I'm on my own, Peter."

"With me behind you . . . it's a cinch!"

"What about Hankins?"

"Hankins . . . Hankins! He's only what I make him."

"So you'd drop him?"

447

"In a second . . . if you and I could work together."

"No dice!"

"What?" He sat forward and stared at her. "Maggie, this is the big time. The U.S. Congress!"

"I know what it is."

"You can't get there without me."

"I'm going to try."

"Think about it, Maggie. We belong together. . . ."

"I've heard that line before."

"I said forget the past. I made a mistake. I apologize for it. Let's put that behind us. It's the future I'm thinking of. You and me, Maggie! Consider it! The Starks and the Camerons working together . . . my political organization and the Lantana's reputation. God, Maggie! We could own the Governor. We could have both Senators in our pockets. One of these days, the President himself would pick up the phone when we called."

"Big dreams, Peter."

"Damn right!"

"Well, like I said, no dice!"

"Why, Maggie?"

"Because I don't want to."

"Don't be a fool, Maggie. Even Dos would tell you to take my offer."

"No, he wouldn't! And even if he did, Dos doesn't tell me what to do. I live my own life. I make my own decisions. It's a brand-new world, Peter. Old maids like me don't have to sit at home with our knitting."

He sat back and laughed. "You're no old maid, Maggie!"

"No . . . I'm an old whore. Remember? You told me so once."

His laughter died. "I'm sorry for that, Maggie."

"You ought to be."

Silence fell between them. Then Maggie reached for the door.

"Wait!" he cried.

"I'm tired, Peter, and I'm flying out early in the morning."

"Maggie! Deal with me! We'll create an empire!"

"I've got one, Peter. I don't need two."

She left him and hurried through the darkness to her car.

He sat behind his wheel, trembling, sweat dampening his collar. "Damn you, Maggie! I'll bring you back to earth! Just wait and see!"

The next day, Peter called Dos. His voice was oily and slick, his tone condescending and polite. "I tried to reason with her," he said. "Maybe you can make her see that the two of us together could be a power to be reckoned with."

"That doesn't concern me," Dos replied.

"You must have some influence with her."

"None that I'd care to exercise."

Peter growled into the mouthpiece. "You Camerons are too damned high and mighty! It's about time someone took you down a notch. Hell! It's about time someone dragged you in the dirt."

"And you're going to try?"

"Damn right! Tell Maggie if she doesn't play along, I'll spread her past all over the front page!"

Dos struggled to keep his calm. "I'll tell her." He hung up and smashed his fist against his palm, thinking how much he would like to be pounding Peter Stark's face instead.

When Maggie landed that night, Dos told her about Peter's call. They were in the parlor, and she walked up to the mantel and stared at her portrait. "Look at that girl," she said, as if she were talking about someone else. "It had to take guts to pose for that picture, even if she did love the artist. And it took guts to steal enough money to cross the ocean in search of him. She felt lost and weak; she thought she needed him. And later, when she fell in love with Bryan, she didn't know how much courage it would take to live openly with him. But she did! She was strong . . . without knowing how really strong she was. And then, when she had to face her mother, feeling guilt and shame after so many years, she found she was able to do it."

She turned and faced Dos. Her face was hard, her jaw set and determined. "I can't let that brave girl down, can I? I can't turn tail and run! I've got to stand by her side . . . match her strength, fight every inch of the way."

Dos's heart filled with pride. But he warned her, "Maggie, Peter will smear the story across the papers."

She smiled, totally at peace with herself. "Let him!"

# 32

Two days later, black headlines told the tale. Preachers did their duty and rose in their pulpits to denounce Maggie, calling her a Jezebel. But strangely enough, their congregations walked away, thinking of her as Magdalene instead; and the Catholic Mexicans were utterly unswayed. Perhaps the sophistication of old Europe still lived in their veins, for peccadillos didn't shock them, and sin played little part in their lives. It was so easily confessed, so quickly forgiven, so wisely forgotten. The revelations of Maggie's past didn't turn the women against her, and, to Peter's dismay, it raised her esteem in the eyes of the men.

Wherever she went, the crowds shouted even more loudly: *"Viva la Doña Águila!"* They mobbed her in every pasture where the crimson biplane touched down, and she found it wasn't necessary to speak. Her appearance sufficed.

The primary was held the fourth Saturday in July. Maggie rose early, cast her ballot, then went back to the ranch house to wait.

It was mid-day before Peter left his home and strolled to the courthouse to vote. In a last-ditch effort to defeat Maggie, he had ordered his men into their cars to scour the district. They prowled the towns and motored along country roads, picking up people and driving them to the polling places; and if for some reason, a poll tax hadn't been paid, there were forged receipts to remedy the oversight. And at Peter's direction, the passengers were pointedly reminded that *el Patrón* expected them to vote for Curtis Hankins.

As Peter approached the courthouse, he noted with satisfaction that the grounds were littered with the sample ballots he'd had printed up—each one carefully marked with a bold, black *X* beside Hankins's name.

He smiled to himself, and later, as he left the booth, someone in the lobby shouted out good-naturedly, "How'd you vote, Mr. Stark?"

Peter formed a pistol with his thumb and forefinger and pointed overhead. "Well, you might say I just shot that Lady Eagle out of the sky!"

Then, tucking his thumbs into his beltloops, he bade the gathering good day and swaggered back out into the sunshine.

The first thing he saw was Maggie's face staring at him from a poster. As he walked by, he reached up and tore it from the telephone pole and dropped it to the ground around the scattered sample ballots.

Maggie had intended to spend the day resting up from the arduous campaign, for she knew that the night ahead, waiting for returns, was bound to be long and tense. But Trev was too keyed up to sit still for

452

more than a minute. He paced and fidgeted, wandered in and out of the house a dozen times an hour, and even fired up one of Dos's cigars, puffing on it until the pungent blue smoke made him dizzy.

Maggie watched him with amusement and finally said, "I'll swear, Trev, I believe you want me to win this election more than I do."

"I probably do, Aunt Maggie. I can't remember when I've wanted anything more. And I think I'm going to go crazy waiting for the polls to close."

She took pity on him and suggested they take a drive. He jumped at the opportunity. They climbed into his Ford and began to wander aimlessly over the ranch. The day was blisteringly hot, and the horizon shimmered like a silver moat encircling the land. Cows huddled in motts of mesquite, seeking the scanty shade, and dragonflies buzzed like iridescent sparks hovering above the rustling grass.

They passed by Bitter Creek, and Maggie reminisced out loud, "When I was a girl, I used to spend all summer here, taking dips and keeping an eye out, scared to death a cowboy would catch me in my birthday suit. I always kept a shift on one of those pepper bushes so I could slip into it quick. And your daddy used to hide out high up in the salt cedars and spy on the Mexican girls when they came down to swim. One day, the branch broke and he fell right in the middle of them. You could hear their screams all the way to the big house."

Trev laughed and tried to imagine the commotion.

Then they drove by an abandoned house. Its roof had long since fallen in, leaving only four bone-white walls of native stone.

"That's where the Starks used to live when Peter's

father was foreman. And Mama and Dos moved in there after the old hacienda burned."

"Is it true that Rudy Stark stole a lot of money from Grandma?" Trev asked.

Maggie gazed at the deserted house. "That's what they say. Mama never talked about it. I think she was embarrassed, because it was more than half a million dollars. Some people thought Rudy stashed it away in banks here and there around the state. But I've always believed it's still somewhere on the ranch, buried under a rock or beside a fencepost. When I was a girl, I used to ride out with a shovel strapped to my saddle and go looking for it. I bet I dug a thousand holes from here to the Ebonal."

"Did you ever find anything?"

"A rusty horseshoe and a handful of arrowheads . . . but not a single penny."

"Maybe one of the hands already found it."

"I don't think so," she said. "Word would've gotten around. I think it's still out there. Maybe one of these days you or your future children will come across it. Oh, wouldn't that be something!"

They rode on throughout the afternoon, and Maggie found it harder and harder to take her eyes off the terrain. Every landmark they came upon—the profusion of lantana blooming at the graveyard; the original mission church built of stone and mortar and still in use; one of the first windmills put up in South Texas; the skeleton of a chuck wagon from the days of the cattle drives, abandoned because of a broken axle, now half-buried in sand—all these and so much more flooded Maggie's mind with memories. The trip was a diary of her girlhood. Here was where she used to take shelter when caught in a sudden summer rain. There was where she fell from a horse and broke her collarbone. And over there . . . she was twelve and saw a handsome cowboy planting fenceposts. He was stripped to the waist and his muscles rippled beneath his sweat-slick skin. And she had felt, for the first time, a flutter of excitement in her breast but was too inexperienced to know what caused it.

"My God!" she said out loud, almost forgetting that Trev was at her side. "I almost hope I lose this election. I must be crazy to want to leave the Lantana again!"

"Don't say that, Aunt Maggie!"

She abandoned her memories and turned to smile at him. "Let's go home, Trev. I'll need some time to get dressed before we go into town to await the outcome."

In front of the *Journal* building, carpenters had erected a platform bearing large blackboards on which the election results would be displayed.

Maggie, Dos, and Trev parked across the street and waited in the car. It was still early, but a crowd had already formed, some milling about in the streets, others settling in for the evening on folding chairs or blankets spread out on the sidewalk. As the sunlight failed, electric lights blinked on, illuminating the blackboards, and soon afterward, the first returns were posted.

Trev slumped in his seat. The figures came from one precinct only, but they showed Maggie trailing by more than a hundred votes.

"Off to a bad start," Maggie said lightly.

"Don't give up so fast," Dos cautioned. "That's only one precinct. And look, it's from Menendez, a Stark stronghold."

At that moment Peter's black Packard with its inky blue windows pulled up at the edge of the crowd. It seemed to crouch in the shadows, looking like a preda-tor lying in wait, a panther set to spring. Its presence brought a momentary hush to the crowd; but soon after, the men on the platform began chalking in new figures, and all eyes returned to the blackboards.

Trev groaned. In the race for Congress, Curtis Hankins was leading by nearly four hundred votes. Maggie's spirits sagged, but Dos, as if he could read her mind, reached across and took her hand. "It's still early. Things'll turn around."

Maggie shrugged. "I only ran to spite Peter. Now, I suppose I'll have to eat crow."

"Don't talk like that, Aunt Maggie," Trev urged, but there was dread and discouragement in his voice.

"I wouldn't mind living in Washington, you know. I loved the city from the moment I laid eyes on it. But . . . the Lantana's plenty for me. It's home. And I've spent far too many years away from it."

But Trev wasn't listening. He was watching the men scribbling in the latest returns. "Look!" he shouted. "Aunt Maggie! You took Rincon!"

And she had. By more than two to one, cutting Hankins's lead almost in half.

"That's Maria's doing!" Maggie whispered. "I'm sure of it! If Peter ever finds out, he'll have Ricardo's head."

Then Ochoa reported, and before Maggie could read the figures, she heard the crowd shout, *"La Doña Águila!"*

Trev let out a whoop. "Aunt Maggie! You're neck and neck!"

"I bet Peter's sweating now!" Dos grinned.

But a moment later, they were cast into gloom as a big block of votes went to Hankins. He led comfortably for the next half-hour; then Maggie edged forward, nearly catching him before Hankins won another important precinct.

Maggie covered her eyes. "God! This is worse than a horserace!"

Suddenly she heard the crowd again. "*Águila! Águila!*"

Madison had gone heavily for her, putting her back in close contention; and as the next hour dragged by and the returns filtered in from distant precincts, she and Hankins played tag, exchanging the lead more than a dozen times.

It was growing late, and all of the other contests had long since been settled; but the crowd lingered in front of the *Journal* office, unable to take their eyes off the boards, unwilling to leave before this last race was decided.

Maggie whittled away at Hankins's slight lead, then pulled in front—but by less than twenty votes.

"We still haven't heard from Carmelo," Dos observed.

"Wait," Trev said. "Maybe that's it now."

A man was chalking in new figures, and they strained to see past him, but even before he moved aside, they knew Maggie had taken the town, for the crowd cheered again, "*Águila! Águila!*"

"My God!" Maggie cried when she saw the board. She had trounced Hankins in Carmelo and shot ahead by more than a thousand votes.

"That's it!" Dos shouted. "He'll never be able to catch you now!"

Maggie crossed her fingers; but she needn't have worried, for she never trailed again.

Hankins made a showing here and there, but it was never enough, and Maggie's lead steadily increased until it was clear to everyone that she had won.

Trev hugged her, tears of joy glistening on his cheeks. Dos kissed her and said, "Maggie! You beat him!"

She laughed and cried and wiped the tears from her eyes. "I can't believe it!"

"You did it, Aunt Maggie!"

She sniffed and studied the figures on the blackboard again. "Well, that shows what a bad reputation can do for you!"

They laughed heartily and hugged each other once more; then Trev said, "Aunt Maggie, go up on the platform."

"I couldn't!"

"You ought to! They voted for you. They'd like to see you!"

"Trev's right, Maggie," Dos said.

"Oh, my!"

"Come on, Aunt Maggie! I'll go with you."

Together, she and Trev made their way to the scaffolding, but before they reached it the crowd recognized her and began chanting, "Eagle! Eagle! Eagle! *Águila! Águila! Águila!*"

Off to the side, the big black Packard backed up and crept slowly away.

The throng cheered as Maggie was helped onto the platform. She waved and waved until her arm grew tired. She tried to keep her composure, but tears blurred her vision, and all she could say was, "Thank you! *Gracias! Muchas gracias!*"

# 33

Maggie awoke the next day still dazed by her victory. She pulled on a silk robe and went downstairs where Trev and Dos were already at the breakfast table. They greeted her with smiles, but instead of joining them, she stood gripping the back of her chair and glanced from one to the other.

"I've just had the most horrible thought," she said slowly. "I don't know the first thing about the U.S. Congress!"

There was a moment's silence; then Dos burst into hearty laughter. "Relax, Maggie. Sit down and have your breakfast. The next session doesn't convene until December. You've got a long time to prepare."

An hour later, she sat curled up in her bed, reading the Constitution for the first time in her life. And after she had plowed through it three or four times, she laid it aside and reached for an encyclopedia and began studying the history of the United States.

In the weeks that followed, she traveled around the state, meeting with other congressmen, picking their brains, learning as much as she could. She learned about power—a different kind than the power owning the Lantana brought. The men she met were reticent at first, suspicious of this woman who was joining their exclusive club, and none of them was quite able to forget the stories about her past that had surfaced during her campaign. But her charm and quick intelligence broke through the barriers of all but a couple of the crustiest and most prejudiced, and she breathed easier knowing she had colleagues to turn to for advice.

Although she still had to face the general election in November, lobbyists began calling on her to press their special interests, for Texas was a one-party state, and the primary was the only race that really mattered. She was headed for Washington; no one could stop her now.

As the summer drew to a close, Trev packed up and prepared to leave for Austin—his last year at the University before heading for Cambridge. Maggie hugged him and kissed him goodbye.

"I'm damned proud of you, Aunt Maggie."

"You'll come see me in Washington, won't you?"

"Just try to keep me away! In the meantime, tell President Harding hello."

As soon as the formality of the November election was over and done with, Maggie made plans to move. It took a dozen trunks to hold all her clothes and an equal number of crates to contain the furniture she wanted to take with her.

On a quick exploratory trip to Washington in September, she had rented a lovely house in Georgetown —small but elegant, with a first floor perfectly suited for entertaining, a cozy upstairs, and plenty of room for the three maids and the cook who were to accompany her.

On the Monday following the general election, Dos drove her to the siding where the Lantana train with its two Pullman cars waited to take her away. Just before dawn, a mild norther had passed through, bringing rains that washed the air and settled the dust, leaving behind a morning sky as blue and clear as Maggie's eyes and a gentle breeze that held only the slightest hint of winter.

When they reached the siding, she took a deep breath of the fresh, sweet air and looked around her.

"Oh, Dos! I'm a damned fool to leave all this!"

"It's not forever!"

She fervently hoped not. Her eyes went to the horizon, and her mind traveled beyond. She could see it all as she had viewed it from the air—the Lantana! Their private kingdom! How fortunate they were to be so blessed!

"My heart's here," she whispered. "I suppose it always was. The Lantana's in our blood—like it was in Mama's and Papa's."

"Like it was in Grandpa's and Sofia's," Dos added. "Maggie! They would be proud of you today!"

A lump filled her throat and she held her brother tightly. "I love you, Dos!"

"I know."

"And I'll be back."

"Of course you will." His voice was tender and soft.

"No! I mean soon! I can't stay away for long."

"We'll be waiting for you."

"And when I come back . . . it'll be for good! I know it will. I want to grow old on the Lantana. I don't want to die like Mama, in a city far away. I want to be here with you and Trev . . . and Trev's

461

family. Oh, Dos! I wish I could take the Lantana with me!"

He reached down, scooped up a handful of sand, and poured it into her palm. She made a fist and held it to her breast.

Silently, he escorted her aboard the train. He kissed her goodbye, stepped back onto the siding, and waved to the engineer.

The whistle blared, the bell clanged, and the Lantana train with the emblem of the Crown of Thorns on its sides was on its way. Maggie leaned from a window and watched until Dos was a mere speck on the horizon.

Then drawing inside, she went to a desk and emptied the silver cigar case that had once belonged to Anne. She opened her fingers and let the sand stream through them into the box. Then closing it, she held it in both hands. She would keep this bit of the Lantana with her until she came back home again.

One of her maids entered and asked her if she wanted anything.

"No, thank you, Dora. I'd like to be alone."

When the maid disappeared into the other car, Maggie settled into an armchair and watched the passing countryside. It was flat, almost featureless, and bone white in the bright morning sun. And she remembered the words of a letter Alex once wrote her: ". . . *this strangely beautiful part of the world. Do others see its beauty as I do? Do you?"*

"Yes, Papa!" she cried out. "I do! I do!"

The train whistled again and clattered past the last fence—the Lantana's northern boundary.

Maggie's hand flew to the garnet lavaliere around her neck.

"I'll be back!" she vowed. "Nothing could keep me away."

# THE BEST OF BESTSELLERS
# FROM WARNER BOOKS

**THE KINGDOM**
*by Ronald S. Joseph*                    *(33-074, $2.95)*
Out of the rugged brasada, a powerful family carved THE KINGDOM. Joel Trevor was willing to fight Mexicans, carpetbaggers, raiders, even Nature itself to secure his ranch. Then he won the beautiful Spanish Sofia who joined her heart and her lands to his. When control passed to Joel's daughter Anne, she took trouble and tragedy with the same conquering spirit as her father. These were the founders—and their story blazes from the pages of THE KINGDOM, the first book of a giant trilogy.

**THE POWER**
*by Ronald S. Joseph*                    *(36-161, $3.50)*
The children of Anne Trevor and Alex Cameron set out at the turn of the century to conquer the world in their own ways. Follow Dos, the reckless son, as he escalates youthful scrapes into crime. Travel with Maggie from boarding school to brothel to Congress. Meet Trev and the baby daughter to whom all the kingdom, power and glory will belong.

**THE GLORY**
*by Ronald S. Joseph*                    *(36-175, $3.50)*
Meet the inheritors: Allis Cameron, great-granddaughter of the pioneers who carved a kingdom in southern Texas. Go with her to Hollywood where her beauty conquers the screen and captures the heart of her leading man. Cammie: Allis's daughter, who comes of age and finds herself torn between a ruthless politician and a radical young Mexican. They were the Cameron women, heirs to a Texas fortune, rich, defiant, ripe for love.